ALL DESIRES KNOWN

ALL
DESIRES
KNOWN

writing as

M. R. O'Donnell

HEADLINE

First published in 1993
by HEADLINE BOOK PUBLISHING PLC

10 9 8 7 6 5 4 3 2 1

British Library Cataloging in Publication Data

O'Donnell, M.R.
All Desires Known
I. Title
823.914 [F]

ISBN 0–7472–0751–8

Typeset by
Letterpart Limited, Reigate, Surrey

Printed and bound in Great Britain by
Clays Ltd, St Ives PLC

HEADLINE BOOK PUBLISHING PLC
Headline House
79 Great Titchfield Street
London W1P 7FN

For
Mike O'Rahilly
and
in loving memory of
Bernie

Lucy had never sunk so low in all her life. Imagine! The Honourable Lucinda Raven, youngest daughter of Lord Mountstephen . . . the brightest and most talked-about young hostess in Dublin society . . . to have to stoop to *this!* Michael would only kill her if he ever found out.

She drew a deep breath and – praying that her veil was ten times more impenetrable from the outside than it seemed to her from within – turned to face the man with whom she had to do this awful, terrifying, monstrous thing.

"I've . . . er, that is . . . I never did this before," she stammered.

He peered at her dispassionately over his half-moon glasses. Thank heavens the light in here was dim. Those eyes had seen everything, every variety of human depravity. Her fall from grace was a drop in the ocean to him. "There's a first time for everyone, my dear," he said mildly. "Let's have a look at what you've got, shall we?" He stretched his hand toward her.

Instinctively she shrank from him. Was he allowed to call her "my dear"?

"Well, I can't compel you," he continued in those unshockable tones – and turned to the woman behind her.

But the woman behind her, an old Dublin shawlie who could sniff a hard case three streets away, nudged Lucy in the back and said, "G'wan, love! May you never tread a worse step than that. Your man has a heart of sugar, so he has." She craned forward to see what Lucy had half unwrapped and then wrapped up again. The chamois-leather alone would have been worth three dinners to her and her family.

Lucy made the most of her slender figure, pressing herself tight against the counter and bending forward to shield her treasures from inquisitive eyes. But there were mirrors everywhere, and glass cabinets – dozens of surfaces to reflect the image of those sparkling jewels and fetch gasps of wonder, not alone from the old shawlie but from the other two customers, as well – a respectably dressed young woman waiting to pop a portable gramophone and four records, and an old man about to part with his teeth.

Such humble transactions gave point to the pawnbroker's next words. Clamping a jeweller's lens between his eyebrow and his cheek, he carried Lucy's offering to the window. "I'm afraid, Madam," he said – she was "Madam" now – "that these are far above my usual

1

class of trade. I could offer you no more than a fraction of their value . . ."

"Sure you're a-a-all heart!" put in the shawlie, quite happy to contradict her previous assertion.

"May I suggest that you try these people, instead?" He wrote *Webb & Co* on a piece of paper and turned it to face her. "They would surely know the value to a pound."

"They'd surely recognize them, too," she said.

"Ah!" He pondered whether he should tell her how to handle old Webb and come away without too much loss of dignity.

Before he reached any conclusion, however, Lucy scooped up the jewelry, stuffed it hastily in the chamois pouch, and turned from him. "I've made a mistake," she said. "I'll come back."

Why did she add that last promise? she wondered as she fled from the shop. All the dragoons in Dublin would never force her back there. Now, in her confusion she turned the wrong way down Eustace Street – though she failed to notice the fact until she was almost at the bottom, near the corner with Temple Bar. She had never been in this disreputable part of the city before and was amazed that she could feel so lost and alien; she was, after all, only a couple of hundred yards from Dame Street, which she knew so well.

She hesitated, not knowing which way to turn now. Somewhere to her right – less than half a mile – was Westmoreland Street, dear, familiar territory, too. The same was true of Parliament Street, which was to her left and probably even closer. But Dame Street, behind her, was closest of all. So, even though it meant passing that unspeakable shop again, she turned about and began to retrace her steps.

To her left was a house that resembled a tavern, though it had no name over the entrance and no sign hung out over the foot pavement. A respectable-looking man appeared at the side-door and stood there a moment, wiping his beard with a little flick of his knuckles – a gesture that was disconcertingly familiar to her, though she could not immediately place it.

Even when he gazed directly at her she did not at once recognize him; all she saw was a man who looked as if he'd just risen after two hours at a groaning table – a man in search of nothing more than a quiet place where he might enjoy a good snooze.

But then she recognized him.

Panic seized her. She forgot she was wearing a veil so impenetrable it plunged this rather bright March afternoon into a deep twilight – which must also explain why she had not recognized him at once. She forgot she was wearing clothes that no one on God's earth – and certainly no one in Dublin – would associate with her. She forgot it was a good ten years since they had last met. All she knew was that she must get as far away from him as she could – and waste no time about it.

2

It was the worst possible decision, for – naturally – the sudden quickening of her pace and her general agitation drew his attention at once. She hadn't gone two steps beyond him before he said – in tones whose incredulity matched hers – "Lucy?"

She hastened onward without turning.

"Is it you?" he continued, raising his voice as the distance between them increased.

She trotted as fast as the hobble of her skirt allowed. A moment later she heard him running to catch her up. "Whoever you are," he called as he drew near, "this bracelet is far too valuable to leave lying on the pavement."

No other words could have halted her so swiftly. She turned and saw him holding one of her bracelets flat in the palm of his gloved hand. She had not even heard it fall.

"Ah . . . why . . ." she mumbled incoherently as she reached for it . . . and then withdrew her hand without taking it. She could not touch him.

Even at the time the turbulence of her feelings struck her as strange. She and he had, in fact, parted the best of friends. A little sadly, perhaps, a little sentimentally, but in a friendly fashion for all that. He had said things like, "The best man won." And she had said something stupid like she hoped they'd all have another life, and then the balance would tip in his favour – the sort of thing one says at awkward partings like that.

So why was she now behaving as if he were some sort of unexploded shell?

It was silly. She must stop it this minute.

"It *is* Lucy, isn't it," he said, still holding forth her bracelet.

She smiled ruefully and nodded – though, of course, he could see nothing of her expression through her veil.

His eyes twinkled and she knew he was about to say something outrageous. "I knew it, the moment you went past me. There's no other woman in Dublin whose walk is quite so exciting as yours, Lucy."

"Dazzler O'Dea!" she exclaimed, taking the bracelet at last. "You're a thundering disgrace, so you are! You never change." How pleasingly calm her voice sounded, she thought, despite all the turmoil.

"No," he replied, a sad light creeping into his eyes, "I never changed."

Only then did she realize what a cunning thing he had done. By coming out with one of his famous "outrageous" remarks, he had allowed her to respond with that sort of half-amused asperity which women are supposed to use on such occasions, when they know the fella means no harm. First he had calmed the emotional waters into which this chance encounter had thrown them. And then – the touch of a master – he tossed after it this little pebble of regret, whose

3

ripples were now just reaching her, ripples she would never have noticed had he not first made all so smooth. "Sure why *should* you change," she said, determined not to let him get away with it, "when all the world adores you as you are! I'm sure they still do – don't they?"

He brushed the jibe aside with a smile, though she could see he was not very amused. "Why did you hurry on by?" he asked. He did not add: "You surely knew it was me." But the accusation hung between them nonetheless.

Her flight had brought her to within a few paces of the pawnbroker's; from his point of view, the dark shopfront framed her, with the three gilded balls suspended menacingly above her. She watched his eyes making all the right connections, finishing with the chamois-leather bag, which she now clutched tighter than ever in her hand. "Ah," he said.

There was no detectable emotion in his tone at all – neither sadness nor (as there might well have been) a grim sort of satisfaction. It was a very workmanlike "Ah," which suggested he was already thinking on her behalf. He concluded by pulling out his watch and saying, "Teatime! There's a very *good* little café up in Dame Street." He raised his eyebrows.

"Oh, I don't know that I ought . . ." she protested feebly.

"What?" he cajoled. "We haven't met in . . . eight? nine? years, and you . . ."

"Ten years," she interrupted. A fraction of a second later it struck her that he had misstated the interval deliberately – to see if she would correct him.

His smile confirmed it. "How time flies when one is having fun," he said bleakly. "But surely you can't just say ta-ta – nice to have seen you. We must do it again in another ten years. Has it really been ten years, Lucy?"

"I've just had a wedding anniversary to remind me," she replied, partly to excuse her precision and partly to remind him of . . . the way it was now.

He stared at her coldly and then said, "Yes. Of course."

"And you?" she asked brightly.

He shook his head, but then immediately made his denial ambiguous by saying, "If we're going to catch up on each other's news – which I really would rather like to do, Luce – we can't stand about out here, in this street of all streets."

She looked about her, reassessing their surroundings in the wake of this condemnation. "Why?" she asked. "Is it especially . . . you know?"

He laughed. "Oh, Luce! You always wanted to know *everything!*"

"No one's called me Luce for . . . ten years." It wasn't true, actually, but it flattered him.

"Well – shall we share this pot of tea or shan't we?"

4

She came to him smiling and took his arm; for some reason all her worries had evaporated. Dazzler had always been able to work that magic, somehow. He'd find a way out of this present mess, too – and without doing anything crass like offering to take her jewels in pawn to himself. "Dazzler O'Dea!" she said. "I thought you were in Cork."

"I was," he replied, giving his hat a tip as he caught sight of himself in the pawnshop window. "But I'm back in Dublin now – for good, I hope."

"You look a lot more prosperous than when you left, I must say."

"Anyone can *look* prosperous, Luce." He nudged her to show he didn't mean it unkindly.

"Ha ha," she said in a tone she hoped would dissuade him from further humour of that kind.

They had reached the corner with Dame Street. She paused and looked back into that alien world. "Is it very disreputable, Dazzler?" she wondered.

"Out with it," he said. "The question you're dying to ask."

She rose to his challenge – as ever: "Was that one of those *houses* you came out of?"

"It was," he replied evenly.

"Oh." She felt herself blush and was grateful, once again, for the veil.

"Hit the nail home," he continued. "What good is a single tap?"

She cleared her throat awkwardly. "It's none of my business, I'm sure."

"It wasn't," he agreed. "Until you made it so. Not that I mind – not in the least. But you've left the furrow half-turned."

After a brief silence she said, "Because the field seems to have an Irish bull in it as large as the Lucan tram!" She laughed, hoping her wit would close the subject, for she fervently wished she had let his challenge lie.

"I'll tell you, then," he said, taking her arm and guiding her down the hill toward Parliament Street where – presumably – this café of his was to be found. "I was collecting the rents for my Uncle Ebenezer. You remember Uncle Ebenezer?"

"I remember your Uncle Ebenezer," she said fervently. "I doubt he ever forgave me."

"He forgot it the next day," O'Dea assured her. "Don't give yourself airs. He's the ground landlord for every building on that side of the street. If I hadn't met you, I'd be calling at every single one of them now."

It was a polished performance, but she remembered that debauched glint in his eye, before he knew who she was. "How is your Uncle?" she asked.

"Not too well, I'm afraid. I'm his leg-man now. He can't get out as much as he once did."

5

"I heard he's in a sedan chair now?"

"Yes. Very sudden." Dazzler was awkward, wanting to move off the subject. "But he has a good nurse. A strong colleen, up from the country, perfectly suited to him."

Lucy wondered what sort of woman at all could be "perfectly suited" to that ogre.

Then Dazzler told her. "She *looks* like the flaming-red-haired temptress beloved of three-volume novelists. But she's the Ice Maiden, herself. No breath of passion has ever melted the frost that rimes her heart."

"My, my, Dazzler – there's passion of some kind in *that* judgement!"

"Tcha!" He began to parody his distress. "I give myself away at every turn! Still, she suits Uncle Ebenezer, and that's all that really matters."

As they passed the Empire Theatre he paused to read the notices. And Lucy seized the chance to take stock of him. His mock grievance – that he gave himself away at every turn – was still in her ears. And all at once she realized it was true. He was no longer very good at hiding things to do with himself. Or had the intervening years taught her to pick them up a lot quicker? That was probably it. After all she had been a mere girl of seventeen, hardly out of the nursery, when they'd last met. And that was now *more* than ten years ago, in fact, for she was now twenty-eight. Twenty-eight years and ten days.

"Sorry," he said as they resumed their stroll – something he would never have done in the old days. Then he had considered his passion for the music hall to be the most natural thing in the world. He probably still did – except that he now realized it was something to say "sorry" about, too.

"You were the last fellow to take me through those doors," she told him. "D'you remember the fuss my father made?"

"Fuss, is it?" he said drily. "He ate me a mile off, the last straw, he called it."

It had been the last straw, too, though neither of them said as much now.

"All those . . . *things!*" she said vaguely.

"Things?"

"Life-and-death things. We thought they were so important."

He made no reply to that.

"And what's important now?" she asked glumly. "Keeping our heads above water. It's all dwindled down to that!"

He held open the door of the café, arching his eyebrows to prepare her for his next question, or the closest he dared get to it: "Michael must be doing well, surely? Consultant general surgeon at Eli's . . . and his practice in Fitzwilliam Square . . ." He helped her into her chair.

6

"You *have* kept yourself informed!"

"My dear Luce, one cannot open a newspaper without seeing either your name or . . ." His voice tailed off as she lifted her veil at last. His jaw dropped and all he could do was stare at her.

"But you've not seen my photograph, obviously," she said in some embarrassment.

"I'm sorry." He breathed in deeply and pulled himself together. "I'd forgotten. Your eyes . . . I'd forgotten. Where were we? Oh yes – you seem to be on every worthy committee going, one or other of you. The Dublin Season has little to do with the Castle these days, they say. It begins when Mrs Michael Raven gives a select little dinner in Clyde Road . . ."

"Would you stop that!" She waved away his blarney with a laugh.

". . . and it ends with a magnificent ball at that same address. Am I wrong?"

The waitress came and took their order, which gave time for her amusement to expire.

Then, like a true devotee of the theatre, he gave her the cue he must have known she needed. He reached forward and tapped the chamois-leather bag. "Does all that expensive *grandeur* explain this little expedition?"

She slumped in her seat and nodded. "D'you know, Dazzler, if I'd met you in Dame Street on my way to that awful . . . *mont de piété* . . ."

"Ah!" he mused, "how much more civilized it sounds in French!"

". . . and if you'd said something like you said just now – about Michael doing pretty well – sure I'd have laughed and said never better!"

"*But ye cot me unawares, a-bending on the stairs* . . ." He half-sang it like a snatch of music-hall song – and then said – yet again – "Sorry!" He smiled sympathetically. "You hardly need distress yourself with an explanation, Luce," he went on. "It's obvious to anyone that keeping up a position in society cannot be done on bread and cheese and kisses."

"It was so easy in the beginning," she said.

"Before the children came along – what is it now? Four?"

She eyed him askance. "Dear God! I'll bet you know their names, too!"

He made an arch of his hands and rested his chin there. He did know their names, she could tell; he was merely wondering whether or not to admit it.

"Alice, Charley, Tarquin, and Portia?" he said. At least he had the grace to make a slight question of it. Then, out of the blue, he added, "What ever possessed you to go to a dingy little back-street pawnbroker like that, Luce?"

"What else should I do?" she challenged. "Take them back to Webb? Say, 'We gave you eight hundred for these – how much d'you

7

want to take them back?' I might as well put an announcement in the *Irish Times*."

"Not at all!" He laughed at her naïvete. "You always were the extremist – all or nothing! Why not do what Lady Ardilaun herself would do . . ."

"Well, she's certainly not hard up!"

"Precisely! Would you ever just listen! Do what Lady Ardilaun would do. Go back to Webb and say how unfashionable these baubles are and how tired you are of seeing yourself in them, and . . ."

She cut him short. "But he'd never offer more than four hundred."

His eyebrows shot up. "You've tried already, then?"

"Of course not. But I know those jewellers. Webb wouldn't give his own mother more than half what she paid."

"Even so, four hundred is not to be sneezed at."

"It's the *other* four hundred that would hurt."

"You could call it the price of keeping up appearances?"

She stared at him in something close to disgust. "It's easy for some to be so high and mighty," she said. "May we talk about something else?"

"Surely!" The smile never left his lips. "Shall we talk about where you might get . . . what shall we say? Six hundred and fifty for them – and the chance to redeem them when needed?"

It was bait, and she knew it – bait of the most flagrant kind. Also it showed her a new side to this man, new since the days when she had known him so well. It was hardly surprising that he should change in ten years, even a man as flamboyant and outgoing as Dazzler, but it made her wonder how well she knew him now – or even whether she knew him at all. The similarities between the man who now sat facing her and the gay blade she had once loved so dearly might be all on the surface – the looks, the clothes, the mannerisms . . . the shared memories. Inside, he might be . . . anybody.

For all her caution, however, she was too desperate to pass his offer by. "Who?" she asked in a whisper. "Where?"

He shrugged, as if he now wished to imply he had not been quite so positive. "My Uncle Ebenezer?" he suggested.

Uncle Ebenezer lived in one of the few remaining private houses in Sackville Street, just beyond the General Post Office; on those mornings when the sun shone, the shadow of Nelson, high on his pillar, laid a dark finger over the façade of the house, which Uncle Ebenezer took as his signal to rise. But he was up betimes on that first Thursday in March, when the Hon. Lucinda Raven was expected to call on a matter of some delicacy. In any case, no sun shone – not for Nelson, not for Lucy – as she stood on the far side of the street, peering at the place through the leafless branches of the trees that grew all down the central island. The cold breeze whipped around her while she fought a powerful urge to turn and flee. Even then, before she so much as set eyes on the old man, she had an intimation that this next hour of her life would change it forever – *if* she went through with this meeting at all.

On the face of it she would be doing nothing more than hundreds of others did every day. Old men pawned their teeth for pennies, just to stay alive; big magnates borrowed in the tens of thousands, to become bigger still – on the security of their existing assets. What was that but a respectable kind of pawning? Her own case, she decided, lay somewhere in between.

There was no doubt that six hundred-odd pounds would see her through the summer and make it another glorious season for Mr and Mrs Michael Raven. And where else might she lay hands on such a sum? Her father was in as parlous a state as she herself. The banks were losing patience . . .

"Pardon me, ma'am, but are you lost? May I direct you?" The gentleman, a Dubliner by his speech, took her unawares.

"Oh, no thank you, sir." She smiled gratefully. "I'm to meet a friend here. I'm a little early for her, that's all." She thought she knew him vaguely, but, of course, in this city, where she knew hundreds by name, she knew thousands by sight.

Still he hesitated. Then, with a swift glance across the street, he tipped his hat and went his way. Was that a knowing grin on his face? Had he actually looked at Uncle Ebenezer's – and leaped to the obvious conclusion? Guilty conscience fanned the fire of her doubts.

That decided her. Momentous, life-shattering step or no – trivial, everyday act or no – she realized she now had no choice but to go through with the whole wretched business. What was the alternative? Reduce the scale of her entertaining? Cut down on her committees and charities? She might as well hang a poster round her neck: PAUPER. A diplomatic illness might serve for a while – an attack of neurasthaenia, say – but only for a day or two; she'd go insane if she had to feign some malady all summer. Besides, Michael's practice in Fitzwilliam Square and his advancement at the Eli depended on her activity as hostess and leading light. Michael himself had said he'd lost count of the number of patients who mentioned her – her tireless work on this or that committee, her *usefulness* (by which they mean that she knew everybody, knew what they were up to, knew whose ear was best for bending in this or that case, knew who was presently allied with whom, and who had fallen out.) "An invaluable woman," was the universal verdict. So a prostrating illness might save a little money, but it would cost them even more in lost income. In short, there was no escape from this present nightmare but forward.

She drew a deep breath and, seeing a lull in the traffic, stepped out across the street.

Uncle Ebenezer, sitting in his wheelchair, well back in the dark interior of his morning room, murmured, "Good. She's decided to burn her bridges at last."

His nurse, Diana Powers, who had just that moment entered the room, was not sure the remark had been addressed to her; but when Mr O'Dea added "Eh?" she replied that she wasn't quite sure what he meant.

"She's been standing there, across the street, for the past five minutes, running over all the other possible ways out of her dilemma."

"Who?" Diana asked.

"The lady who is about to ring the bell."

The clamour echoed faintly from the kitchen, even as he spoke.

"Wheel me to the door," he said.

As the maid passed he told her to show the visitor into the drawing room and to explain that it would be two or three minutes before he could join her. He shut the morning-room door and put a finger to his lips, warning his nurse to be quiet. They hardly breathed until they heard the drawing-room door close.

The maid came to them. "It's a Mrs . . ."

"I know," he interrupted. "It's all right, Sarah. I'll go to her in a little while." When the maid had withdrawn he added, "We'll let her stew a minute or two longer. Tell me Nurse Powers, did you ever come across a surgeon called Raven – Michael Raven?"

She gave a start. Then, seeing it had pricked his interest, she confessed the barest minimum – that she had known a medical student of that name when she had trained at the Adelaide.

The answer did more than merely prick his interest. He spun his chair round and faced her, showing a surprising turn of speed for a portly, sedentary man in his sixties. "Did you really?" he asked. "Sit down, do, and tell me more. The Michael Raven I'm referring to is also a Protestant, so we're almost certainly thinking of the same fellow. What did they say of him in those days? You know he's one of the principal surgeons in Dublin now, I'm sure? Did he show any sign of it then? Did people pick him out as a man who'd go far?"

Diana had regained her composure by now and was well able to talk about Michael Raven without betraying the slightest emotion; in any case, only the most feeble sentimental remnant remained within her these days – enough to make her jump at the unexpected mention of his name, and then die from even that trivial exertion. "There were a fair few like him, sir," she replied.

"In what way? What did they have in common?"

"They were determined to shine. You know that look a man gets in his eye when he means to excel? And there's others, you know equally well, who'll be content to live and die in some wild country practice beyond the McGillycuddy Reeks. But fair dues to Michael Raven, he was unlike the others in one respect – he'd be as friendly to you *after*

10

you were of use to him as he was when he only hoped you might render him some service."

Uncle Ebenezer looked quite toadlike when he smiled. "And were *you* ever able to render him some service, Nurse Powers?"

She raised her eyebrows for – apart from his very first interview with her – she could not ever remember his putting a personal question to her.

"I do not ask idly," he added, "as you shall see if this encounter with Mrs Michael Raven goes the way I expect it to."

"Is that who she is?"

He nodded, not taking his eyes off her.

"The Honourable Mrs Michael Raven," Diana said. "And yes, I did render him some small service. I helped him grind his third-year midwifery and thoracic pathology."

The old man winced. "That sounds rather painful, if I may say so."

The nurse laughed. "The worst pain was no more than pins-and-needles, sir. It involved sitting on the lawn asking questions like 'What four signs distinguish the Tetralogy of Fallot? . . . What, if any, are the cardiac complications of Bright's Disease?' And so forth."

The jargon passed Uncle Ebenezer by but he could not recall a time when he had seen such a gentle glint in the eyes of this cold young lady. "And you have not met him since?" he asked.

She shook her head; her long, severe plait of bright-red hair slapped audibly between her shoulderblades. "Our paths have never crossed," she added, as if he had accused her of avoiding Mr Raven deliberately.

"So you know nothing of Mrs Michael Raven – apart from the fact that she's the Honourable Mrs et cetera?"

"Only what all Dublin knows, sir. That she's *in*. She's thick with everyone . . . has her finger on the pulse . . . you know."

"What they call a proper little *quidnunc*. Yes. Of course, such a way of life cannot be kept up on halfpennies – and hardly on guineas, either, if truth were told. I suspect that poor Mister Raven has been running as hard as he can, merely to stand still these past . . . how many years has it been?"

"Ten years or so," she told him, though she knew it was precisely eleven years and seven months.

"Would you like to be present at this interview, Nurse Powers?" he asked suddenly, taking her aback.

"I hardly think that's for me . . ." she faltered.

He saw a hard little smile twitch at the corners of her lips, though she swiftly pursed them and frowned again. It was all he wished to know for the moment: Nurse Powers and the Hon. Mrs Raven would never form an alliance – and even if they did, in some quite extraordinary circumstances, neither of them would trust it much.

11

"Again," he said, "I do not ask the question lightly – though I have my reasons for not wishing to explain myself to you just yet."

He wanted her to be as surprised as possible at the proposal he was going to put to Lucy Raven – perhaps today, but more likely on some future occasion, when she was well and truly "softened up," as artillery officers say. If Lucy even suspected that the nurse was already privy to the business – that he had sought her approval first – she would probably reject his plan out of hand. Judging his moment, he added, "I would very much like you to be there."

She suppressed another smile and dipped her head, as if she were making a noble sacrifice of some minor scruple out of deference to him.

"Then let us go," he said. "Fuss over me a little. Bring me a glass of water as if it were medicine. For the next half hour I shall cease to be a mere cripple and become an invalid instead."

At the door to the drawing room he paused briefly, looked up at her, and said, "If you ever wonder what really keeps me alive . . ." He grinned and nodded in the direction of their as-yet-unseen visitor.

Uncle Ebenezer drew a deep breath, gave a curt little nod to Nurse Powers, and reached forward to turn the drawing-room doorhandle. Lucy was standing near the window, gazing wistfully at the street, no doubt telling herself she could still back out. Apart from Dazzler's promised word in his uncle's ear the transaction had barely begun. "Mrs Raven!" the old man cried jovially the moment he saw her. "How very kind of you to call after all this time. Of course, it's only yesterday to me, but I know how long eleven years must seem to a youngster like you. And you haven't changed a bit!" He stretched forth his hands, making a sandwich of hers and shaking it warmly, a dozen times or more.

His cordiality made Lucy's opening remark – that this was hardly a social call – seemed frostier than she had intended. But he was not in the least put out."Ah," he said pensively. "How true, how sadly true. Allow me to present my nurse, Miss Diana Powers."

Lucy gave her a vacant smile and inclined her head slightly. Diana said, "How d'you do, Mrs Raven," but did not proffer her hand.

Lucy sat down and said rather pointedly, "It is, in fact, a matter of some delicacy, Mister O'Dea."

Uncle Ebenezer pretended not to follow, compelling her to indicate Diana by a glance. "Oh, you mean Miss Powers," he said dismissively. "Well, have no fear. She's more than a nurse to me. She's my amanuensis, my book-keeper, my conscience . . . in short, my recording angel – and the very soul of discretion, I do assure you."

He spoke with such finality that Lucy realized it would be fruitless to continue to press for her departure. She stared briefly at the young

12

woman, but even so it was long enough for her to feel unnerved by her cold, almost reptilian gaze. Then, turning back to Uncle Ebenezer, said, rather off-handedly, "It concerns some jewelry – a few bits and pieces I've grown rather tired of. They were the height of fashion, of course, when Michael bought them but now they irk me. I was on my way yesterday to see whether Mister Webb at Webb and Co, would buy them back. And then, by the merest chance, I ran across Dazzler." She smiled affectionately. "After all these years! I had no idea he was back in Dublin. Anyway, he suggested you might go rather higher than Webb's. I don't know. I just wondered if you were at all interested?"

The smile never left his face. "May I be frank, Mrs Raven?" he asked in his gentle, rather kindly voice.

"Please," she replied, her heart already beginning to sink.

"There are no friends in business, of course. Yet I am – how shall I put it – *tenderly* aware of the friendship that existed at one time between you and my nephew. I feel, at the very least, that I owe it to you to say I am not in the least bit interested in buying old jewelry. Nor in advancing a payment upon its security."

"Oh," Lucy said flatly. *Advancing* was a good word, though – so much mellower than *lending*. She popped it into memory.

He, meanwhile, was holding up a playful finger. "But I am intensely interested in the reasons behind your desire to be rid of these . . . baubles."

"But I told you – I've grown rather tired of them. I never wear them. They lie in the drawer, year after year, a standing temptation to robbers."

Uncle Ebenezer said nothing. He simply continued to stare at her with a somewhat melancholy expression.

At length Lucy felt uncomfortable enough to add, "In any case, even if there were some . . . some . . ."

"More urgent reason?" he suggested.

"I was going to say more *private* reason, it hardly need concern you. Please, I don't mean that in an offensive way."

"Of course not. I cannot imagine your being offensive, dear lady – even if you wished to be – which is also unimaginable. Oh dear! We are in something of a quicksand here. Let me be utterly, utterly frank then. The fact is, you see, that I have a business proposal in mind, but I am reluctant to put it to you openly because you might not view it in quite the same light as I do. You will not see it as I believe you *ought* to see it. In my opinion, you and your husband are absolutely *made* for the, ah, *situation* I have in mind. However, if the pair of you turned it down, I should – with the greatest reluctance, let me say – be forced to take my proposal to some less worthy physician. You might then see him as competition and – being forewarned – might use your considerable influence to scotch my idea and ensure its miscarriage. D'you appreciate my dilemma?"

13

Lucy discovered that all her misgivings and awkwardness had evaporated. With a grand upwelling of her usual confidence she replied, "Indeed, I do, Mister O'Dea. But I fail to see how a closer inquiry into our circumstances might offer a way out of your difficulty."

"Ah!" His eyes twinkled and he seemed pleased she had made such a sagacious point. "You see . . ." But he bit off the rest of what he had intended saying and relapsed into thought. Then, with a wry little smile he went on. "This is either the moment when you stand up and storm out of my house – or we start to lay our cards on the table. So here we go: If I knew that your husband's present practice, successful though it undoubtedly is, was not yet earning *quite* as much as you hoped for – and certainly less than you require – I should feel much less diffident in laying before you a proposal that would make you richer by far."

Lucy's eyes went wide at this promise. She glanced swiftly at the nurse and was pleased to see that she was equally surprised at her employer's words – though the woman resumed her masklike face the moment she was aware of Lucy's attention. "It would be enough, I presume, to pay *you* a good return as well, Mister O'Dea?" she said.

Again the words seemed to please him. Was she saying all the correct, businesslike things? Or was it merely that she was feeding him the appropriate cues for whatever he wished to tell her next? She had no way of knowing, but he was certainly ready with an answer, every time. "My interest in a continuing return, Mrs Raven, would be modest, I assure you." He smiled almost apologetically at the nurse, as if to warn her that she was about to see him in an unusual aspect. "The truth is that a couple of years ago I acquired a certain property – that is to say, a chain of legal events placed it in my possession. I did not want it, but I had no choice in the matter. Unfortunately this property has proved, as I feared it would, to be something of a white elephant, and I have almost reached the decision to pull its roof off so as to avoid paying the rates, which are quite iniquitous. But I have decided to make this one last effort to use the place. I would be very happy to let it go for a peppercorn rent – even a caretaker lease – merely in the hope of increasing its capital value. There now! I have already said too much, perhaps? You must know which property I am speaking of?"

Lucy frowned and shook her head. "But in any case we already have a home, Mister O'Dea," she objected.

"This is vastly larger than any home in Ballsbridge, Mrs Raven." He sighed and began to quantify his heavy burden: "Sixty-four principal rooms. A ballroom larger than the RDS ballroom at Leinster House. Its own chapel and organ. Ten acres of landscaped garden. A hundred-and-two-acre home farm – that at least has a tenant, thanks be to God. But you see why I call it a white elephant! You can imagine the rates on such a place!"

"I can't imagine which house it could be," Lucy said. "I thought I knew pretty well every last place within thirty miles of Dublin – certainly every one of such grandeur as you have just described."

"Killattin House, for instance?" he suggested with something of a challenging air.

"George and Millicent O'Brien's place?" she said at once. "But that's not empty. Nor, with all respect to them, is it quite as grand as . . ."

"I'm not saying it is. When were you last there, Mrs Raven?"

"Oh . . . heavens – years ago. I wonder if I could even find the place now. It's out near Mount Venus, I think."

His smile suggested she was missing some vital point.

"Millicent's sister Etty is on the Dublin Day-Out committee with me," she added. "Her husband died in that dreadful accident when the drain collapsed in Firhouse last year. They had to take their boy out of Clongowes and send him . . ."

"Or Porterstown House?" Uncle Ebenezer interrupted again.

"Philip and Margaret Flannery's place. But they still live there, surely? Mind you, it's a few months since last I saw them. Their little boy, Ian, had rheumatic fever just before Christmas, poor mite. Michael treated him at the Eli, but he'll never be completely well again, I gather – and he was such an athlete." She frowned. "And come to think of it, Porterstown House is also out near Mount Venus."

He nodded. His eyes twinkled merrily, and understanding dawned upon her at last. "Are you talking about Mount Venus House itself?" she asked. "Good heavens!"

"Quite," he said.

"But you know who built that place – or enlarged it to its present size?"

He nodded. "If I'm not mistaken, it was your father's grandfather's brother – I don't know what that makes him to you."

"My great-great-uncle. Boniface Fitzbutler was his name. The only Roman Catholic in County Dublin they never dispossessed, so it was said. He never had to turn his coat. I always thought he must have been shamefully useful to them. You *are* talking about Mount Venus House – 'jewel of the Dublin Mountains'?"

He nodded. "So you'll understand my reluctance to unroof the place – *and* my eagerness to see it earning a little money for a change."

"But that house has bankrupted everyone who ever owned it, Mister O'Dea."

He pulled a face. "I thank you for the reminder!"

"But it has. Boniface died in Tuscany, living on a remittance from my great-grandfather. Then a banker called Gorman acquired it – I think in default of a loan to Boniface . . ."

15

"Go on! Go on!" Uncle Ebenezer said sarcastically. "You'll cut through to bone anon!"

"I'm only telling you. Gorman was forced to sell the place – within ten years, if I remember. Then there was a shipbuilder from the Clyde – Murchison, was it?"

The old man was becoming fascinated despite himself. "D'you know the history of *every* great house in County Dublin, Mrs Raven?" he asked. "Or is it just that you have a particular reason to be interested in Mount Venus?"

"Both-and," she replied. "I could tell you the history of most of them over the last half century, I suppose. Though it's not the houses, mind – not the bricks and mortar. It's the people. Murchison was a crabby old fellow. My father knew him well – couldn't shake him off, in fact. He kept pestering to be elected to the Kildare Street Club – though he knew fine well they wouldn't let in anyone who lived within thirty-five miles of the Castle. He thought he could buy his way in." She laughed. "But Mount Venus took every penny he had. He's buried in Glasnevin and you'd walk past his grave and never give it a second glance! His wife is still alive. She's companion to Mrs Phelan, the one who owns the big bakery in Grangegorman."

There was a short pause and then he commented, "I notice you say nothing as to the *next* owner of Mount Venus, Mrs Raven."

"Speak no ill of the dead," she replied. "Poor man! A suicide like that can't have done much to raise the value of the estate!"

Uncle Ebenezer gave a mirthless laugh and looked up at Miss Powers. "If ever you think I've grown a little too boisterous, a touch too exuberant, Nurse, you'll know where to apply for a remedy!"

Lucy laughed and apologized. "I just thought it would save my having to explain why my husband and I could not even contemplate taking a lease on the place – despite my family's connections there, Mister O'Dea. Not even on a caretaker basis."

"Ah!" He became businesslike again and, making a bridge of his hands and arms, rested his chin upon it and eyed her speculatively – precisely the gesture his nephew had used yesterday. Did it run in the blood, she wondered, or was it simple mimicry? "Did it ever cross your mind to consider," he asked, "*why* the place seems so cursed? And does it not cross your mind now, Mrs Raven, that there's a world of difference between Mount Venus as a private house, draining the purse of owner after owner, and Mount Venus as a centre of business? As – shall we say – a very select sanatorium, where wealthy invalids are offered one of the finest views in Europe, bracing lungfuls of Dublin Bay air, soft, pure water to drink and bathe in, ten acres of landscaped gardens to wander among, and – to be sure – the very finest medical attention that money can command! And if the prospectus could also add that the whole establishment is under the discriminating management of the great-great niece of the man who built the place . . . ah!" He smiled benignly. "Do at least think it

16

over, Mrs Raven. See what your husband has to say. And let me know of your decision in your own good time. And meanwhile – to tide you over any immediate awkwardness – and as an earnest of my good faith . . ." He reached behind him and drew forth a small leather bag whose contents jingled as he passed it to her.

"Oh . . . you'll want my jewelry then . . ." she began.

But he waved the offer aside. "It's of no conceivable interest to me, dear lady," he said.

"And you don't want me to sign an IOU or anything?"

He looked at her askance. "I am not a moneylender," he said deprecatingly. "I an a man of honour, and I take care to do business only with those of a like character."

She smiled. "You *advance* money, Mister O'Dea!"

"What else can I do with it at my age?" he asked.

When she had gone, he turned to Diana and said, "Well, what d'you think of her? Am I being foolish?" Then, answering himself at once, "I am of course. But is my folly great or small? Do sit down."

She sat where Lucy had dinted the sofa, which struck him as an odd choice when half a dozen equally congenial places were on offer. "I don't think you're being foolish at all, Mister O'Dea," she replied.

"That woman would spend the bank," he said, almost as if he were criticizing Diana for having parted with the money. "That was two hundred pounds in that bag. It won't last her the month – you'll see."

Diana nodded. Her face remained expressionless. He wondered what it would take to make her laugh, or cry, or even smile. "In that case," she said, "I'm at a loss to know why you advanced it at all."

He pursed his lips and scratched his head abstractedly. "Since it seems to be my day for being utterly, utterly frank, Miss Powers, let me continue with you. I have spent all my life in one pursuit – the making of money. And I have succeeded at it, I may say. I have made more money than most men dream of. It is not, however, the only thing I've made. I have also, for instance, made a large number of enemies – and very few friends. I've made several useful discoveries, too – that I cannot take my money with me, for example . . . and that it would be the ruination of my nephew if he were to inherit it. He is – as you have no doubt observed – a weak, shallow, amiable, good-hearted young fellow who needs the discipline of having to earn his daily bread in order to keep him a half-way acceptable member of society." To himself he mumbled, "He'll never be more than half-way acceptable, anyway." Then, to her again: "Even one tenth of my wealth would be the ruin of him."

Diana, leaping to his conclusion – as she thought – said, "D'you mean you actually *want* Mrs Raven to . . . squander it all for you?"

"No!" He chuckled. "Mind you – it would be the fireworks show of the century. But no . . ." His voice became cheerless again. "Did you know that my nephew once 'did a line' with Mrs Raven, as they

17

say? That, of course, was when she was still the Honourable Lucy Fitzbutler.''

Astonishment registered briefly in the nurse's eyes but was quickly masked. "What did Lord Mountstephen say to that?''

"No! – in a word. It broke poor Dazzler's spirit. Even worse, it showed him that the ceiling in society is rather low for people like us. If he had married into the nobility – even the worthless fringe of it like the Fitzbutlers – he might have made something of himself.'' He peered at her intently. "You look dubious. D'you believe people are born what they are and can never really change?''

She shook her head slowly. There was a bitter glint in her eye. "People can change," she said. "And they can *be* changed – by . . . things.''

"Things that happen to them?''

"And things that don't. Is this to be your revenge, Mister O'Dea? Give Lucy Raven enough rope . . .?''

He raised his eyebrows at so direct a challenge.

"I'm sorry," she said. "I thought you were being utterly candid.''

He nodded ruefully. "I did promise as much. So I'll tell you – this is not an act of revenge. Not at all. Incidentally, one of the other discoveries I've made is that you can never get your own back. People try, but it takes years, and by that time anything worth calling 'your own' has moved on. It's no longer there to 'get back' – if you follow me.''

She nodded slowly; an unusually pensive mood settled upon her. "I never thought of that," she murmured.

"To return to my point," he went on, "you can call it an experiment, if you like. I wouldn't quarrel with that. I'm playing God with Mister and the Honourable Mrs Raven – but why not? Their progress has fascinated me for the past ten years – in a passive way, you know. Now I am offered the chance of an active rôle. Who's to say it is not divinely ordained? In theory, their career ought by now to be in full flower. Just consider their assets. He is one of the finest doctors the Adelaide ever produced.'' He lifted an eyebrow at her for confirmation. She nodded but said nothing. Ebenezer went on: "He's a Protestant with little wealth but eminently connected. And she's a Roman Catholic who could hardly be better connected. The Fitzbutlers kept their title when all about were losing theirs. And, in her own special way, she's as talented as he is. You've just seen her in action.''

"She seems to know everybody.''

"And everything *about* everybody. She could weigh the world to an ounce. In my map of Irish society – and yours, too, no doubt – the interior of every continent is blank – with *here be tygers* scrawled across it. But not in Lucy Raven's. She has never met a *tyger* in her life. And add to all that their boundless energy . . . their charm. I don't know what Michael Raven was like in his student days but he's Prince Charming himself now.''

18

He watched closely for her response to this but all she did was grunt.

"In short, Miss Powers, if you wanted to write a prospectus for the couple most likely to succeed, out of all their generation, those two would fit it down to the last semicolon. So what has gone wrong?"

At first she thought the question was merely rhetorical. Then, when she realized he expected an answer, she said the first thing that came to mind: "Ambition, perhaps?"

"Excellent!" He rubbed his hands. "They have overreached themselves, that's all."

"Running before they could walk."

"No – galloping before they could canter, more like it. If she had good reason – the best reason in the world – for cutting down on her social whirl . . ."

"Such as living at the back of beyond in Mount Venus?" Diana suggested with the ghost of a smile.

"Come-come, that's too severe. Mount Venus is close enough for her to maintain all her connections with the mainsprings of power and the wellsprings of information – ha, I like that! – in Dublin. But it is too far for her to be throwing grand dinner parties every week and going to charity balls and concerts every other night. I'm taking a gamble, I know, but it amuses me and I can afford it. I think I have offered them a way of bringing their income and their outgoings more into balance. If I'm right, they'll soar like eagles."

"And how will you make sure they toe the line – if I may ask so bold a question, Mister O'Dea?"

"You may, indeed, Miss Powers. You, especially." He took her hand and shook it between his, as he had done with Lucy's earlier. "For that is where you come in. You're utterly wasted here, looking after me." She drew breath to protest but he held up a warning finger. "And you know it, too. I don't require any more talent than would fill your little finger. So we'll let the good doctor and his wife snap up the bait we've just laid – which they will, you'll see. And then we'll throw in our one little condition – they'll only get the money for the Mount Venus Sanatorium, or whatever they wish to call it, on condition that *you* are its matron."

He had not yet discovered the secret of making her smile, but he realized he had just discovered how to fill her eyes with a blend of astonishment and fear.

Michael knew something was wrong – or at least unusual – the moment he returned home that evening. First the parlour-maid, Bridey, took his hat and gloves with a bright smile on her lips – where no smile of any kind had been seen for many a long week. Then he noticed that a new pair of grey leather gloves lay casually displayed on the stand in the hall; at least, he believed they were new, though it was hard to be sure. Lucy had dozens of pairs, of innumerable colours and shades – lavender, red, black, and, especially, grey; but he could not remember a grey quite so pearly as these.

And to top it all there was Lucy herself, wearing that deep-blue day gown of watered silk with the big, flowing sleeves – the one she'd been talking about for weeks – and kissing him with a warmth he had almost forgotten. It still amazed him that after ten years of marriage the very sight of her could tug at his heartstrings as strongly as in the days of their courtship. Indeed, by some odd paradox of human emotion, the feeling was stronger now than ever. He could fill two sides of foolscap with her faults and deficiencies; he would carry the scars of her wounding words to the day he died; but somehow it only made his feelings for her all the stronger. If their love could survive such challenges, what choice had it but to grow deeper and ever deeper?

Her provocative display of expenditure (or, rather, of *fresh* expenditure – for the entire house was a provocative display of a decade-long spree) did not end there. The sherry she now handed was twice as generous as any she'd poured since the January bills had descended like bolts from the gods. And one sniff was enough to tell him it was his favourite Oloroso, available only in cask from Phelan & Goodbody. The brown "gear oil," as he called it, had obviously been sent back to its proper place in the kitchen.

"Successful day, dear?" she asked with a gaiety that implied she hadn't done too badly herself.

He eyed her warily. If she had spent the last half-hour arranging his reception in such a way as to force him to ask what she had been up to, she could hardly have managed it better. But, since Michael Raven was that sort of horse which can be led to water but cannot be made to drink, he said nothing as to Bridey's gaiety, nothing about the gloves, and not a word about the sherry; as to her new gown, all he said was, "That's a very fetching dress, darling. Is it the one you've mentioned once or twice recently?"

"Yes." Her delight was not as casual as she tried to make it seem. "And it was only ten guineas," she added.

Ten guineas, he thought, would pay a maid's wages for eighteen months – or, in Bridey's case, her back wages for the past nine months and her wages for the rest of the year. "Ah," he replied, knowing he was supposed to fly off the handle and engage her in yet another row about money – whereupon she would no doubt produce some explanation for this sudden affluence and leave him wrong-footed. "That's very good."

Or perhaps he was behaving precisely as she intended? He would not put it past her to have scattered these clues around the house deliberately, to make him believe he was being trapped into an argument she was bound to win. Not that she would do it in a coldly calculating manner – she was too impulsive for that – but, even in her giddiest, most spontaneous actions she never lost that instinct for the phrase or gesture that would incline the world more favourably toward her particular goals.

He sipped his sherry with relish and said, "Mrs Spencer brought her daughter Charlotte to see me today."

"She's the crippled one?" Lucy seated herself. The catlike grace of her movement stirred his loins.

He looked away and gazed around the room – until he realized he was searching for missing ornaments . . . anything she might have pawned. There had to be *some* explanation for this provocative display of fresh funds. "She's a bit of a simpleton, too, I fear," he replied. "We can do something to straighten her back and hip, but nothing about . . ." His fingertips drummed his forehead at the temple.

Lucy had a brief image of those same fingertips exploring young Charlotte Spencer's naked hips and back. The girl wasn't badly crippled and she was excessively pretty; Lucy simply couldn't believe that such encounters aroused no private feelings in any doctor, let alone her husband. One only had to see him among the ladies at any gathering to know how very far from indifferent were his feelings toward them – never mind the passion he could properly show for her. It was the same with priests. She didn't believe *they* were as unmoved as people made out when attractive young ladies brought their risqué thoughts and licentious deeds to the confessional. "Bless me father for I have . . . wait till I scorch the ears off you!"

"She's our first patient from that part of Rathgar," Michael said, seating himself at her side. "Or is it Terenure? The Kenilworth Square set. It would be nice if she started a fashion among her neighbours."

"She must have overcome her husband's opposition," Lucy pointed out. "Phillip Spencer is very staunch Church of Ireland . . ."

His laugh interrupted her. "Protestants are always *staunch*, according to you. Roman Catholics, on the other hand, are *devout*."

She gave him a withering smile and continued: "His brother Albert is a pillar of the Zion Church in Rathgar. Is 'pillar' better than 'staunch'? Anyway, they all strongly disapprove of mixed marriages. They wouldn't give you and me the steam off their porridge if we met socially."

He touched the tip of her nose affectionately. "I realize it's quite futile to ask – but how d'you know such things?"

"Sure everyone knows that," she replied dismissively. "The Spencers make no secret of it, anyway. Quite the reverse."

The children came bursting into the room at that moment. Alice and Charley were arguing over which of them had the more important news to impart; Tarquin waited, knowing that his was important

21

enough to keep. Baby Portia slipped onto her father's lap and got in first of all with: "I caught fifteen fish."

He kissed her and said it was wonderful, then asked Lucy how a child of three could go fishing, much less catch fifteen of the blighters. She explained that the fish were made of paper with pins in them and the fishing line was a magnet tied to a bamboo from the garden.

"They're *real* fish," Portia said quietly.

Alice and Charley stopped arguing and stared at the glass their father had put down for safety.

"What now?" he asked them. "Have you never seen a sherry glass before?"

"That's your bestest Oloroso," Charley said.

"I can smell it," Alice confirmed.

"What amazingly observant children you are!" he exclaimed. "I wonder where you get it from?"

"Phelan and Goodbody," Lucy put in.

"Tilly O'Hare has a new pony for her birthday," Alice said apropos nothing.

Her parents exchanged amused glances, for Alice's own birthday was a mere twenty days away.

"Billy Dalton got a bow-and-arrow set for his," Charley said. "A real one." His tone was more wistful, his birthday being six months away – or behind him, depending on how you looked at it.

"What would an *unreal* bow and arrow look like, I wonder?" Lucy mused aloud. Then, to her elder daughter: "Where are the O'Hares keeping this poor creature, then?"

"In that field by the Wicklow Railway line. And it's not a poor creature. It's . . ."

"What? In that little patch of furze and gravel? Where the poor boys can come out from Rathdrum and Goatstown and torment it with sticks and stones? You need a fair few acres to keep a pony in grass. Why d'you think we gave up the carriage and pair?"

"Francis O'Hanrahan says his father will take me and him to the railway workshops at Inchicore on Sunday," Tarquin said.

"And me?" Charley asked eagerly.

His younger brother turned his great, solemn eyes upon him and slowly shook his head.

"Oh dear," Lucy interposed. "I suppose you'll have to go and sleep at the O'Hanrahans on Saturday night – because the rest of us are going on a little jaunt, straight after church on Sunday, and we shan't have time to take you there then."

The disappointment drained from Charley's eyes and he grinned at Tarquin as if to suggest *he* might be the one who was missing the best of it that day.

"What jaunt?" their father asked. "Is this something you've mentioned and I've forgotten?"

22

"Not at all!" She let her tongue linger on her lip, to tease him. "It's an idea that came to me today – a *mystery jaunt*, as the charabanc company calls it."

"Howth Castle!" Alice guessed.

"No-o-o."

"The Sally Gap?" Charley put in.

"No-o-o . . ."

"Glendalough?" Michael asked.

Lucy realized that if she went on saying no they'd soon guess it by elimination, so from then on she answered all their suggestions with an arch "pro-o-obably!"

Alice tried a new tack: "Will it be a picnic?"

"Of course, dear," her mother said effusively. "We *always* go for picnics in March, don't we. It's the best way to avoid the crowds."

Michael said nothing more about it until the evening's entertaining was behind them and they were preparing for bed. Then he asked if he was to be let in on the secret at all.

"If you want me to spoil it for you," she replied. "Stop fiddling like that! Have you lost something?"

"No." He withdrew his hand smartly from the handle of the drawer to the left of her looking glass.

"You'd hardly find it there, even if you had," she added.

"You weren't wearing your pearls at dinner tonight," he remarked.

"Well," she replied dismissively, "it was only the Brennans and Father Kelly. Besides, Mrs Brennan had hers stolen recently. It would have been rather tactless to make a parade of mine." She smiled, to let him understand she knew precisely what was on his mind but if he wished to talk about it, he was going to have to come out and say it.

"Ah," he said. "How thoughtful."

"In any case, I never wear anything but paste when Father Kelly comes to dine – you know that. Let one diamond show and out comes the begging bowl! Those reformed drunkards must be living in the lap of luxury out there at Stepaside. Did he try to cadge anything off you over the port?"

"He asked could he take a cigar back for Father Ignatius."

"That's not quite what I meant, darling. Could you undo this hook?"

It was not a difficult hook but he knew what she really wanted. A moment later she leaned back against him and sighed. "Don't tarry in the bath."

"Come and join me." He leaned down and kissed her forehead – noticing several more silver hairs among her gold; this time he passed no remark.

"Ah!" she murmured. "If only our bath were large enough!" A new thought struck her. "Actually . . ." she began – but said no more.

"What?" He straightened himself again.

"It'll keep."

"Like your mystery jaunt?"

She laughed. "*Exactly* like my mystery jaunt."

He tarried so briefly in his bath that he was already back in their bedroom by the time she returned from her final check on the nursery. He was sitting at her dressing table, plucking hairs from his nostrils with a surgical tweezers, wiping them in a piece of tissue paper. He knew she detested the habit, especially since she'd bought him a perfectly good enlarging mirror for his bathroom – therefore he was doing it on purpose. Therefore he was trying to distract her from . . . something else. The jewelry drawer, of course!

She laughed inwardly and thought, *What silly games we do be playing on one another!* But she said nothing heated, nothing that would let him come back with the accusation that the drawer was empty. And, indeed, it was empty, for Lucy, infinitely caring of her reputation and realizing that the maids must surely have noticed the absence of her jewelry those past couple of days, had taken steps that would explain it all away. But she wanted Michael to stew in his own suspicions a good while longer yet – he'd remember it all the better *next* time, when the absence of her baubles might not be quite so innocently explained.

"I often wonder," she said, "how the skin inside our noses *knows* it belongs to a man or a woman."

He began making a joke of it. "Moses knowses his nose is . . ."

"And the hairs on our cheeks and chins, of course," she insisted.

He realized that his plucking had served its purpose and so refrained from aggravating her further. "The body must have some way of sending messages to it," he said, "telling it to grow hair or not, as the case may be. Through the nerves, perhaps, or by some as-yet-undiscovered chemicals in the blood? It's hard to see what else it could be." He wrapped up the hair-dappled tissue and offered it experimentally to her.

She pulled a face and backed away. "Don't you long to find out, though?" she asked.

"About the mystery jaunt?"

"No! Whether it's nerves or chemicals – things like that. How can you just dismiss it with a phrase like 'as-yet-undiscovered'? You're handing out advice right, left, and centre, all day long. It could be life or death to someone, yet it's all based on ignorance like that – 'as-yet-undiscovered'! If I were a doctor, I couldn't wait for someone else to find out. I'd drop everything until I'd done it myself."

She slipped onto her stool the moment he vacated it and started to unpin her hair and brush out her curls.

"Who'd pay for the diamonds and pearls *then*, Little Face?" he asked as he came back to her. He took the brush and continued to ply it while she fished out the pins – firm, gentle strokes that sent tingles down her spine.

"Perhaps those sort of things aren't as important as we suppose," she mused.

He stopped and stared at her aghast, feeling her brow as one does for a fever. "Luce?" he asked.

She grinned up at him in her looking glass. "I am tonight!"

"No!" He tried not to smile. "I mean, did I really hear what I think I heard? Did you actually suggest that diamonds and pearls are really not . . ."

"I wouldn't miss them a jot," she said firmly. "Would you?"

He crumpled at the knees and supported himself with one hand on the stool, the other on her shoulder; the brush fell from his nerveless fingers.

"I'm being serious," she insisted.

"Indeed!" He stooped and retrieved the brush. "It sounds very grave to me, too. Quite possibly fatal. Shall I inform your parents? Fetch Father Kelly back. It would be awful to die unconfessed. Or would I do, perhaps? You could surely confess to me?"

"Confess what?" she asked, maintaining as stony an expression as she could.

"Ah!" His eyes gleamed like some villain's in a melodrama. "Everything, of course! A thousand Ave-Marias' worth at least!"

She permitted a half-smile to play about her lips and eyed him speculatively, as if she were wondering whether or not to take him at his word.

Mildly alarmed at the prospect, he went on: "Such a pity Boucicault died. Think what a stirring play *he* could have made of it! Wife – fearing death in a state of mortal sin – confesses all to the only Christian in sight – her husband – a searing catalogue of depravity and transgression! But alas – wife fails to shuffle off this mortal coil – wakes up, fever gone – mad glint in husband's eyes!" He started to brush out her hair again.

She, having no more pins to extract, raised her arms above her head and drew him down to kiss her.

He dropped the brush and his hands stole around her breasts. She sighed and pressed herself firmly against him, feeling him harden there. Yet he did not abandon himself to that most ancient joy. His hands did not take full, voluptuous pleasure in their fondling; rather, he sought to madden her with desire by gently scratching the outer edges of her nipples through the flannelette of her night-dress, increasing the stroke as they hardened and swelled. Unfortunately he was well versed in her ways by now; he knew precisely what he must do to shred the last vestige of her self-control. And he did it then.

She had a moment of sweet retaliation, though – some half-hour later, when all he wanted was to sink in profound, exhausted

25

slumber. "Oh, there's something I forgot to tell you last night," she said chirpily.

He groaned. "I didn't think there was *anything* you forgot to tell me last night. My lack of consideration? No, you said quite a bit about that. My tendency to communicate in monosyllables? No – or was that the night before? I give up – What could it have been, light of my life?"

"I ran across Dazzler O'Dea yesterday. Down near the Halfpenny Bridge. He's back in Dublin again, working for his uncle."

Michael said nothing. He did not even seem to be breathing.

"I got such a shock," she added.

"What were you doing by the Halfpenny Bridge, anyway?" he asked at length.

"Oh yes – that was another thing I forgot to mention. I took some of my jewelry to be cleaned – to Cosgrave's on Ormonde Quay. Amanda Williams says they're awfully good."

"Ah," she said.

She giggled and tickled the nape of his neck. "And *you* hadn't even noticed they'd gone, had you! Be honest now!"

From the moment they could sit up and look at the world about them the Raven children had loved the mountainy road. It was not the quickest way to the valley of Glenasmole (which is where Lucy pretended they were going, since it lay just a mile or two beyond Mount Venus) but they would have sulked all day if their parents had taken any other. A fine day they had for it, too. Spring in Ireland is reckoned to start on the first of February, an annual triumph of hope over experience. That first Sunday in March, however, brought a passable imitation of a bright, if chilly, spring day. A blustery half-gale chased up the Irish Sea, filling the bay with white horses. Overhead, shoals of pale, fleecy cloud alternated with wide lanes of clear blue sky.

When the wind blew southerly, the mountainy road was the best of all for shelter, too, for it meandered along the northern slopes of the Dublin Mountains – the Three Rock and Kilmahogue and Cruagh, whose peaks are, in turn, mere ramparts to the even higher Wicklow Mountains beyond them.

The Ravens were late with their lunch because Lucy and the two girls had an extra homily tacked onto their Mass; Father Kelly's retreat had not attracted as many candidates as he thought it should have done. So it did not help that Michael and Charley had got through Matins in record time – as they always did when the local harriers were drawing the spinneys between Fern Hill and Taylor's Folly. Late or early, however, they devoured their lunch as fast as they decently could. Even so, they were still half an hour behind

Lucy's secret schedule when they left the house at half past one.

Reluctantly the children agreed to sacrifice the first leg of the drive – the not-very-mountainy stretch between Deans Grange and Sandyford – and take a short cut through the suburbs, by Milltown, Windy Arbour, and Rathdrum, joining the road west of Moreen, about a third of the way up the Three Rock Mountain. For Alice there was the compensation of being able to point out the pony Tilly O'Hare had been given for her birthday.

It was a journey of less than six miles, five of them through comfortable, middle-class suburbs comparable to anything you might see around the larger cities in the rest of the kingdom; over the last mile, however, they passed into a land that was unmistakably Ireland, a land that, one suspected, had hardly changed since the Norman Conquest.

It was a place where material comfort seemed little prized. The green slopes and wooded hollows were dotted with limewashed cottages with low ceilings and tiny windows, and roofed with sods or thatch. The people who came eagerly to their doors to watch the fine open landau go by and exchange a little cheery banter with its occupants were bright-eyed and well-fed, but the children were for the most part barefoot and everyone wore clothes so heavily patched that the original garments were no longer recognizable.

"It's like entering a different world," Lucy murmured as they left a small cluster of cottages behind. "And yet so close to Dublin!" She waved a hand over the soot-black huddle of the city, now five hundred feet below them, sprawling over the Liffey plain. With smoke pouring from every chimney it looked like a newly extinguished bog fire – charred but still smoking.

"When we demand Home Rule," Michael said, "we're thinking of people like us ruling the roost. When the English say we'd sink if we got it, they're thinking of people like these with their hand on the tiller."

It was an unusual thing for him to say; like most of their friends, Protestant and Roman Catholic alike, he was an ardent Home Ruler. She gazed back over her shoulder and asked, "How would you prove them wrong?"

He laughed morosely. "I wouldn't even try." A moment later, however, he added with more spirit, "I'd tell them that either they pass control to us by consent or those people will wrest it from them by force. They can have cool friends or fiery enemies on this side of the water. The one thing they can't have is Ireland herself."

"God save us if it ever comes to that!"

Young Alice sighed petulantly, for she knew how this sort of talk could go on and on. "I adore that smell of turf smoke," she said, sniffing the air keenly. "I wish we burned turf instead of nasty, smelly coal."

That started an argument with her mother about whether one

27

should use beautiful words like *adore* about anything so mundane as turf smoke; then her father chipped in with a lecture on something called calorific values. Portia brought it to an end with the announcement that she was hungry again. Lucy tried to distract her by pointing out yet another superb panorama over the entire city of Dublin, but to no avail. Charley tried, too, telling his baby sister she could crow over Tarquin that evening for everything he'd missed. "Look!" he said eagerly, pointing through the bare-branched trees to their left. "See that big house up there? That's Saint Columba's. That's where I'll be going to school one day. And Tarquin. You can tell him you've seen it."

Portia was not very impressed.

In the end it was Alice who managed to shut her up. In a doom-laden voice she said, "You know what's coming next, don't you?"

Her little sister shook her head and waited with her jaw wide open.

"Ghostly Hollow," Alice said in even more sepulchral tones. "So you'd best keep your wits about you."

Ghostly Hollow was their own name for the dark, narrow little valley below Tibradden, where the road plunges steeply down one side, winds along the foot for fifty-odd yards, and then climbs just as steeply up again, crossing the Cruagh road to begin the last leg to Mount Venus.

Portia said she wasn't the least bit afraid of ghosts, but she pulled the scarf tighter around her neck and huddled closer to Lucy, for all that – and there was no more talk of hunger.

At the next junction Charley looked at the fingerboard and said, "Why does *every* road here go to Rathfarnham? You'd think it was bigger than Dublin."

Alice said, "Show off! All you're really saying is, 'Look at me! I can read long words like Rathfarnham!' Nyeah!"

"It's true, all the same," Lucy said, stepping conversationally between them. "The last four fingerboards have all said Rathfarnham."

"Anyway," Alice went on, determined not to be smoothed aside. "Rathfarnham is a suburb of Dublin, so it can't possibly be bigger."

"I didn't say it is," Charley pointed out angrily.

"Did!" It was like the peck of a bird.

"I didn't. I only said you'd *think* it was bigger because all the fingerboards say Rathfarnham and none of them say Dublin."

"Well, I wouldn't think it was bigger because I've *been* to Rathfarnham, so I know it's smaller. Anyway, the word *none* is singular. You should say 'none of them *says* Dublin.'"

Her brother gave her a withering look. "*Them*," he said, "is plural."

Lucy saw a further chance to intervene: "How do you come to

28

know words like *singular* and *plural?*" she asked, silently begging Alice with her eyes to give over.

"From Daddy's Latin Grammar," Charley told her proudly.

Michael gave a start for he kept one or two fairly racy books tucked away amid the decent obscurity of his Latin and Greek tomes. Lucy, who knew nothing about them, said, "Well, I think that's clever, don't you, darling?" The happy relief they heard in her tone, however, had nothing to do with her successful intervention in the squabble; the imposing walls and gables of Mount Venus House had just come into view. The road dipped, though, and the place was soon out of sight again.

And Portia, God bless her, gave the perfect cue when she said, "I need to go."

"If you can hold on for just a few more minutes," her mother replied, "I think we can take care of that – and my! Won't everyone else be surprised!"

The other two children wriggled with delight at this promise of amazements in store. Even Michael, who said, "I *knew* you had something up your sleeve!" settled happily to see what it might be.

And with that, Lucy began what seemed at first like a fairy story:

"Once upon a time," she said, "when the birds ate lime, and the monkeys chewed tobacco, there lived a man called Boniface Fitzbutler . . ."

"Is he one of our Fitzbutlers?" Charley asked.

"All Fitzbutlers are our Fitzbutlers," she assured him. "Anyway, Boniface decided that the Protestants in Ireland were getting too grand altogether . . ."

Michael cleared his throat reprovingly.

She grinned at him and ploughed on: ". . . building themselves grand houses, two and three storeys high and taking all the best views in the country – and passing laws saying Roman Catholics must live in houses of one storey or less."

"How can you have a house of less than one storey?" Charley objected.

"Sure there's no dearth of ditches to shelter behind, is there. Will you let me get on with my tale – because time is running out."

"Ah!" Michael exclaimed, for Mount Venus had just come back into view, prompting him to make the connection. This oblique assurance that the story had a point – which you could guess if you were a clever man like Daddy – held back all further interruptions.

"Anyway," Lucy continued, "he put on his seven-league boots and walked all over Dublin and all around and about Dublin, looking for the bestest view of them all. And first, of course, he tried the Phoenix Park – but hadn't the Lord Lieutenant and the First Secretary got there before him and snatched the cream of the places! Then he tried the Strawberry Beds, only to find the Guinnesses were there before him. The rest of North Dublin was u-u-useless – flat as a Christian

29

Brother's hand, so it was. So he started along the southern hills – the way we've just taken ourselves. But, as you've seen with your own eyes, the Protestants had got there before him once again – Kilgobbin, Fern Hill, Jamestown House, Saint Columba's, Hillcot – and if it wasn't them, it was fever hospitals and Leopardstown Racecourse. There wasn't enough room to slip a house in *sideways!* There now!"

"Did he come along this road?" Alice asked. "I mean, was this road here in those days?"

"Oh, indeed it was. And it's funny you should ask. For poor old Boniface was just on the point of giving up in despair and yielding all the best views of Dublin to the Protestants, when . . . what d'you think happened?"

She needed to spin it out a half-minute longer – until the gates of Mount Venus came into view around the next bend. Michael, realizing what she was at, reined the horses to a halt and said in a worried voice, "I think that gray has cast a shoe. One simply cannot trust these livery . . ."

"Michael!" she exclaimed ominously. "If you don't shake those horses to a trot this minute, *I'll* cast a shoe – straight at your head!"

He laughed but did as she told him. The children, aware that some kind of climax was in the offing and that their father was, somehow, in the know, looked from one to the other to see who would reveal it first.

Lucy continued. "Old Boniface, as I said, was just about to give up – in fact, it was on this very spot where we are now. On this very road! Can't you just see him – trudging wearily along here, all the magic in his seven-league boots used up in his fruitless search, and his feet only *eaten* with blisters inside them. So he arrives at this corner and there's a little voice in his head saying, 'Boniface, old fellow, don't go on! Don't turn this corner. Don't be tormenting yourself with yet another grand villa, built by the other crowd – sure it's bound to be there!' But" – she held up a finger and made an impressive pause – "he wasn't a Fitzbutler for nothing. That little bit of extra spirit, which never deserts us you'll be glad to hear, forced him to take those last few steps and . . ."

The carriage rounded the bend at that moment and she swept a hand toward the road ahead. "There was a fanfare of trumpets from on high and the voices of heavenly choirs rained down in all glory upon the slopes of Mount Venus!"

"But there's a big house there, too," Alice objected.

"*Now* there is," her mother agreed – and waited for the penny to drop.

It did not take long. They turned again and stared at the house, whose upper floor and roof were now in full view over and among the laurels, the massive rhododendrons, and the cedars of Lebanon that filled the slopes of the front garden – all the way down to the romantic, turreted gate lodge, which straddled the entrance like a castle keep.

Again Michael reined in the horses, but this time there was no complaint from Lucy. They sat and gazed at the impressive pile for a long, silent moment.

"And did Boniface Fitzbutler build all that?" Charley asked in an awestruck voice.

"In the year of Our Lord eighteen hundred and four," Lucy assured him.

"Exactly a hundred years ago!" Alice put in.

"He took up his residence here on the first day of September, eighteen-oh-four."

Michael turned to her, amused and not a little bewildered. "Is all this true?" he asked.

"Cross my heart and hope to die."

"And have you any further surprises, milady?"

"Perhaps – it all depends." She grinned. "Let's go and look the place over."

"But the gate's padlocked," Charley objected, for the idea had already occurred to him.

His mother produced a key from the pocket in her muff. "Would you ever see if that fits it?" she said, handing it to him.

He leaped down with glee.

"What is all this?" Michael asked. A certain tetchiness was now beginning to replace his earlier amusement.

"I shan't say a word," Lucy promised. "I don't want to go putting fancy notions into your head, because you'll only say later, 'Well, it was *your* idea, after all.' D'you see?" Almost as an afterthought she added, "Though I've no objection if the house itself should make one or two interesting suggestions to you."

"It works!" Charley swung the padlock and chain free of the gates. When he pushed them open, the shriek of its rusty hinges frightened the horses, who almost backed the carriage into the ditch.

"How did you get the key at all?" Michael asked when he had restored calm once more.

"I'm after meeting the present owner – I told you – or *half*-told you, but you didn't seem very interested."

He leaned over and helped Charley back up into the carriage. "I don't seem to recall," he said. And then the memory returned to him. He turned to her and pulled a face, saying, "Below the belt, darling."

She laughed. "That's a delicate way of putting it!"

They negotiated the potholes and puddles with care; in several places they had to duck beneath low-hanging branches. The drive made a lazy S to the right, ending up square-on to the house, which had been built facing slightly west of north to catch what it could of the late-evening sun.

Decayed though it now was, Mount Venus House was still

31

impressive enough to bring one concerted gasp from all five of them as the carriage emerged at last onto the gravelled sweep before it.

"No wonder old Boniface lies in a pauper's grave!" Michael murmured, running an admiring eye over the mellow façade of ochre-coloured stone.

"Does anyone live in it now?" Alice asked.

"That's a point," her father said. "D'you mean to say Dazzler O'Dea owns all this now? He must have done well down in Cork."

"That's why I said I only half-told you. It's not Dazzler but the *other* O'Dea who owns it – his uncle."

"Old Ebenezer? Aha!' He stared at her, his brow dark with anger. "Things begin to fall into place."

It took her by surprise – until she realized he had jumped to the conclusion that she had borrowed money off the old skinflint. Well, in a way, she had – but only on account – not a loan but an advance. Secure behind the buttress of that vital distinction, she smiled back.

He drove the carriage into the stable yard, where they found some good hay for the horses.

"Can we go inside?" Charley asked excitedly when he returned from closing the stable-yard gate.

"Ask the lady with the seven-league purse," his father told him jokingly – or in a tone any youngster would assume was jocular.

With a magician's flourish Lucy produced a second key."See if that talks the same language as the back door," she said as she handed it to him.

A moment later he gave another shout of glee. His father grabbed him by the collar as he was about to sprint indoors. "Now we all stick together," he warned them. "You never know. Some of the floors may be rotten. The banisters may be rickety. Nobody is to go anywhere unless I'm sure it's safe. Understood?"

The two older ones nodded dutifully; Portia clung to her mother and said, "I want to stay out here."

"I thought you needed to *go*," Lucy chided. "There's sure to be a jakes inside."

"I already went," the child replied.

"Oh dear!" Lucy bent to feel.

"No!" she responded scornfully. "While you were getting the hay."

"Ah!" Lucy picked her up with more confidence then. "Well, if you're afraid of ghosts, you needn't be. Your great-great-great uncle was a very powerful man. He wouldn't let anybody – living or ghostly – harm one hair on the head of his great-great-great niece."

"Was he really our great-great . . . how many greats?" Alice asked.

"Thrice-great – which is much greater than great. You're his thrice-great nephews and nieces – and he built all of this!"

Moving as one, the awe-struck family passed indoors.

Portia struggled to be put down the moment they entered the scullery, antechamber to the great empty kitchens; Alice, by contrast, instinctively sought the comfort of her mother's hand. "Used you to live here when you were a little girl, Mammy?" she asked. She had only lately been able to comprehend that her mother *had* once (rather than "once upon a time") been an actual, flesh-and-blood little girl like herself.

"No!" Lucy laughed. "Thrice-great Uncle Boniface died before the middle of the last century – almost forty years before I was even born. And he was the last of the Fitzbutlers to own Mount Venus."

"It took every penny he had," Michael commented. "And plenty that he didn't."

The drying racks for the plates seemed to go on for ever – mostly empty. Only one small section was filled with a motley collection of servants' crockery. Several unwashed saucepans stood in the dry sink, bright efflorescence of mould fighting with rust for colour supremacy. Michael cranked the handle of the pump, which emitted a loud, grating shriek. Lucy and the two girls covered their ears and squealed their protests in response. Charley then thought it great fun to prolong their agony by giving the handle several more pulls, until his father plucked him away.

"How can a house take pennies you *don't* have?" he asked idly as he opened some cupboard doors and began to root around inside.

His parents exchanged amused glances. "It's a trick they're born with, some houses," Lucy told him. "And, like damp in the walls, you can't easily get rid of it."

"Has this house got the trick?" Alice asked.

Lucy drew breath to answer but Michael cut in: "It's bankrupted everyone who ever owned it. Let's hope it does the same to its present owner."

Lucy cleared her throat meaningfully; he stared back at her, a truculent gleam in his eye. "Don't you agree?" he asked, as if a negative reply would surprise him.

She smiled enigmatically. "Charley," she said, "your bottom is a very tempting target. I should come back out of that cupboard this minute, if I were you." Then, turning back to her husband, she went on, "Perhaps its present owner has found the right use for it at last. Perhaps it was never the destiny of this place to be a private house. Come on – let's explore the rest of it. Charley! I shan't tell you again."

The boy scrabbled out of the cupboard and joined them, saying excitedly, "There's a barn owl's nest in there."

"Ha ha!" Alice said, pointedly not looking at him. "You don't catch *me* out like that!"

He sneaked an arm around her and tapped her on her farther shoulder. Not fooled for a moment, she turned with weary asperity to face him – only to run her cheek directly into his outstretched finger. He giggled with delight and ran off ahead of them into the great hall that opened up beyond the servants' door.

Its magnificence took his breath away. All bickering was forgotten as they stood and stared around them, feeling rather small. Magnificent wrought-iron gates stretched from wall to wall *inside* the portico, which was wide and almost entirely glazed with pale-tinted glass set between slender stone mullions. The floor was of polished marble with a rich inlay of foliage swags and classical medallions; a central cartouche radiated spines of some gold-flecked stone, which caught Charley's attention at once. He asked his father what it was.

"Probably the stone they call 'Fool's Gold' – appropriately enough!" he replied. He was thinking you could tell at once it was a Roman Catholic's house. He'd have guessed as much from the colour on the railings down by the gate lodge. But this hall would have confirmed it to even the most doubting observer.

The walls were panelled in fumed oak, whose rich, russet hue added that touch of warmth which the marble, for all its colour, failed to provide. The staircase itself, however, was of a different wood.

"What is it, I wonder?" Michael asked, trying to score it with his thumbnail and failing.

"Yew," she told him – then, seeing the bewilderment in Portia's face, added, "Not *you*. The name of the wood is *yew*. Irish yew. There's a legend that Boniface cut down a thousand-year-old plantation of it to make room for the house. And he used it to build the staircase."

"A thousand years' bad luck!" Michael intoned.

She laughed. "And the poor man never lived to enjoy it – the bad luck, I mean. But he enjoyed the house itself for the best part of thirty years. Shall we start at the top and work our way down? Or bottom up – like Charley in the cupboard?"

"Bottom up!" Charley said – immediately contradicting himself by racing up to the half-way landing.

"He's learning fast," Michael said with seeming approval.

Lucy raised an eyebrow at him.

"Say one thing and immediately do the opposite," Michael explained, sweeping Portia into his arms and carrying her up to the landing like a sporting trophy.

The ceiling over the hall was flat, divided into squares of heavy italianate plasterwork. In the middle, over the stairwell itself, a rectangular space – a room without a floor, in effect – rose to an oval-shaped dome of clear-glazed lights, culminating, as they had seen from outside, in an ornate copper spire, which was now corroded to a soft grey-green.

"It's got *two* layers of glass," Charley exclaimed in amazement.

34

"That's rather sharp-eyed of you," Lucy said approvingly. "In fact, both my men are quite *sharp* today." She smiled rather deliberately at her husband and then, leading them across the broad expanse of the upper landing, added, "Let's see what's down this corridor."

Michael paused to explain how the double glazing helped to keep in the heat before he hastened to catch her up. "I get the feeling you already know what's down here – and everywhere else in this . . . this *palace*," he said.

"Oh? You believe such knowledge is something one inherits?"

"No." He put down the struggling Portia and took Lucy's arm. "I believe it's something one acquires – like the keys to the premises, you know."

"Ah! You think I've been out here already this week?"

"And haven't you?"

She shook her head. "I'm as excited by its novelty – and its possibilities – as you are, darling. Or ought to be." She threw open the door to what proved to be a large, opulently decorated bedroom – or it could have been an upstairs drawing room, for the carpets, furniture, and pictures had all gone.

"*Ought* to be?" he echoed, staring about him now with a new, speculative light in his eye. "Why ought I . . ." the question tailed off as his mind began to whirr.

"You can see all of Dublin from here!" Alice exclaimed excitedly from her vantage at one of the tall windows. Her younger siblings ran to join her and all three stood, awe-struck and silent for a while.

"It would just about suit a colony of artists," Michael said. "All the principal rooms face north."

"That's because of the view," Lucy pointed out. Then, clearing her throat once again, she added, "It would also suit a colony of patients. What's the first thing *we* do in a room where someone is seriously ill?"

He nodded. "All right, love. I'm beginning to understand." He stared about him, measuring the room with his eye, placing the bed, the day bed, the attendant's bed, a screened-off area for ablutions . . . "Has every bedroom a fireplace, I wonder?" he asked.

She held out a hand to him. "Let's go and see. Come on, children! And nobody's to open any of the cupboards."

Michael raised an eyebrow, for she was not usually so all-prohibitive.

"William Reilly hanged himself in one of the cupboards," she murmured by way of explanation.

The remaining rooms, being empty of all furnishings, detained the party only briefly – just long enough to count them, rough-measure them by eye, and take in their basic appointments. There were fourteen principal bedrooms on the upper floor; four of them – the ones at each end and those nearest the stairwell – had their own private bathrooms, too. All had separate dressing rooms, where a bath might be built in or an attendant might sleep.

"It's a monstrous notion, Lucy," he said when that part of their inspection was done.

"Isn't it just!" She beamed happily.

"Did Boniface put in all those private bathrooms?" he asked. "I didn't think they went in for so much cleanliness back in those days."

"It was probably Murchison did that – the shipbuilder from the Clyde."

"Ah! Scottish Presbyterian, no doubt – cleanliness being next to godliness."

"Not at all." She grinned like the cat with the cream. "He was a Roman Catholic – like all the owners of Mount Venus. Ridden by guilt, you know – wash, wash, wash!"

"Who else owned this place then?" he asked seriously. "I'm sure you know every last one."

She told him the story of the house then, more or less as she had told it to Ebenezer four days earlier.

When she had concluded, he said, "Fitzbutler – bankrupt. Gorman – bankrupt. Murchison – bankrupt. And Reilly . . ."

Lucy cut him short with a wide-eyed warning, though he had not intended to mention the suicide.

"Yes, poor Reilly," he said. "And now it's fallen into the clutches of the most notorious moneylender in Dublin. I'd give all Lombard Street to a china orange that *he* won't let this place drag him down – I just don't relish being the one whose shoulders he's standing upon in order to avoid that fate." He sighed and looked about them. "And yet . . . and yet . . .!"

Alice, who always seemed to know what her father was talking about, no matter how obscure he made his references, jumped up and down excitedly. "Are we going to live here?" she asked. "Is this going to be *our* home now?"

He ran his finger affectionately through her curls. "We're a long way short of reaching that decision, Little Face. Let's see what else there is."

"Won't Tarquin be just *green* when he hears about this!" Charley said happily.

"I'm hungry," Portia complained, rubbing her eyes.

Her mother scooped her up and hugged her tight until her mild, token struggles were over. Then her thumb went to her mouth, her head drooped on Lucy's shoulder, and, a few seconds later, she was fast asleep.

Alice went officiously to pull the thumb out again but Lucy shook her head and half-turned the sleeping bundle beyond her reach.

On the southern side of the corridor, which they explored on their return leg, were eighteen smaller bedrooms, only ten of which had dressing rooms attached.

At each extremity, east and west, a narrow stair led up to the attics, which Lucy let Michael and the two older children go back and explore on their own – after they had completed their tour of the lesser bedrooms.

She went back to the landing, to the huge window that overlooked the entrance portico, and stared down at the city, spread like a map, far below. Would she be here a year from this day? she wondered. Two years? Ten years? Would she and Michael live here all their lives? If a place was going to be *that* important, surely something of significance should already cling about its walls? It should already feel different from any other empty building in the world. She closed her eyes and strained to catch that delicate aura of premature familiarity – but felt nothing. Or, rather, felt only the increasing burden of her slumbering daughter. Then the excited chatter of the other children brought her back to the here-and-now.

"What did you find?" she asked as they emerged onto the landing.

Michael grinned. "A tribute to Ruskin, I suppose. There's morality in every stone – or brick, anyway. The eastern attics contain cubicles for the female servants – three above each of the seven principal bedrooms in that half. The partitions are ingeniously angled so that all three share the light of one window. Old Fitzbutler couldn't tolerate a plethora of tiny windows up there, d'you see, messing up his beautiful fenestration! But in the western attics – no cubicles. Just one big dormitory for the male servants. And between the two there's thirty inches of solid brick – *and* the dome."

Lucy couldn't quite picture it. "Which side gets the space above this vast stairwell?" she asked. "North or south of the dome?"

"Both. The men get the northern bit, the women the southern one. It's where their ablutions are. I've never seen anything quite like it. They've got *piped* water up there – cold and hot! Those Clyde shipbuilders know how to do things properly. I'll bet old Murchison worked out how much of their wages would go in carrying water up to the attics and realized that, if he was piping water up to these two bedrooms, it wouldn't cost much to take it up one more floor . . . pay for itself inside a year. I think we should take up one or two floorboards and see what other surprises he has left behind for us."

His eyes shone. He was like a boy with a new mechanical toy, whose first thought is to take it to bits and see how it works.

"Not today," she said.

He drew breath to assure her that, of course, he didn't mean today – and then realized it would be akin to committing himself to come back here, to invest *real* time, not a spare Sunday afternoon, in this lunatic . . . seductive idea of hers. "Well . . . let's see," he said vaguely.

Portia woke up at that moment, yawned, and said, "I'm hungry," as if her previous statement to that effect had been made only seconds ago.

"Yes!" Lucy said, bouncing her joyfully, "Let's go and eat our picnic now. We can come back another day and look at all the outbuildings and gardens and things."

"I didn't say that!" Michael warned her.

"Of course you didn't," she agreed.

They returned to the kitchens, where they guzzled their sandwiches and relished their tea, which had been kept piping hot all this time in Dewar flasks, "acquired" from the physiological laboratory at the Eli. Then they made a quick tour of the ground floor. As Ebenezer had promised, it sported a larger ballroom than the one at the RDS in Leinster House – not to mention a library (empty) almost as large, a dining room, a banqueting hall, a breakfast room, a morning room, two drawing rooms, a billiards room with its two tables intact but lacking balls and cues . . . on and on it went. At the far end, on the northwest corner, a passage led through – not past, but actually through – the under-butler's bedroom, then the butler's bedroom, to end inside a huge concrete vault containing the silver safe. Alas, it was as empty as the library.

Outside again, as they took the blankets off the horses and removed their nosebags, Michael looked longingly at the numerous outbuildings. Somewhere among them there was, no doubt, a laundry, a steam engine for pumping water, furnaces for heating it and raising steam, perhaps an ancient gasifier . . . an untold wealth of grown-up toys. He drew out his watch, as if it might contradict the evidence of fading brightness along the eastern skyline. "Another day," he murmured sadly, putting it back.

Then he caught a glimpse of Lucy's smile. "*If* . . ." he added heavily.

"Ah, yes!" she replied. "If!"

E vensong was over, the children were in bed and fast asleep. The wind had veered northwesterly during the evening and was now working up to a full gale; it keened in the sashes of the drawing room windows and stirred the heavy velvet curtains. Lucy clutched her silk shawl tightly to her and felt the chill more sharply as she reached up a hand to take the whiskey nightcap Michael now offered her.

"I hope you don't object to it straight from the bottle," he said. "The wretched stopper is wedged tight in the decanter again. They'll have to take it back and regrind it."

"As long as you don't try bicycle oil again!" she pulled a face of comical disgust.

"Will I redden that fire with a spot more coal?" he went on.

Reluctantly she said it was hardly worth it. He laughed and she asked why.

"You're like your thrice- . . . no, twice-great uncle – the illustrious Boniface. There's that story about him buying the Rembrandt, remember? It cost him an absolute fortune – over a thousand pounds. And when he came home he told his cook he only wanted cabbage and bacon for dinner. Doubtless he slept easier for knowing how much he'd saved on port and caviar – just as you'll sleep easier tonight for saving two lumps of coal."

"Ha ha," she said petulantly. "And what's supposed to be my equivalent of the Rembrandt?"

He seated himself in his favourite armchair, facing her, and said, "I was rather hoping *you'd* tell *me*, Lucinda."

She stared into the dying fire awhile, sipping her whiskey in an abstracted manner and relishing its burn in her throat. "I've been thinking about the way they arranged the lesser bedrooms at Mount Venus . . ." she began.

"Lu-cy!" he cried more sharply.

"Very well!" She sighed and turned to face him then. "If you want to know the full of it, I was taking some jewelry to . . ." She hesitated between "be cleaned" and "the pawnbroker" and eventually chose to tell the truth – because, for once, it actually suited her purposes better than the easy white lie: ". . . the pawnbroker, when . . ."

"*What?*" He was aghast.

She bit her lip to stifle the hot defence that rose to her throat. *Hold hard!* she warned herself. She set her whiskey down and asked belligerently, "D'you want yet another flaming argument about the past, Michael? Because let me tell you, it would be a lot more fiery than the two coals I've just saved. Or shall we talk in a calm, collected way about the future, instead?"

"A pawnbroker!" he echoed. "Which pawnbroker, anyway?"

"It doesn't matter."

"It matters who might have seen you going in or coming out."

"I'm not an *absolute* fool, Michael. Occasionally incautious with money, perhaps – but I'm not alone in that tumbril. Just you try casting the first stone!"

He bridled. "I'm sure I don't know what you may mean by that, my dear."

"'My dear' was a dangerous phrase on his lips. Spoken with reined-back menace, it was the verbal equivalent of a Chinese burn.

"Then I'll repeat the question: the sorry past or the happier future?"

"Ah!" He smiled thinly. "The *sorry* past, is it! Well now, if sorrow and contrition and apologies are in the air . . ."

"Then I'll accept them and we'll say no more about it," she cut in quickly. Her eyes sparkled. She smiled and let her tongue linger on her lip – she did not know why except that experience had taught her it had some soothing – or behaviour-altering – effect on him.

This time it almost failed to work; for a long moment he teetered

39

between his anger and a reluctant amusement at her little *coup de grâce*. He was still in that uncertain state when she pressed on: "Anyway, I never got there, so it hardly matters. I ran across old Dazzler O'Dea, as I told you, and we went to some tea rooms nearby and . . ."

"Tea rooms?" he asked, as if the term itself were unfamiliar.

It was a clever ruse for, in her desire to placate him, she said at once, "You know – café – what else can one call it? – that little place down past the Empire Theatre, near the corner with Parliament Street."

He was onto it at once then. "The pawnbroker in *Eustace* Street?" he asked in a tone of horror.

She gave herself a mental kick and said, "Oh, is there one in Eustace Street, too?"

His smile conceded her quickness of wit but he was not deceived. "Don't ever go down *that* street, Lucy," he said.

"Why not? Not that I've ever needed to, mind . . ."

"Just don't. That's all."

She smiled mischievously. "Dazzler told me his Uncle Ebenezer owns half the properties in that street, on the side nearer Jury's."

"I'm not in the least surprised to hear it."

"He was collecting the rents when I met him – or *had been* collecting them."

"Hmm," was all her husband said to that.

She grinned. "I know why you've gone all vague. There's one of those . . . you know – *houses* there, isn't there."

He stared at her blankly. "I'm still intrigued to know how you got from *not* going to the pawnshop in Eustace Street and *not* meeting Dazzler O'Dea down there to . . . well, let's say the ticklish subject of financial need."

Her mind raced but no words came.

"I mean, if he spotted you going in or met you coming out – then it becomes perfectly clear. But otherwise I can't for the life of me see the Honourable Lucinda Raven, whose parents once spurned the impecunious Dazzler O'Dea, calmly volunteering the information that . . ."

"All *right*, Michael. Try salt and mustard, too! There must be something about me that acts like a magnet to *smart* fellows – cunning, tricky, wily fellows. For he was onto it like a travelling rat – just like yourself, now. Enough said?"

He smiled complacently. "You've hardly touched your nightcap."

She picked it up and tossed it down her throat in one, passing the empty glass to him with a truculent flourish. He raised an eyebrow and took it hesitantly from her. "A bird never flew on one wing," she said.

He acknowledged the truth of that with a dip of his head and poured her a second, rather meaner measure.

"So," she went on, "he said his Uncle Ebenezer would prove far more discreet – and more generous – than Webb's or any pawnbroker. That was last Tuesday. So come Wednesday morning I'm standing trembling up near the top of Sackville Street, thinking once I get into the clutches of that old devil, will I ever get out again?"

"And?"

"It turned out he wasn't interested in the jewelry, at all – didn't even look at it! He's changed somehow."

Michael frowned. "But it's gone. Your jewelry's gone. It's not in your box."

"I told you – I took it to Cosgrave's, to be cleaned." She grinned knowingly. "And yes, I *was* telling the truth, too! Anyway, take it from me – Ebenezer O'Dea has changed."

Michael shook his head. "People like that never change. He's noticed what a financial success Miss Huxley is making of her private nursing home in Lower Mount Street. Money can whisper across miles to that man. He's not changed."

"Well," she conceded, "not right down at rock bottom, perhaps. But he's changed in his methods. He'll still grasp every brass farthing he can, but not in his old, skinflint ways. He's bound in a sedan chair now, you know – permanently, I think. And they say his heart's not good – or Dazzler says so, anyway. So maybe the old boy's eyes are trained on first-and-last things these days? Also he has this very good-looking nurse with him, day and night. She might have softened his outlook." Lucy laughed. "Dazzler calls her the Ice Maiden. He said she *looks* like a flamehaired temptress but she's as cold as ice – so it's not hard to guess what went on there!"

"And does this temptress have a name?" he asked.

She frowned and tapped her forehead with annoyance, for Diana Powers's name just would not come to her. It was the same name as one of the big Dublin whiskeys, she remembered. She looked at the opened bottle on the sideboard and said, "Jameson, I think. Nurse Jameson – yes." It didn't sound quite right – but, anyway, what did it matter? "She is rather beautiful," she added, as if that somehow compensated the nurse, *in absentia*, for the failure to recall her name. "Luxuriously beautiful. The first sight of her must have played havoc with poor Dazzler's heartbeat. He's very bitter about her now, anyway."

"Yes – anyway!" Michael interrupted. "What is the oul' rascal's proposal? Why did he give you the key to Mount Venus?"

This was the part where she had to skirt the truth rather carefully. "He made no proposal to *me*," she said self-deprecatingly. "He'd hardly do a thing like that. I'm sure he *has* a proposal and I'm sure he'll put it to *you*, if the time should come. All he said to me was that he'd acquired the property in default of a loan and was rather desperate to turn it to some account. Not a word about poor Reilly's suicide, though. I skirted round it, just to see. He thought the place

41

might make an excellent sanatorium – given the proper medical supervision. If you were interested, he thought we might kill two birds with one stone. That's all."

"It's rather more than *one* stone," he murmured, scratching the bridge of his nose – a gesture with which he always accompanied his knottiest thinking. "Rather more than a million stones, I shouldn't wonder." He began thinking aloud. "If he kept the freehold and charged us a market rent . . ."

She interrupted: "I doubt if old Ebenezer would ever suggest a simple, straightforward arrangement like that. He could get any old doctor to take him up on that basis. He sees us as more than usually vulnerable to . . . how can I put it to avoid a fruitless argument? We're probably amenable to a less profitable arrangement – or more profitable from his point of view."

Michael nodded thoughtfully.

"Although mind you," she went on, "it did also occur to me that his reasons might be more medical than pecuniary. His own suite of rooms with his own lovely nurse – in what will probably be the best sanatorium in the kingdom . . . If you can already hear the wingbeat of Death's dark angel, it might seem an alluring prospect."

But Michael shook his head at that. "Lend us money – and then place himself in our care? I doubt it."

She laughed. "Oh, you may be sure that, in any arrangement he may propose along those lines, we shall certainly lose – not gain – by his death!"

He reached a long arm for the whiskey, feeling now that her last helping had been niggardly. He spotted the name as he held the bottle toward her. "Coincidence!" he said. "Have a drop more of *this* flaxen-haired temptress – although she's more auburn, actually."

She did not correct his little slip about "flaxen-haired" for she was slightly embarrassed – almost as if he had accused her of engineering the coincidence; but she accepted the refill with pleasure. "I must say, I'm in two minds about this whole business," she went on. "I mean, no sooner do I think of Mount Venus and how wonderful it would be to live there, and how the children would adore it, and what a superb sanatorium *you'd* make of it . . . than I remember Uncle Ebenezer!"

"And your flesh crawls!"

She did not at once agree.

"That's what you always used to say about him," he reminded her.

"I know. Funnily enough, though, he doesn't make me feel like that any more. In fact, he was really rather pleasant, if you can imagine it."

"Not easily!"

"Well, he was. Yet he still leaves one with that feeling he'd be absolutely ruthless if you crossed him or if you were at his mercy and didn't do as he said."

They sipped their – by now rather extended – nightcaps in silence awhile. At last Michael said, "I agree! I have the same feeling as you. It's a wonderful opportunity and if any other man in Dublin offered it – Jew, Quaker, or heathen – I'd leap at it. But we'd never know another night's peace if we let ourselves fall into *that* one's hands."

There was no pleasure in his voice at having reached this totally negative conclusion. Indeed, his gloomy tone deepened still further as he went on: "There's nothing for it, old girl. We shall just have to pull in our horns."

"Yes," she said bleakly.

"I'm not compelled to maintain my consulting rooms in Fitzwilliam Square."

"Of course not."

"Most physicians take twenty-five years to achieve what we've tried to do inside ten."

"That's true."

"It was a noble attempt but we just failed to leap the bar."

She nodded but said nothing.

A further ruminative silence descended and there was more sipping of whiskey, this time with little show of relish.

He sighed and sucked a strand of celery from between his teeth. Celery in March! That was the sort of thing they would now have to give up.

She sighed in sympathy and murmured, "On the other hand . . ." before lapsing once more into silence. Surely he must be wondering about the money she'd been spending this past week?

"Mmm?" He looked up at her, but with little hope or even interest.

"You wouldn't actually have to commit yourself," she pointed out.

"If . . .?" he asked.

"Well I mean there'd be no harm in at least *listening* to . . . whatever he has to say."

He agreed that was so.

"At least we'd know *what* we were turning down."

"Quite."

"You could even go back to him with some kind of counterproposal of your own."

He frowned. "Such as?"

"Well, you and Sir William might join forces and . . ."

"That old charlatan! Never!"

"His name still counts for something, darling. And he needn't do much more than lend it to the venture. But we both know half a dozen bankers who'd *fight* each other to lend to a partnership between you and Sir William. *If* old Ebenezer really is so desperate to turn the liability of Mount Venus into a roaring asset, he'd leap at a straightforward offer of a ninety-nine-year lease, wouldn't he? No strings!"

43

He made several dubious noises but she could see he was interested, despite the rivalry between him and his former chief, Sir William Sheehan, FRS FRICP. To rub it in she added, "Besides, suppose we turn down this offer and Ebenezer O'Dea takes it to someone else – Fergal O'Hare, for instance!"

He winced at the very thought. "All right! I'll go and see the old devil. Just see him, though. At least we'll know what we're turning down."

Michael understood what Lucy had meant when she spoke of standing "trembling near the top of Sackville Street"; the following afternoon he experienced the same mistrust of his own self-control, the same apprehensions about dealing with Satan, when he stood at the identical spot, adjusting his cravat for the hundredth time and wondering what lunacy had brought him to the brink of this dire new departure in his life.

Diana Powers, standing well back from the drawing-room window, watched his every move. When at last he squared his shoulders and set out across the street, she turned to her employer and said, "You'll probably be happier discussing this business in my absence, sir. So if I may, I'll take advantage of your interview to slip out and get some more calamine lotion and surgical spirit – also one or two little medical requirements for myself."

She added the last bit because he always became mildly flustered at any suggestion that she was a woman with personal needs.

And, true to form, he gave her leave at once – reluctantly but without question. She hung back until Violet, the maid who was answering knocks that day, had shown Michael Raven in . . . until the study door had closed behind him, and then, pausing only to ask the maid to half-pull one of the drawing-room curtains as a signal that the visitor had gone, she slipped quietly out of doors.

She set off for the medical hall in Abbey Street, filled with self congratulation that, after so many years, the sight of Michael had stirred her so little. What price all that fuss now! There was a time when she could have killed him, would have killed for him, would have died for him. But ten long, bitter years had finally cauterized even the deepest of her wounds. Never again would she be the fluttering, helpless prisoner of that particular weakness, she now realized. All the same . . . she'd take it one step at a time; she had no desire to face the challenge of a full reunion today. The mere sight of him crossing Sackville Street – and stirring absolutely nothing within her – was sufficient.

Her thoughts turned then to old Ebenezer O'Dea's strangely selective embarrassment. She supposed it was because, in the course of her duties, she had to carry out some fairly intimate procedures for him, and so any suggestion that she was something other than a genderless nurse-automaton was cause for embarrassment. And yet his fastidiousness was purely physical; it did not extend to her emotional and romantic nature at all. Every day he would make at least one more attempt to chip away at her adamantine exterior, trying to find out what feelings might be simmering away inside. But fair dues to him, he was the same with everyone else.

People's motives were an endless fascination to him. After the departure of every visitor – even of the plumber who came to unblock a drain – he would call her to his side and hold a little postmortem: What did Nurse Powers suppose was that woman or man really after in life? What would be the ultimate thing they'd strive to achieve? And what huge prize would they dismiss at once – not even consider – because they'd think it was beyond their grasp? At the other end of the scale, what petty inducement would they judge beneath their contempt? And in between, what would they sell their own children to gain? He could also ask some surprising questions – things that would be of no immediate benefit to him to know: "Do you think that lady would enjoy Beethoven more than Bach? . . . Would that fellow be more likely to take a walking tour or go fishing on his holidays?" – questions like that. She often told him he should write stories because he was so interested in all the differences between people.

He replied that what he really wanted was to create some sort of zoo where all the exhibits were humans. There'd be four main sections: Phlegmatic, Choleric, Sanguine, and Melancholic. And inside each there'd be every subdivision you could possibly imagine; so you could compare, for instance, a cautious Sanguine with an outgoing Phlegmatic. And there'd be special demonstrations every afternoon – battles of wits between different types. And there'd be longer contests, too, lasting months or even years, involving factions made up of alliances of many different types . . .

Half way through this absurd fancy he had burst out laughing, saying, "Begod, Nurse Powers! You realize what I'm describing, don't you!"

She had suggested it would make a book to rival *Gulliver's Travels*.

"Not a bit of it," he cackled. "Isn't it Dublin's fair city itself to a T! I have it already, don't you see? I'm living, here and now, in the heart of my own favourite zoo!"

Had that been a genuine discovery, she wondered, or had he begun the entire flummery already sure of its conclusion? You'd never know with him but, either way, the effect was to remind her of her status as just another exhibit in his private zoo – Phlegmatic, for sure; you'd find her somewhere down the little path that crosses over into Melancholic.

It was the same with his proposal to make her matron of the Ravens' sanatorium, or whatever they were going to call the place. On the face of it, his offer was highly flattering to her. He appreciated her dedication, admired her skill, was impressed by her character. He needed to have eyes and ears out there at Mount Venus – who better than she, then? Yet she could not shake off the suspicion that he had no real intention of carrying out his promise. Quite simply, he had noticed how the very mention of Michael's name had startled her; so, later, he had dropped his suggestion out of the blue like that, simply to see how she responded. When it came to the point he'd make himself far too ill for her to leave him, and he'd recover as soon as the position went, by default, to another nurse.

Or so she fervently hoped.

Back in the study Ebenezer was watching young Michael Raven with a feeling bordering on incredulity. Here was a man so hopelessly in debt that he ought not to show his face outdoors except on moonless nights between midnight and four in the morning; his hair should have turned white months ago, and it ought by now to be falling out by the handful; dark rings should circle his eyes; his cheeks should quiver with one continual tic. How dare he have fingernails ready for the cutting when they should be half-way down to the quick! How could his voice possibly be so calm and unflustered! And why – above all – should his prime concern now be the *naming* of the new institution on Mount Venus? The fellow had not mentioned money once! Was he the greatest fool Ebenezer had ever encountered – certainly in such a relatively exalted position? Or the wiliest rascal with whom it had been his privilege to lock horns? Time would tell – though Ebenezer doubted that this interview would.

"*Clinic* is a possibility," Michael was saying. He wondered how much longer the old boy would put up with his irrelevant discussions. "It's curious how words change meanings, isn't it. A *clinic* used to mean a bed-patient. I remember dear old Professor Sahl saying, 'I treat my ambulatories in the morning and my clinics in the afternoon.' But when I trained, the word usually referred to a sort of adjunct to a hospital where particular conditions were treated – consumptives' clinic, eye clinic . . . and so on. Nursing mothers' clinic – that was another. Usually they were free, too, for the poor. But now I see the word used more and more for describing a superior sort of sanatorium . . ."

"Superior?" Ebenezer questioned. "You mean it can charge higher fees for the same services?"

Michael laughed but did not directly answer. "It's because *sanatorium* has changed meaning, too. To most people nowadays it's where consumptives go for the open-air cure."

"Does consumption pay well?" Ebenezer tried again. "The open-air cure sounds as if it would be cheap on coals, anyway!"

"We could build a separate house for consumptives at the upper end of the gardens."

"Build?" the older man echoed in horror. "My dear chap – the whole idea is to employ the *existing* white elephant, not give him a

46

mate to breed with! Are there enough consumptives in Ireland to turn the whole of Mount Venus into a consumptives' clinic?"

"Lord! There are enough to fill it a thousand times over – but not enough rich ones, I think. The rich all go to Switzerland, which is what any sensible physician would continue to recommend."

To Michael's surprise the other beamed broadly at hearing this. He raised his eyebrows in a questioning manner.

"I'm glad you're thinking along the right lines at last," Ebenezer said. "So tell me, what is the next most lucrative ailment, eh?"

"Why *ailment* in the singular, sir – if I may ask?"

"Ah! I understand, of course, that to have an entire *clinic* – shall we settle on that word for the moment? – to have an entire clinic devoted to a single disease or condition would be rather dull for you. But it might have distinct advantages in *my* specialism – which is accountancy. We could order medicines and equipment in gross at considerable discounts, for example. And – correct me if I'm wrong – but just suppose our clinic became renowned for treating this one condition, would not your colleagues, throughout these islands, be under a strong compulsion to send any patient who presented with that condition . . . that is the correct medical usage, is it not?"

Michael grinned and said it was. Now he understood, too, why Lucy said the old boy's manner had changed, at least superficially.

"Would they not be compelled," he repeated, "to send such patients to us?"

"No doctor can be *compelled* to do anything, sir."

"Come, come, Raven! I speak of *social* compulsion, of course. If Lady Ardilaun brought her niece to you and said she wanted to send the girl to some exclusive clinic in Switzerland, are you going to tell her she could save a farthing or two by sending her to the Adelaide? Especially if the Swiss people were to send you a little *bonne bouche* by way of a thank-you?" He peered intently at Michael. "And don't tell me they never do such things!"

Michael shook his head awkwardly – not quite in denial. "There is usually an introduction fee," he said – his tone suggesting that was something altogether different.

"Ah! You are quite right, young man!" He smiled as if the discovery surprised him more than somewhat. "It *is* important to get the name absolutely right. *Bonne bouche* is dreadful. *Bribe* would be appalling! But 'introduction fee'!" He blew a kiss at the ceiling. "*Quelle finesse!*" He rubbed his hands and became serious again at once. "So ideally we need to find a common ailment of the rich – something that would keep us in funds for the next thirty years, and upon which you could write the definitive textbook before you retire."

He had offered the last item as a kind of jest but the sudden gleam in Michael's eye made him think again. He wondered how far he could push it before even this remarkably ambitious (and therefore, in some respects, blind) young man saw the funny side of it. "There'd certainly be a knighthood in it," he mused. "But you'd probably earn that anyway, no matter what you did. Let's pick a *royal* disease! There must be a list as long as your arm. Then you'd land a viscountcy at the very least. Lord Raven of Mount Venus in the peerage of Ireland – eh?"

The young fellow smiled at the words, but not – Ebenezer noted – at their absurdity; his smile was of simple modesty!

Ebenezer pushed further. "Best of all," he reflected, "would be one of the *imaginary* diseases. I often wonder about *neurasthaenia*, you know. D'you think there really is such a thing? It amazes me the way it stalks the land, singling out the better-off sort of female with time on her hands and corsets of an unbelievable ferocity."

The suggestion raised no more than a faint smile of distaste. Ebenezer changed tack. "Or these multitudinous diseases connected with the heart – there seems to be a new one every week. They can't *all* be real, can they?" He waited for the silence to force young Raven to respond – and he had no doubt the fellow *would* respond for he had seen a flicker of interest, hastily suppressed, at his mention of the word *heart*.

"For example, sir?" Michael asked.

"Blood pressure, for instance," the older man replied vaguely.

He laughed dismissively. "We've been measuring that for over a hundred years."

"I know. Your colleague Doctor Heffernan . . ."

"Excellent man," Michael interrupted mechanically.

"Quite. He took mine only last week. Said it was nice and low – subnormal. Congratulated me, in fact. But he also warned me not to consult a physician in France or Germany – if I should think of travelling abroad. He said *they* would regard it as a *very* grave matter."

Michael nodded. "And, indeed, they prove it to their own satisfaction by killing off several thousand patients a year with their rather drastic 'cures' for this nonexistent disease!"

"Aha!" Ebenezer pursed his lips. "I'm obviously barking up the wrong tree. I thought that if our clinic could specialize in a non-disease, we couldn't do much harm. But you seem to imply that treating diseases that don't exist can be dangerous?"

"I would compare it to mending an unbroken spoke in a wheel of a gig that is trundling merrily along."

Ebenezer chuckled at this and then, making a steeple of his two index fingers, rested his chin gravely upon the point of it. "Good," he said at length. "I'm satisfied at least that there's no cant in you – none of that highfalutin nonsense about doctors being angels of mercy . . . the Lady with the Lamp . . . all that sort of thing. So enough of this sparring! Let us turn to matters of substance. The questions, it seems to me, are these: Do we concentrate on one or two specialized conditions – presumably non-infectious? Or would we do better to set up a sort of hospital-in-miniature out there and treat all comers? Does the altitude and view – and remoteness from the city's vapours – offer particular advantages? Will you maintain your connection with the Eli and merely administer Mount Venus – or will it become your full-time dedication? I want to know what each of these choices is likely to cost and what return we might expect on our outlay."

"Here and now?" Michael asked in consternation.

"Hardly!" Ebenezer laughed. "But take out your notebook. I want you to go away with a list of such questions – drawn with all the precision we can manage, between us. And I would like the answers by this day week."

The hour that followed was one of the turning points in Michael's life; even as he lived through it he was aware of that. Until that morning his approach to financial matters had been based on a rather static view of money. Insofar as he thought about the stuff at all, he would have likened it to a pool that fills at one end and empties at the other. The flow could be as lively or as sluggish as you liked, but the pool stayed more or less the same. But Ebenezer O'Dea's questions made him realize just how much improvement was possible in the way of navigation and irrigation (to pursue the same metaphor), not only upstream of the pool, but downstream, as well. The first man who ever realized that penned-back water could turn wheels as well as flow prettily away could not have felt more excited by the discovery than Michael Raven was when he left that house and wandered in a daze down Sackville Street, unaware of time and place until he reached the Liffey's banks.

Ebenezer, too, was sunk in thought – until a rather strange action on the part of Violet, the maid, caught his attention. She wheeled his sedan chair back into the drawing-room and immediately half-drew one of the curtains.

"I don't want that," he told her. "Lord, isn't there little enough sun with the month that's in it!"

"But Nurse Powers asked me to do it, sir," the woman responded. "As a signal, you see, that your man was departed."

He pretended to accept this explanation but the moment he was alone he poled his chair over to the window in question and, reaching up with his walking stick, pulled the curtain wide open again.

A few minutes later he was pleased to see Nurse Powers walking slowly up the opposite pavement staring at the drawing-room windows every so often – and far more often than she would if her interest were merely casual. "I knew it!" he murmured happily. Diana Powers and Michael Raven were more to each other than mere ships that had passed in the night! Her behaviour now confirmed it.

His mind raced off down familiar, well-oiled grooves.

azzler O'Dea swung his cane with panache – or perhaps merely elan – as he strolled up the tree-lined island that ran down the centre of Sackville Street to the north of Nelson's Pillar. He noticed the young woman waiting to cross but did not recognize her as Nurse Powers until too late – that is, until she turned and recognized him. Her masklike face remained as impassive – and as beautiful – as ever. Such a waste! he thought. The sight of a comely nun always produced the same response in him. Unemployed loveliness on such a lavish scale was a taunt – a sneer against manhood in general, and the manhood of Dazzler O'Dea in particular. Diana Powers was like someone who, having accidentally acquired a superb rod and line, baited the hook and cast it in the waters – but then, having no liking at all for fish, abandoned it in favour of some other amusement. One day she'd go too far. She'd fish out of her depth and catch a shark, or some monster of the deep too big to ignore – a creature that would take a terrible revenge on her. Or so he hoped.

Knowing it was a hopeless cause, knowing he was heading directly for one more rebuff, one further humiliation, he nonetheless flashed his most engaging smile and said, "I never saw you looking so grand, Nurse Powers. Will you not let me in on the secret?"

In fact, as he realized when he came to a halt at her side, she was not looking too well at all. Perhaps she'd landed that shark already! Whatever about that, *something* had at last cracked her flawless exterior – not into smithereens but enough to open a gap or two. And through them he glimpsed a nervous, hesitant young woman he'd never seen before. To his surprise he found he was suddenly quite concerned on her behalf; he would never have believed he could entertain such a genuine feeling for her. "I'm sorry," he said. "Pay no heed to my blather. Are you feeling quite well? Will you take my arm across the street?"

"No." The refusal was direct enough but she spoke it hesitantly and with none of her customary chill. "I just . . . I'll be . . ." She glanced again at the curtain that was supposed to signal Michael Raven's departure. Surely he couldn't *still* be in there? Not after two hours. She herself could hardly stay away much longer, not without some thundering good excuse – of which her mind was, at present, a total blank. Had Violet simply forgotten to do as she was asked? Or had himself come into the room and told her to draw it back again? In that case, God send she hadn't explained to her master why it was drawn; he'd be onto it like a terrier with teeth to spare.

The pause gave Dazzler the chance to discover his more usual self. A vulnerable woman – especially one who had flaunted the old don't-touch-me as blatantly as Diana Powers had done – was like bad meat to a fly where he was concerned. All she needed now was a little push and who knew what beans she might not spill.

"Ah," he sighed, "I know this feeling so well. I call it the Sackville Street Panic. You stand out here with your heart like lead, thinking can I possibly *face* another day with the oul' fella in there? How sweet the city air smells by comparison! How bright . . ."

"Oh no!" she exclaimed, horrified to think he could have mistaken her hesitation for disloyalty of that kind. And so – as he had hoped – it provoked her into revealing things she would otherwise have kept to herself. "To be honest with you, Mister O'Dea," she said, "your uncle is, at this moment, interviewing a . . . a person in connection with a new scheme of his."

Dazzler was cockahoop. His first thought was to tell her he knew all about it – had, indeed, put the notion into the old boy's head. Not only would it encourage her further confidences, it would show her he wasn't just the errand boy she clearly took him to be. But, like any good chess player, he rapidly thought through several of the moves that might follow this original revelation. One possibility was that he would tell her she was wrong if she supposed Michael Raven was still in there, for hadn't he passed the man not five minutes since, wandering in a daze down Sackville Street.

And that was where he decided to hold his tongue instead. The woman's agitation was so unusual, he suspected he would learn more if he said nothing. "Oh, really?" was all the prompting he gave her.

And it was all the prompting she needed, too. "Naturally it involves a certain advance of capital," she continued.

"How surprising!" He grinned – and was astonished to see the ghost of a smile twitch at her lips. The arctic icecap was breaking up with a vengeance today!

"And one of his conditions for advancing it – I should first explain that it's for a private sanatorium of some kind – one of his conditions, as I say, is that I should be taken on as its matron."

"You sound as if you'd rather be pelted for a month with wet fish."

She actually laughed! A single, harsh bark of a laugh, but a laugh nonetheless. It seemed to surprise her as much as it did him; she nipped it off at once and was left looking marooned. Dazzler took a further gamble. "I'll be honest with you now," he said. "I know the proposal you're referring to. In fact, 'twas meself first put it into the quare fella's head – because, you see, 'twas also meself was after meeting the lady . . . tskoh! Why go all about the bush like this! I met the Honourable Lucinda Raven – there now!"

The moment he started on this revelation he knew why he had decided against it earlier – and why he ought to have stuck by that decision. For how on earth was he going to explain the fact that Mrs Raven had apparently volunteered the intimate details of her financial plight to him – an utter stranger for all Nurse Powers knew? There was no time to devise a watertight lie. It would have to be the truth. He reached that conclusion just as he was telling her he had met the Honourable Lucinda Raven; without a pause he continued: "I knew her when she was still Lucinda Fitzbutler. In fact, between you and me and these four trees, we did a line together before his lordship gave me the Grand Oul' Order of the Boot. I only mention this to explain why she confided in me certain facts that wild dogs wouldn't have got out of her in the ordinary run of things."

Nurse Powers just stood there, mouth agape, drinking in every word; he could not believe his luck in striking a topic that could so capture and hold her interest. Under his breath, but intended for her ears, too, he added laconically. "Mind you, it helped that she was just emerging from a pawnshop at the time – with a face on her like a plate of mortal sins."

For the second incredible time within the space of five minutes Diana Powers burst out laughing – and it was no bark this time but a genuine silvery peal. "Oh, Mister O'Dea!" she exclaimed, giving him that reproachful smile women use when they don't really mean to admonish.

By now there was nothing he would not dare. "I'm sorry," he replied, pretending to take her chiding seriously. "I know how you *hate* to laugh. I'll guard me tongue more carefully in future, so I will. Anyway, where was I? Oh yes. Her Honourable Majesty informed me, between bites of a sticky bun, that a million pounds would just about paper over the worries on her life. And so – to cut to the discovery scene at once – I remembered that great white elephant out at Mount Venus, which my uncle got when Reilly . . . er, defaulted last year."

He wished he hadn't brought that up, for he could tell that Miss Powers remembered the suicide; she was her usual solemn self again now – all his good work undone.

"So," he concluded swiftly, "that is why Michael the Magnificent is talking with my uncle about setting up a sanatorium out there – though if you suppose they are engaged in discussion at this very moment, you are mistaken, for I saw the man myself, not ten minutes ago, walking into the coffee rooms at the Metropole and looking as if he'd stopped a twenty-pound hammer between the eyes."

The relief in her face when she heard that Michael Raven had departed was so overwhelming that it encouraged Dazzler into yet another flight of wild surmise – and yet another gamble. Halfway across the street he took her arm – ostensibly to warn her of a speeding bicyclist, whom she had not, in fact, noticed – and said with a laugh, "Wouldn't it balance the pyramid nicely if it turned out you and the good doctor did a line once, too!"

Angrily she pulled away from him and stamped across the remainder of the street until she gained the farther pavement, where she turned and reeled him off a piece of her mind.

Had she been her old, cold self, he would have felt mortified; he would have kicked himself all week. But there was just a shade too much fervour in her remonstration for him to take it entirely at face value. Secretly, too, he exulted that he had at last found a trigger to release the passionate Diana Powers he had long suspected of hiding inside the starched uniform of the nurse. Therefore, having risked so much already, he decided on one last fling of the dice. "I only mention it," he said evenly as he caught up with her, "because – as I'm in that predicament myself, and am none too happy about it – I feel very keenly the want of a supporter who knows what it's like." His smile pinched his eyes to lazy slits as he concluded: "You may come to feel the same yourself in time."

She hesitated a long moment but then, dismissing him with a contemptuous "*hah!*", spun on her heel and strode confidently up to her employer's front door.

Violet opened it with an apologetic tilt of her head that – she hoped – conveyed everything.

Dazzler, remembering Diana's hesitation, calmly followed her inside, knowing he could now afford to bide his time.

Lucy kept her impatience in check for as long as she could, but when bedtime came around and an unusually pensive Michael had still volunteered nothing more than the bare facts – that Ebenezer O'Dea was keen to turn Mount Venus into a clinic, preferably with him, Michael Raven, at its head, but with A. N. O'Other if he refused the offer – she could contain her curiosity no longer. "Ninety minutes was a long time to be telling you that place would make a grand clinic," she remarked as she rubbed the goose grease into the knuckles of her fingers; the wrinkles there were already beginning to distress her. "Was there talk of hard cash anywhere in it?"

Michael shook his head. He was already between the sheets, sitting up and trying to read a paper on high blood pressure in kidney failure. "He's too clever for that. In fact, I caught myself thinking – somewhere about half-way through our discussion – that I was probably talking to the cleverest man I'd even encountered in my life. Does he give you that feeling?"

"What, that he knows just the right words to hold your interest? No, *more than* hold your interest – to grip you, to recruit you."

"Yes – recruit you! That's it. If the army had him as recruiting sergeant, the whole country would be in uniform."

"And no king's shilling on the table, either! You'd see the flash of it a dozen times but when you put out your hand, it'd be gone. Well, if it wasn't cash, my love, what *did* he offer you by way of inducement?"

"Fame. Immortality. A peerage!"

She laughed. "All of which are well within his gift, of course!"

But he did not share her merriment. "In a curious way, they are." He laid the paper aside. "Let me tell you how it went."

"Please!" she said heavily. She screwed the lid back on the grease and crossed the room to join him.

"Oh," he said, "I know you've been eaten alive all day with the curiosity, but I've been trying to work out what he did and how he did it – and I'm still not sure."

He lay on his back, looking up at the ceiling; she snuggled at his side and, clasping his hand, brought it up to her lips. Yet for some reason these intimacies made her feel more remote from him than before. "Go on," she prompted.

"He played the cynical card for all it was worth," Michael began. "He treated medicine as if it were nothing but a system for squeezing as much money out of patients as possible. Money, money, money – that's all you heard. He wanted to be told the most profitable disease. Or even *non*-disease."

"Mmm?" She stopped stroking his hand for a moment.

"He thinks neurasthænia is probably a nonexistent disease – the way it goes about the country striking down only those ladies with time on their hands and enough wealth to indulge it."

Lucy chuckled and began to caress his hand again. "Don't you think he's right?"

"Probably – in that particular case, anyway. But I think he had quite a different purpose in bringing it up. He wanted me to be very sure that *profit-profit-profit* was his sole consideration. In a way he was telling me I'd be free to make whatever I like of the clinic – assuming I agree to take it on at all, of course. If I do, I'll be free to specialize in any area I like. Or none. It's every doctor's dream, naturally – and that old skinflint knows it. But first he put that band of iron around the whole business: profit!"

"And would it be best to specialize, d'you think? Or make it a general establishment like the Eli? Does it depend on physical size? Mount Venus'd be about half the size of the Eli, wouldn't you say? The actual building, I mean. Is that too small to run as a general clinic?"

He lifted his hand to her forehead and ran his fingers briefly through her hair. "I say – you're as taken with the whole idea as I am! Aren't you afraid of losing touch with . . . well, Dublin in general? All the busy-bee things you get involved with?"

"Too many," she replied.

He cleared his throat. "I gave up trying to convince you of that five years ago – if you recall?"

"Just as I gave up trying to convince you that you couldn't practise surgery *and* follow every other branch of medicine, from obstetrics to physiology. And now it looks as if you were right to keep up with all those specialties, as much as you could. You didn't answer my question, however."

"No," he sighed. "I would if I knew what to say. I just cannot seem to decide."

54

After a silence she gave a little chuckle and said, "At the risk of trying to out-cynic old Ebenezer, it would be a wonderful wheeze to invent a bran-new disease and become the world's leading centre for curing it! What could it be? It'd have to be the next stage onward from neurasthænia. Neura-something. Neura-itis? Neuremia?"

"Neuritis and neurosis – they already exist, I'm sorry to say. Someone's got there before you. The trouble with this cynical approach is that there's more than a grain of truth in it, to our undying shame. We *do* care for reputation, and it isn't always for the highest motives. We do want to put our name on a new disease. We do want our lucrative list of patients. We do wonder if we're in the mainstream or some backwater of medical progress. It would be foolish to deny it. Professor Whatsizname may *claim* he discovered Panacea Ninety-nine out of pure love of humanity, but let some rash journal credit Doctor Whatyamacallim with the discovery, instead, and you'll soon hear a different tune!"

Lucy, tiring of the one position, turned on her back and settled herself upon him, laying her head beside his. "And d'you think you may have chosen a backwater in becoming a surgeon?" she asked.

She felt him nod. "Me and just about everyone else," he replied. "The whole of medicine as we presently know it may turn out to be one vast backwater. I've often thought that the coming thing is not the medicine of the body but the medicine of the mind. To be sure, we've still a long way to go with the body, but at least we know enough to realize where to turn next. The future obviously lies in chemistry – understanding the chemistry of life. But where d'you start with the mind? I was talking with Henderson this afternoon about a case he's just taken on – a man paralysed all down one side of his face."

"A stroke?" she suggested.

"Apparently not. No other signs of a stroke. It happened to him suddenly in the middle of an argument with his daughter. As far as medical science – bodily science – can tell, he's as fit as a fiddle. But that doesn't cure his paralysis. So we call it a neurosis – to give you an example of the word. What it really means is that we can neither explain it nor cure it. We don't even know where to begin. Where *does* one begin?"

"Ask the daughter," Lucy suggested.

She meant her words light-heartedly but Michael gave out a toneless whistle of admiration. "You're probably right," he said. "You see – it's nothing like medicine as we know it. It's something entirely new. But wouldn't it be exciting to be one of the pioneers!"

She shivered with a pleasure that was borrowed from his eagerness. "And to be given your own clinic in which to do it!" she added.

"Precisely!" He breathed a deep draught of satisfaction. "Of course, it couldn't be our bread and butter, not for a year or two. But we could start with, say, four beds and slowly work up the numbers."

"And what would our bread-and-butter cases be?"

"Well," he said diffidently, to indicate that these were mere preliminary thoughts, "Mount Venus divides naturally into two wings, one each side of that central lantern. If we say males to the west, females to the east . . ."

"As it was with the servants in the attics."

"I never thought of it," he said, "but yes – just like that. We have thirty-four beds to distribute among our medical patients – and the architecture more or less forces us to make it seventeen male, seventeen female. We could easily find seventeen male cardiacs." He explained why it would keep the accountant in Ebenezer O'Dea happy to specialize in that fashion. "But heart disorders are an overwhelmingly male condition. Women don't suffer until they're practically senile. So I doubt we could fill all seventeen female beds with cardiacs. Seven would be more like it."

"We suffer from plenty of other complaints, though," Lucy pointed out.

"Gynæ-obstet," he murmured. "We could easily fill ten beds with gynæcologicals. And if we could concentrate on circulatory disorders in that field . . ." He paused and then laughed.

"What now?" she asked.

"Ten years ago you could still hear old buffers like Sheehan complaining about specialisms like gynæcology, cardiology, splanchnology, and so forth. He said he needed a new set of teeth every time he came away from a medical meeting. And now here *we* are, already splitting gynæcology up into subspecialisms! Can the day be far distant, I wonder, when we call a plumber to mend a leaking main only to have him say, 'Sorry – I'm a *hot*-water plumber. You'll have to call in a cold-water specialist for this!' And how could we possibly complain!"

"So – I'm sorry, I've lost the thread now. Are you saying we should or shouldn't specialize in . . ."

"I think we should. If we can get a good gynæ man – someone like Walshe at the Rotunda, say . . ."

"He'd be excellent," Lucy put in. "His father was chairman of the old grand jury for County Kildare. The Walshes have very good connections through the whole of west Leinster, in fact, because his mother was one of the Kilkenny Butlers – the legitimate line."

Michael cleared his throat. "I was thinking more of his medical pedigree, actually."

"Besides, his wife, Janet, is absolutely sweet. We'd get on like a house on fire. Her mother used to . . ."

"Lu-cy!"

"Sorry!" She made a pantomime of buttoning her lips. "You were saying – Walshe – good man . . .?"

"Yes, and more to the point – I happen to know he'd be very interested in a position that allowed him to focus on circulatory disorders, within his particular field."

"But could the two of you manage thirty-four beds between you? It's a bit of a tall order, isn't it?"

He nodded. "We'd need two juniors as well."

"And how many nurses? I say – it's starting to grow at a frightening pace, Michael."

He chuckled drily. "Isn't it just! The very least, I'd say, is one nurse to every three beds. One to every six at night."

They continued in this fashion for some time, turning pipe-dreams into firmish plans, deciding who would lodge where and how the rooms they had seen on their first – and so far only – visit could be adapted to new purposes. They decided they would need at least three dozen nurses, with a dozen more on rapid call, since many of the patients would need round-the-clock care. Two junior doctors might also prove insufficient – "but we'll leave it there for the moment," Michael concluded. "We don't want old Ebenezer to die of heart failure before we even start!"

"Oh, and we mustn't forget the . . . *neurotics?* Is that the right word?"

"That's what they call them."

"No wonder they feel ill!"

"They won't necessarily be bed-patients," Michael pointed out.

"But they'll still need beds! I think we ought to go back to Mount Venus – without the children – delightful though their company is – and have another good think about what goes where."

"Take Philip de Renzi with us, perhaps?"

"The architect? For heaven's sake, no! My father is not exactly worldly-wise, I grant, but even he will tell you: Never let an architect within a mile of a building until you can tell him *exactly* what you want to do with it. They're fed on oats, those fellows. We'd see nothing but de Renzi's heels. Will we go back there tomorrow?"

Michael, still chortling at her dismissal of de Renzi and his whole profession, shook his head. "There's something else, even more important, we should do first. If I let Gill take my sessions tomorrow, we could go into town and have a talk with O'Dwyer and look at the legal aspects of the whole business." In a different tone he added, "We'd have to settle his bill first, I suppose."

She shook her head. "Fifty on account will keep him sweet. We could manage that much, I believe."

There was a pause; then he said, "D'you realize, this clinic will be the first thing we've undertaken together, Lucy? Up until now it's always been the two of us in tandem, which isn't quite the same thing, is it."

"Mmmm," she murmured, lifting his arm around her and leaving his hand loosely on her belly. "Talking of doing things together . . ."

"We never do," he replied.

"What?" She moved his hand for him.

57

"*Talk* of doing . . . *things* together."

"How would it help?" she asked, turning over upon him and settling with a sigh. She still suffered from that strange feeling of remoteness with him, however. It was a gap that physical intimacy alone could never bridge.

Ebenezer chose the moment with all his usual care. He waited until Diana Powers brought him his bedtime cup of cocoa – the last chore of her long day – and then asked, "What d'you imagine Michael and Lucinda Raven are doing at this precise moment, Nurse Powers?"

Diana, who had spent more than a decade trying *never* to imagine what Michael and Lucy were doing at any sort of moment, precise or vague, closed her eyes and swallowed hard. From the instant that Violet's wet little gesture of apology made it clear that the old fellow *knew*, she had been dreading a question of this kind. She had waited for it all day yesterday and it had not come – and again all today, and still he held his peace; so she had had all the time in the world to prepare an answer. In fact, she had prepared so many that they all deserted her when she most needed them. Her instinct as Diana Powers was to carry the aggression into the other's camp; her training as a nurse forbade it. Racked between the two she had no recourse beyond simple honesty. She inhaled deeply and, plumping up his pillows to avoid having to meet the challenge of his gaze, said, "Is it still the time for being utterly frank, Mister O'Dea?"

"Oh dear," he replied. "That sounds ominous. Do go on."

"Well, if they've any sense," she continued, "the pair of them are laughing at the folly of it all – the very idea! However, from what little I know of them, they'll be doing no such thing. They're probably covering sheets of paper with lists and numbers – so many patients, so many doctors, so many nurses – and dreaming dreams any grown man should be ashamed of putting into their heads."

He beamed with pleasure – as he always did, oddly enough, whenever she was severe with him. Often, she thought, he provoked her to it deliberately, just for the perversity of it. "Don't you think all great enterprises start from a little germ of madness?" he asked. "Can you imagine anything more lunatic than building ships of iron? Or burning coal and selling the resulting gas and waste products for ten times what you paid the coal merchant for it? The first people who got those two ideas were lucky not to have been put away safely, don't you think? Of course, now we know it works, we *all* wish we'd been the ones to think of it!" He took his first sip of the cocoa and exhaled with relish. "But enough philosophy," he said. "More to the point, what sort of clinic or sanatorium – is it sanatorium or sanitarium, by the way?"

"Either," she replied. "Though nowadays sanitarium usually means an isolation hospital for consumptives."

"And what d'you think they'll aim at?" he repeated.

"Sure I haven't the first notion," she told him with a light laugh, implying that she thought his question more jocular than serious. "Can you tell me why you chose *them*? Out of all the likely people in Dublin . . ."

"They are the *most* likely," he interrupted to assure her. "They started from nothing, and just look how far they've come! Ten years ago had anybody ever heard of the Honourable Lucinda Raven?" His eyes dwelled in hers for a moment and she felt sure he was mentally adding, *apart from yourself, of course.* He went on: "And come to that, what was Michael Raven then? An above-average medical graduate with a long, hard haul ahead of him. A cart-horse for work, a Derby winner in his ambition. Ambition, Nurse Powers! I tell you, the sight of a pretty girl may stir a young man's blood – but it is as nothing compared with what the word *ambition* does to mine! No – not the word – the thing itself . . . that fluid . . . that electricity which just seems to pour out of those two – but especially out of her! She's not even aware of it, I think. And if I'm right there, I hope she never will be. But it draws me to her as a lantern does a moth. I want to know all about her. When did she start? Was she like it even as a child? If they gave her a Shetland, did she want a Connemara? If they gave her a Connemara, did she pine for a thoroughbred? And how did she set about acquiring young Michael Raven, eh?"

This time he avoided her eyes altogether, which was as significant in its way as a forthright stare would have been; he pretended to relish his cocoa again, taking a deep gulp at it this time.

"You think she singled him out, do you?" Diana asked lightly. She sat in the wicker chair at his bedside and took up the book from which she read to him each night. At the moment it was a translation of Balzac's *Old Goriot*.

"Ah!" he said, as if she had homed in on an important new point. "You're right. How astute you are! Perhaps she didn't single him out. Perhaps there is some unconscious process at work among all such people – indeed, among all people of every kind. Attraction and repulsion. Rather like magnetism and iron filings – you've seen the trick, I'm sure: iron filings on a sheet of paper, a bar magnet beneath it, and, hey presto! – they all line up. Scientists will tell you it proves something about lines of force, but I'll tell you what intrigues *me* about that simple experiment: The magnet doesn't know the iron filings are there, and the iron filings don't know the magnet is there. How could they? They're on different sides of the paper! But the magnet goes on sending out its lines of force just the same – and the iron filings go on lining up. *They can't help it!* They have no knowledge of the magnet yet they're in thrall to it all the same. That's the really fascinating thing to me. You see the parallel with a woman

59

like Lucy Raven, I'm sure? Where she moves, the world lines up."

Diana made a noncommittal noise and fidgeted with the unopened novel.

Ebenezer appeared not to notice. He drained his cocoa and said, "Believe it or not, I never desired to make a fortune. It has come to me almost by accident, you know. And because it's not what I wanted . . . I mean, not what I set out to achieve . . ." His voice tailed off. Either he had lost the thread or he saw all too clearly where it might lead and so gave up following it. Instead he pursued a different hare. "I know what my nephew's probably told you," he said rather sternly. "A nurse gets paid thirty pounds a year. She works eighty hours a week and gets one day off a month. But her employers can charge half a guinea a day for her services. Dazzler thinks *that* is the calculation behind my desire to set up this new clinic. Am I not right?"

She stared at him evenly. "I have no idea, Mister O'Dea. He has never discussed it with me. But if he had, the question I would now ask is: 'Is he right?' Since you raise the matter, let's deal with it."

Her directness took him aback; it was the first sign that the taciturn, undemanding Nurse Powers was not going to be quite the easy accomplice he had hoped for. "Very well," he replied, eyeing her warily, "just for argument's sake, let's suppose he is. After all, that's the way the noble Margaret Huxley makes her living."

Diana drew a deep breath. Her nostrils flared and she had to fight to rein in the anger that would have prompted her to speak far more harshly than she did when she finally answered him. "Matron Huxley," she said quietly, "has a considerable private fortune. Most of her income has been devoted to the cause of nursing. She has made the nursing course at Dun's the best in the kingdom. If you carry through your scheme to appoint me matron of this new clinic and you desire to know what sort of matron I'll be, study Miss Huxley – for I hope I shall be in her mould."

He smiled warmly, having recovered all his poise. "Excellent!" he said. "You qualify more and more with each day that passes, Miss Powers. However," he added, almost as an afterthought, "the fact remains that Miss Huxley does not pay her nurses more than the going rate, which is less than half what a railway porter earns. And *they* are about to strike for a forty-four-hour week."

Diana decided not to let herself be drawn again. She knew he was only testing her. "This is fruitless, Mister O'Dea. You said just now that you did not set out to achieve great wealth. What *did* you set out to achieve, then – if I may ask?"

"Ah! I just wanted a fight." He chuckled, as old men do at the follies of their youth. "I wanted to be able to look back on it all and say no man ever bested me."

"And can you?"

His eyes twinkled. "I wonder?"

She smiled back, feeling it was safe to push him a little further. "Surely you know a thing like that?"

"I thought I did, Nurse Powers. If you'd asked me that same question a year ago, you'd have heard the most confident *yes* ever. But that was when I was walking around this city, early and late, just looking for fights. You understand what I mean – battles of wits, not simple brawls."

"Of course."

"But losing the power of these old shanks" – he thumped his nerveless thighs with his clenched fists – "has given me a different perspective. I used to think it was, literally, a battle of wits. Mind against mind. Intellect versus intellect. My logic against theirs. But now . . ." He patted his breastbone. "I see it's all in here – in the heart. In the spleen. In the blood and bowels. Can you understand what that does to a fighter like me – to realize I've been barking up the wrong tree all my life? How trivial is the power of the naked intellect when set against the majesty of just one concealed emotion! Love. Hate. Or, above all, ambition!" He laughed and said, as if it were a biblical quotation: "*And the greatest of these is ambition!*"

Until that moment Diana had taken his conversation to be nothing more than the close-of-day ramblings of an old man – not tedious, but playful. However, when he spoke of the majesty of emotion concealed – of love and hate – she felt the hair bristle at the nape of her neck and it was as if she stood suddenly at the mouth of a cave – huge, dark, and terrifying. Her mind was all at once full of whispering voices, telling her to go forward, promising her enlightenment out of that darkness, peace in the heart of the terror, and the small, unimportant life she craved in the midst of its hugeness.

Her pulse delayed a beat and then thumped double tides. She had been staring at his head on the pillow so long that her peripheral vision became exhausted – the black lines of the cast-iron bedhead, the faded curlicues of ancient wallpaper, the bucolic little painting beneath which he liked to sleep . . . all vanished in a sort of shimmering blackness. There was a faint whirring in her ears. She shook her head and brought herself out of that semi-trance. Some recollected duty came to her aid. "Will I read to you awhile, sir?" she asked.

He shook his head. "I don't want to go on with that book – that oul' man helping his daughter claw her way up the social ladder by sacrificing himself." He shook his head in disgust. "Anyone could tell you how that will end up. You didn't say what sort of clinic the Ravens are going to choose."

"Sure how should I know! I've not seen him in more than ten years and I met her for the first time last week – the first and only time."

"Have a wild guess at it, then, and we'll see how good your intuition is."

She pulled the sort of face nurses pull when they're humouring a patient – and want the patient to know it. "Well, when I helped him cram his thoracic pathology, he said it was the best, or most interesting – something like that. The area where the future of medicine lay – the heart and circulation. So, if her Honourable majesty hasn't managed to change him too much, that's what he'll go for."

He pinched his nose until white patches showed along his nostrils. "The area where the future lay?" he echoed thoughtfully. "Perhaps that is what attracted him to the heart and blood circulation – or whatever you call it. Has that situation changed in ten years? Where does the future lie *now*, d'you believe?"

Diana's intuition was good enough at that moment to warn her that these were no idle questions. Somehow he would take her answers and use them against her, or, at least, not to her benefit. How? She could not even guess; but intuition is not designed to answer questions of *how*; it merely warns us *that*.

Wildly, she picked the least likely area of medicine in which Michael might conceivably take an interest: "Something to do with the mind," she told him. "Every issue of *The Lancet* these days seems to carry an article or letter on medicine and the mind. So – if all Doctor Raven wants is to leap onto the bandstand and hog the limelight – he'll make Mount Venus a clinic for the treatment of mental disorders."

"A bedlam?" Ebenezer asked in surprise.

"No." Diana was delighted she had got him to take this absurd flight of fancy seriously. "The treatable disorders – hysterical paralysis, compulsive overeating – or compulsive self-starvation – irrational compulsions of every kind – kleptomania . . . lots of things called something-mania that have nothing to do with being a maniac in the popular sense."

Now that she had warmed to her theme she eyed him shrewdly and added, "It would suit you ideally, Mister O'Dea. All those little quirks of human behaviour, which interest you so deeply – you'd see every last one of them, and more, all magnified a thousand-fold."

He laughed and wagged a finger at her, meaning he wasn't beyond realizing when she was seeking to distract him from some earlier purpose. "We'll see, Nurse Powers," he said. "So, to sum up: You have a main bet to win on heart-and-circulation and a place-bet on some highfalutin kind of loony bin – is that right?"

She shrugged.

"That's the fourth time you've smiled this evening," he pointed out. "If I may risk a personal remark, you have one of the most beautiful smiles I've ever seen."

Despite her enormous reserves of self-control Diana felt herself blushing furiously – partly out of annoyance, but partly in pleasure, too. Worse, she suspected that the annoyance was felt by a Diana who was already dying, while the pleasure lay in a different self – one who was just coming (or coming back?) to life. She was not sure she welcomed either development. "Why did you want me to guess what sort of clinic the Ravens will decide upon, sir?" she asked.

"Oh, as I said – to test your intuition. If you're right, you're obviously the perfect candidate for matron – from my point of view, anyway. I shall need someone out there with a first-class intuitive understanding of the good doctor."

"And if I'm wrong?"

"Ah!" He tilted his head sadly. "Then we shall have to look elsewhere, shan't we."

And that was it! All he had wanted, she now realized, was a graceful way of bowing out of his commitment to make her matron of the Mount Venus Clinic, come what may. He had trapped her into providing his excuse in advance. If only he knew how little she relished his offer in the first place! And thank heavens she had chosen the "loony bin" suggestion. The Michael Raven she knew had been a hearty rugby footballer who thought a good long swim off the arctic icecap would cure all mental disorders. The very last thing in which he'd choose to specialize would be disorders of the mind.

She slept easily that night for the first time since the old man had proposed banishing her to Mount Venus as matron of the clinic.

An excited Philip de Renzi leaped from the carriage the moment they turned the final bend in the drive, when the whole of Mount Venus came into view. He stood on the gravel, legs apart, coat unbuttoned, fists on hips, and let his eye wander several times up and down the massive façade. "What a *dinosaur!*" he said at last, in an odd blend of mockery and praise. He ran to catch up with the carriage, arriving just as Lucy was stepping out; she had his tape and sketchbook under her arm.

"Doesn't it just ooze with self-satisfaction!" he said, giving her a truculent grin. "Is that why it appeals to you?"

"Philip!" She smiled thinly as she passed him his paraphernalia. "You are not the only architect in Dublin." She took the key from her purse – the front-door key this time. "And nor do we have all day for idle nonsense of that kind."

He was not the least bit abashed as he followed her up the front steps, admiring her figure and the subtle displacements of her bustle. "Then it must be true," he went on. "I was told a kinsman of yours was the original builder."

She turned the key in the lock, which had been kept well oiled. "The history," she said, "is immaterial."

"Which is more than one can say of *this!*" He hammered the stone jambs with his gloved fist. "Even with the roof off, it would stand another century." He turned his back to the doorway and stared out

63

over the city. "I'll bet you can see Ulster on a clear day," he went on. "This is what architecture's all about, you realize. The utilitarians may say it's for keeping the wind and rain at bay. The romantics may say it's about building public theatres for private lives. But *p-shaw*, I say!" He spoke the word with deliberate comedy. "Yes – *p-shaw!* Architecture is about power. It's about ascendancy. And no one knew it better than your old kinsman, Lucy. When the builders packed up and the gardeners moved in and he stood here for the first time as master-in-possession at last, he knew he'd joined the Irish Ascendancy. This house is a fanfare of welcome in brick and stone."

"Philip!" Lucy said sharply. "You are not being paid by the word."

He spun round, eyes gleaming with excitement. "I'm being *paid?*" he asked breathlessly.

"Eventually," she replied, compressing her lips so as not to smile. "Give me the end of that tape. Let's start with the hall, front-to-back."

For the best part of the next hour they recorded the principal measurements of the rooms on the ground floor, which gave de Renzi little scope for his blarney. When they reached the library, the third room to the west of the central hall, he pointed out that one run of floorboards, about two feet out from the rear wall, had been lifted and nailed back with round-headed wire nails; all the other boards were still held by the original square-headed floor brads. "It was the same in the other rooms, too," he added. "Shall we investigate? There's no obvious reason for lifting just that run of boards. Shall I get your driver and the gardener to prize up one or two of them?"

"What gardener?" she asked.

"Dear Lucy! Isn't it obvious that the grounds are being cared for by *someone?* Otherwise this place would be like Sleeping Beauty's palace – we'd still be hacking though the thorns to reach it."

She gave a small, self-disparaging laugh. "It never crossed my mind. We didn't see anyone when . . . oh, of course, that was a Sunday."

"The gravel was raked, too."

"Yes, all right, Philip! I'm blind. Leave it at that."

"We'll need a crowbar, too," de Renzi said as he wandered off.

While he was away she flipped through his sketchbook, admiring the skill that could doodle the plan of a complicated house like Mount Venus in the absolute minimum of lines and make a better go of it than she would manage in a whole day with ruler and compasses. What *was* it about the freehand line that was so much more arresting than the perfection of one drawn by ruler? And why were some freehand lines better than others? How did Philip's lines manage to sing and sparkle whereas her own always looked wobbly and incompetent? Even when they were children there had been that difference.

"Penny for 'em?" He caught her unawares on his return.

She dropped the book guiltily. "I was just thinking how beautiful your drawing is – and why are freehand lines so much more interesting than lines drawn with a ruler?"

"Ah!" he said, rubbing his hands with glee – and making her instantly regret having started this hare.

"Did you find the gardener?" she asked, swiftly heading him off.

De Renzi made a vague gesture over his shoulder. "He think's he knows where to put his hands on a crowbar."

"What's his name? Does he live in one of the outhouses? How old is he?"

"Slattery. Yes. And in his sixties. That's a most profound observation of yours, about lines . . ."

"I was afraid of that." She edged toward the door. "Let's start on the upstairs."

"They'll be here in a mo. I'd only have to come down again. About the lines – it's the same with people, don't you think? People and the lives they lead. Some try to live dead straight, dead by the rules – and *dead* is the proper word for them, too. Whereas all the more interesting people – people like you and me, that is – have lives full of wobbles and kinks, and thin bits and thick . . . and so forth. We have that indefinable but instantly recognizable panache of the freehand drawing, don't you think? I suppose that's why all the moralists throughout history – the ruler merchants – have always had such an uphill struggle. We – interesting people like you and me – absolutely *know* they're barking up the wrong whatsit."

Lucy seated herself on one of the broad window sills; a playful smile twitched her lips. "De Renzi," she said with theatrical weariness, "if this is the start of some sophistical seduction, I can save you a great deal of mental effort now and even more emotional distress in the hours to come."

Their eyes met, and did not waver. She could see that her frankness had taken him aback. True, they had occasionally indulged in jocular, near-the-bone conversations before now – of the "Ah, Lucy, if only you had married me . . .!" kind; but she had never said anything so direct before. However, his whole attitude, from the moment he had assisted her into the carriage in Clyde Road that morning, had been crying out for some such reproach from her. How would he respond? she wondered. Hurt? Blustery? Embarrassed?

He clearly decided to bluff it out. "I wish you hadn't said that, Lucy." He shook his head as if she had committed some grave folly.

She chuckled. "I'm quite sure you do, Philip. But now we know where we stand, don't we. So we can each get on with our proper business."

"How I wish that were true!" He sighed lugubriously. "Unfortunately, what you have just said is what *all* the ladies say – at the outset."

She laughed merrily and rose to her feet again. "You're impossible," she told him, in a tone that was dismissively cordial. "You imagine that enough waves will eventually wear away the cliff."

He remained sombre. "I imagine no such thing," he replied. "D'you want to know what particular delusion leads inevitably to every woman's downfall?"

"It's not of the slightest interest to me, I assure you." She heard Glynn, her groom, and Slattery the gardener making their way along the corridor outside. "But tell me if you have to," she added quickly.

"Tell you what?"

"This . . . female delusion or whatever it is. You won't give me peace until you've got it off your chest, I know."

"Ah, yes. All you women seem to believe that the prime mover in any seduction is the *man*."

She gave a little laugh of protest. "But every book you ever read . . ."

He cut across her. "That's why they're called *fiction*, Lucy." He smiled as conjurors smile when they produce missing cards from impossible places.

And she was prevented from replying by the arrival of the two men, complete with crowbar, nail bar, and a short oak plank. His insinuation rankled all the more for her enforced silence.

When the introductions were over and Lucy had explained her presence to Slattery, the gardener, the two men set about lifting one of the floorboards. They used the short plank as a fulcrum for the bars, to protect the neighbouring floorboards; de Renzi found the marks where the boards had been prized up last time and told the two men to put their bars in the identical places, to avoid fresh damage. Lucy, notwithstanding her annoyance at the man, applauded these precautions.

The nails, being round, were soon eased out again. De Renzi made sure they were all freed before he risked lifting the board; by then Lucy's patience was at breaking point. But when the board was lifted and laid on its back beside the hole, the sight that met her eyes was utterly mystifying.

"What on earth are they?" she asked.

Two parallel bars of some dull, yellowish metal – probably copper, to judge by the streaks of verdigris – had been let down into the joists, three inches apart. They were square in section and measured about an inch on each side; and they obviously ran the full length of the room. Indeed, if de Renzi was right about the lifting of the other floorboards, they probably ran the entire length of the house.

"'Tis the ilictric," Slattery told them.

Lucy, who had half-knelt to touch the bars, plucked her hand back at once.

De Renzi laughed. "They won't be alive, don't worry." He touched one of them to prove it – gingerly at first, then with confidence. "Do you know anything about this?" he asked Slattery.

"There's no sign of electrical apparatus in the house, so why these conductors?"

"Sure 'twas Mister Reilly's doing, your honour," the man replied. "He had them bars laid under the floors of every room in the house, so he did."

"Shortly before he . . . passed on?" Lucy asked.

"So he never got around to installing any apparatus," Philip mused. He turned again to the gardener. "Did you say *every* room in the house?"

The man nodded. "Even the servants' quarters above in the attics, sorr. And the stables beyond."

De Renzi gave a low whistle. "That'd be around two thousand feet of one inch copper bar . . . *four* thousand, actually, because it's double. It must have cost a small fortune!"

Nobody responded to that comment, for it touched all too closely on the cause of Reilly's sad end.

"I wonder if old O'Dea knows about it," he mused, also to himself. Then, turning once more to Slattery, "Is it connected to some apparatus in the outbuildings? Or had he no time for that, either?"

"He had and he hadn't," the man replied. "There's a shteam engyne for the raising of the water beyond. And the boss set an ilictric yawk foranenst it. For the fly to be turning, d'ye see, to make the ilictric. But he never had time to get the belt made up, so it's after lying there all them months, and never once did it turn, I want to tell ye."

The architect's eyes glowed with excitement as he said to Lucy: "Let's go and see!"

But she shook her head and told him Michael would be furious if anyone else were the first to discover such a marvellous toy. "Besides," she added, "we have a lot more measuring to do yet."

The groom and the gardener removed the nails from the floorboard and left it lying loosely back in place before they returned to their labours. Lucy and de Renzi continued with their measurements, making such good progress that, by the time they broke off for a picnic luncheon, they had only the principal bedrooms and the servants' attics to complete.

They made a start on the magnificent bedroom at the western end. After taking the two major dimensions Philip tried to open the cupboard door. "Here's a rum thing," he said.

Lucy cleared her throat. "I gave orders for it to be screwed shut."

The penny dropped. "Reilly?" he said. "Is that where he . . ."

She nodded. "You can take the dimensions off the cupboard in the next room. They're identical. Actually, let's break off and eat. I'm peckish, aren't you?"

A feeble sun broke through the misty veil of clouds, reaching long silver fingers down the slopes of Cruagh. It encouraged Lucy to suggest that they should take the hamper out to the conservatory.

As they set off across the terrace de Renzi ran his eye over the line of the outbuildings, which were all to the west of the main house, and said, "It's cleverly done, I'll grant him that, but it's a house of its times, Lucy. We'd do it very differently these days."

"In what way?" she asked cautiously, for she could smell an approaching architect's fee three miles downwind.

"It's the dilemma one gets with all north-facing houses," he replied. "Your man faced it north for that view, of course – he could hardly have done otherwise – but the sun, with all its colour and life, lies to the south. So he tucks all the outbuildings away over there to the west, where they'll act as a break on the prevailing wind, and he puts this sheltered terrace here between the house and the conservatory. But that's his only concession to a private life."

She opened the all-glazed door and ushered him in ahead of her, his hands being full of hamper and basket. She caught up with him and, still on the move, whisked a cloth from the basket. She managed to spread it over the rusting cast-iron table before he set the rest of the things down there.

"A tablecloth?" he asked in amazement.

She grinned. "Civilization comes to south County Dublin! How would *we* build such a house nowadays? You said we'd manage it all differently."

"They were very public people a hundred years ago. Outward show was all-important. Private domestic comfort meant much less to them than it does to us. We'd put the offices, the gun room, the business room, the billiards room on the north side. Never mind that it's the main façade. And we'd have a garden room and a morning room and an informal family drawing room here on the south side. It's an entirely different attitude. You see! One don't need books to tell one how people lived in past ages. Just look at the buildings they left behind them. They'll spill the beans at once."

She laughed as she began to set out their little banquet. "Can one even discover what they *thought?*" she challenged him.

"Especially what they thought, Lucy," he replied. "Do you notice anything about the arrangement of the staircases on this side of the house?"

"Only that they're the most inconvenient things I ever saw. You could shell those eggs if you like – I hope they're hard-boiled enough." She pulled out a bottle of Chablis and looked at it askance. "I gave no instructions to include that!" she added.

"I'll throw it away if you wish," he offered as he started to peel the eggs. "Is that all you noticed – that they're inconvenient?"

"From our point of view they are. If a nurse is tending to a patient in *that* room there" – she pointed to a window at the south-eastern end of the house – "she can look in on all the other rooms on that floor except the last three. And how does she get to them? She can't even reach them via the main part of the house. She has to come all the way back to this end, go down to the ground floor, go all the way back again to the far end, and then go through what was obviously someone's bedroom to reach a staircase – the *only* staircase, mark you – that leads up to those three rooms. I ask you! What *were* they thinking of!" She handed him a chicken drumstick and a sandwich of chutney.

Throughout her exposition the smile on his face grew broader and broader. When she finished, he laughed and said, "No, Lucy – ask yourself! Isn't it obvious what they were thinking of?" He bit off a good mouthful of chicken and chewed with relish.

She strode a few paces toward the house and stared at it thoughtfully – or as much of it as was visible through the lichen-streaked panes of the conservatory. The twinkle in his eye had alerted her to the fact that they had somehow strayed back to his favourite topic. "I see," she said at length. "I suppose the bachelors were all at this end while the spinsters were safely locked away in those three awkward bedrooms."

"Which, as you pointed out without realizing it, were accessible *only* through the housekeeper's bedroom."

"Dear God!" she murmured, taking her first nibble of chicken.

"And that honestly never struck you?" he asked.

She took a larger bite and chewed it thoroughly as she returned to the table. He helped her into her chair and filled her glass with wine before sitting down himself. "I suppose if I'd really thought about it . . ." she said vaguely.

"There's no such arrangement at Lucan, I know!" he remarked. "How did ye manage there?"

Hermitage Lodge, Lucan, was her parental home. The de Renzis had lived just over the hill in Leixlip and Philip, though a Protestant and four years her senior, had often come over to play – until he went away to school. They had seen little of each other during their teens, which did much to explain their present, rather unconventional, relationship. The provocation behind his words almost led her to assure him that Hermitage Lodge offered a hundred ways for young bachelors to reach young spinsters, if they were so minded; but then she realized what he'd make of it. "Sure what are dungeons for," she observed blithely. "To get back to Mount Venus, can we knock a hole in the wall at the end of that corridor?"

She could see he was about to make some flippant reply – probably to the effect that he never answered professional questions during his luncheon hour – when some other notion struck him. He eyed her thoughtfully and said. "You *have* changed, Lucy," in a tone that implied reluctant approval.

A little knot of fear twisted itself inside her. She realized suddenly that she could talk flippant nonsense with Philip de Renzi all day long, even if it was larded with heavy hints of a seduction that would never take place; but a serious conversation was altogether different –

69

a door into unknown territory. Her spirit shied at the prospect. "Have I?" she asked lightly. "I suppose one does. May I ask you a question?"

He realized he was being snubbed – in a way – and a touching sadness invaded his eye. "Fire away," he said morosely.

"How many of your friends' wives have you actually seduced?"

That certainly jolted him out of the mood into which he was threatening to settle! "Eh?" he gasped.

She smiled sweetly.

He frowned. "Is that my reputation?"

"It is with me," she told him. "The way you carry on – what else can you expect?"

He relaxed somewhat. "Sure it's all a cod," he said dismissively. "You know yourself now – it's a cod."

"D'you carry on the same with other ladies, married ladies – your other friends' wives?"

The form of her question seemed to puzzle him. "Is that how you think of yourself, Lucy?" he asked. "Is Michael my friend while you're just his wife? Didn't I know you long before I knew him?"

She realized that somehow, despite her best efforts to return their conversation to its usual, lighthearted level, they had once again strayed into serious realms – and this time there was no backing out. "I think marriage changes all that, Philip," she replied.

"Ah," he said, but whether he agreed or disagreed she could not tell. "D'you remember that game we used to play – where we turned the nursery table upside down and tied a sheet across the legs and sailed for Africa?"

"And you'd never let me be captain. And when we got to Africa I was never allowed to be the lion, either. How could I ever forget! Anyway, what about it?"

"The point is that if we'd sailed off for Africa in a real dinghy, down the Liffey and out on the open sea, we'd have been shouting 'Mama!' before we even reached Shackleton's mills."

"And so? I still don't see . . ."

"And so games are *not* a substitute for the real thing. They are a way of avoiding the real thing – because it is too frightening to contemplate. Childhood games . . . grown-up games. There is no essential difference as far as I can see."

Alice ran her eye down the list her mother had left lying open on her escritoire: Dublin Day-Out, Ranelagh Female Rescue, City Drinking Trough Foundation, Cats' and Dogs' Home, War Widows, Mendicants Society, Eli Lying-In Clinic, Ladies' Literary Prize, RDS Ladies' Committee . . . on and on it meandered, in no particular order, through some two dozen worthy committees, societies, and causes. She counted them. Twenty-five, actually. A quarter of a hundred! Why did a quarter of a hundred sound so much more than two dozen, when there was only one in it?

Too late she heard her mother approaching along the corridor outside; she turned about, full of guilt, even though they had reached the compromise agreement that she could read anything left open on the escritoire – on the strict understanding that everything else was private. As far as Lucy was concerned, however, it was a bit of an empty gesture; the only truly private material anyone would find in her escritoire – even in the secret drawer – was a starkly damning set of domestic accounts, stretching back over the decade of her increasingly debt-laden marriage. She had read enough three-volume novels to know the utter folly of committing private thoughts and feelings to paper, where venial servants, jealous lovers, and husbands with murder in their hearts could discover them at the worst possible moment.

Lucy chuckled when she saw what Alice had been reading. She told her: " 'Neither a borrower nor a lender be.' Or so Shakespeare said. But he left out the most important one – never a *collector* be! That's what I'd add." She slipped an arm around the girl's shoulders. "Aren't you shooting up fast now you've turned nine!" she added.

Together they stared in silence at the list, which, in Lucy's rather extravagant hand, filled two columns and the whole of one side of a sheet of notepaper. She heaved a sigh and said, "The question is – which ones do I give up?"

"That one." Alice pointed to the printed heading – Wellington Dower House, Clyde Road, Dublin. (Telephone 101).

"Yes!" Lucy sighed heavily. "It's certainly starting to look that way. The thing is, you see, if we give up *that*," – her fingertip rested on the address – "I shall be compelled to give up many of these as well." Her nail ran a wavy line down the gutter between the two columns. "And it's not a simple question of giving up the least worthy, for they are often the ones where I can do the most good."

"Which is the most worthy?" Alice asked.

Her mother pursed her lips in thought. "The War Widows, I suppose. But there you are, you see – the committee is really just a cypher, there. Whereas the least worthy, I'd have to admit, is the Drinking Fountain . . . *No!* The Literary Prize – which is supposed to encourage literary activities. In Dublin that's like setting up a committee to encourage heavy drinking – so I daresay we can safely cross that one off. I only joined because Lady Sheehan was on it, too. Such a *useful* woman!"

She picked up a pencil and drew a line through the name – a vigorous line that sang and sparkled; briefly she remembered Philip de Renzi and his sketch plan of Mount Venus – and his little sermon on rules and freedom.

"What does the Female Rescue do?" Alice broke into her reverie;

71

she had a picture of a female throwing wide a bedroom window while smoke billowed from the parlour window below – but she couldn't imagine her mother and her friends dashing down the street with ladders, somehow.

"It rescues females," Lucy said lightly.

"From what? Fire?"

Her mother nodded. "And brimstone."

"Are you going to give that up?"

Lucy shook her head dubiously. "It's a good source of cheap labour – of which we shall need plenty. They might even pay us a fee to train up some of the girls – often that's all they lack, a bit of training." She turned the list over and left it face-down, as if pushing temptation from her. "There is so much to consider with each and every one of them, you see. It's like asking a surgeon does he want to do without his scalpel or his scissors or his suturing needles or his seekers . . ."

"What are seekers?"

"I don't know, but it's what your father has in his tools of the trade." She realized the analogy was all very remote from the girl's own experience so she tried again. "If you were going to sew something, which would you rather do without – needle or thread?"

"Thread," Alice replied at once, almost without thinking.

"Why?" a surprised Lucy asked her.

"Because I could always pull a bit of thread out from somewhere it wouldn't show," she replied, as if it were too obvious to need saying.

Lucy laughed. "I don't know where you get them from, my love. Not from me, and that's for certain!"

"Get what?"

Lucy tapped her daughter's brow. "Those things inside there. Actually, I came up to find Tarquin. I suppose he's in the attic. It's the one thing I really *dread* about moving to Mount Venus. Here there are only twenty-one rooms for him to hide in. Out there we could be hunting him all day. Lord alone knows how many rooms there are out there!" She wandered back into the corridor as she spoke.

After she had gone, Alice murmured, "One hundred and seventeen, actually."

Hand comes out of bush holding clonker, wrote Tarquin. Then: *End of Scene three*. He glanced up at the clock to see what the next scene would be called and then, at the head of a fresh sheet of paper, wrote: Scene four. He enjoyed writing stage directions because you could leave out *a* and *the* and no one could tell you off for being slovenly; that was the proper way to do it. Also stage directions were actions, which he greatly preferred to words. In fact, this play he'd been working on for the past month or so, was called *Actions Speak Louder Than Words* – which he'd also chosen because he could trace it directly out of Vere Foster's *Copybook of Decorative Penmanship*. (His next play would be called *The Pen Is Mightier Than The Sword* for the same reason. *Writing Is Almost As Important As Speaking*, however, did not immediately suggest a very exciting plot, so he might not write that play at all.)

"*There* you are!" Lucy exaggerated her breathlessness after her brief climb to the attic, just to show Tarquin what a nuisance he was being. "What on earth are you doing up here when you should be down in the gig? Is that my notepaper? Are you the one who's been pilfering it under my nose? And here's me blaming the maids for making spills of it to light the fires. That costs a farthing for half a dozen sheets, you know – it doesn't grow on trees."

"Daddy said paper is made from trees," he told her.

"Not that paper," she replied, knowing what a mistake it was to get involved in discussions of this kind with him. "It's made from rags and costs a great deal more than paper from wood pulp."

"Rags cost more than trees?" he asked incredulously, squaring up for a good old ding-dong.

"Never you mind. It's a puzzling world at the best of times. We can continue this discussion in the gig. Everyone else is waiting."

"I don't want to go."

"That has nothing to do with it."

"I want to stay and write Act Aye-Aye-Aye-Aye."

Lucy's eyes raked the ceiling. "It's about a drunken sailor who sees double and talks double, I suppose. The only trouble is that you'd stick it for half an hour and then you'd get bored and go and torment the life out of Alice – and the house would be in smithereens by the time we came back."

"I won't, I promise," he said. "I've just got to the exciting part where a hand comes out of a bush holding a clonker."

"Whose hand?"

"I don't know. I just thought it would be an exciting thing to happen."

"Oh . . . very well!" She heaved a great sigh and pretended to yield. As she went out by the door she added, "Daddy will just have to get that steam engine going on his own." Before she had reached the bottom of the attic stairs Tarquin had slipped his hand into hers.

"I hope you've left *your* clonker behind," she said.

He smiled, slightly against his will, and murmured, "*Exeunt*."

A s they drove in past the gate lodge at Mount Venus, where Sean Slattery, the widower-gardener, lived, Lucy drew a deep breath and closed her eyes. Michael stared quizzically at her and then asked, "D'you always do that?"

"Do what?" She opened her eyes and stared innocently back, as if she had no idea what he was talking about.

"I've seen you do it on several visits. As we drive in, you shut your eyes and hold your breath."

Her smile was like an owning-up. "The first time we came here – four weeks ago to the day, isn't it? – I seemed to feel . . . I don't know. Something. A presence. Welcoming us."

He chuckled. "The shade of your twice-great uncle Boniface? Surely you don't believe in all that . . ."

"I'm not saying it was him. You're putting words into my mouth. All I'm saying is that there was a welcoming *presence*. An aura – call it what you will."

The gig rounded the final curve and the by now familiar façade of Mount Venus came into view. Michael reined back the horse and gazed at it, running his eyes the full length, several times. "Shades, presences, auras . . ." he said dismissively, "call them anything you like, it's all so much folderol. I refuse to believe in them."

The children, solemn as judges, listened in silence.

"You don't think houses have a sort of personality? Surely they do! Some sort of remnant . . . what's another word for aura?"

"Mood?" he offered, losing interest.

She looked away in exasperation. "Actually, I think there's something malevolent about this house."

"Malevolent?" The word surprised him. "I thought you said it was welcoming." He clucked up the horse and they turned toward the stable yard.

"No. The welcome is just floating in the air – nothing to do with the house. The house is definitely malevolent – in fact, it's *doubly* malevolent, because it *looks* so warm and friendly."

"Ah ha, I know what you mean there!" he cried. "It's exactly like . . ."

She cleared her throat significantly, thinking he was going to say "like Ebenezer O'Dea."

". . . Like the Viceregal Lodge," he said.

It surprised her as much as her earlier words had surprised him.

He continued: "I remember when Fritz Hedermann came to give his lecture on hormones last year, we went for a stroll through Phoenix Park and he simply couldn't believe it. After all he'd heard about eight centuries of British misrule he expected the Lord Lieutenant to live in some mighty fortress or a grand, swaggering sort of palace like those strutting stucco mansions that have transformed Berlin. But there it is – a modest country house for a minor English squire." He smiled acidly. " 'Doubly malevolent because it looks so friendly' is a good way of putting it. I must remember that."

"Mount Venus has ruined everyone who ever lived in it," she said as they drew to a halt. "Are you going to unharness the horse?"

He shook his head. "Just unhitch him. Charley? Go and shake some hay into the manger."

74

"And then can we gather some firing for the steam engine?" the boy asked as he went to obey.

"We shan't be steaming her today, old scout," his father told him.

Tarquin shot a look of bitter accusation at his mother, who shrugged apologetically and said, "I didn't know. I thought that's what we were coming out here for." She turned to her husband. "Why not?"

"Too dangerous. I want an engineer to look at that pressure vessel and certify it before we do anything like that," Michael said as he led the horse into the loose box. "All we're going to do this afternoon is strip it down and oil and grease every moving part we can reach."

Tarquin turned angrily on his heel and stalked off across the yard. "You said we were going to fire it up," he complained.

Lucy made a few ineffectual noises but Michael had the remedy; he let the boy get to the steps that led up into the shrubbery behind the conservatory (which they had since discovered was called the "winter garden"), and then called after him, "Tarquin! Are *you* going to open up the stuffing gland or will I let Charley do it?" He winked at Charley to recruit him into the conspiracy.

Tarquin halted with one foot on the bottom step. "Open the what?" he asked warily.

"The stuffing gland!" Michael made it sound like the sixpence in the Christmas pudding.

The boy took his foot off the bottom step and made a dignified return to the bosom of his family. "I suppose I'd better," he replied magnanimously.

"What's a stuffing gland?" Lucy asked quietly, while he was still out of earshot. "If it's not an indelicate question."

"A most useful phrase – obviously – describing a rather common-place device. Let's go and change."

The children took the key and ran ahead of them to open up the house. As they approached at a more leisurely pace Michael took Lucy's arm. "Not getting cold feet, I hope?" he asked. "By the end of this year – if we take the plunge – there'll be over a hundred people living here. So – no matter how malevolent this house might be, it'd have a job to ruin all that lot."

"I know." She sighed. "It's first-night nerves, that's all." She smiled to herself, for the phrase was one of Dazzler O'Dea's. "I mean it's fear of taking such a very public step into the unknown. If we come a cropper, the whole world will know . . ."

"Only Dublin," he pointed out.

"Dublin *is* our world. To go back to your very first question, the reason I shut my eyes and hold my breath is that I had a very strong feeling of some friendly . . . I know you don't like the word 'aura' – but some friendly . . . *thing*. A spirit of reassurance. And I don't want to lose touch with it."

What she really meant was that she didn't wish to insult it or

75

alienate it by some careless action – but she knew he'd only scoff if she said as much.

"I'll agree with you *this* far," he said after a moment's thought. "One could say that this location – this actual site out here at Mount Venus – must have cried out to have a house built upon it. I mean, that's the sort of thing one says – 'the site cried out for a house' and so on. We don't mean that an actual voice came welling up out of the ground. It's just a manner of speaking. And you could also say the house, in turn, just cried out for twelve acres of landscaped garden – which is what ruined Gorman. Then along came Murchison with his shipbuilder's ideas – he sees a house that just cries out for piped water, steam engines, hydraulics . . . and it's heigh-ho for a poor-man's grave in Glasnevin. And finally the mysterious William Reilly . . ."

"And by now the house is crying out for blood!" Lucy put in.

"Nonsense!" he laughed indulgently. "William Reilly bought a house with one of the finest views in County Dublin – with twelve acres of superbly landscaped grounds . . . every modern convenience, except electricity. What does such a house cry out for? Entertainments! Grand garden parties. Grand balls. Soirées. Baronial feasts. That's what beggared him. So tell me, my dear – what was the one thing all these ruined men had in common?"

"They were all Roman Catholic?" she offered.

"No!" He laughed again. "They all failed to see that *investments must pay for themselves* – no matter what."

They had reached the back door; she put her hand to the knob and held it, wanting to finish this conversation before they rejoined the youngsters. "But how does *any* big country house pay for itself? I don't see that at all."

He glanced up at the sun – or where the sun would be if it weren't veiled by high sheets of bright cloud. "I want to get on with that engine," he said. "But I'll prove it all to you later. We are not in the same kettle of fish as those previous owners of Mount Venus."

For the rest of the visit he and the two boys had the time of their lives taking the steam engine to pieces and lubricating everything in sight. They freed it up so well that, when it was all reassembled, Michael got the flywheel moving as fast as he could manage and it took almost two minutes before it came to a halt once more. Lucy and the two girls spent the time taking down old curtains and, if they were worth saving, listing them for later inclusion in the laundry book; Portia, who could already write the numbers from one to nine, was allowed to make the entries on a loose sheet of paper, which her mother would later compile for the book. They were duly impressed when they saw how well the steam engine turned.

These good works lasted much longer than they had intended and so they had to make the entire journey home in the dark. "At least the rain held off," Michael said when they reached Donnybrook and were still dry.

"I think Mount Venus is a very friendly house," Alice said suddenly. "Because we all work together when we're there, and it brings us together. So there – that's what I think."

"And what do *you* think, Charley?" Lucy quickly made a game of it, knowing they were growing tired and irritable.

"I think it's quite an *old* house," he said gravely.

Nobody could think of any comment to qualify that.

"And Tarquin?" Lucy said.

"I think it's an apple pie," Tarquin said – and giggled his head off.

Charley was tired enough to join him rather than start an argument. "I think it's a rhubarb and blackberry tart," he said – and laughed uproariously.

"I think it's a swan in the evening," Alice put in, subtly changing the game to a competition of inventiveness.

Later, when they were all happily and soundly asleep, Lucy said to Michael. "Alice was right about Mount Venus in one way – it *has* brought us all much closer together. I mean, we *do* more together. And have you noticed how much less they quarrel among themselves nowadays?"

"They aren't the only ones," he said significantly.

"That's true," she conceded. "Perhaps the Ravens will be the ones to break the curse they say is on Mount Venus. There'd be a sort of justice in that. Oh yes – I'd almost forgotten! You were going to explain to me how big mansions like Carton and Russborough are investments that pay for themselves."

"I'd rather we dropped it," he replied in a tone that merely encouraged her to press him the harder.

"You won't like it very much," he warned her.

"Let me be the judge of that."

"Well, as you said yourself – all the previous owners of Mount Venus were Roman Catholics. That set me thinking. And I believe you've accidentally hit on something important . . ."

"Oh yes – if I hit on something important, it *must* be accidentally!"

"Aah diddums! That's not what I mean. I mean you make a statement for one purpose and it actually fits another purpose better."

"*Your* purpose, of course."

He dipped his head modestly. "As it happens – yes. Anyway, all the previous owners of Mount Venus were ruined, I believe, because they made the same mistake most people make when they think of those big country mansions. They suppose that life in them is one long round of luxury, comfort, pleasure, and . . ."

"I certainly don't!" Lucy interrupted him. "And I've stayed at a fair number of them in my time – freezing cold, draughty, damp . . . I've never had a hot dinner at Carton – lukewarm cutlets in

77

congealing gravy. Eurgh! And going to bed in any Irish castle is work for mountaineers."

All through this outburst his smile grew broader. "Yet again you make my point for me, darling," he said. "If not for comfort and pleasure – what are they for?"

She had to think. "For meeting in, I suppose," she offered at length.

"Meeting who? Or whom?"

"People of their own class. Family – and the vague tribe called *kinsmen*."

"For what purpose do they meet?"

She laughed. "Is this a catechism?"

"Sort of. I'm trying to show you that you already know the answers. What do they meet *for?*"

"Dinners and dances. Marriages. Funerals. Hunts, point-to-points. Shoots. Fishing parties. Long 'week-ends,' as they call them nowadays."

"And in passing – while all the eating, drinking, dancing, and slaughtering is going on – what is the steady background to it all?"

"Gossip."

But he would not agree there. "Much more than that. You know yourself how it goes:

"–What's your opinion of young Freddy so-and-so . . .?

"–I'm wondering if Lady Sarah whatsername would make a suitable wife for Peter?

"–We need a good, steady chairman for this regrettable but necessary Board of Inquiry. Would you happen to know of one?

"–I had a strong tip yesterday about Consolidated Zinc . . .

"–That howling ass Marksby wants to join the club. I can't oppose him openly, so I was rather hoping you might . . .?

"–and so on. It's one great *octopus* of a club, Lucy – with eight *hundred* tentacles, if not eight thousand! It's a vast, secret committee that never adjourns. And that's what all those great country houses are *for*. They're private committee rooms. And of course they pay for themselves! Time and again with each new generation."

Glumly she added the only point he had omitted to make: "Unless they happen to be owned by Roman Catholics!"

He nodded sadly. "I entirely agree. So that's when you want six thousand acres paying good rents instead – which is the one thing Mount Venus never had. They were doomed before the ink on the conveyance was dry."

She brightened a little as his point struck her: "And so a first-rate clinic full of wealthy invalids should do even better than six thousand acres!"

He put his arms around her and hugged her tightly to him. "If it doesn't, by God, it won't be for want of trying!"

"So – you'll sign on the dotted line tomorrow?"

There was a pause before Michael finally committed himself. "Yes," he said at length. "Barring any last-minutes accidents. Old Ebenezer says he wants to meet me out there tomorrow. He wants to discuss the arrangements for the nurses. Most peculiar."

"Is it? You yourself have often said – nurses are far more important than doctors. If he's really intending to become a patient out there . . ."

"We've no certainty of that."

"No, but if. Surely it's a very reasonable thing to do."

Michael shook his head, somewhat at a loss. "I just have a feeling he's got some trick up his sleeve. D'you want to be there, too?"

She kissed him lightly on the cheek. "Not to Mount Venus. I'll come to Sackville Street for the signing but I'll go to Lucan in the morning – tell the mater and pater. They'd never forgive me if they heard about it after."

Michael drove the gig out to Mount Venus; alone he could manage the journey in just under thirty minutes, fifteen of them being spent on the final mile, a long haul up the hill from Rathfarnham. April was already living up to her reputation, ambushing him with quick showers all the way. However, when he reached the crest, overlooking the picturesque little villages of Tallaght and Oldbawn, the Clerk of the Weather lost the element of surprise, for Michael could now see what was coming his way for at least the next hour, spread across the skies down to Carlow and Kildare: a vault of cerulean blue, mottled with sepia rainclouds, some trailing squid-inky tentacles down to the ground. One, over Kiltipper, which would reach Mount Venus in about five minutes, wore a diagonal snippet of a rainbow arc, like the sash of some ancient Hibernian order.

It was a heavy shower, too, and it caught him just as he was entering by the gatelodge. He pulled off the drive to the left under the shelter of a giant thuja, which must have been planted when the house was still building. As he sat there, waiting for the downpour to pass, he realized he was grateful for its intrusion. The unease he felt about this meeting with Ebenezer O'Dea had, if anything, intensified between last night and this morning. He thought he and O'Dwyer had closed off every possible avenue by which the old rascal could exploit their partnership and turn him and Lucy into virtual slaves. It had been the most unnerving month he had ever lived through (and he had lived through some pretty unnerving months lately, too!). Worst of all had been the way the old fellow yielded on every point they raised. They had expected him to bluster, to fight back, to protest that they were behaving as if he were a seven-times-convicted felon who could not be trusted an inch; but instead he had met each new condition with unfailing courtesy and had even congratulated them for their businesslike approach!

At one stage a baffled O'Dwyer had said, "It's as if he still had some weapon up his sleeve, so devastating he can afford to concede every other point with good grace – for it'll make no difference to the outcome when all the dust-sheets are off."

Such remarks, Michael felt, were designed more to shield the lawyer against future recriminations than to guarantee him and Lucy a good night's sleep – which the ignorant layman might suppose to be the fundamental reason for hiring a lawyer in the first place!

I can still turn back, he told himself as he watched the next band of blue sky creep up over the laurels on the far side of the drive. *I am still a free man*.

In the strictly technical sense it was true; the final instrument was to be signed in Dublin that very afternoon. But to speak of "freedom" was to ignore the fact that ruin and disgrace were creeping up behind him – to turn back now would be to take their hot breath full in the face.

Not for the first time – indeed, not even for the hundred-and-first time – he ran through the bright features of this new venture, starting with "a clinic of my own" and ending, somewhat shamefacedly, with "a brake on Lucy's extravagant forays into Dublin," meaning both the city's shops and its society. He had paraded the list for his comfort so many times by now that he could get through it quicker than Lucy could polish off her rosary beads, which was a fairly difficult bench mark to beat.

It did no good. The blue was now overhead. The drops that still fell came from the tree, not the sky. And he knew from the fresh ruts in the wet gravel that a comfortable four-wheeler had gone up the drive already this morning.

Ebenezer O'Dea was waiting.

"He's sheltering under that cypress or whatever it is." Ebenezer offered Nurse Powers the binoculars. "Care to have a closer look at your future master?"

"It's a thuja," Diana said. She took the glasses but let them hang a moment at her side. Why did she continue to say nothing? She could spike the old man's guns this minute by telling him that she and Michael Raven had been lovers . . .

No! That would be like tipping the executioner to make a good clean cut. Besides, it wouldn't stop there. He'd find out about the baby, too, and then he'd have power of life and death over her. No one would ever know about Mick.

She could not help wondering, though, how different things might be at that very moment if she *had* told Michael that Mick was on the way. She might now be sitting in that gig at Michael's side and the Hon. Lucinda Fitzbutler, spinster, might be nurse-companion to the old boy, instead. *She* might now be standing here, dreading the moment when he'd goad her to put the binoculars to her eyes.

No, again!

Life was never so generous with its ironies. Remember the man who, when the gypsy told him he'd die on French soil, emigrated to America, collapsed on the street, and was carried into the nearest house – where he died a few minutes later. What house? The French Embassy! So – no matter what had, or hadn't, or might have happened between her and Michael Raven, with or without the intervention of every breed of dog in the Kennel Club register, Life, the Great Unequalizer, would somehow have arranged for the Hon. Lucinda Fitzbutler to end up as Lucy Raven and for Diana Powers to remain Diana Powers. She rummaged for the pain behind the thought but it was a sore she had scratched too often for it to yield even that perverse satisfaction one more time.

"Under the thuja," Ebenezer reminded her.

"I know." She raised the glasses to her eyes at last.

The old man chuckled. "*Under the thuja*. It sounds like the title of one of those romantic songs Dazzler's always humming." He began to parody the genre: "*Under the spreading thuja tree – I loved you and you loved me* . . . How would that continue?"

The sight of Michael, standing all alone in the gloom with the rain sluicing down around him, helped her shut her inner ears to Ebenezer's jibes. Little things about Michael – gestures she had forgotten, or had forced herself to forget – came flooding back now with a sharpness that hurt. When he toyed with his ear like that it meant he was anxious; she did not need the eightfold magnification of the binoculars to show her the fear that haunted his eyes. When he glanced at the house he seemed to look directly at her.

"Lucy Raven told me she thinks this house is haunted," Ebenezer said suddenly. "D'you believe in ghosts, Nurse Powers?"

"We die a little every day," she told him, glad to be able to lower the binoculars at last. "Sure we haunt ourselves better than any old apparition." By her knowing smile she managed to imply that she was referring more to *his* past life than to any skeleton in hers. Their relations had changed subtly since he had told her she was to be the matron of this new clinic. She could be bolder with him, she found, in an indirect sort of way – and he appeared to enjoy it.

"Arrah, 'tis the God's own truth, I want to tell you!" He spoke in a quaver to emphasize this new parody. Then, in an altogether crisper tone: "Capital! Here's Dazzler in the nick of time. That boy will be late at his own wake."

"As long as I live to see it, I shan't mind that!" Diana said tartly.

He swivelled from the window and stared at her. "How now?" he asked.

"Isn't he the seven plagues of Egypt all rolled into one," she said.

Ebenezer's eyebrows shot up. "I'll have his guts for garters," he promised mildly.

"Please!" She shook her head. "That's a battle I'll fight for myself."

They watched the two gigs, Michael's and Dazzler's, pass out of sight around the western end of the house. Diana realized that her remarks about Dazzler gave her the perfect opportunity to speak out at last – obliquely giving her employer a piece of her mind. She could tell him that when Dazzler had heard how she once helped Mister Raven with his cramming at the Adelaide he had leaped to all sorts of scurrilous and unwarrantable conclusions. ("So unlike his uncle"!) And he'd gone on behaving in that childish way ever since. Wouldn't that box the old fellow in – all four sides, top, and bottom!

She let precious seconds tick away while she said nothing. And then it was too late. Two pairs of boots echoed across the uncarpeted hall outside. Male laughter chased the dying tones. A fresh downpour peppered the windowpanes. The door handle rattled.

Diana drew a deep breath and turned to face him at last.

Lucy stepped off the Lucan steam tram and set out on the one-mile walk through the village. It took her the best part of two hours for she was greeted every yard of the way and invited to step inside at the threat of each passing shower. In her wake people told each other she was a grand sort altogether, hadn't changed a bit, was great gas, one of nature's gentlewomen, a star. They meant that she never gave herself airs, never stood on her dignity – that she knew them all by name and remembered all life's peck of troubles that had been their share. And it was all true. Even now, twelve years after she grew up and left to get married, she could still walk down the street and name the family behind every door – even people who had arrived after she left. But it would never have occurred to them that for Lucy Fitzbutler (as they still thought of her) no other mode of behaviour was possible. To know who lived beneath each roof was for her a kind of compulsion. Some people could manage the world blindfold but not Lucy; she had to *know*. An anonymous house would fill her with unease. It would be the first small crack in the foundations of her influence.

But the good people of Lucan all thought it was simple noblesse oblige.

Because she had to catch up on so much news the luncheon gong was ringing by the time she walked up the drive to Hermitage Lodge – where a new surprise awaited her.

"Dazzler!" she cried out, the moment she saw him standing at the open french window. "What are you doing *here* of all places? I thought you'd be at Mount Venus."

He grinned. "Now which is the bigger surprise – to find me here? Or to find I'm not there?"

She knitted her brow, not seeing any essential difference.

"I'll explain both," he went on, standing aside to let her pass. "I'm here on a small matter of business with your father. He's gone out, by the way. And I'm just about to take lunch with your mother and aunt."

Lucy's face fell. "Which aunt?" she asked under her breath.

"Maude."

She brightened again. "That's all right. It's Gertrude I'd rather not meet just yet." Her smile helped him guess it was a delicate matter of an overdue loan.

She slid out from under her cape and gave it to him to drape over a wicker chair on the verandah; also her rain hat and umbrella. She struggled heartily with her galoshes before yielding the delicate service to him. When his finger lingered in a dainty caress about her ankles she reached down and pinched him hard.

And that was the moment her mother chose to enter the room. "I can't seem to find Maude . . ." Her voice trailed off as her eyes took in the scene. "Well, well!" she said coldly. "What are you doing here – apart, of course, from" – she waved a catty hand at the two of them – ". . . *that?*"

"Mama!" Lucy smiled her best-tempered smile, refusing to be provoked. "I thought I'd come out and tell you all the news. But I suppose Dazzler's beaten me to it. I had no idea you and he were on terms."

"On terms?" Her mother bristled.

Lucy's smile broadened further still. "Or" – she mimicked her mother's earlier wave of the paw – "however you might describe it."

"Mister O'Dea has business with your pater." She paused to let her daughter peck her cheek. "And *he* has, for some reason, chosen this moment to go and see Mister Lamb. He'll come back in two hours, reeking of beer and pickles, I'm sure."

Lamb was the manager of the Lucan branch of the Royal Hibernian Bank.

Lucy raised her eyebrows at Dazzler.

"Oh, just some properties that your father and my uncle are, er, involved with in Chapelizod," he told her vaguely.

"Death by a thousand cuts," Lucy said brightly.

"Whatever that means," Lady Mountstephen added.

Her daughter's smile grew weary. "It's ten years since I left this house, Mama. I do know something of the world and its ways. I have debts of my own, now." She winked at Dazzler.

Her mother saw the gesture and bridled once again. "When did you not!"

Lucy glanced at the other two, several times, in quick succession. "If I'm in the way," she said sweetly, "I'll go."

To her surprise her mother – who was never flustered – was flustered; it had never seemed possible to Lucy that Mama might have romantic leanings, much less that she could be charmed by a rogue like Dazzler O'Dea. She supposed that *she* was the only female in the family who was quite as foolish as that.

Or *had been* quite as foolish as that. She glanced at Dazzler now, a quick up-and-downer, and came to a sudden conclusion about him that had perhaps been bubbling away for weeks inside her, ever since that surprise encounter in Eustace Street. Even in the emotional confusions of that meeting she had been aware that he was somehow different; but she had assumed it was merely because he was older – changed in the way anyone might change after rubbing shoulders with the world for ten years or so. Yet now it struck her that the differences ran much deeper. The gay dog, the feckless man-about-town, the blade who could make your heart leap at the very sight of his smile – *that* Dazzler O'Dea had since become "legs, eyes, and ears" to his Uncle Ebenezer. The work had corroded his very soul. And whenever their eyes met she could see that he knew it. He could remember the man he once was but he had no way of going back and recovering him now. All he could do was make a parade of the old outward signs – the dress, the panache, the bonhomie. Actor-manager Dazzler put on a round-the-clock show of those pyrotechnics that Dazzler, the Young Prodigy, had once lavished on the world without charge. Now it came with a price, even if it was Dazzler himself who usually ended up paying it.

Her heart ached for the young genius she had once loved – but her pain arose from her insight that he was now nowhere to be found, outside the pages of her old diaries.

These thoughts flashed through her mind in the twinkling of an eye – so that her mother's next words came only a few embarrassed seconds after Lucy's offer to depart. "Ah, Maude!" Lady Mountstephen was relieved to see her sister wandering up the verandah. "The gong rang ages ago. Where have you been?"

"You've got aphids on your roses," Maude said.

"Hallo, Aunt dear." Lucy kissed her warmly on the cheek. Aunt Maude's dour pessimism had always cheered her, for nothing in all the world could be quite as bad as Aunt Maude's voice painted it. "There are aphids everywhere. We were just talking about that – in a way. Aphids can take many forms."

The soup arrived and Lucy went to wash her hands. When she returned, Dazzler was charming the two older ladies with an account of the new show at the Empire. Maude was right – the soup was cold; it could hardly have been more than lukewarm when it arrived. Lucy stirred it about and tried to scoop up the liquor before the congealing fat spread itself evenly over the surface again. At last, with only a quarter of it gone, she pushed the plate aside. "I've a touch of diuresis today," she explained, knowing that her mother would never look up the word. To bandy medical terms across the table was bad enough, especially if they shrouded what sounded like indelicate conditions. Lady Mountstephen merely smiled with distaste and pursed her lips.

It left Lucy free to turn to Dazzler and say, "So what happened at Mount Venus this morning? I'm sorry I wasn't there."

The smile left his countenance, replaced by a shifty, slightly worried frown. "It was most extraordinary," he replied.

"Oh?" Lucy was suddenly all attention; she, too, had stopped smiling.

"Is your husband at all . . ." He hunted for an apt word. "I hesitate to say 'unwell,' Mrs Raven, but has he been at all . . . I mean acting at all strangely lately?"

"Of course not." Lucy gripped the edge of the table. "What happened? Just tell me what happened."

"Well, the purpose of this morning's meeting . . ."

"Yes! Tell me that for a start," she interrupted. "Your uncle wouldn't explain why he wanted yet another meeting out there. As if we hadn't already . . ."

"It was to introduce the matron," Dazzler interrupted.

Lucy was nonplussed. "Matron?" she echoed. "What matron?"

"The new matron. The first matron . . ." Dazzler, pretending not to understand her bewilderment, was enjoying himself hugely. "*The* matron. What else can one call her?"

"Well, one could give her a *name*, for a start. Michael never even mentioned . . ."

"Diana Powers," he said. In the corner of his eye he saw Lady Mountstephen give a start; he did not think Lucy noticed.

Lucy's eyes narrowed as comprehension began to dawn upon her. "But that's his own nurse. I met her." She smiled faintly. "The 'flaxen-haired temptress.' I don't know why you called her that – her hair is flaming red."

"I never called her flaxen-haired," he assured her.

"Oh?" She shrugged. "Someone did. Anyway – what happened?"

"Did my son-in-law accept her?" Lady Mountstephen asked eagerly.

Lucy, surprised at her mother's interest, resented her intrusion at this point. "Just a moment," she cut in. "First of all, why is your uncle insisting on this particular woman? I thought he was highly pleased with her work. Why does he want to let her go?"

"He doesn't, Mrs Raven," Dazzler assured her. "You see, he intends to be the first patient to take up residence at Mount Venus."

"Permanently?"

"What does 'permanent' mean when you're half-paralysed and sixty-five?"

Lucy was slightly relieved. "So she'll be matron in title only. She'll continue to be his nurse, in fact." She gave a brief, humourless laugh. "No – in fact, she'll be his spy."

"Oh," he said magnanimously, "we are all spies, surely! At the risk of contradicting you, I think he intends her to be matron in the full sense of the word. She's to have charge of all forty nurses . . . or however many are finally enrolled."

"And keep an eagle eye on the doctors – especially on Michael – and report everything to your uncle!" Lucy added bitterly.

"Has Nurse Powers agreed to this extraordinary arrangement?" Lady Mountstephen asked.

Dazzler turned to her. "She said she'd leave the decision to Doctor Raven – I mean, Mister Raven."

"So she knows her place at least!" Lucy tried to retrieve the initiative. "And what did my husband say? I suppose your uncle left him no choice in the matter."

"He would have left him no choice," Dazzler agreed. "But there's the extraordinary thing, you see. Mister Raven entered the room. He took one look at Nurse Powers and cried out 'You!' She replied . . . I think she was feeling a little unwell for her voice was very faint – and also because of . . . well, something that happened a few moments later. Anyway, she replied, 'Good morning, Mister Raven' – rather faintly, as I said. And then my uncle, realizing that no formal introductions were needed, said, 'I'd like you to meet the nurse who is going to be matron at our new Mount Venus Clinic when it opens.' That was all."

"That was all?" Lucy echoed.

"I mean that was all he said. That was all he got the chance to say. Mister Raven simply turned on his heel and walked out of the house. But even more extraordinary – in my view – was the behaviour of Nurse Powers. She burst into tears and ran away."

"She followed him?" Lucy asked.

"No. Just out into the garden. She got soaking wet and then returned half an hour later, completely restored to her usual ice-maiden self." He turned to the two other women, who were following the exchange with rapt attention. "You'd have to know her to understand how amazing her behaviour was. She is normally – I mean *at all times* – the coolest, calmest, most collected person you could ever hope to meet. For her to register the slightest feeling . . . mild annoyance, say, or passing amusement . . . is the equal of an emotional *outburst* in any other mortal sinner. So for her to break down and cry is like the end of the world."

Lucy had time to gather her thoughts during this long aside – which was as Dazzler had intended it. However, he could hardly have guessed that she would leap at once to the attack. And now he saw a side to his old flame he had never seen before; he knew she had a hot temper, but a cold one was new to him.

"All right, Dazzler," she said calmly. "You've had your little moment of fun. Now let's . . ."

"I'm sure I don't know what you mean," he began to bluster.

"Oh yes you do."

86

The maid came in with a plate of cold tongue. Lady Mountstephen raised a single finger and she understood she was not to bring the vegetables until rung for.

Lucy continued in the same calm manner: "It is quite obvious to me what has happened. My husband and Nurse Powers clearly know each other. Or *knew* each other at some time in the past.'

Lady Mountstephen, who was also seeing a Lucy who was new to her, shifted nervously, and this time her daughter noticed. "Oh?" she exclaimed, turning to her mother with a challenging stare.

The woman sighed and glanced nervously at Aunt Maude. That made Lucy round on her, too. "And you also know of it, Aunt?" she said.

"It was before he met you, my dear," Aunt Maude assured her.

"I'll tell her, Maude, if you don't mind," Lady Mountstephen put in. Turning to Lucy she repeated the assurance: "It was before you even knew Michael – when he was a medical student at the Adelaide. Diana Powers was a nurse there."

"You might at least have told me," Lucy complained.

"But how was I to know they'd ever meet again, dear? Much less in circumstances like *these*." She passed the accusation on in Dazzler's direction. "As I say, it was all over and done with before Michael met you."

"*What* was all over and done with, may I ask? Was it puppy love, or something rather . . ." She broke off and sighed. "What a pointless question! If after ten years apart *he* stalks out of the room and *she* bursts into tears, it was certainly not puppy love. Dazzler! If I didn't *need* you from time to time, I'd cut the head off you this very minute."

He started to smile, thinking the worst was over – until he saw the glint in her eye and realized she meant it. Her mother, too, was about to tell her not to use such a coarse expression – until she saw that same hard gleam.

"And now," Lucy said, "you will each tell me what you know."

On the steam tram back into Dublin, Lucy worked out the things Dazzler had failed to tell her, too. There must, for instance, have been some conversation between him and Michael before they met this Diana Powers person, otherwise he'd never have come hot-foot to Hermitage Lodge. Probably Dazzler said, "What – Mrs Raven not with us, today?" or some such remark, and Michael would have explained that she had gone to see her parents. Then Dazzler would have remembered some business that would take him to Lucan – like the overdue payments on the properties in Chapelizod – and then it was but a seven-mile hop across country and he'd be there before her, bloated with surprise and innocence, but bursting to tell her nonetheless.

Yet had he told her *all?* Had he even stayed long enough to witness it all? She did not doubt that Michael had been shocked enough to walk out of the meeting before it even began; but had he later cooled down and returned – perhaps even after Dazzler had left in high glee for Lucan? And Nurse Powers – what had *she* done after she dried her tears? Dazzler had said nothing as to that.

More to the point, perhaps – what had she done *before* this morning's meeting? Michael had called only once on Ebenezer O'Dea in Sackville street; all their other business, whether in Dublin or up in the mountains, had been mediated by Dazzler. On that one occasion, about a month ago by now, Nurse Powers had not been present, though the meeting had lasted some time. Who had contrived her absence – herself or the old man? In short, who was manipulating whom?

Though the possibility that anyone might manipulate Ebenezer O'Dea was remote, it was, nonetheless, just possible that Nurse Powers was the instigator, the prime mover in everything – perhaps even with the old fellow's connivance. The moment he told her that Michael Raven was to be the medical director at Mount Venus, she could have started to scheme her way into becoming its matron. She would have kept herself out of sight until Michael was so deeply committed to the plan that he could not back out. Ebenezer's sense of malice was great enough to make him connive at her conspiracy.

But what would be her motive? Revenge against Michael for having jilted her? Or did she still love him? Did she see this as her chance to win him back?

Revenge or love – both were powerful enough to drive a woman to folly; yet somehow, despite the fact that she had met Nurse Powers only the once, and so briefly at that, she could not imagine the woman being moved by either. In fact, she could not imagine any intelligent woman behaving so stupidly – not when there were so many subtler and more satisfying ways of achieving the same ends. Dublin was small; its society was a schemer's hothouse, where the most exotic plans could be coaxed into bearing fruit.

All in all, then, it seemed far more likely that Ebenezer's long shadow fell over the whole episode, from first to last, and that poor Nurse Powers was, like almost everyone else in his life, a mere catspaw. With his amazing alertness to others' discomforts, he had somehow twigged that Michael Raven was more to her than a mere name in the medical register. He had then wormed the whole story out of her. Then, realizing what a useful pair of eyes and ears she would make, he had insisted on this otherwise strange condition.

If that was so, then he must be fairly sure that Nurse Powers's love for Michael had cooled beyond reviving – or that the desire for vengeance would encourage her to speak out where the natural loyalties that exist between doctors and nurses might otherwise enjoin silence. It amused Lucy – in a grim fashion – to realize that, no matter how she approached this mystery, it boiled down in the end to one simple question: Did Diana Powers still love Michael in her heart of hearts, or had it all turned to hatred and thoughts of revenge?

She was surprised to discover that she could not say which of these unpleasant alternatives she would prefer. Of course, she wished most of all that neither was the case – that the intervening decade had made Nurse Powers completely indifferent to Michael. But then Ebenezer O'Dea would not have thought her worth the trouble. He would certainly not have *insisted* upon her appointment. It was only the fact that she had betrayed a strong feeling of *some* kind for Michael that the old fellow was playing this game.

In the end she decided she would prefer a lovelorn Diana Powers to one who was torn by hate. The woman might still light a sentimental candle in her heart for the young doctor-to-be who had once meant so much to her, but Lucy was absolutely confident of Michael's love and loyalty – not because their marriage was a bouquet of everlasting roses but precisely because it was not. They could fight like Kilkenny cats. They could say things to each other that would kill mere friendships for ever. She had on several occasions plotted his actual murder – and made no doubt that he had done the same toward her. It had been the most wonderful discovery of her life – the day she realized that, for her and Michael, love and hate were not opposites but actually part of the same magnificent emotion; their love was grand enough to encompass their hatred and give it scope.

She would not, however, concede the same greatness of spirit to Diana Powers – or, indeed, to any other woman. You had to live with a partner for ten years and more, loving him to insanity for his good points, seething with fury at his bad ones, slowly reforming him where he was amenable to reform, and even more slowly accepting him where he was not . . . you had to shed many a tear of regret (and happiness), to give out many a shrill of rage (and ecstasy), before your soul grew large enough to envelop it all.

Besides, she'd seen enough women throw themselves at Michael, all to no avail, for her to feel sure that even the dearest old flame could never singe his loyalty now. Pretty young things, witty young wives, wealthy widows still young at heart – all had tried their luck, their charms, their reputations . . . and all had failed.

Besides, what was the alternative?

A Nurse Powers who continued to live in Sackville Street would be a far greater threat. Michael would, in the nature of things, have to make frequent reports to Ebenezer O'Dea; there was also his one weekly session at the Eli, which he intended to keep up; so there would be plenty of opportunities for brief, sentimental reunions. But *Matron* Powers, in daily touch and (again, in the nature of things) almost daily conflict with Medical Director Raven, under the same roof as Mrs Raven – to say nothing of the patients, nurses, and

89

servants, all on the *qui-vive* for a whiff of scandal . . . Lord, wouldn't they be only mad to stand within three feet of each other!

In fact – and this was Lucy's final thought as the tram rumbled along Bachelors Walk – if Michael did finally accept Diana Powers as his Matron, that atmosphere of "forbidden fruit" would constitute the greatest danger; for nothing is so repellent to a man that a dash of prohibition won't add the spice of attraction to it. She decided she must be especially warm and friendly to Matron Powers. Indeed, she and Michael, both, must be warm and friendly to Matron Powers; for nothing is so attractive to a man that a woman's wholehearted encouragement will not kill his enthusiasm for it inside a week. Madge Ireland had completely cured her husband of fishing by saying things like: "Now I don't want you moping about the house and getting under my feet this weekend so you're to go off fishing somewhere, there's a lamb." And Melissa Condron had cured her brother's drinking, after everyone else had failed, by constantly topping his glass up to the brim and shouting out for all the world to hear: "Watch Liam drink this, everyone. He's amazing. He can put down gallons and yet remain steady as a rock. You'll see! Go on, Liam – show them!"

As the tram drew close to O'Connell Bridge she glanced across the Liffey at the clock on the Ballast House and was amazed to discover she was in good time for the meeting with Ebenezer. The tram went on up Sackville Street to terminate at Nelson's Pillar but she decided to alight at the bridge and walk up the street, looking at the shop windows. She wondered if Michael was going to turn up at all. As she rounded the corner from Bachelors Walk she glanced behind her, because if he was intending to sign all the deeds and agreements today, he'd be crossing the bridge about now.

She searched earnestly but saw no trace of him.

Partly as a game, then, and partly as a test of her own knowledge of him, she tried to imagine the thoughts that had gone through his mind since the shock of seeing Diana Powers again had sent him scurrying off like that. Would he have called it "scurrying off"? To be quite candid, that response from him had surprised her.

Last February she had enlivened a dull dinner party by inventing a new game, which she called "Know Thy Spouse." It consisted of posing half a dozen imaginary situations and asking husbands and wives to confess what they would do if faced with them – and to guess what their partner would do; the guessing and confessing, of course, took place when the ladies retired to the drawing room while the gentlemen stayed for their port and cigars. The situations ranged from the absurd – like seeing an unattended elephant in St Stephen's Green – to the near-the-bone – like opening the spouse's wallet or handbag and finding the stubs of *two* theatre tickets for a recent performance of which the finder knew nothing. The Ravens had won hands-down, much to everyone's annoyance, so Lucy rather prided herself on knowing how Michael would behave in even the most unusual circumstances.

Now, walking up Sackville Street, she guessed that Michael would have got over his shock very quickly. He'd have driven, say, half a mile in the gig and then turned about and come back to beard the lion in his den. And the lioness. Dazzler, bursting to get to Lucan and break the news to her, Lucy, had left almost immediately – and so would have missed Michael's return. Michael might even have seen Dazzler's gig rattling away in the opposite direction. During that cooling-off he'd have realized he had no real choice, anyway. He could accept the directorship at Mount Venus – with Diana Powers as Matron – or he could go to the bankruptcy court – and wind up in a modest practice in some missionary outpost of the empire. Being the man he was, he'd have returned to the meeting bristling with apologies and bursting with charm.

Then, during the delayed interview that followed, he'd have asked old Ebenezer if Nurse Powers had been given any choice in the matter. In fact, he'd probably have insisted on seeing her alone, so that no question of coercion could arise. What else might they have said to each other then? Lucy seethed with anger, mostly against herself, for Michael had asked her to accompany him that morning but she, weary of meetings at Mount Venus, had preferred to visit her parents instead. Now she'd give all her jewels to have been hidden somewhere near the two of them when that painful reunion took place this morning.

No – she mustn't start thinking like that. Spying . . . suspicions . . . they were corrosions to eat up love faster than anything.

All the same . . .

"Lucy!"

She spun round and found Michael almost treading on her heels. "Darling!" Her whole face lit up. "I looked for you just now . . ."

"And stared right through me!" There was no smile on his lips.

"Did I? I'm sorry. I was miles away – but I was thinking about *you*, in fact. You and . . . what happened this morning at Mount Venus. Dazzler told me all about it, of course. He couldn't wait! You must have mentioned that I was going to Lucan?" Michael nodded gravely, confirming that much of her guesswork at least.

"He was beside himself with glee," she added scornfully. "But what happened after he left?" Her merry smile returned. "Did you turn about and go back again? I've been playing 'Know Thy Spouse' solitaire, trying to guess. I guessed you went back and asked to speak with Nurse Powers alone – to see if she was being coerced. Did you?" She tried to let him see she was not worried, even if he had.

And still he did not smile. "Why did you tell me she was flaxen-haired?" he asked. "And that her name was Jameson? That was so unnecessary, Luce."

"Unnecessary?" The word had no meaning for her in this context –

91

as if he had called her actions "mauve" or "grassy."

"It has cut me to the quick, I can tell you," he continued.

They were beginning to attract attention from passers-by. "We can't talk here," she muttered. "We've got twenty minutes. Let's go up the pillar."

They walked in silence the couple of hundred yards to the entrance, where they paid their pennies and started on the long, spiral climb to the platform at the top. She went first. Michael took the steps two at a time, but slowly, because he had to keep down to her pace; he deliberately overventilated his lungs – though as unobtrusively as possible – so that he would hardly be out of breath when they reached the top. She, for her part, became aware that she was deliberately clenching the muscles of her b-t-m with each step so as to make her fashionably tiny bustle wiggle more fetchingly. She almost laughed aloud. They were each, in their different ways, being childish – and both would have died rather than admit as much!

As luck would have it they were alone when they gained the platform at the top. Both were badly out of breath, though they struggled valiantly to conceal the fact. After a long glance northward, pretending to be interested in Carlingford and the Mountains of Mourne – which were clear enough to prompt Michael to mumble that rain was on the way – they moved round to the southern side and, as one, sought out the roseate slab of Mount Venus among the tree-girt slopes of the Dublin Mountains. When they found it, each wanted to say something profound – being stirred by the thought that that place could be the making of them – or the breaking; but the right words eluded them both. The notion carried too many overtones.

"It looks small enough from here," Lucy said at last. Michael grunted his assent. It was the best they could manage.

"Now!" she continued in a brisker tone. "I don't believe I did say she was raven haired . . ."

"*Flaxen*-haired," he snapped.

"Flaxen-haired," she echoed, as if he were being tiresomely pedantic – which annoyed him all the more because that was precisely the burden of his complaint. "I'm sure I said *flaming*-haired, because that's what Dazzler called her to me when I hadn't even met her. The flaming-haired temptress. And flaxen and flaming aren't a million miles apart. And anyway – *I* wouldn't call her raven, flaxen, or flaming. In my view her hair is a rather dull chestnut, completely lacking in lustre. And I thought the same even before I knew you and she were once engaged."

He drew a deep breath, held it a while, and then expelled it again.

"Michael," she said. "I was joking."

He nodded abstractedly. "Many a true word . . ."

She gripped his arm. "You mean you *were?* You and she were actually . . ."

He shrugged awkwardly. "Who can say? It's not just . . ."

"Who can *say?*" she echoed, cutting him short. ' I'm sure if I'd been engaged before you came along, *I'd* jolly well be able to say!"

"Ah, but then you were born lucky," he sneered.

At any other time she would have relished an argument with him. Their eyes would flash, pulses race, cheeks glow – and making it up afterwards was always such bliss! But there was no time for all that before their meeting with Ebenezer O'Dea, which was now due in ten minutes. "I never thought so until I met you," she replied quietly.

Her unprecedented mildness after such a challenge surprised him. He glanced at his watch and exclaimed, "Oh, damnation take this meeting! So much to explain and so little time to do it in!" He smiled wanly at her. "You have absolutely no grounds for worry – at least there's time enough to tell you that."

"Then what else do you need to tell me?" she asked. "To explain more would be like accusing me of disbelieving you – and I don't. Truly, I don't."

"Let's go, then," he said. "Let's give that old rascal the surprise of his life by turning up a minute early."

"He'll assume we did it a-purpose, to unnerve him."

Michael laughed at last. "He'd assume that anyway, no matter what we did." He glanced once more at the panorama before starting on the downward climb. "That was a singularly pointless exercise," he commented.

She laughed. "I think it was the exercise that took the starch out of us, my dear. Perhaps we have learned something after all."

There were times when Michael wished he was a Roman Catholic; it would be so comforting to be able to make the sign of the cross. He'd heard tales of a nun at the Loreto who made surplices for choirboys out of bolts of some incredibly expensive cloth; she used no patterns, they said – she simply made the sign of the cross with the scissors and cut straight into it. There were, he thought, moments in a Protestant's life when some equally soothing gesture would be the greatest balm; and this particular moment, when he stood with pen in hand, about to sign the agreement with Ebenezer O'Dea, was one of them.

He continued to hesitate. He dipped the pen in the ink yet again, and, yet again, he touched the nib to the side of the well, allowing half the charge to drain back. He closed his eyes briefly, as if praying – though no prayer would come – and then at last he signed with a flourish. "Done!" he murmured. The half-circle of his R projected like a gross caricature of a female breast over the v of Raven.

"And it didn't hurt a bit, eh?" Ebenezer signed his own name in a modest, crabbed hand in the space beneath Michael's. The attendant

93

lawyers beamed and breathed sighs of relief as they administered the blotting paper.

Lucy had been watching Diana Powers all this while, though the nurse had been studiously avoiding her eye ever since she and Michael had entered the house. She could wish that the woman was at least ten years older, with a corresponding number of inches on her hips, waist, and neck; she would not have denied her the red hair but she would have liked its glow to be dimmed – the glow that made adjectives like "flaming" come all too easily to mind. She would have preferred, too, that the woman had been a Roman Catholic and had trained at the Mater or the Coombe, where her chance of meeting Michael at that impressionable age would have been precisely nil. She could have wished for . . . oh, so many changes but it was all too late by now.

Her misgivings surprised her for on paper she held all the cards. In fact, she held the entire pack, so that it was absurd to think of their forthcoming life at Mount Venus as some kind of game where one or other of them might win the odd trick. The notion of life-as-a-card-game lingered in her mind while they waited for Michael to give the document one last skim-through. Seen in that light, the only cards Nurse Powers held were for a game of *Hearts* that had ended rather abruptly over a decade ago; the new game was *Happy Families* and – as everyone knows – the two packs had not a single card in common.

This play of ideas did not amuse her as much as it ought, and it comforted her not at all. A great sense of foreboding had hung over her ever since Dazzler had told her of that morning's events at Mount Venus. She could soothe herself a hundred ways to Christmas but her mind always returned to the central and inescapable fact – that Michael had taken one look at Diana Powers and had fled without a word. No comforting fantasy could accommodate the intensity of that reaction – all the more so because it was entirely unpremeditated. He could not have known she was there, so his response was *pure* – untainted by any calculation of self-interest or consideration for wife and children. It was Michael the Unready, Michael in his innermost self, who had bolted like a terrified rabbit; only later had a more calculating part of him reasserted its control and forced him back to do the urbane and civilized thing.

Too late, of course. The harm was done by then. The truth was out. During that brief interval the veneer had been stripped away and the primal self stood revealed. How could she recapture what he would hardly ever let her see – that primitive, unreasoning creature at the core of him?

When Michael dipped his pen in the ink for the second time, and primly drained half of it back into the well, she glanced at Dazzler – and found him staring at her in much the same way as, she imagined, she must be staring at Nurse Powers. Suddenly it was like looking at a negative of a familiar person or scene. When, as a girl, she had seen her first negatives, she had refused to believe that Papa had the face of a nigger-minstrel or that cypresses and yews made brilliant white spikes across the landscape. Now, too, her mind could see the superficial likeness between the two situations – Lucy–Dazzler and Michael–Diana; but the one was a complete negative of the other; so here, too, she refused to accept that any true correspondence existed.

No power in creation would ever revive the romantic feeling she had once felt for Dazzler O'Dea. And as for running from him in fear . . . her thoughts ground to a halt. Hadn't she, indeed, found herself face to face with Dazzler, little over a month ago in Eustace Street? And hadn't he called her name and hadn't she, too, bolted like a frightened rabbit – in spirit if not in fact?

It ought to have soothed her that Michael's response had been so like her own, but it did not. She sought for some essential difference between them. At last – being unable to find any, and thus becoming more annoyed with herself than ever – she brushed the whole stupid train of thought aside. What was the point of those idle speculations? When the bugles sounded, she'd know well enough what to do.

Michael signed, and it was done. The lawyers gathered the papers and retired.

Lucy gave Dazzler her warmest smile, which she then trained on Diana Powers, as well.

The nurse risked the briefest glance in her direction and was at once trapped by the brilliance of Lucy's grin, which took her aback.

"Isn't it exciting!" Lucy exclaimed. "It's like setting out on a great adventure, all of us together." She held out a hand to Diana. "I had no idea, when last we met, that we were to become such close associates, Miss Powers." Almost as an afterthought she added, "I don't suppose you did either." She managed to inject the slightest note of doubt into the question, but not enough to provoke an answer. Then she turned to the two O'Deas. "Come on, Dazzler – don't tell me you haven't got a bottle of bubbly tucked away somewhere, to celebrate a moment like this!"

She hoped to embarrass him, of course, but he clapped his hands and drysoaped them, saying merrily, "I never could hide a thing from you, Luce!" He pulled the bell sash beside the fireplace and within moments Violet appeared, bearing a tray on which rested a magnum of champagne and five glasses.

Lucy, despite her smiles, was furious – for now it must seem to the others that she and Dazzler had contrived it between them. The idea that she might have guessed at finding such an unlikely commodity under Ebenezer O'Dea's roof – and that it should actually be held in readiness just outside the door – was so remote as to be unthinkable; she did not wish anyone to suppose there was the slightest degree of collusion between her and Dazzler on any conceivable topic. No one was ever going to say, "You started it first!"

Dazzler had meanwhile popped the cork and charged their glasses with the expertise of long familiarity.

"To Mount Venus!"

Five sparkling glasses rose in unison: "To Mount Venus!"

"God bless her and all who sail in her!" Dazzler added, breaking up their solemnity.

Michael picked up the metaphor. "She'll be the finest ship that never sailed. And we'll do more for our patients' health than any cruise on the seven seas."

"Hear-hear!" Diana said, not realizing that hers would be the only voice.

"Hear-hear!" Lucy put in belatedly. She challenged Dazzler for support.

"There-there!" he said impishly.

"One point we didn't actually settle," Michael said. "We're agreed that Nurse Powers will make a splendid matron, but there remains the point I raised this morning. She cannot be both matron to Mount Venus and nurse to Mister O'Dea."

Ebenezer chuckled. "I fear we were not entirely frank with you this morning, Raven," he said. "We told you we intended to advertise for a successor. In fact, we had already done so – as a result of which we interviewed a lady this afternoon who seems suitable in every way. She starts tomorrow."

"Do we know her?" Lucy asked at once – using the verb in all its subtle bourgeois shades of meaning.

"*You* probably do, Mrs Raven," he replied. "Her name is Lynch. Mrs Lynch. And she comes from a village in County Kildare called Prosperous – a happy omen, I feel."

Lucy's eyes narrowed, for these details rang a bell with her. "Was she widowed last year?"

Ebenezer's eyes raked the ceiling "You *do* know her!'

"I think I've heard of her." She turned to Michael. "You remember that surgeon – Tom Lynch, was it? Or Tim Lynch? Lived out near Rathfarnham. Resigned from Saint Vincent's under a rather mysterious cloud . . . about two years ago. No one would quite talk about it, though you could see everyone was dying to. They bought a cottage on the Liffey at Millicent – which isn't so very far from Prosperous, is it. And Myles Boylan told me he died last year. *Helen!*" she cried triumphantly. "Helen Lynch! Am I right?"

Diana Powers stared at her in reluctant admiration.

"Don't ask her size in gloves," Michael warned the company. "She'd only tell you."

"So!" Lucy ignored the jibe and continued addressing Diana. "If Nurse Lynch is coming tomorrow, *Matron* Powers might be available from lunchtime onwards?"

Diana gave her the briefest of nods and eyed her warily.

"Then perhaps we could all meet at Mount Venus?" Lucy went on, adding for Ebenezer's benefit, "Unless the boss-man has any objection?"

He waved his hand, conceding he had none; the exchange between the two women seemed to fascinate him.

"All?" Diana echoed.

"Yes. I'm meeting the architect there after luncheon. Philip de Renzi – you may know of him?"

Diana shook her head.

"Salt of the earth, of course," Lucy went on. "But he suffers from a serious delusion, common, I believe, to many in the architectural profession: He thinks he knows what we want even before we tell him of it. I say we want such-and-such here and so-and-so there and I can see his eyes go all glazed and I know he's only waiting for me to stop so that he can tell me what is actually going to go where. But I'm sure he'd listen much more to you than he ever will to me. D'you think you could possibly spare the time to put him back in his place, Miss Powers? Tomorrow afternoon, say?"

Diana nodded gravely.

To Lucy that brief nod was the most encouraging event of the entire day; and the best thing of all about it was the fact that the new matron did not even glance in Ebenezer O'Dea's direction before she agreed.

Lucy met Diana off the train at Dundrum. She felt nervous enough to ask whether she had had a comfortable journey. Diana looked somewhat surprised and said it was hardly fifteen minutes from Harcourt Street. Lucy, who never went by public conveyance unless it was quite unavoidable – as with her visit to Lucan the previous day – looked suddenly thoughtful. "I'd never realized that," she said. "Perhaps Mount Venus isn't quite as remote as I'd supposed. Until now it's felt as if we're sentencing ourselves to exile in Ultima Thule."

"The desert were a paradise, wert thou there – wert thou there," Diana replied – so conversationally that Lucy did not recognize it for a quotation until she repeated the last three words. "Burrrns," she added, giving the name its Scottish pronunciation.

"Ah," Lucy replied. Then, thinking that sounded rather bald, added, "They say he's not quite proper for a lady to read, but even so I find him hard going."

Diana said nothing, but managed to do it in a rather triumphant manner. The self-sufficiency she radiated was awesome, Lucy thought. Also it occurred to her that if Diana was going to spend the day making oblique remarks like that, forcing her, Lucy, to say the first thing that came into her head, and then responding with a kind of smug silence, she would seize the initiative in a most unfair manner – exposing nothing of herself, risking nothing.

She was not going to allow that to happen.

97

They emerged from the station and Lucy indicated her carriage. She had the hood half-up today, keeping off the occasional shower but letting in the healthy fresh air. As Diana climbed the steps ahead of her, Lucy found herself inspecting her figure with a man's eyes – her lissome figure in graceful, willowy motion. How would . . . well, Dazzler, for instance, look at Diana Powers in this *interesting* situation? She knew it was interesting to men from the number of times they tried to engineer it. Try as she would, however, the imaginary man behind her eyes was not Dazzler but Michael; and then her spirit refused to continue the inquiry. It merely sulked within her, sputtering with anger at the realization that Michael would be presented with *interesting* opportunities of this kind every day from now on – whether he wanted them or no. And even, to be fair to Miss Powers, whether *she* wanted them or no. For the first time in her life she gained an inkling of what the great Catholic theologians had meant when they spoke of women as *occasions* of sin rather than as agents. For agents have some say in the matter; they are, by definition, an agency – they make things happen. But occasions . . . well, they're just . . . *occasions*. Happenings. They just happen. They *are*. Simply by existing they cause all the trouble.

And so it would be with Diana Powers as matron at Mount Venus. She wouldn't need to wish for anything; her mere existence would be an *occasion* of . . . all sort of things that she, Lucy, would rather not have to think about or worry about or be on the *qui-vive* to detect.

"I think I may have found our first patient," Diana said as soon as the carriage moved off.

"Good heavens!" Lucy felt an instinctive desire to reject anything that would hasten the day when the clinic would start to function, to settle to its alarming routine. "It'll be weeks before we're ready for patients, Matron."

Diana nodded, as if that were a point of view she could just about understand – without actually sharing it. "In an ideal world, yes, Mrs Raven. It's something we shall have to consider. Do we get ready first – down to the very last kidney bowl and bronchial inhaler . . . and forty nurses eating their heads off – before we open our doors? Or do we open a single wing first – a single room, even?"

"Well!" Lucy said coolly. "If people go discovering patients all over the place, we shan't have much choice, shall we!" She smiled to soften the words now they were safely uttered. "Who is this patient? A lot might depend on that, of course."

The horses plodded up the hill toward Ticknock. They passed the gates of a large house and for a moment Lucy could not recall who lived there – a moment of panic. The ultimate horror story for her was Rip van Winkle – to wake up in a familiar world peopled entirely by strangers.

98

"She's a Mrs Doherty," Diana replied. "I'm afraid I know little else about her beyond the fact that she has a delicate cardiac condition and needs rest and later re-examination. I only heard of her last night, as a matter of fact. I went back to the Adelaide, to see a young cousin of mine who's starting training there."

"A nurse?"

"No. A doctor. And I ran into Matron on my way out . . ." She broke off and gave a little laugh. "It's funny. She was such a hard, intimidating woman – Miss Rivers – or seemed so, when I was a nurse there – and actually, she's quite sweet and charming."

"You're no longer a challenge to her, that's all."

"Challenge?" Diana echoed incredulously. "Believe me, Mrs Raven, the last thing that was *ever* on my mind was to challenge that gorgon!"

"Oh, but I don't mean wilfully challenge. One can challenge just by existing, don't you think? The Adelaide was her territory. And still is, come to that. Everyone on it – patients, nurses, and doctors – is a potential challenge to her possession of it, whether they will it or not. Even if, as you say, it's the last thing on their minds. You see what I mean?"

Diana stared up at the Three Rock Mountain, whose familiar outline looked wrong from this unfamiliar angle. "Yes, Mrs Raven," she said at last. "I do see what you mean."

"But to get back to this Mrs Doherty, was it Matron Rivers who told you of her?"

Diana, still thinking over what Lucy had said, merely nodded.

Lucy continued: "Don't you find that rather odd? In my experience, generosity is a flower that blooms only on the lower slopes of the medical mountain."

Diana smiled, somewhat reluctantly, and nodded again.

"Doherty . . . Doherty . . ." Lucy repeated. But the name did not suggest any immediate links with possible rivals who might want to get a stalking horse into the new clinic.

"That's something else that never even crossed my mind," Diana said.

They reached the junction with the mountainy road and the horses immediately picked up a trot. The mood in the carriage changed with the smarter pace. They stared down over Dublin in silence awhile, broken at last by Lucy, who said, "No matter how often one sees it – and we're going to see it every day very soon – that view still takes the breath away, don't you think?"

Diana nodded. "All those houses . . . and people. All that struggle! The unending struggle."

"And somewhere down there – at this very moment – there's a handful of people – half a dozen, perhaps a dozen – who want us to fail at Mount Venus. And maybe three times that number who haven't yet decided whether to support us or throw in their lot with the enemy." She leaned forward and gripped the edge of the carriage, staring intently at the smudges that were bricks and mortar down there, as if they might somehow yield up clues to that secret band.

Watching her, Diana felt the hair prickle on her neck. She had an intuition that, whether they liked each other or not, they were now inextricably yoked together. They needed each other as desperately as any two human beings possibly could. The success or failure of the Mount Venus Clinic was in their hands – far more than it was in Michael's or Ebenezer's or any of those important people they had persuaded to sit on the governing medical committee.

The intuition was too grand to take in all at once. All she could express in actual words was the thought: "I don't think Doctor Raven has quite the same view of the matter, you know."

"The same jaundiced view, you mean." Lucy turned to her, smiling once more. "Do you think I'm jaundiced, Matron?"

"Oh no, not at all, Mrs Raven. I'm sure you're right. I have to admit that when Matron Rivers mentioned Mrs Doherty my only thought was, *How kind of her – she's not a bad old stick, really!* But, as I say, I'm sure you have the truth of it. If not about Mrs D., then about someone. They'll try to slip a stalking horse in somehow. The nurses, too – we must be careful about them."

"How many have applied?"

"Oh, dozens – it's one of the few respectable ways in which young spinsters can get out of their parents' . . . er . . ."

"Clutches?"

Diana smiled. "I've only seen two so far. But in view of what you say, Mrs Raven, I think we both ought to interview all applicants in future."

"Doherty!" Lucy cried triumphantly. "Tell me – is there a Doctor Lucas still at the Adelaide?"

Diana nodded. "The consultant cardiologist."

"Hah!" Lucy rubbed her hands. "And Rebecca Lucas is his wife?"

The other shrugged. "I have no idea. He wasn't married when I did my training."

"I'm sure of it. And her maiden name was . . . Doherty – voilà! I think we've been offered old Lucas's sister-in-law."

Diana closed her eyes and then laughed coldly. "The duplicity of people! And she was nice as pie to me – Matron Rivers." She pulled a glum face. "So I suppose I'll tell her we're not quite ready?"

"Not at all!" Lucy cried spiritedly. "On the contrary – wheel her in! What a feather it would be in Michael's cap if he actually found something wrong with her heart! You know how cardiac conditions can lie undetected for years – especially among ladies of the leisured classes!" She soaped her hands excitedly at the prospect. "If we hadn't arranged to meet Philip de Renzi, I'd be tempted to say let's turn about and collect her this morning!"

100

To her amazement, Diana Powers actually laughed – a genuine laugh at last!

And as for Diana herself, she became aware that her eyes sparkled. It was a sensation she had almost forgotten. And she gazed out of the carriage, seeing the landscape not as an unknown country that no amount of familiarity would ever naturalize for her but as a potential home. For the first time she faced a future that was not a bleak repetition of the past, or, even worse, a *disguised* repetition of the past. Somewhere out there, among all those ill-wishers, all those uncertainties, an incredible hope was beckoning.

Philip de Renzi stood in the portico of Mount Venus House, legs apart, hands on hips – a masterful pose altogether, he told himself. Not that he was feeling especially masterful that day, he was simply trying to imagine what it would be like to be the owner of a great mansion like this, to have all those thousands of tons of carefully arranged stone, timber, plaster, and glass at your back, and to stand here, lord and master of it all, with the whole of Dublin at your feet.

He tried. He willed himself so very hard to be such a man . . . and failed. It was like diving into the sea, into some rocky pool, and pretending to be a fish – or imagining what it must be like to be a fish. You'd flog your brains to think *fish*, and all the while a most un-fishlike panic to breathe air again was growing inside you, getting in the way. And so it was now, on the grand steps of Mount Venus. Think *rich*, he told himself – but an ever-swelling desire to breathe the sweet air of realism again kept intruding. What happened in the mind of a rich man when he looked at a tree and said, *I own you!* Surely realism gave the tree a say in the matter, too? And didn't the tree reply, *All you own is the right to cut me down. If you don't exercise it, your "ownership" is meaningless. But if you do . . . what then do you own!* Realism was like the slave whose task was to murmur, "You are only mortal" into the ear of every Roman general who rode in triumph through the Eternal City.

Did rich men have a special valve in their minds to shut out the voice of that slave?

Philip heard the approaching carriage and he abandoned the pose at once. He stuffed his hands in his pockets and leaned against one of the pilasters beside the door. While he waited he practised the slight head movement that would make his hat appear to doff itself of its own accord; that was always a good one with the ladies.

The ladies, God bless 'em! He closed his eyes and fought off the threat of weariness as familiar arguments in all-too-familiar voices rattled round inside his skull: "Philip, you should get married. People are starting to talk. Of course you can afford it! You're well able – it's just a feeble excuse. And as for saying you never meet the right woman – well, 'feeble excuse' is about the kindest judgement one could pass on *that* nonsense!"

Yes, Mama. Yes, Aunty Ethel. Yes, Nanny Hawkins . . . Would they ever stop!

What if he told them the truth – that the only woman he'd ever wanted to marry was Lucy Fitzbutler? That'd put the cat among the pigeons.

Or probably it wouldn't. After all these years, they'd say, he was just using that as an excuse, too. And perhaps they'd be right. What was reality – once you started digging as deep into the mind as all that? It dissolved into something more properly called *habit*.

The carriage drew to a halt and he roused himself from his annoying reverie just in time to remember the trick with the hat. "Good morning, ladies!" he called out, straightening himself with such vigour that his hat spun right off his head and fell in a couple of somersaults before, by the greatest fluke, he caught it with the merest flick of his fingers.

The ladies laughed; Lucy applauded. "Practice makes perfect!" she called out.

"As the surgeon said on his ninetieth birthday," Philip replied, sauntering to the edge of the top step to receive them.

A moment later the whole day seemed to rearrange itself in some subtle way around him. He knew Lucy was bringing out the new matron to meet him, and so he was expecting some grim old battleaxe in black bombazine. The lissome figure and graceful, willowy poise of the young woman who was at that moment descending backwards from the carriage towards him, held him spellbound. And when she turned to face him, still laughing at his quip, her eyes sparkling, he thought he had never seen anyone quite so engaging in all his life.

It was so unwelcome that he actually turned his back on her as she advanced up the steps. Good sense persuaded him to complete the movement, however, so that, to them, he appeared to spin idly on his heel.

"Matron, I'd like to present Philip de Renzi," Lucy said gaily. "A childhood sweetheart of mine, presently masquerading as our architect. Philip, this is Miss Diana Powers, our Matron-elect, or however one might express it."

On impulse Philip raised her proffered hand to his lips and pressed a symbolic kiss within an inch of it. She stared at him in surprise, looked deep into his eyes . . . and all at once the smile faded from her countenance and the gaiety fled from her eyes – to be replaced by a kind of pent-up anxiety, cautious and watchful. Lucy saw it but pretended not to. The sun came out – in almost perfect opposition to their change in mood.

As they passed indoors Philip became entirely businesslike, a paragon of an architect blessed with intelligent clients who knew what they wanted. Lucy, who had never seen him so impersonal before, was full of admiration, until she realized he was making the same impression on Miss Powers. She wondered whether Philip realized it, too, and, if so, was he doing it deliberately? Or was it that he had no alternatives to offer between the paragon and the gay buffoon who had greeted them on the steps? The temptation to stir the pot, be it ever so slightly, was great, but she resisted it.

The only problem he was not able to solve (because it was personal rather than architectural) was where the Ravens should live. On the one hand Lucy was afraid of getting so swept up in the affairs of the clinic that her life outside it would cease to have much meaning. So they ought to adapt one of the outbuildings as living quarters for the director and his family. On the other hand, that would mean setting aside a bedroom for the director for those occasions when some desperately ill patient required him to be seconds rather than minutes away. And bedrooms and long hours of waiting around were apt to give people ideas, especially if . . .

She did not complete the thought, however. She wanted to try to stop thinking of Diana Powers as a rival, as the Other Woman, as an enemy. Of course, the terms in which she expressed the problem to Philip were nothing like so direct. They had repaired, once again, to the winter garden, where they were sharing the hamper Lucy had brought.

"It's the children, mainly," she said. "Our generation, I believe, is coming increasingly to see children as part of the family – which is an idea that *my* parents, for instance, still find quite shocking. They have little enough life in common with each other, never mind their children. To them children were damnable accidents who were left more or less alone to grow up any old how, as best they could. But Michael and I have positively enjoyed bringing our four out here with us and feeling they're really quite an important part of it all."

"Yes, Lucy, you're a wonderful mother!" Philip risked something dangerously close to a genial wink in Diana's direction. He was overcoming the shock of being so instantly attracted to her and was trying to find a civilized way of neutralizing it entirely. "But what's the point of telling us all this?"

I mean, what are you hoping we won't notice? he thought to himself.

"Oh, simply that – in one way – we want to live in the main house itself . . . carve out some small family dwelling in a corner somewhere, if that's possible?"

"Perfectly."

"Oh, Philip, don't be so smug! The purely architectural possibility or impossibility is neither here nor there. It's a personal dilemma. The other argument is that it would immerse them much too much in the day-to-day business of the place, which would not be a healthy way to grow up. So perhaps we ought to adapt one of the outbuildings for our own quarters?" She turned to Diana. "What does our matron think?"

Diana understood very well the true nature of the fears that lay behind this camouflage. At once she made the point about the need for a bedroom for the director on those nights when he could not go too far from a critically ill patient; if she had said nothing about it, her omission would have been glaring. "The disadvantage of that," she added, "is that it would mean sacrificing a room that might otherwise be housing a fee-paying patient."

Philip, who had been amazed that Lucy should canvass anyone else's opinion on a choice that affected her own family so intimately, began to glimpse the vaguest hints of an answer to his earlier, unspoken question about what she was trying to hide. "One of the previous owners was good enough to give us a ready-made answer," he pointed out. "The arrangement of the rooms and staircases for the governess and the young spinsters provides a perfect little family quarters. It even has its own bathroom."

"Well . . ." Lucy shrugged the problem aside. "We shall have to see what Michael says."

"Governess and young spinsters?" Diana echoed. "It sounds intriguing."

Philip explained the architectural underpinnings of morality to her, more or less as he had to Lucy on an earlier visit.

"What a waste of effort!" Diana commented. "If love laughs at locksmiths, it's unlikely to have been daunted by a slumbering governess and the odd creaking stair. However, you do bring the discussion to a point *I* wanted to raise. Something of a similar nature will have to be devised for my nurses, you realize."

"You already have it," he pointed out. "There's only one staircase leading up to the old female servants' rooms."

"But I'm unhappy about that, Mister de Renzi. If there were a fire, they'd be trapped and killed. There must be a fire escape, too."

He smiled, as professionals always smile when an amateur finally catches up with some problem they themselves have long ago resolved. "Not one, but two," he replied. "I'm afraid the entire back to the building is going to be disfigured with outside fire escapes – which will, of course, extend all the way to the attic floor."

Diana closed her eyes and sank into thought.

"Better?" Philip prompted.

"No," she said glumly. "Worse! One single staircase can be controlled. I mean, notwithstanding what I said about locksmiths, one does stand a slight chance of controlling a single stair. But three!" She raised her hands in a gesture of hopelessness.

"But the fire escape doors will be barred from external entry," he explained. "Only your nurses will be able to open them – and only from the inside."

"Precisely!" she said – in the tone professionals always use when some amateur gets the point at last.

"Ah!" he said, swallowing hard.

Lucy couldn't recall the last time she'd seen him redden like that.

"We're not all sugar and spice and all things nice," Diana added.

"Does it matter?" Lucy put in.

The other two stared at her in surprise.

"I mean, how old are they?" she asked.

"In their twenties," Diana replied. "Some in their thirties."

"Well, then!" Lucy waved the problem airily aside. "It's hardly our business, is it? No doubt it's different in a teaching hospital, where the governors are *in loco parentis*, as it were. But we are a commercial enterprise. Surely people must recognize that – including the nurses who come to work here? We can't waste our resources on policing our employees' morals in their own time. D'you suppose Guinness worries what its workers get up to once the whistle goes?"

Diana swallowed heavily. "I suppose I'd never thought of it – but even so, it doesn't seem right."

"Make a rod for your own back if you wish, Matron," Lucy said. "But all the laws in the world can't stop the Liffey from reaching the sea, so it's a waste of time passing them."

The other two exchanged surprised glances. "I must admit it, Matron," Philip went on. "I find the Roman Catholic approach to life and its problems refreshingly free of cant and humbug at times, don't you?"

"There's something in the air, or the water, or *somewhere* in this benighted country," Michael said at the end of one particularly gruelling day. "It's not as if it's difficult to work out how a thing *ought* to be done. We all know how we *ought* to have set about establishing Mount Venus – dammit, we even sat down and solemnly agreed: First we do A, then we do B, and only then do we start on C. And what happens?" He choked briefly on his own enthusiasm.

Which gave Lucy a chance to slip in a sideways word: "Matron couldn't help it. It wasn't her fault. You surely can't blame her?"

"Of course not." He recovered his breath. "That's actually my point. It's not her. It's in the air, as I said at the beginning. And it's *not* just with Mount Venus. It's with everything in life. D'you remember that day, when Portia was on the way, when we set off for the donkey races in Blessington and ended up singing songs round Billy McReevey's piano in Castleknock – never having got within ten miles of the donkeys? That's the sort of thing I mean. That Irishman who invented the submarine – whatsizname in Lahinch in County Clare – I'll bet he sat down intending to write a patriotic address to Daniel O'Connell or something. He just got distracted on the way and somehow ended up with working drawings for a submarine. That's

105

how things get done in this country."

"Well, at least they get done." She folded down the last of the six dozen bedsheets she had marked that evening and added it to the pile. "There!" She pinned down the marking-ink bottle and screwed the top back on with a flourish. "*Now* let them say they don't know which sheets are ours! I think we've done wonders." She rubbed the corners of her eyes and yawned. Even tiredness had a morally good feeling about it nowadays. "We said it would be two months before we were ready for our first patients, and, thanks to Matron, we've already got six."

"And we accepted our first on the very next day!" He pushed the two piles of applications farther onto the table and a little farther apart: the short-list and the rejects.

"Mrs Doherty wasn't a patient, she was a spy. We had to accept her – and a jolly good thing it turned out, too! She'd be dead by now, but for you – even Ben Lucas had to admit it."

"It was hardly as dramatic as all that," he said modestly. The size of the rejects pile worried him. All those hopes being dashed. All those desperate young women, frantic to escape the life-sapping tedium of their middle-class homes, so awful that the ill-paid drudgery of nursing was a paradise in comparison. He could imagine them rushing to intercept the post . . . extracting the letter from Mount Venus . . . carrying it upstairs and locking the bedroom door . . . opening it with trembling fingers, hearts leaping out of their breasts . . . and then the tears, the floods and floods of tears. And the aching, empty days that would follow – filled only with the knowledge that they were no damn good. No damn good! No damn good!

"Well, I know different," Lucy said as she rose and crossed the room to stand behind him. "Are those the nurses – or applicant nurses? Or just builders' bills? We're going to drown in paper soon."

He touched the pile that worried him. "It's not that they're no damn good," he said. "It's just that these others are better. How can we help them understand that? They should go on trying. I think I should write to each one personally."

"Michael!" She laughed, not thinking he could mean it seriously. "You can't possibly afford the time."

"I'll have to make it somehow," he told her. "I'm haunted by the picture of a poor young girl getting an impersonal rejection from us and concluding she's utterly useless – and then accepting a proposal from the first chump who comes along with a spare ring in his pocket. We'd have ruined her life – just for the want of a little note from me. I have to do it, Lucy."

She put her hands round him and hugged his head to her breast. "Oh, Michael – you are just too good for this world, sometimes! Listen. Life is hard and life is brutal. Why hide it from them? If young women want to quit the charmed domestic circle and plunge

106

into the waters of life, they must learn how cold it is. Would you be equally worried if those were all young men being turned down for a clerical position?"

He chuckled. "Of course not! Men have to learn to take that sort of thing."

"And so must women. We're a lot tougher than you think, you know."

The odd thing was – he *did* know! He had watched Lucy and Diana over these past weeks – and their growing band of nurses – working themselves until they dropped, which was always long after he was ready to throw in the sponge. And how severe they were with one another, too! Petty faults that he and, he believed, most other men would have let pass were pounced upon mercilessly; they let *nothing* pass them by.

Lucy sighed. "It doesn't matter what I say, does it! You're still going to write your feather-bolster notes to each and every one."

He leaned tighter into her embrace, relishing her softness – God's joke on Adam, of course, all that softness He hung about them. "It's a matter of courtesy, love. Put it no higher than that."

"Aargh!" She grasped his ears and shook them to the point where discomfort shaded into pain. "How can anyone love such a stubborn, awkward, unreasonable . . . knobbly creature! What was my transgression, Lord?"

"Put yourself in the place of one of those poor girls. I know it's hard, because *you* were brought up on a system of benign neglect. If your parents ever ran across you by accident, they said, 'Hallo, little girl, and what might your name be?' But these poor creatures" – he tapped the pile of rejects – "they live with personal gaollers in a kind of lifelong prison."

"And what might you know about it?" Lucy was struggling not to laugh, for his description of her upbringing, though a wild exaggeration, of course, was not entirely wide of the mark – close enough, anyway, to stir ancient resentments.

"I've attended some of the interviews," he replied. "I've seen the desperation in their eyes. The longing to be free." He reached for his fountain pen and opened the drawer where the notepaper was kept. "I must write those notes, love. I needn't say much. Just . . ."

Lucy pushed his pen back in his pocket and gently closed the drawer, making him pluck his hand away from it. "Alice can write them tomorrow," she told him. "She has a fair enough hand for that. A little note saying, 'Please do not be too disheartened by this single rejection. I was most impressed by your application and certainly believe you will find a place somewhere. You had the misfortune to apply for one where the competition was extraordinarily high.' Something like that, eh? Alice would love to do that for you. And all you need do is sign it."

He turned his head to the left and pressed that ear to her bosom,

107

listening to her pulse – no *thrill* in the diagnostic sense but an unending source of thrills to him. "You *have* got a heart, after all!" he murmured.

She cuddled his head against that bosom, caressing him gently with its softness. "Pray continue your examination of my organs, Doctor Raven," she said in a voice deliberately husky. "Who knows what you may find!"

"O-o-oh!" He collapsed away from her where he sat, drawing the word out in an octogenarian quaver. "Trapped again!" Then he rose, all sprightly, and took her in his arms. "You've changed," he said.

And so she had, of course. And she knew it. And she also knew what he believed to lie behind it all: the daily competition with Diana Powers. How smug it must make him feel! And how uneasy he would turn if he knew the real cause! For it had nothing to do with the matron at all. It was having Philip de Renzi around – desperately trying not to fall in love with Miss Powers by fanning the much weaker embers of his ancient, and merely sentimental, attachment to her, Lucy. It was having Dazzler drop by at frequent but always unexpected moments, full of his blarney, and making outrageous suggestions that would leave him panicstricken if she ever said yes.

"Are you complaining?" she asked, taking his hand and leading him toward the stair.

"No," he replied.

"I should jolly well hope not!"

This was one of the highlights of the day – leading him up the Young Bachelors' Stair to bed . . . and thinking of a particular young spinster, alone in her bed, not a million miles away . . . and wondering if she ever pictured this little scene to herself . . .

Lucy felt sure she must.

Ebenezer O'Dea sat in the drawing room of his private suite at the western end of Mount Venus. By his own macabre choice it was the room with the cupboard where Reilly had hanged himself; the door remained fastened with the screws Lucy had ordered.

At that moment Ebenezer was staring at the plans Philip de Renzi had laid before him some ten minutes earlier; the young man himself had tactfully withdrawn to the farther window and was pretending to take an intense interest in nature . . . or distant Dublin as it neared the end of a working day . . . or anything, in fact, but his professional fate, which now lay entirely in the old fellow's hands.

The westering sun lay across the "blue" prints, making folds in the paper, shadows of ivy leaves, and accidental lenses in the panes seem more important than the carefully placed lines and textures of the architect's draft. And perhaps they were more important, too,

Ebenezer thought. *Something* had to be; there must be more to life than this.

He could make neither head nor tail of the drawings, though it was not for lack of expertise. Down the years he had pored over dozens of plans, and had learned to soak up every detail and ask the most pertinent questions; often he'd caught those smart young fellows out, too – sent them back to their drawing boards with orders to return when they'd clipped a hundred off the estimate. And he could still glance at a wall and give you its weight in bricks. So it wasn't that he lacked the knowledge. Rather it was interest – he could no longer drum up the interest.

He looked at de Renzi, impassively dying a thousand deaths over there – then again at the meaningless drawings – and so out through the window and over the plains of Kildare. Was it clear enough to see all the way to the Curragh? They said you could if you went up on the roof. He ought to go to the races at least once before he died. Have a little flutter for the first time in his life. Lay out money with a ten-to-one chance of losing every penny – that would be a memorable first for him! But seriously, he ought to try it just once. Watch the horses go round, one of them carrying . . . what – say, twenty pounds of his? Would it still hurt to lose twenty pounds? He didn't know. Dear God – once it would have hurt to lose twenty farthings! However, it would be one way of finding out if twenty quid still meant anything at all to him – put it all on a horse and die of an apoplexy when it came in last! What a way to go!

De Renzi cleared his throat, as if it were something beyond his control.

"I know. I know." Ebenezer sighed. "Come and explain it to me instead."

He watched the young fellow forcing himself to saunter, trying to make his gestures imply he had a dozen clients on his books at that moment but, of course, he could always find the time for *you*, Mister O'Dea!

Why could young people never see the one glaring step they ought to take next in life? De Renzi should be throwing himself heart and soul into this remodelling of Mount Venus. He should have no time for anything else. No time for his suave, sterile little courtship of Lucy Raven while her indulgent husband just smiled and shook his head. Nor any time for running round like the White Rabbit when Diana Powers hove into view. He could make himself rich enough to keep an obliging young lady in a discreet little apartment in Rathmines, which would free him entirely from such pointless emotions until it was time to take matrimony seriously. That was what he, Ebenezer, had done – though the moment for serious matrimony had never quite arrived.

Philip finished his explanation and waited with bated breath for the explosion that would surely follow. He'd spoken to brother architects about old Ebenezer O'Dea, so he knew what to expect. He'd be nice as pie for half a dozen meetings, until you were too deeply dug in to extricate yourself without heavy loss, and then he'd start to pile on the demands, the insults, the disclaimers . . . until you were glad to get out with the shirt on your back.

After a long silence Ebenezer looked up at him and said, "Perhaps I am going mad after all, de Renzi."

"Sir?" Philip eyed him with alarm.

"All my life I've made money by knowing my limitations. People call me a man of business. Would you call me a man of business?"

"At the very least, sir."

"Sit down, do. These plans are fine, by the way." He pushed them nonchalantly aside. "And the estimates are about what one might expect. You might have another go at the flooring man, Dunne. He did a similar job for the RDS at a much keener price than this. However, I leave that to you. I was saying – I am most certainly *not* a man of business, and never have been. I have always lent money to men of business – and let them do all this worrying for me. All I wanted was my four percent." He smiled mischievously. "Or however much it was."

That smile made Philip's heart drop a beat. *Here it comes!* he told himself. *The smiling coup de grâce*. But nothing followed.

Ebenezer saw the young chap wince and knew that further conversation would be pointless; de Renzi was not really listening to *him*, to the things he was struggling to say; de Renzi was waiting for a different Ebenezer O'Dea to appear, the one he'd heard so much about, the one half Dublin walked in fear of (and the other half despised). He rounded off his thought as swiftly as possible: "So why, in the evening of my life, do I suddenly plunge myself into it – up to the elbows, eh? Riddle me that, ye Trinity scholars!"

Idly Philip began rolling up his plans; open they seemed as naked and vulnerable as babes on the hillsides of Sparta. "Perhaps, sir, being so much in touch with death – in a place like this – you feel an urge to do many things you have previously avoided?"

Ebenezer gave him an encouraging nod; perhaps there was hope for the young man yet.

Philip went on: "My ambition, for instance, is to sail right around the coast of Ireland. Not a race, you understand. Take a year about it – put in at every bay that seized my fancy. If I still haven't done it by the time I reach seventy, I shall begin to feel a touch desperate, too."

It was a courtier's performance, Ebenezer realized – talking about being "in touch with death" but adding "in a place like this" to remove any personal reference. And then picking the age of seventy – a safe half-decade older than Ebenezer – it was all so dreadfully tactful.

There was suddenly nothing more he wished to say to de Renzi so he fell back on old reflexes. "Are you in for this big job at Merrion Gates, by the way?" he asked.

Philip shook his head. "It's a bit beyond my capacity, I'm afraid, sir."

"Nonsense, my boy!" Ebenezer rejoined affably. "Never under-puff yourself. With this Mount Venus feather in your cap you'd be admirably placed. You do a good job here and I promise you – I'll put in a word in the right quarter."

Mrs Lynch, the nurse who had replaced Diana Powers, came bustling in at that moment. "Time for our enema," she said breezily from the door.

"Friend or enema!" Ebenezer murmured, giving Philip a wink.

And though Philip chuckled heartily – and genuinely – enough, he left feeling doubly worried. The old bastard had *never* been as pleasant and as easygoing as this with anyone before; it left him feeling he was being well and truly softened up for one almighty trouncing.

"*Our* enema?" Ebenezer shouted angrily after de Renzi had gone. "If you call it that once again, Mrs Lynch, I shall insist on giving you one, too. Anyway, I don't need an enema today."

His deliberately vulgar threat, intended to shake her out of her self-righteous omniscience, had not the slightest discernible effect – no sigh, no tut-tut, not even the teeniest compression of her lips. She was a write-off. He longed to hear about her late husband – that business about ambushing girls in the country lanes round Rathfarn-ham and Tallaght and knocking them off their bicycles, but she ignored every approach he ever made to the topic. The best thing about her was that she made him feel young again; the worst was that "young," in this case, meant about six.

A write-off. She would have to go. He needed a proper confidante, a female more pliant to his will.

Toward the end of May the builders completed the installation of the new hydraulic lift for patients. It was an open-fronted box of the paternoster type, wide enough to accommodate a stretcher and two bearers, and it travelled between the far corner of the entrance hall, the one to the right as you came in, and the blind end of the stairwell gallery immediately above it. There was a gallows-like device of iron in one corner of the platform from which dangled what looked like a pull-chain for a water closet; the harder you pulled, the faster the platform moved, though even its fastest was only a snail's pace. There was also a fixed lever on either floor so that it could be sent up and down unmanned. They tested it with sacks of potatoes, two frightened dogs, and, finally, the first building worker rash enough to mutter within the foreman's hearing, "Jaysus, the feckin' thing works!"

And so, with the afternoon almost gone, the moment arrived for its official inauguration – an honour that Ebenezer O'Dea had arrogated to himself as founder of this whole feast. The gardener and odd-job-men refilled the reservoir in the roof, using a hand pump, and then Mrs Lynch, looking dauntless, wheeled his sedan chair onto the platform. But when she felt it wobble gently beneath her and saw strips of vertiginous daylight all around its edge, she stepped back onto terra firma – or galleria firma, perhaps – and uttered the rashest promise of her life: "I'll just run downstairs and catch us if we fall, Mister O'Dea."

"Good idea!" he called after her. "Don't run now. I'll allow you time to get there. And be sure to stand *immediately* underneath the contraption as it descends." To Matron Powers, who was standing near by, he added under his breath: "God send it's as easy as that."

Diana suppressed a smile. "You're very hard on her, Mister O'Dea."

"One way or another, she'll have to go."

"Go on – she's an excellent nurse. And a doctor's wife, too – or widow."

"Would you have her on your staff?" he challenged.

Diana, knowing the question would never actually arise, said, "Of course I would."

"Readee!" came a trill from below.

"Are we standing directly beneath us now?" Ebenezer called back, grasping the pull-chain with demonic glee.

"Away now, Mister O'Dea!" Mrs Lynch giggled at the top of her voice.

The actual descent seemed a bit of an anticlimax after that. Ebenezer, having been coached by the builder, pulled only gradually on the chain so that the platform descended smoothly, and infuriatingly slowly, from view. "Where's the flames and the reek of brimstone?" he called out. The spectators on the gallery crowded the rope that provided some sort of minimal guard around the opening.

"A suitable device for any teetotal household," Dazzler commented as he stared down into the void.

Diana smiled briefly at him while Philip, at her other side, thought desperately for something even wittier to say.

"Now up we go again!" Mrs Lynch's warble rose through the opening. "Time for our little nap."

"Not at all, woman!" was Ebenezer's testy response. "Sure where's the point in going downstairs if you're only going to turn round and go back up again? Is it the Grand Old Duke of York you'd have me turn myself into? I'll go and sit awhile by my own front door, if you don't mind, and enjoy the evening sun. So off with you – out of my way!"

112

The argument about whether the summer evening was warm enough to permit this dangerous variation in the day's routine somehow became confused with a parallel argument about which direction the Grand Old Duke had taken before his volte-face; Ebenezer was glad to concede the latter as long as he won the former, and a moment later he was seated outside in the tranquil evening air and feeling more at peace than he had done for weeks.

Occasionally over the next ten minutes his calm was punctuated by the return of Mrs Lynch with a rug for his knees, then a woollen scarf, then a deerstalker hat – but at last he was confident enough of her absence to throw them aside again and draw a deep breath of contentment.

Miss Powers had said she'd accept La Lynch into her coven! He could hardly believe it had happened at last. Ever since they'd moved to Mount Venus he'd schemed to find ways of trapping her into such an unlikely promise; but he had never dreamed it would come about as easily as that. Opportunity – that was the point. You had to recognize an opportunity when it was still just a little dot on the horizon; and you had to grasp it, by the throat if need be, when everyone else thought it was still miles away.

He beamed happily and stared out into the trees on the far side of the carriage sweep. Oak, lime, beech, elm, a pair of walnuts, a Morinda spruce with its long, pendulous branches, a monkey-puzzle, killed out at the bottom by creepers of Russian vine . . . and, of course, ash. Only the ash boughs were still in bud. Oak before ash, we're in for a splash. He glanced up at the sky, which offered no prospect of a splash; it was one mighty vault of darkling blue, mottled by a few wisps of streaky cloud, turning from peach to gold in the evening sun.

Six weeks ago he couldn't have identified a single tree with confidence – well, oak and ash, perhaps. And monkey-puzzle, of course. But the rest would have been simply "mature woodland" – the estate agent's contemptuous dismissal of distinctions that had no value in cash.

Any old stick will do to beat a dog – any old tree will do to sell a house. Moral maxims for estate agents.

A dog, a woman, and a walnut tree – the more you beat 'em, the better they be. Moral maxims for life.

A picture came into his mind of beating La Lynch with a hazel switch but he dismissed it with self-contempt. He didn't dislike the woman – certainly not to that extent – he just wanted her . . . not to be there. He entertained a much more enjoyable fantasy then: a conjuring trick that went wrong. The magician made her disappear effectively enough, but when he said his *abracadabra* and opened the cabinet door – she was *still* not there. Hee hee! He chuckled aloud and soaped his hands with joy as they searched high and low for the vanished old shrew.

And then he heard it: a woman's voice, coming from somewhere down the drive – a plaintive, angry whine that took almost a minute to resolve itself into words. By then she had come into view.

She was a young woman of average height, dark-haired and modestly attired – that is, neither in hand-me-downs nor in the height of fashion. Something above a servant girl yet not quite a lady. It was curious, he reflected, how one could tell so much about someone who was still over a hundred yards away. Indeed, one could tell more. She was hot, for instance. Her face and forearms – the half of them that showed between the lace cuffs at her elbows and the lace fringes to her gloves – were pink, and she held her bonnet in her hands and fanned her head with it. Perhaps she was drunk, too? She did not look like the sort of woman who would talk to herself at the top of her voice without the assistance of a strong beverage.

She had not noticed him yet. She was standing there, one fist on her hip, surveying the place slowly from left to right. She was also, no doubt, recovering her breath, for it cannot have been easy to toil up the drive, giving out at such volume.

She saw him then, and clamped her hat back on her head with an oddly defiant gesture. She shook her head to settle her long black hair – but succeeded only in showing how unruly it was. She resumed her walk, approaching him directly; and she resumed her giving-out, too: "I want to see them! Show me! Show me this *compe-teeeeshun* that's so kiln-fired wonderful! I want to see the wings and haloes on them!"

She was not drunk, Ebenezer decided – just hearty. A drop taken, as they say. She was also quite pretty – though her features were too interesting to be dismissed as *merely* pretty. Her jaw was firm; her lower lip positively sulky; her cheeks looked as if they'd keep their roses even after she cooled down – assuming this young lady ever reached a state you might call cool. And her eyes gave off sparks you could light tinder with.

"And would you be one of the patients in this zion?" she asked as she came to a halt at the foot of the steps. "Is it true the nurses here all have wings between their shoulderblades?"

Opportunity! he thought. If ever opportunity was a mere dot on the horizon, it was so at this moment!

"How strong are your arms?" he asked. "Would you hold the chair back and wheel it, with me in it, down the side of the steps there?"

She tilted her head and gauged the task.

"They're after making a slope for me," he added, "but isn't it only half-done – like everything else in this place."

That note of criticism tipped the balance for her. "Sure I can," she said, and a moment later her strong arms and back had him safely delivered onto the carriage sweep.

"You may push me around to the lawn on the sunny side there," he told her. "What's your name?"

"Birdie," she replied. "'Tis Bridget, really. Bridget Kelly."

114

"Then surely it's *Bridie*, not Birdie?"

"God I know that. But I do be having trouble with the writing at times. I have the letters but not the ranking of them, so I haven't."

He chuckled with delight. "So you write Birdie for Bridie!"

"I did the once – and it shtuck." She laughed at herself. "They say it suits me better. Am I to know who you are, sir?"

"I'm Ebenezer O'Dea." He looked up swiftly, over his shoulder, to see what response his name might produce. When her face remained a blank some imp made him add, "Ezeneber to you, I suppose."

Birdie, hearing "I's a neighbour to you, I suppose?", stared at him in amazement. "Be all the holy! How in the name of God did you know that?" she asked.

"'Tis a gift," he replied modestly, not quite sure what she meant, anyway.

"I live just down there in Tallaght," she went on. "You could call that 'neighbour,' I'm sure."

He saw her confusion then and burst into laughter. "Oh please!" he prayed aloud. "Don't let this stop!" To her he added, "And I suppose you applied for a position here as nurse?"

She scrabbled in her pocket and produced a bit of paper, now rather dishevelled, which she thrust into his hand. It was, of course, Alice's carefully written letter of rejection, signed with a flourish by her father.

"A bit the worse for wear," he commented, then, smiling up at her, "rather like yourself, Birdie – if I may be so frank?"

They had reached the lawn at that end of Mount Venus by now. Some previous owner had made a rustic table by putting a ring cut from a large beech onto the stump of a pine. Three oak benches completed the arrangement. He had stared down at it longingly for weeks from his drawing-room window, which was immediately above the place.

"Will we sit here?" she asked, and not waiting for a reply, helped him out of his chair and onto one of the benches. The firm grip of her hands and the smell of her sweating body reminded him of all he had forgotten about being young and close to a girl – which was odd, he immediately thought, for he had often been as close to Nurse Powers – who was assuredly not *old* – and those thoughts had never arisen. "I said a bit worse for wear," he reminded her.

She stared off into the shrubbery and murmured, "Sure I've no head for that stuff at all." Then she glanced toward the house. "But I'd never have got up the courage without it." She smiled wanly at him.

"Now that I do find odd, Birdie," he told her. "You strike me as not at all the sort of woman who needs spiritual support in order to do what she knows is right."

She grinned as if he had caught her out in a fib. "You're the quare one altogether," she said. "Sure what do you know about me?"

"More than you'd think. And will I tell you the best thing of all about you?"

"What?"

"How much d'you know about me?"

"God! Nothing at all!"

"You've never even heard my name – Ebenezer O'Dea? It means nothing to you?"

"Divil a thing!"

"*That*," he said triumphantly, "is the best thing of all about you!"

The window of his drawing room shrieked open. "Mister O-Dea!" Mrs Lynch shouted down in horror. "*What* are we doing out there?"

"Mrs Lynch!" he called back affably. "Would we do us a little favour? Would we ever go to Matron Powers and say, 'The moment has come!' Can we remember that? *The moment has come!*"

"Don't move!" was the peremptory reply. "We're coming . . . tskoh! I mean *I'm* coming down!"

The smile vanished from Ebenezer's face and, turning to Birdie Kelly, he seized her urgently by the wrist. "We haven't long now," he said, speaking rapidly. "You're going to have to think fast and make up your mind like *that!*" He snapped his fingers.

Birdie nodded. "Who was that woman?"

"Mrs Lynch, my present nurse. You're about to spare her life if you'll just say yes. Will *you* be my nurse instead? I'll pay you better than a nurse – as well as your uniform, linen allowance, bed, and the run of your teeth. Yes or no?"

Birdie eyed him askance.

"Listen till I tell you," he went on. "Have you never wished you could go away somewhere and be among people who never knew you – so that you could start being yourself at last? Don't you ever feel that all the people around you know you only too well? They know exactly what you're going to say and do and think and wear and eat and . . . all that sort of caper. Did you never have that feeling?"

She continued to stare at him, amazed, just as when he had earlier told her, out of the blue, that they were neighbours. "Every hour God sends," she breathed.

"Well you've found the place where you may change all that. There's no one *here* knows you. Accept this position and you can be anyone you like – even your true self, God save the mark!"

"And you?" she asked.

"My ambition is more modest, Birdie. I just want there to be one person in all the world who's never heard of me, who doesn't know my reputation, who's prepared to accept that when I smile I'm not mentally selecting the poison I intend to drop in their nightcap – in a word, someone who'll take me exactly as I now am."

Birdie swallowed heavily. "And that someone is to be me?"

"Isn't that your choice, colleen," he replied.

116

At heart, you know," Ebenezer said, "all I really want is for people to be happy." It struck Birdie as the oddest thing she had heard yet. "Lar Lynch," as he called her, had spent a tearful hour being dosed with cups of hot tea by an icily furious Matron who couldn't bring herself to say a civil word to her employer's new nurse. And as for that Doctor Raven's wife – they had taken one look at each other and . . . *help!*

"All I wanted," Birdie complained, "was four shillings and tenpence a day, a crust of bread, and a place to lay my head."

Ebenezer laughed loudly. "Four and tenpence! D'you think this is a *maison de plaisir!* Let me tell you – a staff nurse in any Dublin hospital earns less than two shillings a day. There's not a matron in Ireland earns more than half a crown."

"Jaysus, Mary, and Joseph!" Birdie exclaimed.

"So I don't know where you get your four and tenpence a day from."

"Only two shillings?" she asked, still shocked. "A florin! Are they all a few cards short of the full deck or what? They could earn five times that as a clerk in an office."

"So you should be careful what you wish for at your age," Ebenezer went on. But somehow she could tell he wasn't really interested in her wishes. He just wanted to make his own points.

"Why did they take so bad against me?" she persisted. "I intend them no harm. Sure how could I and I knowing divil a thing about them."

He saw it was his chance to tell her all about "them" – or as much as he desired her to know – for he was keen to set her off down a path of his own choosing. To his annoyance, however, he actually found himself getting interested in the girl for her own sake. Who was she really? Where had she come from? What background had she, what learning? And what had she done with her life until now? It still went hard against the grain with him to want to know such things for their own sake; he soothed his conscience by assuring himself that the answers might come in handy one day. "Does that really surprise you?" he asked

"Birdie" was a good name for a girl with a brain like hers. She didn't answer the question at all. She hopped onto the twig of that one word "surprise" and sang her own tune upon it: "I'll tell you what *did* surprise me. Didn't I think they'd all be Protestants here. Yet no one axed me what I am. Even you never axed me. That was a surprise, so it was."

"The only way religion matters here is to know who's available for duty, and at what hours, on a Sunday."

"I'd be available *all* hours, so," she said grandly, "for I lost my faith entirely." Her tongue lingered truculently on her lip, challenging him to follow up this provocation. It was the sort of coquetry she might use in different circumstances, and for a different purpose, with a much younger man; it interested Ebenezer that she should bother to parade it for him – as if she thought winsomeness might win him. Was she aware of it? he wondered. Or were females handed a certain set of gestures at birth, which they used willy-nilly, in circumstances of wildly different suitability?

He raised both hands in a grand, Henry Irving sort of gesture – fending off the Foul Fiend. "Pray do not tell me, child, that you are . . . an *atheist!*"

She giggled and squirmed with delight. "I am so."

He switched moods at once, becoming offhand, dismissive. "Well, that counts as Protestant in this country. You know yourself, now – you have to be kicking with one foot or the other."

"And which foot do you be kicking with?" she asked boldly.

He shook his head and grinned. "I'm on the jury – and they haven't brought me all the evidence yet."

Birdie was suddenly filled with chagrin for it seemed to her a perfect answer to an old and vexing question – much more interesting and mature than to proclaim yourself an atheist. It made her wonder how old she'd have to be before such answers came easily and naturally to her, too; and it made her fear she'd never reach that age. "Don't give out to all the world what I said, now," she entreated.

"I'll never pass on *anything* you tell me, Birdie," he promised.

"Nor I won't neither – I mean things you may tell me."

"I'm sure," he replied, meaning he was sure it would be the first promise she'd break. He certainly trusted it would be so, or all his hopes of her would be dashed. "Let me tell you about our merry little community here."

She giggled at the word. "And yourself the father abbot!"

"Not at all. I'm the patron."

"It's not pattren, it's pattern. And you shouldn't say modren, either. It's modern. A professor told me that once."

For a moment she vanished from him. There was a faraway light in her eyes, at once nostalgic and awkward. She suppressed it quickly and returned to him with a smile, winsome again. "Sorry!" she said.

Suddenly he decided on a complete change of tactic with her. Sternly amused, he wagged a finger an inch from her nose and barked, "Stop it this minute, Birdie!"

She gulped and stared back at him wide-eyed – though more in amazement than alarm. "Stop what?"

"You know very well. Stop pretending there's nothing but little bits of fluff there between your ears. You don't deceive me, colleen. You're as cute as a pet fox, sharp as a Sunday collar. Well, I want to tell you this – you may behave like that with all the rest. You'll get away with it there, for they're so possessed by their own guilts and fears – which I'd tell you *all* about if only you'd hold your whisht – they're so burdened with them they won't see through your masquer- ade. But *I* do. And I know full well – there's a *mind* behind those big cute eyes, a mind sharp enough to shave the hairs off the divil's chin. So there, now! Will I tell you all?"

He didn't know whether or not it was true; he suspected it might be – even if she herself didn't know it. But the reprimand was flattering enough to make her stop and think. He saw a speculative light in her eyes and guessed she was wondering whether this new version of herself was not one she might actually rather enjoy playing. "Is it Blarney Castle where you were born?" she asked, both pleased and flustered.

"Will I tell you?" he repeated.

"May the tongue blacken and wither in my throat if . . ."

"It will be enough simply to hold it still, Birdie," he said. "Now let's begin at the top – Doctor Michael Raven."

"Oh God yes, isn't he very . . ." Birdie snapped her hand to her mouth.

"He's very dedicated to his profession, his wife, his children, and, not least, to this clinic. He's a Protestant, well liked and professionally respected on all sides. He has no head for money at all. His wife is the Honourable Lucinda Raven, née Fitzbutler. Her father is Lord Mountstephen. They live at Hermitage Lodge in Lucan."

He noticed her lips move silently as she mouthed the address in concert with him. He made no remark upon it then, though; and he was certain she had no idea she'd done it.

"Lucy Raven could tell you the seed, breed, and generation of every man, woman, and child in Dublin. And she's as sharp as yourself with it." By way of illustration he told her how Ben Lucas at the Adelaide had tried to infiltrate his sister, Mrs Doherty, into the clinic as a patient – and how Lucy had seen through the stratagem the moment she heard of it. Birdie was duly impressed. "If only she could sit herself down and *apply* all her knowledge," Ebenezer went on, "she could ransom an empire. Instead, she and her husband have piled up debts enough to turn an emperor pale – the extent of them certainly frightened me! And then, thirdly, there's our matron – Diana Powers. She'll turn thirty in July, the age when a spinster knows for certain-sure she's on the shelf."

"Could you imagine!" Birdie could not help exclaiming. "And her so beautiful-looking and all!"

He pressed on: "Will I tell you something a thousand times more interesting than that? Diana Powers was Michael Raven's sweetheart when he was a student and she a nurse at the Adelaide!"

"Holy hour!" Birdie's jaw hung slack and her eyes were enormous.

But behind the conventional parade of amazement he could almost hear the brain-cogs whirring. "And the Fitzbutlers all Catholics to a man!" she said. "How did they all three tangle themselves up here at all?" Her eyes narrowed – forced to it by a savage grin. "Is it *her* revenge – the spinster's on the wife?" Then it turned to contempt: "Or is it himself – cutting his cake and keeping it?" This flood-tide of

119

gleeful speculation ebbed when she saw him shaking his head and smiling, waiting.

"It is none of these things, Birdie," he told her. "Matron would rather work for any other doctor in the medical register than Michael Raven – and he would rather have an empty-headed old bat like La Lynch as matron than Diana Powers."

She returned to her earlier question: "Then why are they here at all?"

He tapped his breastbone with his index finger and smiled.

"But why?" she asked. The hair threatened to bristle on her neck; suddenly she did not really want to know the answer – nor to know any more about these unfortunate people and the quagmire of their emotions. But – as almost always happened with her – the *other* half of her spirit immediately rebelled against this faintness of heart; *it* wanted to know everything. It longed to be dealt a hand in that very grown-up game.

"Because people work best when heart and head are at war, Birdie. I don't know why, so it's no use asking. I simply know it's so. Diana Powers will work her fingers to the bone to prove that's *all* she cares about now – that Michael Raven means nothing to her. And he will do the same. And Lucy Raven will go out of her way to cooperate with them both. This place will run like the Ballast Office clock. The three of them know what the world is saying and thinking about them – all the dark thoughts that ran through *your* mind just now! And don't trouble yourself to deny it."

She grinned ruefully and nodded.

"So they'll sweat blood to show the world it isn't so. That was my idea, anyway. But I didn't tell you the full of it even yet. My nephew Dazzler – Bobby O'Dea – you'll meet him tomorrow, perhaps. He was the one who drove off while La Lynch was throwing her fits. Anyway, he once did a line with the Honourable Lucinda."

"Did you ever!" Birdie exclaimed, though her capacity for surprise was becoming exhausted.

"They'd have been married if Lord Mountstephen hadn't stepped in and told her to think of Michael Raven instead."

"And she did? That's not like her." She grinned feebly. "Or is it – I mean, I don't know her."

"No, of course you don't," Ebenezer agreed. "The short answer is, I don't know. Maybe her head had already told her Dazzler wasn't the man for her – which is certainly the truth. But sure head and heart are old rivals for the soul."

"Isn't that the God's truth!"

"So who knows what resentments still smoulder away underneath it all?"

She grinned, truculent once more. "There's one man does, I'm thinking – Mister Foreman of the Jury!"

He shook his head and patted the wheels of his sedan chair. "I need

120

eyes and ears, Birdie. I need a flighty little shlip of a nurse whom all the world will think of no account whatever. A woman with a mind too sharp for the divil – who can make others think there's nothing but fluff between there and there."

Birdie felt her heart drop a beat and then work double-quick. "Is it only eyes and ears?" she asked.

He breathed out a sigh of relief and sat back in his chair, relaxing at last. He had not been mistaken in her. "I *still* didn't tell you the full of it," he went on. "There are things I didn't know when first I hatched this scheme. I didn't know that the architect I employed – or was guided to employ by Lucy Raven – was, in fact, her playmate from childhood. I believe she was his first and deepest love, though, as a man of honour, he'd never declare it. Also because, whatever the romantic inside him might say, the practical man is mightily smitten by Diana Powers! That's happened since they met here, obviously. And something similar has happened with my nephew and our beautiful matron, too – though Dazzler's interest in women (it's only fair to tell you) is always rather narrow and – how may I put it delicately? – single-minded."

"Jaysus!" Birdie snapped at last, punching her fist hard into her open palm. "Wouldn't you wish we could be like the flowers and trees – and leave all the work to the wind and the bees?" She heard the doggerel she had accidentally created and laughed. "Give me two more lines and we'll send it in for a fiver."

"But since we can't be as casual as the flowers and the trees," he said, "we need to keep our eyes and ears open, eh?"

She remembered her earlier question then and repeated it: "Is it only eyes and ears you're after needing?"

He shook his head. "There's a brain in it, too – and a tongue betimes."

For a long while she said nothing – just stared out of the window.

"What are you thinking, colleen?" he asked at length.

"I'm thinking, Mister O'Dea, that four shillings and tenpence is not enough."

"I'll make it five, then," he replied without hesitation.

"Done!" she said.

Like a scouting Hun, Matron came striding up the corridor to Ebenezer's room. Her peremptory knock produced a rather wheezy cry of "Not yet!" which she heard as "Yes!" Faster than a scalded cat, Birdie Kelly sprang back from the bed and stared at her in awe – this beautiful, queenly woman, magnificent in her rage, which was all the more impressive for being so quiet, so self-controlled. And when the majestic apparition hissed in an angry

121

aside: "Tuck those blankets back in!" she could not obey fast enough.

"Did you make up this bed?" the Matron went on in the same imperious manner.

"Hey, Miss!" Ebenezer called angrily. "I said not yet!"

Diana stared at him coolly before acknowledging her fault with the briefest dip of her head. "I'm sorry, Mister O'Dea. I was sure I heard yes. However, now that I am here . . ."

He interrupted: "Go back outside this minute and knock and wait to be invited to enter."

Birdie froze in mid-tuck and stared from one to the other, each equally awesome in their anger. And she wondered which of them could possibly win, for she could not imagine either of them losing.

"Go back outside?" Diana asked, as if she could not believe he had said it.

"Go! Back! Outside!" he echoed tendentiously.

Diana squared her shoulders. "If I go out of that door without saying what's on my mind, I'll go for good. I'll pack my bags and you'll never see me again."

For a moment Ebenezer teetered on the brink of telling her she could quit for all he cared, but in the end his wiser self prevailed. "Say what you must, then," he snapped. "Be quick about it and then go."

"Very well." She drew breath and gave Birdie a venomous glance. "How dare you engage this . . . this . . . *tart* without consulting me?"

"I'll engage whomsoever I like, Miss Powers," he snapped. "And I'll break whomsoever I wish, too, so take . . ."

"Tart, is it!" Birdie exclaimed. "Are you after calling *me* a tart? Well, no one can say black is the white of *my* eye!" She began rolling up her sleeves.

Diana looked at her in alarm. "What are you doing, woman?" she asked.

"I'm going to bate that word back down the lying throat that uttered it – and maybe a few teeth along with it." She was slight enough in her build but the gestures were those of the brawniest washerwoman.

Diana turned pale and took a step back – a small one in the physical sense, but a huge one in the verbal battle she had entered this room determined to fight. "Well now," she said in an emollient tone, "perhaps I did stray a little too far in what I . . ."

Ebenezer chuckled and soaped his hands. "And I with a ringside seat!" he chortled.

Diana rounded on him. "It's you I have a quarrel with, Mister O'Dea, not this young . . . lady."

Birdie, her sleeves tucked up by now, advanced around the foot of the bed. "What I done," she declared, "doesn't make a tart of any woman. Even a dog gets two bites at a bone."

"I have no quarrel with you, Miss Kelly," Diana shouted at her, taking another nervous step nearer the head of Ebenezer's bed. "I'm sorry I used that ill-advised word. It was the heat of the moment."

Ebenezer chuckled again.

Diana flared up at him afresh. "You're the cause of it all. I ask you again – how dare you take *anyone* in – even the queen of England herself – on to *my* staff without consulting me?"

His humour vanished. He eyed her up and down coldly. "In the first place . . ." he began.

But Birdie punched Diana hard on the arm. "Make a fist!" she challenged. "First to draw blood and honour's done."

Diana, smarting with the pain, thrust a finger at Birdie's face. "That's enough of that, young woman!" she snapped. "I'm *not* going to fight you so don't be absurd! I've said I'm sorry, which is the civilized thing to do. If you intend to live among civilized people from now on, then the sooner you learn civilized manners, the better."

Birdie's expression went from pugnacious to smiling without pausing for the smallest fraction of a second at the intermediate stages of doubt. "God but you have the right of it!" she declared. "And I like the fool at court!" She grasped Diana's hand and shook it warmly. "Mind you," she added, "I want to tell you this – a good go with the fists is the mortar of many a friendship." And then, to Diana's bewilderment, she grabbed her arm and hugged it as if they were playground chums at school.

Diana looked to Ebenezer to exert some control over this wild . . . *thing* he had brought among them, but the smile was back on his face again. "You'll find her a hard one to hate," he said.

"Hate, is it?" Diana struggled to extricate herself from the unwelcome embrace. "I never said I hated anyone – not her, not you. What I *do* hate is your behaviour. When you behave as if . . . well, as if you can just go ahead and do this sort of thing" – she waved a hand vaguely in Birdie's direction, having at last untangled her arms – "without a by-your-leave, then, by heaven, I see red! Or am I the only one in this room magnanimous enough to offer an apology when one is due?"

His smile turned thin. "I am not aware of having done anything that requires an apology, Matron. I have discharged my nurse – my medical nurse – *your* nurse, if you will – and I have returned her to your staff. I have declared myself to be fit again and in need of nothing more than stimulating company, someone to push my chair about and tuck me into bed, and read me bits of the newspaper, and fetch and carry my meals . . . all of which – and more – I find in the admirable person of the young lady to your right."

"So!" Diana stared from one to the other. "She is not, in fact, a nurse, then! You are not a nurse at all, Miss Kelly?"

123

"There's some who aren't and some who never will be," Birdie said gravely.

Diana persisted. "She will never wear a nurse's uniform while she works at Mount Venus? She will never call herself nurse?" She looked from one to the other all the while, seeking confirmation. "And she'll never go and sit in the nurses' common room as if she had the right?"

And she'll be paid double what any matron is paid! Birdie thought – but kept her counsel.

"No one has suggested any of these things," Ebenezer told her. "Miss Kelly is my companion. You simply jumped to conclusions and you came barging in here without a by-your-leave. So the question is, Miss Powers, are you only magnanimous enough to apologize the once?"

Diana ignored the provocation; she certainly had no intention of apologizing. "My nurses will still make up your bed each day and give you your baths and enema."

He shook his head. "No more enemas! And no more nurses who think my name is *we* and *us*. I'm not an invalid, Matron."

She tossed her head. "We shall see about that, Mister O'Dea. Here at Mount Venus it is for Doctor Raven to decide who is and who is not an invalid."

After a pause he said, "Talking of Doctor Raven, er, I assume you have consulted with *him* about all this?"

"Hah! 'All this,' as you call it, lies entirely within *my* sphere. Doctor Raven would never dream of interfering with the running of . . ."

"But I'm sure that, like you, he's wishful to be consulted. I take it you have *consulted* with him at least?"

Diana hesitated.

"Oh dear!" Ebenezer pretended to be distressed. "So at any minute he, too, may come barging in here shouting 'How dare you!' at you! Then I suppose you'll *both* have to appeal to the court of last resort." He grinned. "I mean, of course, the *owner* of this magnificent establishment!"

Diana turned and left without further argument. At the door she paused long enough to say, "I meant every word – about Miss Kelly and the subject of nursing."

After she had gone, Birdie slumped on the bed and said, "Now I'll never get round the good side of that one."

"You will, of course," Ebenezer assured her. "Especially now you know the way."

Birdie frowned.

"You just did it, colleen! Like a good boxer – you feint with the left and let her have it with the right. You roll up your sleeves one minute and hug her to death the next. She has no way of dealing with behaviour like that."

124

Birdie grinned at her own quite unintended cleverness. Then she pulled out the blanket where Matron had made her tuck it in tight, and she stuck her hand back in. "More?" she asked.

But Ebenezer shook his head. "That woman has left a sour taste in here. Later, perhaps."

Lucy was in the linen closet with two of the new nurses, Patricia Hennessy and Mollie Brennan; they were taking the sheets out of the baskets that had come back from the laundry and going through them one by one, holding them up to the light. As they worked they talked about the topic of the week at Mount Venus: Birdie Kelly.

Diana, walking down the corridor outside, paused and listened. She did not feel she was eavesdropping, for the door was open and she stood in full view; however, to avoid any later suspicion, she took up the notebook and pencil that always dangled at her waist and made a few jottings. She wondered if Lucy Raven knew yet – had she twigged?

"Tallaght is only a small village," Lucy was saying. "It should be quite possible to find out anything one wants."

"Send Mrs Lynch," Patricia suggested with a snigger, in which Mollie soon joined.

"Why d'you say it like that?" Lucy asked.

Often, Diana mused, the woman herself was the last to realize.

"Ah she's giving out up and down the banks about her dee-motion," Mollie said.

"And being dee-mo-ted by *what?*" Patricia added. "By a parisheen of a colleen reared on soot!"

"But she's sharp," Lucy pointed out.

"Oh God, Mrs Raven, she'd shave mice in their sleep."

"And a flirt, too," Mollie put in. "She'd court a haggard full of sparrows if that was all there was in it."

If Lucy Raven knew already, Diana thought, she was being very cavalier about it – flapping the sheets around like that, putting so much vim into everything. *Look at the bloom on her cheeks!* she told herself. *And the sparkle in her eye! Sure what else could it be?*

She decided it was time to reveal her own presence. She cleared her throat to be sure the three women turned and saw her finishing her jottings; then she breezed in with neither frown nor smile, saying, "If the poor girl's ears are burning, she needn't wonder long. Just let her open her door down the passage there!"

The two nurses stiffened and looked contrite. Lucy smiled, though it annoyed her to always be giving a dozen smiles to Matron's one. "Could you hear us?" she asked.

"Like bells across water." Diana closed the linen-room door.

125

"Oh, don't!" Lucy begged. "It's so *airless* today."

The nurses exchanged surprised glances for the window was wide open and a stiff breeze, cool for the end of May, rattled around the courtyard outside. Diana smiled knowingly. She remembered a Mrs Geoghegan who had complained of the same feeling – "and I like an egg in a slow oven," was her way of putting it – before *her* first; and she had no idea of the connection, either. "Very well, Mrs Raven," she said and opened the door again. You'd think women had no idea how babies were made.

Lucy continued: "I'm sure *I* don't mind that girl hearing my opinion of her. She has no place in a clinic like this. Reared on soot is right. And as for nursing experience, she couldn't even dress a wasp sting. Oh – and look – they've torn that sheet. Put it aside, Hennessy."

Diana, who was determined no one would ever mention Birdie Kelly and nursing in the same breath, said, "She's not engaged as a nurse, Mrs Raven. I have made that abundantly clear to Mister O'Dea and to your husband. Mister O'Dea calls her his companion. He claims to find her cheerful enough in her prattle – which is all the treatment he believes he needs."

Nurse Hennessy, keen to support this obviously official line, said, "Sure she has him in kinks of laughing half the time."

The final sheet passed its inspection. "Very well," Diana said briskly, as if she had been waiting for the moment. "Hennessy to the sluice room – you know what to do there."

The nurse, aware that she had somehow erred, dipped her head and left, giving Lucy a wan, over-the-shoulder smile.

"And Brennan take six pairs of these sheets and help Talbot change the beds in the east wing." Diana took out her notebook again and stabbed two little ticks in it; the nurse counted out the dozen sheets meanwhile. "And then Mrs Lynne is to have a bed-bath and Mister Enright may have a proper bath today," Diana added as Mollie Brennan left.

Lucy watched in reluctant fascination. This woman who dispensed authority as though it were part of the air she breathed – had she been hiding all the while inside that unobtrusive, self-effacing nurse who had so recently tended Ebenezer O'Dea down in Sackville Street? In fact, Lucy had only noticed her then because Dazzler had called her the red-haired temptress.

"Inspecting the sheets is hardly nurse's work, I know," she said before Diana could make the same point. "We really need to distinguish more between what the maids are to do and what's for the nurses. On the other hand, little moments like that, snatched from the hurly-burly, do enable one to get to know them better."

Again she smiled broadly and again Diana did no more than stretch her lips wide for about half a second. She seemed to have something on her mind today.

126

"You certainly discovered their opinions of our latest . . . addition," Diana commented.

"You, on the other hand, sound as if you're beginning to approve of her slightly," Lucy challenged.

"As long as no one calls her a nurse. And at least I no longer have Mister O'Dea camping in my ear, grumbling about Mrs Lynch." She gave a sour laugh. "Instead I have Mrs Lynch camping in my ear, grumbling about Mister O'Dea!"

"Well – Helen Lynch is a good deal easier to send her about her business than Ebenezer O'Dea." Lucy consulted her watch. "Would you like a cup of tea, Matron? It's almost time." She saw the woman's face preparing to decline the offer, but then, with a sudden reversal, she smiled – and for slightly *longer* than half a second! – as she said, "Perhaps I will, Mrs Raven. Shall we take it in my chambers?" She knew Lucy wouldn't turn down the suggestion – she hadn't seen the rooms since the week they moved in.

They walked in silence along the passage to the head of the main stairs – silence as far as they were concerned, though the bustle of the clinic was all around them.

"Too much racket!" Diana said severely when they started down the stair. "I shall speak to them about it. Nurses can be busy without advertising the fact to the whole wide world. Just listen! Close your eyes and you'd think you were in the Dunleary coal harbour!"

"I rather welcome the hurly-burly," Lucy said – then, realizing that her remark sounded critical of the matron, added hastily, "now and then, of course."

"Really?" Diana asked in surprise, which compelled Lucy to explain.

"I suppose it's because of all the associations . . . things hovering around this place . . . sort of in the air, you know."

Diana said nothing but it was clear she did not know.

"A forebear of mine built this house," Lucy added. "And then there were all the bankruptcies. Not to mention the suicide. I had qualms – before we moved in, I mean – about all those unhappy ghosts we'd be sharing the place with. But now, of course, it seems absurd."

"Ah," Diana said.

"The bustle helps, you see. All that *busy*-ness."

"Mmm."

"How often one's worst trepidations turn out to be groundless!"

Lucy had no idea why she had felt it necessary to make this last statement; she immediately wished she hadn't, for it seemed to be a comment – a devious comment, too – on her present "trepidations" about Diana rather than on her vanished fears concerning Mount Venus and its tangled associations.

They had reached the private door to the matron's chambers; she turned and stared at Lucy – a calm, expressionless gaze – before she

127

let her in. The quiet that descended as she closed the door behind them was almost tangible. "What a relief!" Lucy commented.

The questions seethed in Diana's mind – one question above all. But how to steer the conversation around to it? She lit the wick on her spirit stove and set the water to boil in a copper kettle.

"Little Birdie Kelly is, indeed, a bit of a puzzle," Diana mused.

"Have you had much to do with her?" Lucy asked in surprise.

Diana shook her head, but then half-contradicted her own gesture. "Enough to know she's a bit of a puzzle. When I went to complain to Mister O'Dea last week – the day he engaged her – I, er, made the mistake of calling her a . . . *tart*." She whispered the word now though she had shouted it then.

"To her face?"

Diana nodded glumly. "I was so angry! Anger is not good for one's dignity. Of course, I apologized at once but . . . well, what d'you suppose *she* did?"

"Burst into tears?"

"Not that one! No, she rolled up her sleeves and offered to fight me!" Diana parodied Birdie's pugilistic gestures, making Lucy laugh. "And then, when I asked her to try and behave like a civilized being . . . she smiled the sweetest smile – she really has a lovely smile, you know – and flung her arms about me and hugged me half to death!"

"No!" Lucy almost shrieked with disbelieving laughter.

"The thing about her is, you see," Diana went on, "she has no real control of herself. Civilized control – d'you know what I mean?"

Lucy frowned. "Sort of."

"I mean . . . there must be a dozen times every day when you want to hit someone – or hug them. I know I do. But we don't give way to such impulses, do we. We let a frown or a harsh word serve for a punch, and give an encouraging smile instead of a hug. But Birdie Kelly feels no such constraints. Perhaps that's why we're all so down on her – especially we women."

"Especially?" Lucy echoed.

"I mean, we're supposed to be the gentle sex, the retiring ones, the angels – and we know we're not really like that at all, don't we! A lot of the time we *long* to behave the way Birdie Kelly *does* behave. Don't you agree?"

"You *do* like her," Lucy said in amazement.

This time Diana did not smile along with her. "Enough," she agreed, "to feel worried at the *use* old Ebenezer might make of her."

Lucy swallowed heavily and said, "I beg your pardon?" – rather nervously.

The copper kettle began to sing. Diana said slowly, "I'm breaking a confidence now – but only because I feel the other party has absolutely shattered his half of it."

128

"Ebenezer O'Dea?"

"Yes. The only reason I am matron here is that I was to be his eyes and ears. Not to put too fine a point on it – I was to spy on you and Doctor Raven for him."

Lucy stared at her aghast. "And you agreed?"

"Of course not. He thought I did. He didn't even ask – he just assumed. So I let him. And when he found out I never had . . . pfft!"

"Birdie Kelly!"

"That's what it looks like. And that's why it's important for me to understand the girl – even though the prospect fills me with . . ." The word *loathing* seemed too strong but none other occurred to her. She shivered. "And it's not alone me," she went on. "It's true of every other woman under this roof. You heard Brennan and Hennessy just now. She stirs something very . . . *awkward* in each of us. Something we don't wish to acknowledge."

Lucy felt a little out of her depth; she was used to much shallower character readings than this. "Like what?" she asked. "What d'you think she represents for us? The triumph of the upstart? The victory of the grasshopper over the ant?"

"Chaos," Diana replied simply.

Because she did not elaborate on the idea, Lucy was forced to consider the word itself: *chaos*. An image appeared before her mind's eye of "the parisheen," in Patricia Hennessy's vivid phrase, and suddenly she knew what Matron meant. The dissolute face of the Kelly girl, her sullen, sensual bottom lip, her drunken eyes, the voice that never stopped – splattering odd notions around the place the way birds splattered their lime . . . chaos-in-skirts! "I know what you mean," she said.

The water began to rise to the boil but Diana ignored it. She said, "I remember walking with my uncle down Patrick Street in Keelity, when I was about fifteen. Keelity Town – d'you know it?"

Lucy shook her head. "I went through it once on the way to Ennis." She hid her amazement as best she could, for Diana Powers had never before shared a personal memory of any kind.

"We came to O'Connell Square and there was a fellow there giving out about gambling – a ragged preacher standing on the courthouse steps, and the peelers just leaning against the pillars and smiling. Anyway, he called gambling by every name under the sun. You'd think it was that original sin which drove Adam and Eve from Eden. We listened for a while, my uncle and I, and as we moved along he said to me, 'You have to make allowances, Diana. Last year that fellow lost all he had in just three days at the Galway Races.' And I've never forgotten that. I wouldn't say this to any of the nurses when I hear them taking a high moral tone over Miss Birdie Kelly – and I've heard a lot of high moral ground being claimed since *she* appeared – but it does make me wonder whose hearts should be searched and what allowances should be made."

Lucy swallowed heavily. "Myself among them, I suppose," she said.

Diana smiled sadly and shook her head. "*Ourselves* among them," she replied ruefully. "Why do I look at that face on the girl and recoil? What do I see there that fills me with such unreasoning . . . dread is too strong a word. Discomfort is too mild. Something in-between. Alarm, perhaps. Foreboding? No, I hope it's not fore-boding." She trained her great, solemn eyes on Lucy as she added, "And I'm not alone, am I? I'm right about that. All the women here feel it. Birdie Kelly, by her very existence, makes us aware of something we'd rather shut our eyes and ears to."

Lucy cleared her throat. "I've never heard you talk like this before, Matron."

Diana's gaze did not waver. "I realize it should be you, as the married one, to suggest this first, not me – the spinster – but there it is. D'you think, in private, we need be quite so formal? I *think* of you as Lucy Raven, not Mrs."

And *still* she did not really smile! Lucy was amazed at the woman's capacity for remaining impassive yet without seeming unfriendly. She herself smiled broadly. "I have been on the point of suggesting it . . . I cannot tell you how often, er, Diana. There!" Sheer nervousness made her add, "If we had been any two *other* women . . ." And then she realized she could not possibly complete the sentence. *Please don't let her pick it up!* she prayed.

Diana's feelings, however, were precisely the opposite. Now that *half* the idea was born, she could not possibly leave the whole of it in limbo.

The kettle was now boiling vigorously. She heated the pot and emptied the water into the slop bucket. Then three spoons of tea. Then the boiling water, enough for a cup each. Normally she would have capped the wick and left the kettle to cool, but this tête-à-tête was suddenly looking like a two-cup affair.

For Lucy the unfortunate reverberations of her last few words died away quite satisfactorily while Diana pretended to be engrossed in the midmorning ritual. For Diana they rang a crescendo that demanded to be silenced. "You mean because I was once Michael's sweetheart?" she said with brittle offhandedness as she set the teapot between them to draw. She busied herself with the cosy, to avoid the other's eyes.

But Lucy's eyes were closed at that moment, and she nodded – squaring herself to face it. "I'm glad one of us had the courage to say it out loud at last!" She turned her gaze on Diana again.

But Diana just stared out of the window. "In a way I'm rather sorry," she murmured – in a tone so neutral that Lucy could not tell whether it might have continued ". . . sorry I did" or ". . . sorry you did." She asked why.

Diana felt the teapot through its cosy, as if that would tell her whether or not it had drawn sufficiently. "We were keeping such wonderfully stiff upper lips until now – like proper little West Britons! In our heart of hearts we all want to be proper little West Britons, don't we!"

At least it was a public display of emotion of *some* kind, Lucy thought. Even if it was a rather bitter sarcasm! She decided – or, rather, some instinct urged her to feel – that if one card was laid on the table, the whole pack should go down. She laughed. "You wouldn't have thought so if you'd seen me and Michael on the day we finally signed all the deeds that established Mount Venus! Proper little West Celts, we were! We almost didn't sign, you know. And we had the divil's blessing of all arguments – and all over you!"

Diana's eyes went wide with shock. "Mercy me!" she exclaimed. "Whatever for?" She could not entirely suppress a tiny feeling of elation, but it did not make her proud.

"Dazzler described you to me as the red-headed temptress, and I, in my turn . . ."

"Did he, indeed!" She bridled.

"Sure you know Dazzler," Lucy added contemptuously.

"I'd know his hide in a tanyard," Diana said with some spirit, "which is where I'd like to see it at this moment, I may say. Red-headed temptress, indeed!"

"Ah, he likes a rag on every bush – or he likes the world to believe he has. I paid him no heed at all. But anyway, as I was going to say, I'm sure I passed on his description to Michael. This was before either of us had even seen you, mind, so there were no names in it."

"Were you really going to pawn your jewels that day?" Diana gave a hint of a conspiratorial smile.

Lucy waved a dismissive hand. "I'll do all the *mea culpas* you want, afterwards. Would you ever let me just finish?"

Diana pulled her mouth into an upside-down U. "Sorry!"

"But somehow Michael got the idea I said *flaxen*-haired temptress – which I'm sure I didn't. And then, of course, when he finally met you – out here at Mount Venus – on the morning of the signing . . . well! I was lucky to come away with my scalp." She smiled yet again. "And that's why we nearly didn't sign."

Diana poured the tea. "Help yourself to milk and sugar," she said – and then, without the slightest change in tone. "Aren't we the foolish ones!"

"In what way?" Lucy added the merest dash of milk and declined a biscuit with a wave of her hand.

"Oh . . . you know. The thoughts we must each have been harbouring about this . . . situation. Did you think I coaxed old Ebenezer into it?"

"He knows about you and Michael, of course?"

"Of course. *And* I didn't need to tell him! That man would find a guilty conscience in a new-born baby."

The word made Lucy hesitate – but not so positively as to dispel Diana's doubts. "That's why the oul' fella insisted on me as matron," she added, "as I was after telling you."

Lucy covered her hesitation with a frown, saying, "What were we talking about a minute or so ago? There was something I wanted to say. We keep leaving things before we've really . . ."

"Dazzler?" Diana suggested.

"Oh yes! Did he also know about you and Michael – from the beginning, I mean?"

Diana knitted her brows, trying to recall how it had all come about. "He guessed it, I think, that day Michael came to see Mister Ebenezer for the first time. Himself guessed it then, too – because I couldn't face Michael again, you see."

Lucy glanced sharply up at her. "Couldn't face him?"

"Well," Diana responded defensively. "Wouldn't you have been the same if someone had told you Dazzler was going to pay a call on *you*?"

"Ah, so you know about that, do you."

"Dazzler made certain sure I did!" she replied heavily. "Wouldn't *you* have been the same?" she repeated her question. "If you'd known you and he were to meet again?"

"I don't know," Lucy replied evasively.

"How *did* you meet again, if I may ask?"

"It's no secret," Lucy assured her. "I bumped into him in the street – near the pawnbroker, if you really want to know." She grinned to show the admission no longer worried her.

"And you went straight up to him and greeted him like any old friend?"

Lucy hesitated just a little too long to come out with the lie – which she had fully intended telling. "No." She lowered her eyes and took her first sip of tea. "Lovely! Is that Bewley's Oriental?"

Diana nodded. "You understand a little of how I felt, then."

"But I only walked a few paces beyond him – pretending I didn't recognize him. Then I turned and greeted him like an old friend – like the old friend that he is – though I'd not trust him farther than he casts his own shadow – but then I never did trust him, not even in the old days, when we were set on getting married."

"Were you and he actually engaged – if I may ask? I seem to be doing a lot of . . ."

"Of course you may, Diana. Don't keep seeking my leave. There's no point in not telling each other everything now. The answer is Dazzler and I weren't officially engaged – but that was only because my father would never have countenanced it. In our own minds we were, beyond any doubt, engaged." She took another sip and added, "May I ask about you and Michael, then?"

"A bad right I'd have to say no! We were engaged and there was a ring in it." She glanced involuntarily at the third finger on Lucy's left

132

hand and then looked studiously away – but not before Lucy saw the gesture.

"Merciful hour!" she exclaimed in horror, holding her hand out rigid and staring at her engagement ring. "You mean . . .?"

Diana nodded gravely. "D'you think I could be sitting here telling you *any* of this, Lucy, if there was the slightest twinge of a feeling left? A feeling of that sort, I mean? I could have sued Michael but I was too bitter for that. I flung that ring in his face, instead."

Tell her you cried yourself to sleep every night for years, too, she dared herself. *Tell her you went and bought another ring the very twin of that one! Tell her you're wearing it at this moment – and tell her where!* But she was too proud of the cool, collected image she now bore in the eyes of the world to dent it so frivolously.

"I had no idea," Lucy said, barely speaking above a whisper. "I was heartbroken to give up Dazzler – it's hard to believe that now, isn't it! I cried myself to sleep on many a night, I can tell you – even after Michael and I were married. I didn't begin to love Michael until after Alice was born." She smiled wryly. "So now you know all!"

Diana hated Lucy Raven more at that moment than at any previous time in her life. How dare she tell *all* the truth like that! It was only because she had won. She had Michael now, while Diana had nothing. She could afford to be as magnanimous and honest as you like, because what did it cost her? Nothing!

Diana smiled – a warm, sweet smile for once. "Talking of having Alice," she began . . . and then noticed Lucy looking around, searching for something. "A *chocolate* biscuit?" she suggested. "I'm sure I have a packet put by somewhere."

But Lucy was shaking her head. "It sounds idiotic, I know," she said. "But have you e'er such an article as a radish in your little larder out there?"

"A *radish?*" Diana asked in amazement.

"Yes. I just suddenly thought it would be rather nice to eat a radish. The season is so short."

"Well, I'm sorry, but I haven't. Shall I see if Slattery . . ."

"No, don't bother! I've plagued him enough already. What were you going to say about Alice?"

"Oh . . ." Diana thought swiftly. "Er . . . I was just wondering if she'd like to come into Dublin with me tomorrow – my afternoon off? We could go to the stuffed-animals museum, or whatever she'd like."

Diana put her hand to Ebenezer's door and turned the handle slowly. It was locked. Equally slowly she allowed the handle to return to its usual position; then she looked all about her and, seeing no one, laid her ear to the wooden panel, choosing what looked like its thinnest part. Faintly, from the bedroom beyond, she heard strange muffled noises and grunts, though they were less strange to one who had herself given many an enema to Ebenezer O'Dea.

She smiled a grim smile. So the old man had decided he could do without enemas, eh! And now he was too proud to admit he had been wrong. Well, it was only a matter of time before he'd grow weary of the incompetent, untrained efforts of Birdie Kelly!

For the next half hour or so she found occupation in that same wing of the clinic, until she was called away to discuss a new patient with Michael. When she returned she surreptitiously tried the door again and found it still locked, though silence now reigned beyond. Her face was grim as she stood her ground, a few feet from the door, resolved to wait and pounce the moment Kelly appeared. Enema or no enema, a locked bedroom door was something she was not going to tolerate at Mount Venus. A few moments later she heard the snib shoot back inside; then the front castor of Ebenezer's sedan chair come nosing out into the corridor.

"Jaysus, did I leave it locked?" Birdie said before she even saw the matron standing there – so, Diana realized, she must have spotted the handle moving. The girl tried pushing her cap slightly less awry and tucking stray wisps of hair respectfully under it – all while she continued to steer the chair with the other hand. She succeeded only in running it into the skirting opposite the door.

To Diana's surprise Ebenezer said nothing; if a nurse had done that, he'd have eaten her a mile off. But he just sat there, looking all rubicund, eyes slightly distant, saying "tut-tut!" several times in a jocular fashion. The suspicion flashed through her mind that he might be a little tipsy, though he had never shown any tendency toward the bottle during the months he had been under her care. His cheeks were hearty-looking, though.

"We could have been burned in our beds!" Birdie added – to take the sting out of the most obvious reprimand Matron might give her. No doubt about it – when self-preservation was the order, Birdie Kelly was a quick little thinker.

"Would you like a thinner blanket, Mister O'Dea?" Diana leaned over him to feel the weight of his present one. "It's a warm day and there's hardly any breeze."

He realized she was checking on his breath, so he gave her a short, deliberate blast, saying, "Syrup of figs, I believe." Then he turned to Birdie and added. "See? That's the sort of thing I mean."

The girl looked at the matron as if she were an exhibit in a waxworks and nodded. Diana gained the uncomfortable feeling that none of her usual disciplinary tricks – most of which she had learned from Matron Rivers in her days at the Adelaide – would be of the slightest use with this one. Perhaps her insistence that the title Nurse and the name Kelly should be kept in different universes had been a mistake? What discipline could a matron exert over the companion to

134

the owner of the building in which they both happened to work?

She wondered whether even a straightforward woman-to-woman approach would be of any use; what qualities of womanhood did she have in common with this . . . "parisheen"? It was the only name for her.

"I'd like a word with Miss Kelly," she said evenly. "Can I send one of the nurses out to sit with you?"

"Which one?" he asked suspiciously.

She gave him a soothing smile. "Rest easy, now! Mrs Lynch has gone back home for the week. She's selling her house and contents on Friday."

"I'll buy the lot and donate it all to her if she'll promise not to return here," he said.

"I'll send Nurse Walker." Diana chose the one who happened to be nearest. She found occasion to warn her to keep the old fellow out of doors for at least the next half-hour. Two minutes later she showed Birdie Kelly through her matron's office and into her private chambers, a sanctum none of the nurses had yet been privileged to see.

"Be the holy fly but this is great!" Birdie exclaimed, looking about in delight. "You're in God's pocket here. You'd expect it of Mister O'Dea, of course – the great lob of money *he* has. He told me – he never yet shook the hand of a bank manager. Could you imagine!"

Diana sighed and stared at her in bewilderment; where did one begin even?

"Did I say something wrong?" Birdie asked.

"Were you never taught respect for any one or any thing?" Diana asked.

The woman pressed her lips stubbornly together and then opened them briefly to say, "Well, I was – to tell God's truth, now."

Diana gave up for the moment. She smiled and said, "I expect you'd like a cup of tea. I know I would."

Birdie nodded and let slip the briefest of smiles. "I'll give my tongue to the cat if it'll help," she said.

Diana swilled out the teapot into the slop pail. She ought to have done it that morning, immediately she'd finished with the pot, of course. It annoyed her to reveal even that small degree of slovenliness to Kelly – though she knew very well that the girl hadn't even noticed. "Why did Mister O'Dea say just now, 'See? That's what I mean!'? What *did* he mean?"

"Ah – being an invalid, like," she replied. "Haven't you some grand oul' books here!" She plucked one from a shelf.

"Are your hands clean?" Diana asked nervously.

"Indeed I washed them after the work *they* were at!" She sniggered and began turning over the pages. "All them herbs – and are they all for curing the sick?"

Diana ran to her and snatched the book away. "Not that one!" she exclaimed. "It's rather . . . well, it's quite rare."

From the blush on her cheeks Birdie knew it had some personal significance; it must be a book Doctor Raven gave her once. It crossed her mind to come out with a straight question. It would be the sort of thing people round here expected of her. But that brought her back to old Ebenezer's point, too, so she said, "He says as soon as you're in a sedan chair and people have to stoop to pass the time of day, they start to make you out a babby. They talk louder. They talk over your head to the nurse." She did an adenoidal lower-class imitation of a West Briton accent, itself already adenoidal enough to grate: 'Ay suppaws he enjize his waawks'."

Diana could not hold back a laugh. "I know exactly what he means," she said ruefully. "It's so easy to fall into those ways – patronizing the invalid. Don't you find?"

"Shouldn't you say *patternizing?*" Birdie asked.

Diana stared at her, nonplussed. "Not where I come from," she replied, and was surprised to see a brief, superior smile twitch at the other's lips. Talking with Birdie Kelly, she realized, was like walking through treacle with will-o'-the-wisp. "Patternizing or patronizing," she went on, "it is something we all have to train ourselves not to do. Not always successfully."

"He says I never do it."

Diana nodded and remarked, with a certain emphasis, "That's *one* thing at least you don't have to learn, then."

"Learn, is it?" Birdie asked.

"Yes – didn't you come here in the hope of becoming a nurse?"

"Ah!" The girl smiled wanly. "Many are called but few are chosen. The sun has the day but it leaves the night to the moon."

Diana began to wonder if the schoolmaster down in Tallaght had devised a system whereby he taught his pupils a thousand sonorous – but empty – sayings for them to trot out at awkward moments. "You mean you've given up the ambition?" she asked.

"Sure how will I ever learn a stroke here, with every hand against me?"

"Oh, come!" Diana returned to the kettle, which had burst into a whine. "That's going it a bit strong."

"They are, so!" Birdie insisted. "They'd take the pennies off my eyes at my own wake if they could. That Mrs Lynch – she said if she had a brain like mine, she'd drown it in a thimble. And the face on her when she said it! As long as five wet Sundays."

"Don't you understand how she feels, and her a doctor's wife, too? When a slip of a thing half her age and no nursing training at all . . ."

"Isn't that the truth!" Birdie exclaimed, as if Diana had been listing points in her favour. "No one can say black is the white of *my* eye!"

Diana just stared at her. "You keep saying things like that. You said it the other night. What is it supposed to *mean?*"

136

"Did I ever deny I had no training? Didn't I come marching up that drive – a week ago this very day – asking for nothing else but to train as a nurse?"

"Asking at the top of your voice!" Diana commented.

"Sure there you are!" Birdie spoke as if the matron had just hammered home the final nail in her, Birdie's, argument. "I couldn't put it better myself. Training! That's all I wanted – at the top of my voice. Is it my fault that, in the heel of the evening, the quare fella himself would set me on in place of oul' Mrs Lynch? And now they'll not talk to me. Where's the justice in that?" She looked around the room. "Have I leave to sit, ma'am? My knees think the chairs are all sold on us."

"Of course," Diana replied. "By the window, there – forgive me. You have a way of dragging the hunt through ten parishes when . . ." She bit off the rest of the saying. Metaphors, she realized, became an infectious disease around Birdie Kelly. She drummed her fingers on the copper handle of the kettle.

"A watched pot," Birdie said as she seated herself.

"It's true, too." Diana folded her arms across her starched apron front. "So tell me something about yourself, Miss Kelly – all the things I would have asked if you had been taken on as one of my nurses."

"You mean am I Protestant or Roman Catholic?" Birdie asked hopefully; she'd been longing for a chance to try it out only no one had asked her.

"If you think that's the right place to start," Diana conceded.

"Well I'm on the jury!" she replied proudly.

Diana frowned. "I'm sorry?"

Birdie began to panic; she couldn't recall quite what old Ebenezer had said next. "Sure the case has only just begun," she added.

"Oh, I see!" Diana said – being totally absorbed in filling the pot now, for the water had just boiled. "Yes, I do see," she added a moment later, as she brought it over to the table. "And where were you born? Tallaght, was it?"

Birdie crossed her fingers behind her back. "That's where my mammy lives now."

"And your father?"

"Oh God, ma'am, we've not seen him since Moses was in the fire brigade. The less I'd praise him, the less I'd lie."

"Oh, I am sorry to hear that."

"You're alone on the island, so – ma'am," Birdie assured her. "Ill got and ill gone, we say. He used to bate the priest's share out of my mother and me."

"Dear me! So you grew up without a father?"

"I grew up without *that* father." She glanced over her shoulder. "But my mammy's one of *those* women, you know?"

"Not really." Diana pulled the cosy over the pot.

137

"Like Lanna Mochree's dog," Birdie said. "She'd go a furlong with all the world. I was never short of a father, anyway. You have one of each, yourself, I daresay?"

"Ah . . . yes."

"And brothers or sisters? I have none, myself."

"The same with me," Diana admitted, wondering how the girl had managed to turn an interview into a confessional – and how to reverse the process.

"Sorrow take him! I'd have had two but he kicked them out of her," Birdie added casually – leaving Diana struggling for some way to indicate that the explanation for her own lack of siblings did not lie in *that* direction.

She gave up and instead asked, "Did they put you to any trade at all? I mean, what gave you the idea of becoming a nurse, of all things?"

"Sure I have a wild and aching foot," Birdie replied dryly.

"You can read and write, obviously."

"Indeed I can. And figure three columns to the one tot. And set a table of silver. And cut hair to please any lady. Not to mention hoeing turnips and drawing nine pints to the gallon."

Diana could not help but chuckle at this eccentric list, but she began to feel certain of something she had merely suspected until now – namely that Birdie Kelly knew very well what effect her naïve conversation and behaviour had on others. It was not entirely a façade but there was that element about it. Somewhere behind the Birdie Kelly she paraded before all the world was a woman no one at Mount Venus had yet seen, except, perhaps, Ebenezer O'Dea. Yes, if she, Diana had the wit to spot it, he most certainly had. The question it posed, however, was less easily answered: How to deal with it? Should one call her bluff or give her enough rope to hang herself one day?

She decided it was too early to choose; there might be other, subtler ways. For the moment she thought it best to play along. "An impressive list," she commented. "And obviously – to your way of thinking – it all pointed in one direction: nursing. All these skills, you told yourself, are a mere preparation for the most difficult and demanding of all the skilled callings that are open to a woman?" She gave a brief, sympathetic smile, and, raising the teapot, asked, "D'you like the milk in first?"

Birdie shook her head abstractedly. The matron's sudden resumption of command unnerved her. She ran for cover – as a lizard may shed its tail: "Did you ever hear the like of it for lunacy, ma'am! And the divil mend me for it if I'm here now without a friend!"

"Would you like to learn at least the rudiments of nursing?" Diana asked as she passed the girl her cup.

Birdie accepted it with a murmured thankyou and added her own milk and a generous dollop of sugar, gazing around the room the

138

while. "Have you e'er such a thing now as a little book on the business?" she asked. "Something that'd get me started, as the divil said to the hedgehog."

"I have the Royal Humane Society's handbook on first-aid. That wouldn't be a bad start. But you should also know it's not an easy path to tread. Well – no path is easy, of course, but nursing is particularly difficult. What do you *really* want to be? D'you know yet?"

"Anything but rich," the woman replied at once – and without any of her usual saucy sparkle.

"Oh?" Diana prompted. "Why not, pray?"

She nodded her head in the direction of Ebenezer's suite and said, "How that oul' wan can sleep of a night I'll never fathom. He'd skin a flea for a halfpenny and he has half Dublin just waiting a chance to skin him for nothing – him that couldn't lepp an inch now and must send eyes and ears out into the populace to watch his back for him. I'd liefer have one good friend in all the world than all the money besides."

The skin prickled round Diana's back collar-stud when she realized what plea the other was making. Or was it a bargain she offered? She was a past mistress of ambiguity! "I'm sure you know how to go about it," she murmured.

Birdie nodded. "Slowly, I'm thinking."

"Slow but sure," Diana said.

"You have it, ma'am! Slow and steady wins the race – with good grace. Isn't it a great gift – the gift of knowing the right words!"

Birdie Kelly had the right instinct when she came looking for work in an institution that was still in the pangs of its own birth. If there had been the full complement of forty or more nurses, and rooms filled with patients, and a long-established routine . . . chains of command . . . and all those hierarchies-within-hierarchies that humans love to complain about even as they add another tier to the edifice . . . they would have quelled even her anarchic spirit. But she had the good fortune to arrive at Mount Venus when all was in a flux, and when the principals felt their lives were in a kind of double jeopardy, professional and personal.

She understood that Ebenezer O'Dea wished it so – indeed, had *arranged* it so, and would not have laid out a penny on the place if all had been calm and normal. She admired him for it, too. She thought it wonderful – godlike, even – to look down on people's lives like that and force them together against their will. And they to be knowing that if they failed, they were done for. It must be especially satisfying to achieve such a thing when you were nearing the end of your life while they were all in the prime of theirs. To be rich enough to do a

139

thing like that! If she were rich (never mind what she'd said to Matron Powers!), it was exactly what she'd be doing with her money – putting the wrong people together and watching the sparks fly – and catching the sparks – and starting a great fire – and raising steam – and driving a grand engine like Mount Venus to glory. Except, she had to admit, if *she* tried such a thing, they wouldn't progress beyond the flying sparks; her life was full of them! And dead embers.

She even understood that she, too, was one of godlike Ebenezer's pawns. And her not yet in the prime of her life, even! But understanding is one thing, feeling is another; and there was never the slightest contest between the two where Birdie was concerned. Understanding folded his tents and slunk away the moment Feeling poked her nose round the door. And because she was with Ebenezer almost night and day, because he (apparently) took her so much into his confidence, she came to *feel* that she, too, sat in the royal box beside him, a simple handmaiden to his schemes. She was his subject, perhaps, but never one of his objects.

He was the genius of the western world, she thought. All her life she'd had this conviction, vague in its focus but powerful nonetheless, that *something* was missing – whether in her or just in her life she could not say. That was part of the vagueness. Sometimes she thought she wasn't quite "all there," as the saying goes; other times she was almost certain she *was* all there but that part of life had been locked against her – that the door was near – that the key was actually somewhere in view, if only she could wipe this mist from her eyes!

All around her she saw people making improvements in their lives, some ploddingly, some by leaps and bounds. But she, whether she plodded or leaped, seemed only to move from mess to mess; they weren't even disasters – something you could look back on with a shameful sort of pride and say, "I ruined *all* that!" Hers were just stupid, eejit messes.

Another thing she was beginning to notice – a patt-*ern*, as she had proudly learned to call it – was that wherever she went, the women always took against her. Even when they didn't know her. In fact, especially when they didn't know her. They'd take one look at her, recognize something there that'd put them in a holy fright, and they'd bring out the ice. Then bit by bit they'd change, most of them. One would make a friendly overture. Then another. Then they'd find she didn't bite and the horns on her forehead were a trick of the light. And so they'd turn a little warmer. But even then there'd be a kind of disappointment – as if they really wanted her to be . . . whatever awful thing they thought they saw at first. A she-divil or something. They seemed to want some woman to be a she-divil *for* them, tell them all about it, keep them safe. Often she had invented she-devil stories just to keep them happy; now there were times when she didn't know what the real bits were any more. The odd bout of hearty

140

drinking didn't make it any easier to separate fact from fantasy, of course.

When she was a little girl it had been the other way about. Women would only look at her and want to pick her up, buy her a hoop or a bullseye, take her picking berries, listen to her chatter. How could a little girl know tricks that the woman she grew into had forgotten? Often she tried to remember them, those tricks. Life was all tricks when you got down to it. And she was stupid to have forgotten them.

All of which goes far to explain why she was not in the least surprised when first Matron and then Mrs Raven became a little warmer to her. Mrs Raven came along one afternoon, when she was sitting in the shade with Mr O'Dea on his own private bit of the lawn, reading bits of the *Commercial Register* to him, which he enjoyed for her mispronunciations as much as anything.

"Mister O'Dea," she said. "I'm sure you can manage without Miss Kelly for half an hour? May I borrow her to go and cut some flowers for the rooms? I've hardly had a chance to speak to her since she arrived."

Birdie realized she could learn a lot about *successful* lying from Mrs Raven, only first she'd have to learn to coo like a dove and put a bent tip on every challenge – two gifts that seemed to elude her, for all her effort.

"There's a basket for you, dear," Lucy said as they set off toward the greenhouses. "I always think this is one of the *special* moments of the day – setting forth with an empty flower basket. It must be one of the most ancient of all human satisfactions – going out foraging – don't you think? Modern life simply doesn't provide enough of it. We're summoned by whistles and dispatched by bells. All those factories where machines rule the day . . ."

"You'll rue the day!" Birdie murmured.

"Eh?"

"That's my mammy's pet saying, ma'am – you'll rue the day! I'd like a farthing for every time she said it to us childer." Then she remembered she'd told Matron she had no brothers or sisters – which was also true in its way. She waited for Mrs Raven to say something like, "But I thought you told Matron . . ." – which would prove they'd discussed her.

But Mrs Raven said not a word about it – which proved nothing either way.

Instead, Lucy sighed and said, "We must pick some of the wild flowers, too, and things that have run wild. Those bottle-brush flowers, the polyganums there, for instance. We have to go carefully with the glasshouse stocks, you see until we can build them up properly for next year. Did you ever know this house while it stood empty?"

"Empty of the quality?" Birdie asked. "Sean Slattery was never gone."

"You know him then?"

Birdie chuckled. "I'd know *his* shadow on a furze bush. I know the flat of his hand, too – just the way he'd be knowing the flash of my heels. Sure weren't we always in and out of here."

"So you grew up in Tallaght – or this part of the world, anyway?"

They entered the courtyard, where several patients were sitting, ripening like melons in the sun, with the nurses tending them like so many stately gardeners.

"That's a brave sight of people there, ma'am!" she commented. "'Tis one I never thought I'd meet in this old place. I've seen deer *asleep* on them old stones."

"Peacocks!" Lucy said suddenly – thinking that if Birdie Kelly wished her conversations to flow like a stream full of sudden waterfalls, she could have it so. "We must get some peacocks. They're so soothing to watch, and so majestic."

"They have a cry on them like a banshee," Birdie warned.

"Only when they're seeking . . . only for a brief season," Lucy assured her.

At the top of the little flight of steps that led to the greenhouses they turned and looked briefly at the scene once more.

"And now you're here by right," Lucy said. "One of us, eh? No need to show a clean pair of heels to old Slattery when you meet. Did you ever think *that* would befall you when you came up here to play?"

"Play is it?" Birdie laughed. "Sure we came here to feck apples and potatoes!"

Her smile was so frank and open, so devoid of guilt or naughty chagrin, that Lucy understood, quite without the need for words – in her bones, so to speak – a way of life in which theft was just another skill, like washing and ironing. "You really shouldn't say things like that," she told the girl.

"It's the God's truth, ma'am. Potatoes, apples, berries – they only rotted where they grew if we didn't take them, so where was the harm?"

"Well, well . . . it's all water under the bridge now, I suppose." Lucy gritted her teeth. She had never met anyone with whom it was so difficult to start a conversation – no, to *steer* a conversation. She could start them at the rate of a dozen a minute!

As they walked into the cloying humidity of the greenhouse Lucy decided to try an approach she rarely risked with anyone: the direct question. Before their meeting was concluded she rather wished she hadn't; but at first it augured rather well. "Forgive me if I seem rather personal," she said as she handed the girl a flower knife, "but when you came roaring up the front drive like a heifer calf that first evening . . . I mean, did you honestly believe that was the best way to go about seeking employment here – in *any* capacity, whatever –

142

never mind in the saintly profession of nursing?"

At last there was guilt in the girl's face – that naughty chagrin whose lack had shocked Lucy earlier. "I own I was a touch hearty that day, ma'am," she confessed. "Hadn't I written affydavies for a whole raft of places – and some with not even the courtesy to send a word back."

"They were surely the places to go roaring at, then. For I know we answered every letter we got."

"Ah but ye were so near, ma'am. Besides, wasn't I sure 'twas on account of me being a Catholic. I thought this was surely the kind of a place where there'd be Protestant nurses and Catholic scullery maids." While she spoke she looked all about her, eyes taking in everything.

Most of the glass on the side away from the house was misted over with a greenish limewash. Naturally the eye was then drawn to the few missing panes, where a view out was possible. Through one of these Birdie now saw Matron Powers, walking up the back path to the kitchen garden; she was carrying a small bundle under one arm and Birdie thought there was something surreptitious about her gait. She was just about to draw Mrs Raven's attention to the sight when the woman said, "So you just wanted to come up here and make a nuisance of yourself."

"The way of it was, ma'am – I did," she admitted.

Lucy showed her a chrysanthemum she had just cut. "Snip them as long as you can, dear. We can always shorten them back in the house. You must have been very surprised, then, when Mister O'Dea offered you the pick of the positions here?"

Birdie put a hand briefly to Lucy's wrist. "Now, d'you know what I'm going to tell you, ma'am?" she said.

Lucy shook her head.

"You could have flattened me with a feather!"

"I believe you, dear. But I'd love to know how he described the work to you."

"Sure there's little mystery in that. You could say it all while a cat would be licking her ear."

"The actual looking-after him – yes. That wouldn't take long. I mean, it's not as if he's really ill. Being a cripple isn't being ill. But the rest of it – the organization of the clinic . . . the nurses . . . Matron – did he explain any of that?"

"Well now, ma'am, the first drop of broth is the hottest, they say."

Lucy sighed and set her basket down. Before she could speak, however, Birdie cut in with: "Begging your pardon now, ma'am – little right I have to ask such a thing, I know, but if we're all allowed a personal question, is it on saint you are?"

Lucy stared blankly at her as she repeated the nonsense in her mind's ear.

"On saint," Birdie repeated. "Looking for a little bundle of joy?"

The penny dropped. "*Enceinte!*" Lucy repeated, torn between outrage and wild laughter. "Really!"

"You're not, so," Birdie guessed.

"Whether I am or not . . . I mean – good heavens! Did no one ever teach you proper respect, girl?"

Birdie held her head high. "God they did, ma'am. And isn't it the highest aspiration of the respectable woman?"

Lucy gave up. "Anyway," she said, "what makes you ask?"

"Sure the way you'd be putting your hands to your hips – fingers looking back. I've seen women do that when they're on saint, as they say."

Lucy sat down and slumped a little. "Is it so obvious," she sighed. Of all the conversations she had expected to have with the Kelly girl, this had been nowhere on the list. "Are people talking about it?" She nodded toward the house.

"Oh God, ma'am, I want to tell you the truth now. My bible on it! The thought never darkened my mind till I saw you set down your basket not half a minute since. Is it yourself that's surprised?" Birdie took a seat, legs out straight, ankles crossed, and twiddled her thumbs, smiling happily to prove she did not mind this sort of talk one bit.

Lucy glanced nervously toward the house, for the panes on that northern side were not limewashed. She could still hardly believe she had stumbled into this conversation. "Not in my heart of hearts, I suppose," she said reluctantly. "Penny on the drum, I've suspected it for some time. But, what with the move up here, and selling up the old house, and the unending upheaval of setting up this clinic . . . you know . . . it was easy *not* to be certain. You understand? Things are not regular at such times." She smiled wanly, quite embarrassed now at having spoken at all.

"Is it unwelcome it'd be?" Birdie asked, so gaily that Lucy feared she might have answers for that problem, too.

"Well," she said uncertainly, "I do allow the year that's in it could be better chosen. You know yourself, there's so much to *do* here."

"Sure how would that prevent you, ma'am?" Birdie said with all the confidence of the seasoned spectator. "It's no sickness, so it isn't."

"Aren't you the hurler on the ditch!" Lucy exclaimed, resentful that one who'd never crossed that Rubicon should dismiss it so lightly. Then, however, she recalled the point she had started to make and so changed her tone. "But you're right, really. It's no sickness. It's a great inconvenience and it sets you low at times – but it *isn't* a sickness. You seem to understand that, and I certainly understand it, so all I can say is it's a great pity that certain medical gentlemen who

144

ought to know better but alas never will – not at first hand, anyway – believe it's worse than dropsy, cholera, and smallpox, all rolled into one."

"Fancy!" Birdie's voice was heavy with sympathy. "And him your own husband and not believing a word you say!"

Lucy held a finger toward her. "I named no names, Miss Kelly. Remember that. He's not alone. He's one of a legion. And fair dues to him, I never complained when we sent out the bills for his attendance upon ladies I knew were no more sick than I was. I never said we were taking money under false pretences." She shook her head at the harshness of poetic justice. "None of which is any help now. Listen – this is a terrible thing for one woman to be asking of another, but I'd be very much obliged to you if you could possibly, *possibly* manage to keep this discovery to yourself? If word of it leaks out, I'll be treated like an invalid from now until November. There! Now you know *when* it's to be, too! I couldn't bear to be treated like that, not with all there is to do here. Can we keep it a secret, just between us, for as long as nothing shows?"

Birdie nodded happily. "That's a quare thing I want to tell you, ma'am," she said. "I'll babble my heart out from breakfast till supper, and from astronomy to zebras, but I never yet saw the pleasure of gossip. 'Did you see what I saw beyond in the wood-shed? . . . Whose bicycle was that outside Ma Dignam's when himself was on night-shift?' All that fancy caper. I never saw sense in it yet."

Lucy smiled gratefully. "I can believe that, Miss Kelly. There is something in you that is . . ." She shrugged and did not finish the thought. "Anyway – my secret is safe, eh?"

"Isn't it what I'm after telling you. But what about Matron? Wouldn't she be on to it like the tinker's dog?"

Lucy nodded glumly. "I'm sure she already has her suspicions. I gave her the chance to come out with it the other day. But either she hasn't an inkling or she didn't wish to say. But you're right – one misplaced word to my husband and the sky would fall in! I'll have to bite the bullet and speak to her."

Birdie decided to mention that she'd seen Matron herself a short while earlier, stealing up the back path. Their foraging among the flowers had carried them farther into the glasshouse so from where she now sat she could actually see the kitchen-garden entrance. She was just about to speak when she saw Doctor Raven go striding in through that gap, bold as you'd like.

"What now?" Lucy asked, having heard the intake of breath.

"I was just thinking, ma'am – would you like to see where we came, feckin' apples and blackcurrants, me and the gossoons?"

Lucy laughed, glanced at the clock over the stables, and said another time perhaps.

145

S ome of the nurses at Mount Venus took their hygiene training so much to heart that they developed a strong prejudice against the commercial steam laundry – at least when it came to the more intimate clothing, next to the skin. If microbes could lurk all unsuspected in the most innocent-looking pork pies and the crispest summer salads, how could they possibly *not* revel in all that delicious sudsy water? So, until such time as the clinic's own laundry began to operate, they took to washing out their personal underthings and hanging them on makeshift lines in their attic rooms. Matron, however, put her foot down at that and decreed that they must put them out in the yard with the small amount of domestic laundry that was already being washed on the premises each day. The fastidious nurses had feet of their own to put down, however; they were horrified at the thought that all their most intimate garments might be flapping away in the kitchen-courtyard breeze where all the world might see them.

Old Slattery provided the answer when he suggested that the nurses might hang their bodies in the old pheasant-rearing run, foreanenst the north-looking wall of the kitchen garden, where none but himself and the boy might get the odd glimpse of them among the green leaves of the "convulsions" that had climbed up the wire netting. This compromise was duly agreed.

Michael knew nothing of the arrangement; it was the sort of thing that Diana regarded as falling entirely within her own province and altogether too trivial to bother the medical director with. She herself had little patience with the nurses' fastidiousness. Those same nurses would happily boil surgical implements and bandages to make them sterile once more; why they should believe that boiling water at Mount Venus was more effective than boiling water down in Rathfarnham was beyond her. However, there came a day when she had an embarrassing little accident and was rather glad of the camouflage provided by the old pheasant run and its almost permanent display of "bodies." She washed several items of underwear at the same time, so that the one in question should not be too obvious. She also removed her name-tapes. By then it was mid-afternoon.

She made sure every nurse was busy at some task before she set out with her guilty load. She was also careful to inquire about Birdie Kelly – and was glad she did. Someone said that Mrs Raven had "borrowed" her to go picking flowers in the glasshouses. On hearing this news, she chose a roundabout path to the walled garden, for the direct one would have led her in full view of the two flower-pickers. As she went she wondered why Lucy Raven had taken the Kelly woman aside today. It could not have been on the spur of the moment, anyway, for, according to her informant, Mrs Raven had gone out of her way – choosing the moment when Ebenezer could safely be left on his own bit of lawn to snooze in the shade. Was Lucy seeking information of some kind? Or did she want to use the woman as a private channel to Ebenezer? Or perhaps it was something much vaguer – perhaps Lucy, too, was fascinated by Birdie Kelly, by that hint of something savage, something ungovernable about her?

It was odd, Diana thought, how often the Kelly woman had been on her mind since that extraordinary interview, two days ago. She was everything Diana abhorred in a woman – pleasure-seeking, self-indulgent, ignorant, opinionated, cunning, unreliable, fanciful, fond of the bottle . . . She did all her thinking on the tip of her tongue. And yet Diana found herself wanting to protect the creature – or, if not exactly protect, to help her be less like all that, more like the others.

Inside the walled garden she had a quick lookaround for old Slattery and, finding herself alone, scurried across the open ground to the old pheasant run, which was built against the far wall. Its wire-netting frontage was now thickly matted with vines of convolvulus, or morning glory, but there was a gap that served as an entrance down at one end; the wire-netting door that had once closed it had long since rotted away. Safely inside, she walked swiftly to the laundry that already hung there, about thirty yards up inside the run. It was a rather severe collection of black and navy-blue stockings and other unmentionables, all in pristine white. Navy-blue and white were the two colours she loathed above all for undergarments – not for others but for herself.

She chose the first empty line beyond them and draped her things over it: a chemise, a pair of lisle stockings, and an embroidered camisole – all peachy pink; they stuck out like Howth Head. She searched for a spare peg or two, found none, and decided to leave it to chance. The gentle southwesterly breeze hardly stirred the air on this side of the wall, anyway – especially behind that sheltering tapestry of climbers. Briefly she pretended to inspect the other laundry drying there – most of it already dry, in fact – just in case anyone should have noticed her presence; then she made her way back toward the entrance.

Halfway there she spied a movement beyond the festoons of morning glory. She went swiftly to the netting, found a gap, and peered through. It was Michael – and he was striding directly toward the pheasant run! Realizing she could not now leave by the way she had intended, she hastened back again, past the hanging clothes, making for the farthest end of the run, hoping bleakly that she might find another way out up there.

"Matron?" Michael called out as he drew near the run. "Are you in there?"

She doubled her speed – though even then she was telling herself how absurd it all was . . . and hadn't she every right to come out and inspect her nurses' laundry . . . and weren't her own unmentionables all nice and anonymous among them. But these reassurances made not the slightest impression on her terror. The thought of standing there, facing him, among all those feminine inexpressibles was . . . she shuddered even to picture it.

"Matron?" It was slightly more annoyed now.

She arrived at the far end of the run, much more out of breath than her brief sprint would justify. And there was no way out! She looked around in panic, for it was unthinkable that Michael would come all this way and not even glance inside the old run. A rotting incubator stood in the very far corner. About four foot high. If she took off her cap, she could crouch down behind it.

And if he spotted her, she could embarrass him by pointing out that even the most august matron has to obey calls of nature – and she doesn't like to be shouting out "over here!" while doing so.

"Miss Powers?"

He had arrived outside the run, at a point just beyond the laundry lines, and there he stood, trying to peer inwards through the vines.

"Diana?"

The intimacy shocked her, though it was spoken in a kind of stage whisper through a gap in the greenery. She heard him move away – and prayed he was going back to the walled-garden entrance.

But no such luck; he was going down the side of the run, making for the former doorway. Her panic returned as she realized she could not possibly pretend to be obeying a call of nature behind the derelict incubator. She ran to where there was no opening in the netting, put her hand to it in desperation – and almost laughed aloud in her relief. It was so rusty that only the creeper was keeping it up. Here it was not morning glory but traveller's joy and wild woodbine, forming a dense wall through which hardly any light penetrated. If she could hide among it, she would be concealed from all sides unless he came right up close – and even then she could slip outside long before he approached. Quickly she scrabbled a gap between the wire and the wooden post, using hands and boots.

When it was open to the ground she slipped out into the dark-green embrace of the climbers – and just in time, too. Her cap was knocked awry so she took it off and folded it inside her navy-blue bib, where its brilliant white would not give her away.

"Diana?" he repeated as he advanced up the run. But now his tone was that of a man who no longer expects an answer. There is a subtle difference between checking to ensure that you are alone and checking to see whether anyone else is there – and Michael's tone expressed it perfectly. She parted some stems of sweet woodbine and watched.

He was standing among the laundry, grinning as Aladdin must have grinned in his cave, the moment after crying "open sesame!" Gingerly he reached out a hand and touched one of them, a busk; he ran the backs of his knuckles tenderly up and down its silky panels.

He started at some noise and stared guiltily over his shoulder, back toward the door gap. Then he relaxed and reached somewhat more

148

boldly for a black lisle stocking, letting it run through his fingers. Then another. Then another . . . Shimmies, busks, corsets, stays, stockings, bust-holders, bandeaus, convenients – all swayed about him with an enticingly disembodied choreography as he drifted trancelike among them, running his fingers through them with a strange mixture of bawdry and reverence.

Diana watched, appalled. And amused. Diana watched at war with herself. All the tensions of these past few weeks – of being Matron who walks alone, the jilted spinster who sleeps alone, the rejected lover who weeps alone – came to a point in that moment. She wanted to step out of hiding – never mind how she might explain it later – and bellow in her most matronly thunder: "*Doctor* Raven! Pray *what* is the meaning of this?" But the warring faction in her soul heard the ridiculous pomposity of those words and – though she still wished to step out and confront him – urged her to do it with laughter . . . to join him, even, and start a madcap dance among the inexpressibles. And so, perfectly stretched between those two irreconcilable yearnings, she stood her ground and watched.

He brushed against a stocking that was not dry – one of hers, of course. Peach-coloured lisle. Nor was it pegged to the line like the others. It came away, wrapped around his cheeks like a boa. He stopped at once – and so did her heart. Someone must have told him they'd just seen her coming into this kitchen garden, so it would hardly require a Sherlock Holmes to put an owner's name to any wet garment found hanging here – despite their lack of name tags.

She watched with bated breath while he made the obvious connection. Oh Lord, oh Lord, have mercy! She felt sure he was going to look up, give a mischievous grin all about him, and come stalking her! She felt among the growth behind her, gathering up vines of traveller's joy, ready to make a bolt for it.

But he did none of those things. He clearly decided she had returned to the house before ever he entered the walled garden. And so there he stood, legs braced slightly apart, eyes closed, head bowed, while he slowly raised her stocking to his lips and reverently kissed the toe of it.

She watched, horrified, as the kiss lingered on. The drowsy scent of woodbine assailed her, drifting around her cheeks with soporific heaviness.

Now he stretched the garment out between both hands – a strange, almost priestly gesture – and ran his lips tenderly over its surface, from ankle to knee. Her heart dropped a beat and then caught up in double time as a sympathetic tingle ran up her calf, too, from ankle to knee.

Ankle and knee had their memories, also – ankle and knee and thigh . . .

Suddenly she could bear it no longer. As silently as she could she edged her way backwards out of the thicket. From there it was but a hen's race to the path that led down past the volunteer potatoes, behind the weed-choked blackcurrant bushes, whose fruit was just beginning to colour, and so at last to the path that crossed the garden parallel to the pheasant run. There she remembered to take out her cap and put it back on. She hoped it would make her Matron again – and that Matron would know what to do in order to banish the frightened but excited woman who had just witnessed the collapse of her carefully constructed world.

Matron was sure she did. Matron said to turn about and face it like a Christian. Matron stood at the centre of the garden and called out "Doctor Raven?" in the calmest voice you ever heard.

But when Michael Raven appeared once again at the pheasant-run entrance and said, "There you are!" – Matron withered on the summer air and Diana smelled the wild woodbine all about her once again. "I was just on my way to inspect this temporary drying yard," she said, wondering how she could possibly sound so calm and collected.

"Ah." He rubbed his hands. "Someone told me you were already here."

"What does it look like?" she asked. "Is it all neat and tidy – or stuff all over the place?"

"I don't know." They were close enough now for ordinary conversation. "I've only just got here myself."

The flat banality of their conversation made her want to scream. As she came up to him she had to fight an impulse to grab him by the arms and shake him furiously, crying, "I *saw* you, Michael! You can't go back on it now!"

But where was the point? He couldn't go forward, either – or, rather, she wouldn't let herself even contemplate what "going forward" might mean.

She poked her head inside, gazing past him, and said, "Oh, well, it doesn't look too bad – and who can see it, anyway!" She smiled at him. "It's just too hot to be all right and proper today, eh? Is there a tap over there by the potting shed?"

There was. It ran almost too hot to bear for about five seconds and then turned refreshingly chill. They had no cup and so had to drink like wayfarers at a roadside freshet.

"A drink from out the hand," he gasped as he straightened himself and turned off the tap. "No water tastes better, does it!"

"Whoooo!" She plucked two rhubarb leaves and handed him one, fanning her face with the other as she collapsed on a bale of straw set against the potting-shed wall, ready, no doubt, to spread under the strawberries. "Let's rest awhile our weary limbs."

His eyes filled with doubt. She knew he wanted to question the wisdom of it – but she knew, also, that he'd never be the first to put that notion openly between them. "Why not, indeed!" he said, sitting as far from her as was comfortable.

150

He leaned back, rested his left heel on his right knee, and fanned himself with his rhubarb leaf for a while. Then he murmured, "I think it's all going rather well so far."

"We haven't actually killed anyone," she agreed.

"I'm not talking about the clinic, Diana," he said quietly.

"Ah," she said. Had it not been for the panics and passions of the past ten minutes, her heart might have stopped for several beats at that moment; instead she amazed herself – and misled him – by her calm. "D'you think it wise to talk about it now, Michael?"

"Well . . . ." He smiled wanly at her. "A decade on. We are both a decade or so older." It was the wrong response; clearly he had prepared himself for a more spirited reaction than she had given him. Aware of it, he began to extemporize – to depart from his prepared script. "I find it gets in the way sometimes – memories, I mean. Memories get in the way. And it's because we're not doing anything to drive them out. No!" He barked the word angrily and tried to swat a fly on his raised knee – but succeeded only in breaking the leaf and wiping some of its sap on his trousers.

There are times, she thought as she watched it spread, unnoticed by him, *when I am so glad not to be married.*

"Not drive them out," he went on. "Supplant them – put something in their place. We need a new kind of friendship to put in their place."

She became vaguely aware of something within her that wanted to punish him – for what he had just done with her stocking, she assured herself. After all, what punishment could there be now for a treachery that was ten years old? "I don't wish to put anything in their place, Michael," she murmured; her voice had a sudden, silky quality that even she had forgotten.

He eyed her nervously – which emboldened her to continue. "I have memories I shall carry with me, and treasure, until I die. I shall treasure them in my dying hour."

It wasn't true! Of course it wasn't true. Except, when you act something with utter conviction it achieves a kind of ephemeral truth.

"Oh Diana!" he said miserably.

Her spirit exulted in his misery.

"But I'm *happy*, Michael," she said. "I wouldn't have it otherwise. And I certainly don't want to put anything in its place. But – just to make this clear, my dear – I wouldn't take you now if you were free as a linnet. We were *never* intended to marry, you and I. I believe I was never intended for marriage at all. *This!* What I'm doing now." She touched her matron's cap and bib. "This is my destiny. Oh goodness how grand!" She laughed. "Let's just say I'm happier at this than I fear I ever would have been if you had put a second ring around my finger."

He remembered the first ring – the engagement ring she'd flung in his face that bitter afternoon – and wanted to explain why he'd given

151

it to Lucy so soon after. He was sure she must have noticed it and had a grand tale all ready.

But, as if she knew what was on his mind, she grinned at him with a hint of impishness the world had not seen for a decade or more, and, loosening the stud of her starched collar, she slipped two fingers down in front of her throat and slowly hauled out a long chain of gold filigree – at the end of which sparkled the duplicate of the diamond ring he had given her all that time ago.

"Eh?" He frowned at it in disbelief – and was just about to ask her if she and Lucy had discussed it . . . and had Lucy, incredibly, given it back to her – when she murmured, "I've worn it ever since, Michael."

He gazed at it, dumb with misery, and lowered his eyes. Perhaps he had dreamt it all. "I was an utter swine," he said, barely louder than a whisper. "I should never have let myself be talked out of it."

She looked at him sharply; like many a free, good-looking woman of her age, she had heard many a line from married men. "You don't give the impression of being unhappy, Michael."

He shrugged. "I'm not. But one happiness doesn't drive out another. We're not so limited in that capacity."

"Like the Blessington tram, eh?" she sneered. "Always room for one more on top!"

He looked at her in amazement, which gave way to a certain smile.

She realized then that her words had a meaning she never intended, but she managed not to blush. Instead she shook her head and said, quite calmly, "No, Michael. Don't give it a thought. The moving finger wrote . . . and all that."

His face fell.

She reached out and patted his knee. "If you want something to put in the place of all those old memories . . ." She stretched her left arm toward Mount Venus, whose upper floors were visible over the sun-drenched southern wall; the cordon pears and espalier apples were, she noticed, fast swelling to ripeness. Meanwhile the fingers of her right hand fed the chain back down inside her bodice. His surgical eye had gauged the length of it to a fractional inch; his human eye goggled at the realization of where the ring must now be hanging. He could see it nestling there in the shame-filled dark of his mind's eye. No other image could have tormented him with so precise a recall of that thrilling softness.

"The clinic, I mean," she said when she realized mere pointing had not been enough.

"I can't say it's no help at all," he admitted dourly.

"What about the baby, then?"

She held her breath. The words had just slipped out. She had thought them but never meant to say them.

He frowned in bewilderment.

She inhaled deeply, committed to it now. "Lucy's new baby!" she said, smiling as if she thought he must surely be teasing her.

The blood left his face; his jaw hung slack.

Diana turned pale, too – hating herself now for having done this to him. "Has she not told you yet, then?" she asked.

He shook his head. After a silence he said in a dazed sort of voice. "Has she told you?"

"My dear!" She tilted her head to one side and stared at him, eyes large with sympathy. "She hardly needed to. Look at her skin! Look at her eye! Who's the doctor here, anyway!"

The macerated leaf fell from his shaking fingers as he turned and stared at Mount Venus.

"Perhaps Lucy herself doesn't know," she offered. "Women often don't, you know. And what with the disruption of the past weeks . . . it doesn't exactly make for regularity . . ."

"Stop!" he cried – and stared at her in such anguish that she wanted to reach out, touch him, hit him, kiss him – anything to make him look away.

"She hasn't said anything yet?" she asked, not really meaning it as a question, but feeling a bald statement might sound presumptuous.

"But we've been so *careful!*" he said, with a vehemence that astonished her.

A moment later the implications of his words struck her and she could only stare at the ground in embarrassment.

"She can't be," he added, and his tone now was slightly more cheerful – enough, anyway, to recruit his own good spirits once more. "No!" He chuckled as people do at a false alarm. "She can't be. For one thing, we were too . . . I mean – we know what we're doing after all these years. And for another thing, she'd have told me."

Diana rose and dusted her uniform down, a habit rather than a necessity. "It sounds as if it wouldn't be the most welcome event in the calendar," she remarked.

"What do *you* think!" he exclaimed. "With the clinic filling as fast as we can renovate each room . . . new staff . . . new equipment. And us still feeling our way. To have Lucy off the best part of a year to have a baby would be . . ."

"It's not a sickness, Michael," she reminded him.

"Who's the doctor here, *Matron?*" he asked sharply.

"And who's the woman here, *Doctor?*" she replied evenly.

She could see him wanting to ask her what *she* might know about being pregnant and bearing a child . . . and she watched his courage fail him. On that particular point he just wasn't quite sure enough. She saw no harm in feeding a doubt like that. "Sometimes," she added "man's idea of 'being careful' is not the same as God's."

Later that evening, when the last rounds were done and the whole world tucked up asleep, she returned to the pheasant run to retrieve her laundry. One stocking was missing. She did not bother to search for it, though; she knew more or less where it was already.

When Lucy had finished trimming the flowers she carried them through to the nurses, whose task it was to arrange them in the various rooms. When she reached the last room she realized she had not seen Michael on her round. She asked a nurse, a new one called McSharry, if she knew where he might be. The woman replied plainly enough that she did not, but she spoke with an odd kind of smirk. Nurse Brennan, lately promoted sister, took charge and told Lucy, in a tone that was meant to make Nurse McSharry feel small, that Doctor Raven had gone in search of Matron, who, in turn, had gone to inspect the nurses' washing in the old pheasant run.

Moments later Lucy, then on her way back to her office, came across Diana herself, tallying off some new supplies; they exchanged smiles but did not pause for a chat – though Lucy was longing to tell her about the baby and beg her not to say a word to Michael. Almost immediately after that she glimpsed Michael, too, going into one of the patients' bedrooms at the farther end of the corridor; he had his back to her.

And there the matter would have died had it not been for that ghost of a simper on McSharry's lips when she had claimed ignorance of Michael's whereabouts. And Sister Brennan's withering glance. Clearly the nurse had supposed there was something to hide. Did they all know, then, of that long-dead romance between Michael and Diana? Lucy's spirit sagged at the thought. As if life weren't difficult enough already!

Then it dawned on her that the alternative was even worse. If they knew nothing of ancient history, then Nurse McSharry's simper could only mean that . . . she hardly dared frame the thought in words . . . there must be something in Michael's and Diana's *present* behaviour to warrant a giggle.

For the next hour she fought an increasingly forlorn battle to suppress the thought. Unfortunately, she discovered that although she might suppress the words, she was powerless against the images that plagued her: the great beds of uncut grass in the untended portions of the old kitchen garden, the high wall, the balmy air, the sheltering curtains of morning glory that festooned the open side of the run . . . and, worst of all, the potting shed! How many romances had she read in which veils of discretion were drawn over the tale the moment the two clandestine lovers drew near the potting shed!

For a while the sheer absurdity of it – and the comforting thought that such things only ever happened in romances – was enough to restore some calm. But still the doubts grew until, at the very end of the day, she was no longer able to hold herself in check. She had no

154

idea what she expected to discover in the walled garden, yet she knew she would not rest until she'd seen it for herself.

The moment she stepped outdoors, however, and felt the whole bright sky above her – God's eye, as her catechist had assured her – she saw what a silly expedition it was; not to say dangerous. An unconfirmed suspicion might prove the worst suspicion of all. So she stopped when she reached the glasshouses, telling herself they were her real reason for coming out here; she'd just slip inside, cut enough to fill one more vase, and then go back to the house. She had her hand to the door when, in the corner of her eye, she saw a sudden dart of red. She turned and saw it was a fox, a big dog fox, streaking down an unweeded path toward the gateway in the kitchen-garden wall. A moment later it turned and vanished inside.

An omen? God speaking in one of His famous mysterious ways? Or just sly Reynard going about his business? On any other day she'd have no doubt it was just Reynard, tempting fate in his usual bold fashion. On any other day she'd lift her skirts an inch or two and run after the cheeky fellow. She saw it as her chance to restore this day to its proper balance – to make it, indeed, a day like any other. She lifted her skirts an inch or two and ran after the cheeky fellow.

A hound, or a good gamekeeper, would have discerned its tracks through all the long grass; Lucy lost them after a couple of dozen paces – by which time she was far enough inside the walled area to be able to say to herself, "Well . . . now that I'm here . . .!"

For a while she stood where she was, looking around at the wasted two acres. Even before they moved into Mount Venus she had wanted to get a farmer in and till the old vegetable beds – put the whole lot under potatoes, just to clear the weeds; but Ebenezer had refused to approve the expenditure. She fanned the near-dead embers of her anger, giving herself one more reason for standing there today. Then, reluctantly, she yielded to the compulsion that urged her to walk the last fifty paces to the pheasant run.

It was stifling inside, she discovered; the heat simply poured down from the underside of the corrugated-iron roof. The green light made the heat seem unnatural, for green shade usually offers a welcome coolness. The ancient sawdust floor, now rotted to a dark brownish-grey, was pockmarked with footprints. What might she have expected to see there, anyway, she wondered as she sauntered up toward the laundry lines – the imprint of Diana's body, obliterating the marks of her nurses' feet? She shook her head angrily at the image; such thoughts did nothing but degrade her. So why was she continuing to walk toward the stockings and the shimmies? Her mind was a blank as she watched her toecaps peep alternately out in front of her hems, carrying her forward nonetheless.

"Little mice," Aunt Gertrude always called them. "Never let a man see more than your little mice!"

She glanced up at the sky but the sky could no longer watch. A

155

great weariness of prohibitions overcame her. She did not want to flout them; she just wanted to be unaware of them. Unaware? No, idiots were *unaware*; she wanted to be *not*-aware, to live in a sort of knowing oblivion. Like a child again.

"How Irish!" she said aloud as she came to a halt among the inexpressibles. "Well, there they are!" She continued speaking aloud. "And what did you expect, eh? Scarlet hose? Lace? Silk roses?"

The heat made her want to tear off her clothes and feel the cooling breezes on her skin, the way she had when they were children. They? For a moment the plural puzzled her. Then she remembered: herself and Philip de Renzi, of course. Those dear dead days of innocence!

A habit that was now ingrained made her run her eye over the name-tapes: McSharry, Talbot, Geary, Anderson, Hennessy . . . she made a tight orbit round the festooned lines and came to a group, a little apart, that had no name-tapes.

No name-tapes! When she and Diana finally got around to writing the ten most serious *Thou shalt nots* of Mount Venus, *Thou shalt not let thy clothes be without name-tapes* would be high among them. Whose could these garments be – all in pink, too? Lisle stockings – or, rather, a single lisle stocking – a chemise, and an embroidered camisole. They were a puritanical lot, these nurses, even the Roman Catholics; she could not imagine any of them wearing such a garment – or, to be precise – she could not see them parading it so publicly. And a *single* stocking, too. Carelessness? Slovenliness? "Arrah sure, the other one'll do me a day or so yet!" The accent was unmistakably that of Birdie Kelly, which would also account for the bold parade of embroidery. And she'd come out here without pegs to pin them up. Birdie Kelly beyond a doubt!

She lifted the camisole to look at it more closely; it was still slightly damp in the fold where it had touched the line. Lovely material – a long-staple cotton. (It was only amazing what you could learn in battles with the Rathfarnham Steam Laundry!) And art-silk needlework.

She redraped it slightly askew, where the fold would dry, and made her way back to the entrance. Already she was rehearsing the friendly warning she'd give Miss Kelly and preparing to answer her counter-objections: "Sure aren't my stockings pink and the others blue-black! And which of them colleens has silk flowers on her camisole?"

Part of her now rebelled at the very idea of reining in that splendid wild spirit of Birdie Kelly's. "Dear Birdie," she murmured. "It's more than this place you have split in two!"

When she reached the entrance to the run she was surprised to see Philip de Renzi coming toward her. She waved but he was not looking her way at that moment; his eyes were fixed on the potting shed. When he reached a point immediately in front of it he stopped and began to count the number of bricks along one complete course.

It surprised her. She could now look at a pile of sheets and guess its number pretty accurately. She thought architects ought to be able to do the same with bricks in walls.

"Four hundred and seventy-four!" she called out to tease him.

He turned and stared vaguely in her direction; obviously she was not as visible as she had imagined – or the sun was too directly in his eyes. She stepped out into the day, wondering how she had ever thought it hot. "Shame on you!" she called out.

He trotted a few paces and then ambled the rest of the way to where she stood. He looked French, she thought – like a French artist, in his white cotton cravat, white cotton suit with tan stripes, and panama hat.

"Any architect worth his salt should be able to look at a wall and tell you the number of bricks like *that!*" she explained, snapping her fingers on the word.

"Ah!" He was quick to pick her up. "Well, of course, I can look at the wall around this garden and tell you straight away – eighty-four thousand, six hundred, and ninety-five. Ninety-six if you count the broken one in the entrance. It's the piddling little things like that" – he jerked a thumb at the potting shed – "which tend to confuse."

"Do not denigrate the humble potting shed, Philip." She offered him her cheeks in turn. "Without it many a romance would flounder."

She meant romantic novel, of course, but he took the word in its literal meaning and eyed her askance. Then he grinned. "D'you mind if we give all that sort of thing a miss today, Luce? It's just too hot."

She punched him playfully and told him he was incorrigible. Then, in a more serious tone, she asked, "What are you doing here, anyway?"

He stared at her as if he thought he had more right to ask that question of her. "I need two hundred bricks of that pattern." Again he pointed at the shed. "They were probably fired here on the premises. They're no longer obtainable, anyway. I was thinking of demolishing the whole shed, to give us a stock for all our repairs and making good down at the house. And you?"

"Seeing if the nurses were abusing their privileges."

He frowned.

She stepped back inside the run and pointed at the laundry.

"I say!" He tipped back his hat and grinned salaciously.

She liked that honesty in him. All the other men she knew, including, sad to say, Michael, would behave as if the lines held nothing but handkerchiefs and workmen's overalls – though they'd sneak many a sidelong glance when they thought no one was looking. Dazzler had that honesty, too – though he'd make a show of it, whereas Philip just let it show without fuss. "You want to go and count them, too, while the mood is on you?" she asked.

He laughed as he eyed her nervously, wondering how much

genuine permission was conveyed along with the sarcasm. He played for safety. "There's supposed to be an old incubator somewhere in here – must be up the end there. I thought I'd give it a quick look."

Clever! Lucy thought as they set off through the green heat to find the thing – if it existed at all; she certainly hadn't noticed it when she was up that end of the run.

She remembered an evening early on in her marriage when she'd thought Michael was going off to sleep – only to discover that he was watching her undress through flickering, all-but-closed eyelids. Once she'd got over the shock she'd come over and stood beside his bed and really given him something to make his eyelids tremble! Then, after they'd finished laughing, he'd confessed that when he was a boy he'd almost died of exposure while hiding high up in a tree one night in the hope of watching a couple of maidservants undressing in their attic room. The sheer effort, and the fiendish ingenuity, men were capable of expending in the hope of such trivial rewards was staggering. Philip, for instance, had obviously come toiling all this way for a glimpse of the laundry – counting the old bricks was a feeble excuse. Why didn't he just buy a few pairs of stockings and hang them up in the privacy of his own bedroom whenever he felt the need? And as for this tale of an incubator . . . well! That was desperate.

"There she is!" he cried, walking straight past the lingerie in a bee-line for the old apparatus, mouldering away in the far corner.

Feeling rather humble and small, Lucy followed in his wake – until she realized that, if he was in the *habit* of coming up here for nefarious glimpses, of course he'd know all about the incubator. "Haven't you seen it before?" she asked slyly.

"No," he said abstractedly, taking out his pocket knife and opening the blade that looked like a marlin spike – with which he began to test the soundness of the wood. "Margaret and Philip told me about it. He said if you didn't want it, he'd offer a bob or two for it."

"Philip and Margaret Flannery – just up the road here?"

"Porterstown House. Yes. That's a thing I meant to say – I've rented a set of rooms in their west wing, as they rather grandly call it. Old annexe would be more apt." He paused in his testing, to see how she took this news.

"I know one person who'll be pleased," she said in as neutral a tone as possible. "Diana Powers."

It hurt to see how his eyes gleamed at the name. "D'you really think so?" he asked. "Has she said anything to you about me? I can't seem to get near her." He patted the incubator and folded his pocket knife again. "Not bad at all, considering. D'you think you'll ever use it here?"

She shook her head. "I'm sure the Flannerys are welcome to it. How long have you been their tenant?"

158

"Resident architect, actually," he replied. "They want me to lay out an italianate garden."

"And you'll take on work of that kind?" she asked in surprise.

He gave a hollow laugh. "I'll take on work of any kind, Luce."

She thought he was going to add, "as long as it brings me near Diana," or something to that effect. Instead he continued: "Oul' Daycency isn't spending a penny on bricks and mortar in Ireland these days, or hadn't you noticed? Why should they? We can all see the writing on the wall. So we architect-fellows are really rather glad when somebody says to us, 'Here, brush my coat for me, there's a good chap!' In short, yes, I'm happy to design a garden for the one family in south County Dublin that can't read writing on walls. And, to answer your original question: last Tuesday. I'm sorry I forgot to mention it." Then, no doubt feeling his answer had been rather self-pitying, and quite against the devil-may-care reputation he sought to cultivate, he panted like a lap dog and gabbled "CanIhavea-pieceofcakenowplease?"

She laughed and punched him on the shoulder.

"You're in a highly aggressive mood today, Luce," he complained, only half-jokingly, as he rubbed the spot. "Has Uncle Ebenezer been putting his foot down again?"

She shook her head but said nothing as to that – not wishing to pursue it. Instead she waved a hand at the washing lines and asked, "If you were all on your ownio here, Philip, what would you do at this moment?"

"This." He grinned back at her, over his shoulder, while he walked up the line, holding out his hand at half-stocking-height, letting one after the other flow through his fingers and fall back to swing gently in the breezeless heat.

"Why?" she asked, laughing.

"I haven't the faintest idea," he replied, as if it genuinely were the profoundest puzzle. He was about to return in the same way, brushing his hands through Birdie Kelly's things – or what Lucy had decided were Birdie's – when he noticed they were different in character from the rest. "Whose are these?" he asked.

A little imp made Lucy reply, "Matron's, of course."

He plucked his hand away a split-second before he touched the singleton stocking and flushed bright red. When he fell in at Lucy's side again he had recovered sufficiently to give a little theatrical bow. "Will you women ever tame us?" he asked.

She grinned and took his arm. "I hope not."

After several paces he paused and looked back over his shoulder. "Why only one stocking?" he asked.

She drew breath to parody his earlier assertion that he hadn't the faintest idea, but the little imp got to her again and she maintained an embarrassed silence.

Philip stared at her in horror. "She's not missing one . . . I mean . . . " But he couldn't come out with it all.

Lucy, still teasing, pretended to be flustered. "I know nothing about it," she replied breathlessly. "Ask her if you really want to know."

Philip was silent after that.

She felt quite ashamed of herself by the time they regained the cool of the hot afternoon. Only the thought of Philip's face when he at last realized how utterly successful she had been – for once – in pulling his leg prevented her from blurting out the truth.

After they had quitted the walled garden entirely, Birdie Kelly waited in the potting shed a further five minutes before she, too, dared emerge. She stared cautiously all about her, fanned her face, and set off briskly for the big house. Now she had *two* interesting assignations to report to the oul' darlin' beyond.

O nce upon a time," Lucy began, though she had no idea how to continue. She glanced swiftly into four eager pairs of eyes, trying to gauge their degree of tiredness. A short tale or a long one? Portia was plainly tired. A short one, she decided. The Mouse's Tale from *Alice*. "Fury said to a mouse that he met in the house . . ."

A collective groan went up. "We had that last week," Charley complained. "And it's too short," Portia put in.

A medium length one, then. "Once upon a time there was an unhappy king and the reason he was unhappy was because he was all misshapen and crippled. He had only one eye, and a crooked back, and one leg was shorter than the other."

The children settled happily in their twin double-beds; eyelids drooped; thumbs stole into mouths. They had not heard this one before – which was hardly surprising since Lucy was making it up as she went along, though the idea had come to her out of the blue after her conversation with Philip that evening.

"His courtiers tried comforting him in the way courtiers always do. They pointed out that if one leg was shorter, the other must be longer by way of compensation – and isn't nature wonderful! But the poor, ugly king didn't think nature was at all wonderful – especially when he remembered how beautiful he had been as a young prince."

Tarquin interrupted: "How can he be beautiful as a prince and grow up to be . . ."

"If you'll just keep quiet, you'll hear. It was all because of his bravery, you see. He was not only the most dashing and handsome prince that ever was, he was also the bravest – especially when the court went out hunting – and most especially of all when they went hunting wild boar."

"Are there wild boars in the Dublin Mountains?" Tarquin asked.

"There used to be," Charley told him.

"I expect they got eaten up in the Famine," Alice put in.

"D'you want to hear this story or don't you?" their mother asked.

They were chastened for as long as five seconds, long enough for Lucy to continue. "And one day they all went hunting in a part of the forest where there was a particularly fearsome wild boar."

"What was he called?" Portia obviously felt she had not been contributing enough.

"Uncle Ebenezer." Alice giggled.

"And the ugly king is Pappa," Charley added. "And I know what's going to happen because an old witch is going to make him handsome again like Pappa is."

"You tell it, then," Lucy challenged him.

After a long silence he apologized.

"No more interruptions?" Lucy asked.

Four heads shook in ragged unison.

"There are no witches in this story. The people in it are themselves and not anyone you know in disguise. There *is* a moral, however, right at the end, but I shan't tell you what it is. We'll just see which of you is clever enough to spot it – and you won't do that unless you listen very hard. Also you've now wasted so much time I'm going to have to skip over all the blood and gore there was when the prince went after the wily old wild boar, all on his own. Suffice it to say he made a shocking hames of the whole business and the wild boar left him for dead."

"Was there blood all over the forest?" Charley asked. "Were his bowels all yeurgh?" Tarquin added. They were both looking at their sisters, hoping to provoke a reaction there.

"That's enough!" Lucy said. "If you're very very good, I'll put all the gory details in next time I tell this tale. Anyway, they gathered up the bits of the prince – the once oh-so-handsome young man – and sewed them back together as best they could. And, wonderful to relate, he survived! Alas, he was no longer handsome. In fact, he was very much as I described him before you started interrupting me." She challenged them to try it again.

Silence.

"So the years rolled on and people began to notice that the line of royal portraits in the royal portrait gallery stopped at the previous king – and the coins of the realm and the postage stamps all bore the old king's head still. And, of course, people began to snigger, saying the present king was afraid to have his portrait painted. So, when word of this reached the king – *despite* the noble efforts of his courtiers – he sent for the best portrait painter in the country and said to him, 'I want you to paint me *exactly* as you see me – warts and all, as Oliver Cromwell said.'"

She waited for questions, interruptions . . . but silence continued to reign. She had them at last.

"Of course, the best portrait painter in the realm didn't get where

161

he was by obeying wishes of *that* kind! He said yessir, nosir, three-bags-full-sir, but he painted the king as the handsome fellow he would have been if he hadn't met with that dreadful old wild boar. And the king was absolutely furious! In fact, you could say he waxed exceeding wroth – and kings don't do that very often! He ordered the painter to be executed and decreed that the painting should be burned. However, being at heart a merciful man he softened the sentence. The painter had one of his eyes put out and one of his legs cut short and he had to wear a cushion on his back for the rest of his life. Also the king rescued the painting from the flames and had it carried to a high tower – where he used to go and gaze at it from time to time."

Portia sighed – fast asleep.

"So the king sent for the second-best portrait painter in the country and he said to him, 'I want you to paint me *exactly* as you see me – warts and all, as Oliver Cromwell said.' And the second-best portrait painter said yessir, nosir, three-bags-full-sir and, remembering what happened to his colleague, obeyed the king to the letter. But when the king looked at the result and saw the missing eye and the hump back and the short leg he . . . well, I'm sorry to say he waxed exceeding wroth once again! So the second-best painter had his eye put out and one leg shortened and . . ."

"How?" Charley dared to ask.

"You remember how we got the dining room table legs short-ened?"

His eyes went wide with glee and he pulled the sheets up under his chin and held his breath to hear more.

"And this time the painting *was* burned. So then the *third*-best portrait painter was sent for. And once again the king said, 'I want you to paint me *exactly* as you see me – warts and all, as Oliver Cromwell said.' And what d'you think the third-best portrait painter replied?"

"Yessir, nosir, three-bags . . .' The three piping voices tailed off when they saw their mother shaking her head.

"He said, 'I'll naturally do my best, sire, but it'll have to be rather a quick job. For some odd reason I suddenly find myself exceedingly busy!' And when the king saw the painting, he clapped his hands with joy and immediately dubbed the artist a knight of his court. So, what d'you think the painter had done, eh?"

Alice said, "He painted the king, warts and all, only the king had meanwhile realized how unfair he'd been to the second-best painter."

Lucy shook her head. "Life isn't like that, darling. What he did, you see, was paint the king out hunting – actually taking aim with his musket, so that his one bad eye was closed, and his short leg was up on a tree stump, to steady him, and he was bending right forward with one elbow on his knee, so no one could see his back was bent! And the moral of *that* tale is . . .?"

They sort of half-guessed it but none was going to risk putting it into words. Three pairs of eyes gleamed in the lamplight, desperate to hear it.

So she told them: "When life seems impossible, there's always a third way out."

W hat weird and wonderful surgical procedures have you been filling our boys' heads with?" Michael asked Lucy as he came back from saying his goodnights in the nursery.

She stared at him blankly, having forgotten the interruptions to her tale by then.

"Carpentry?" he prompted. "Cutting down table legs?"

"Ah!" She laughed as the memory returned. "The usual fairy-tale stuff: capricious monarchs, beastly punishments, and nature red in tooth and claw. Why people refer to ideal marriages as 'fairytale' is beyond me. Fairy-tales are full of violence and hidden carnality . . ."

"Not unlike ideal marriages!" he commented. "What was your story in particular? Mother Goose . . . or Grimm . . .?"

"It was grim, all right." And she went on to give him the gist of it.

After a moment or two of thought he said, "Don't you realize that violence and hidden carnality are mere venial sins compared with what *you* have managed to smuggle in? Would you like a sherry?"

She rose and punched him playfully on her way to the tantalus. "Why don't you just ask me to pour you one?"

He watched her fill his glass, take one for herself, hesitate, and then put it back. "I don't feel like sherry tonight," she said.

So she did know she was pregnant.

"A beer?" he suggested. "I'll tip down and get one cool from the cellar."

She shook her head and smiled, barely perceptibly, as she handed him his drink – suggesting that the topic was too trivial to waste further breath upon. She told herself she'd go to quite some length to conceal her condition from him, and for as long as possible, but alcoholic beverages were beyond those bounds. "What dread subversion have I managed to smuggle into my fairy-tale marriage?" she asked.

He frowned. "No – not our marriage, just into your bedtime story." Then he grinned. "Although, come to think of it, perhaps you were right first time. Tell me – *what* dread subversions have you introduced into our fairy-tale marriage?" He put his glass down and reached his arms toward her.

She was never more wary of Michael than when he wanted to hold her on his lap while they talked. He made it hard for her to avert her face and even harder to get away. He *knows*, she thought – and immediately wondered why he had said nothing about it before.

163

Perhaps he was having second thoughts about whether or not it really was a sickness. Perhaps some part of him knew that a century and more of medical wisdom was simply wrong and that expecting a baby was, in fact, quite natural for a woman. But, knowing Michael, it would not be a simple acknowledgement, it would be something forced on him by a greater exigency – such as the fact that the clinic could not *afford* for her to be "confined" for the rest of the year. Being Michael, too, he would keep the two kinds of understanding in different wings of his mind, far from any common meeting-ground. Often enough she had seen him give himself permission to undertake tasks, though suffering from a complaint that he knew full well ought to rule them out completely. He was not so foolish as to try to reconcile the irreconcilable; he was wise enough to keep his two minds apart. And let others bear the consequences.

"I do love you, Michael," she said. It surprised him – even shocked him – and she realized how long it had been since she had spoken those treasured words. "Mm-hmm?" was all he replied.

"Why," she went on, "is it subversive to suggest that a good carpenter could shorten human legs in the same way as a table's legs? That's just playing with words. I could tell you far more subversive thoughts than that! D'you know what would be *really* subversive in medicine?"

He raised his eyebrows. *Give a woman enough rope* . . . was part of his philosophy.

"To sit down at the patient's bedside and say, 'Well, Mister Sullivan, we don't honestly know what's wrong with you. All we have is a list of symptoms (which you've been good enough to provide us with) and we've found an impressive Latin tag to tie round them. But the *real* cause of it all is far beyond our present understanding. And, given the complexity of living things, it probably always will be. However, here's a bottle of coloured water – see how you go!' Shall we ever be as honest with our patients as that?"

Michael laughed – a little nervously, for Lucy had never spoken quite like this before.

"And I'll tell you another thing," she went on now that she had the bit between her teeth. "How to subvert religion. D'you know what would subvert religion? If all the archbishops in the world got together and said, 'Listen O ye faithful! Haven't we been telling you for two thousand years that God is Absolutely Unknowable? And don't you know what Absolute means? It means you haven't the luxury of asking questions about Him. So we'll stop trying to guess whether He approves of this or disapproves of that, if you'll stop asking us to tell you. Instead, just look at the world about you – His world – and make your own guesses for a change.' D'you think they'd ever put themselves out of business like that? And then there's the law. D'you know what would subvert the law?"

She drew breath to tell him but he put a finger to her lips and murmured. "All right. I take your point: Truth is a great destroyer of mankind's yearnings. I've never seen you so intense."

She realized her heart was beating rather fast. It surprised her. She frequently got carried away on flights of fancy while telling the children a bedtime story, but it had never happened before during ordinary grown-up conversation – especially not with Michael.

"In fact, you've changed a great deal since we came to live out here at Mount Venus," he said. "Are you aware of it yourself?"

She leaned against him, resting her head on his shoulder, and spoke softly into his ear. "In what way? For better or worse?"

He thought for a moment and then gave out a short explosive sigh. "Comparisons are odious. You've adapted, not simply changed, you've . . . adapted – there isn't another word."

"We have to survive," she said. "You mean I've only given two dinners since we came here – instead of two a week? Did you think I used to give dinner parties and sit on all those committees and pounce on every latest bit of Dublin crack because I *enjoyed* it?"

"Yes!" He was astonished that she could suggest anything else. "Didn't you?"

"Well of course I did. But that wasn't my *reason*. Enjoyment just made the activity palatable. God, but I sound like a hoor! What I'm saying is – down there in Dublin, when you had your consultancy and your practice, survival depended on knowing people – and being known – and knowing what was going on. And in our case letting Protestants know that Catholics aren't contagious."

"Ah g'wan – you enjoyed it!" he teased.

"I never denied that. I enjoyed it too much. But up here survival is different. Here . . ."

"I know all that," he interrupted. "Here it's smooth organization, a contented staff, and watch every penny. A woman of your intelligence would see that at once, and a woman of your character and energy would adapt to it at once. I'm not dismissing the achievement – in fact, at times I'm lost in admiration. But still that's not what I mean when I say you've changed." He lifted his hand to her head and patted it. "I mean up here. You analyse things now that you used to take for granted."

She laughed dryly. "I never had time to do otherwise."

A thought flew past her mind's eye – a big thought, so big she could not even see its shape. But one of its eddies caused her to add: "Actually, I'm wrong there. Time isn't in it. It's something to do with this place itself. Something to do with Mount Venus House."

"Ancestral ghosts?"

"God no. Nothing of that sort. But the place as it is now. Being in a house full of so many other women. I suppose it's not having gone away to boarding school myself. It makes you think of *purpose* in life. What's *their* purpose? Those nurses will work till they drop – and for

165

what? Two shillings a day! The meanest labourer gets five. Why do they do it?"

"Because . . ."

She thumped her arm against his chest. "No – I know why. I wasn't really asking. It's because people don't really want comfort or luxury or idleness, they only think they do. What they really want is fulfilment. All our nurses could sit at home, practising their accomplishments, baiting traps for husbands – and all in far greater comfort than they have here. But there's no fulfilment in that."

"Also," he said, "two shillings a day does help keep out undesirable women. The seven shillings a day the nurses *don't* earn is like a subscription to an exclusive club. It excludes – for example – the Birdie Kellys of this world!"

Lucy shivered. "Don't talk about *her!*"

He lifted her a foot or two off his shoulder so that he might look into her eyes. "Eh?" he asked.

She snuggled back into his embrace. "Among the women at Mount Venus she's the most thought-provoking of all."

He chuckled. "That young lady provokes many things in my mind – but thought is well down the list."

"Oh?" She stiffened warily.

"Anger. Rage. Bewilderment. Dread . . . and all stations to Curiosity."

"And hatred?"

"No! I leave that to the other nurses. They loathe her beyond words."

"You shouldn't say *other* nurses – not if Diana's about."

After a pause he said, "Now that's a funny thing. Matron is the one person who'll stick up for her. She's lent her a book on first aid, you know?"

"Why d'you find that odd, Michael?"

"Well! The ice maiden herself! Even Dazzler O'Dea called her that. And Birdie, who is . . ."

"Was Diana always the ice maiden, Michael?"

His adam's apple plunged up and down; his throat was full of sinewy noises. "No," he replied simply.

"Would it embarrass you to tell me about her? The way she was? What she meant to you?"

Every muscle in his body was tense now. "Do you really want to know?"

"Not at all," she said. "But I want to hear you tell me."

"I don't see the difference."

She sighed. "I mean, if you had it all written down in an old diary and I came across it, I'd not bother to read it. Michael Raven aged twenty-odd doesn't much interest me nowadays. But Michael Raven rising thirty-seven . . ."

"Thanks so much for the reminder!" he interjected.

166

". . . talking about those dear dead days *would* interest me. It's funny – the things one must explain to a man you'd never dream of needing to explain to another woman!"

He shifted her a few inches on his lap, murmuring, "Whew! I'll tell you one thing – Michael Raven *aetat* twenty-odd could have supported the *processi falciformidae* of Lucy Fitzbutler *aetat* twenty-odd for far longer than is the case today!"

"That's a gallànt start!" she commented.

"Would you tell me about Dazzler then?" he asked.

"Dazzler!" she exclaimed in surprise. "Anyway, I *did*. Ad nauseam, I would have thought. But you never said a word about Diana."

There was a further thoughtful pause before he said quietly, "Whose name should I have said, then – if not Dazzler's? Why did it surprise you that I chose him rather than . . . well, who?"

She laughed and hugged him hard. "Oh, Michael! You should be a doctor of the mind, not of the body. To you all hearts are open, all desires known, and from you no secrets are hid."

This, she realized, came perilously close to mocking the Book of Common Prayer; but it added so many prongs to her veiled attack that he did not know which to fend off first. "Let's wait until we're in bed," he said. "It's a more suitable time for grown-up fairytales."

She nuzzled his ear with the tip of her nose. "You sound like a barrister pleading for an adjournment."

He chuckled, turning her accusation into a shared joke at his expense, which, of course, enabled him to ignore it thereafter.

She rose and smoothed her dress down. "Maybe a small sherry," she said, returning to the tantalus. "Since you seem unable to drink yours without company!" She waved a hand at his almost untouched glass.

He pulled a face and laughed again, as if she had hit him below the belt. "I was suffering from a rare disease," he explained. "Elephantiasis of the lap. But I seem to have found the cure."

"Good!" She toasted him ironically with her thimbleful glass.

"You're in an odd mood tonight, darling," he said. "You're not ill, are you?"

She swallowed the sherry down in one small mouthful. "No, Michael – that's one thing I'm not!"

N ow!" Lucy said as she snuggled back into Michael's arms; but all he did was yawn rather ostentatiously. "You promised," she added. "You bought my silence all evening with that promise, and if you think I'm going to go to sleep without hearing your opinion of Miss Kelly . . ." She chose not to mention his promise to tell her about Diana, too.

167

"Oh very well," he groaned. "But I warn you now – it wasn't worth waiting for. I neither like nor dislike the Kelly woman. As a person she hardly exists for me. I mean our spheres never cross from one week to the next. But what I do resent is the effect she's had on the *other* nurses."

"Ah-ah!" Lucy warned. "I told you! Never let Diana hear you lump her among them."

"All right – her effect on the nurses. It's Birdie-Kelly-this and Birdie-Kelly-that from dawn till dusk. And I'll bet they spend half the night at it, too – tearing her character to shreds. Did you keep chickens at home?"

"Chickens?" she echoed in surprise.

"Yes. Did you ever stand and watch a run full of hens?"

"Oh yes. At Philip's place. The de Renzis always kept hens."

There was a hesitation before he said, "Ah, of course. Well, did you ever notice how they'd sometimes all pick on one particular hen and make her life a misery? The other hens, I mean. The cockerel never seemed to take part. Did you ever see that?"

She chuckled.

He asked why.

"You won't believe it," she replied, "but Philip had one hen that the others persecuted like that. And one day she laid all her innards along with the egg – all her egg-laying bits, anyway. They hung down out of her tail like a shambles. And the other hens pecked her to death. Or we thought they were going to. They pecked all those bits off her . . ."

He interrupted queasily. "The children would simply love this story – why don't you save it for them?"

"No, but listen – this is the bit you won't believe. The hen didn't die. Instead, over the next month or so, she grew wattles under her beak, and a bright red comb, and long arched tail plumage, and she, or he, began to crow and fight the other cock and generally lord it over the very hens who used to persecute her before she changed sex. So all I can say is, our heckling nurses had better take care!"

"And then the five little piggies flew home!"

"I said you wouldn't believe me, but you can ask Philip. By the way, he's renting a set of chambers from the Flannerys at Porterstown House. He told me this evening."

"This evening?" It surprised him. "I didn't see him here this evening."

"I met him out in the kitchen garden. He wants to demolish the potting shed to reuse those small yellow bricks."

There was a longish pause before he said, "Well, that's what *he* was doing in the kitchen garden."

"I chased a dog fox in there," she told him. "But I couldn't follow his tracks. The grass is so beaten down – you'd think half Mount Venus has been in there today."

Would he now tell her about being in there with Diana? she wondered.

He said: "The nurses, I expect. It seems they hang their intimate laundry in the old pheasant run to dry."

You'd think he was talking about the habits of the natives on some remote spice island.

"So I discovered," she said. "Not just the nurses, either. There was some rather fetching underwear in pink there, too."

The advantage of lying against him like that was that she could feel the tensions come and go; he almost trembled with it when she mentioned Birdie Kelly's underwear. She could not believe it – especially as he had been as relaxed as anything when speaking about the woman herself earlier.

"No prizes for guessing whose it was!" she added heavily.

"Really?" He sounded bored but his muscles were still tense.

"She brought no pegs. She just flung them doubled-up over the lines. Slapdash. Bright colours. Birdie Kelly or I'm no judge."

He laughed – and then coughed while continuing to laugh.

"I can't think what's so funny," she said coolly.

He apologized. "It's just that I was out there, too, this afternoon – when you and the Kelly woman were picking flowers. I waved but you were too busy talking. I was looking for Diana. When I saw the laundry I was sure it was hers – the coloured stuff."

"Diana?" Lucy echoed incredulously. "Never!" Then, realizing she had missed an opening, she did an about-turn: "On the other hand, Michael, you probably know more about it than me!"

He laughed again, rather more thinly, and said, "Are you sure it was the Kelly woman's?"

"There was only one stocking there," she told him. "That's what my Aunt Gertie used to call slut's economy – washing only one stocking because the other would last a day or two longer. It's hardly Diana's way, now is it?"

"No . . ." he said vaguely.

"And did you in fact meet her?"

He breathed in deeply, as if consigning all their previous conversation to limbo, and said firmly, "Yes. We had quite a talk, too. A personal talk, I mean – our first since . . . well, since our paths have crossed again."

She let out a long breath she had not realized she'd been holding. "And?"

"And we decided we'd been coping rather well with the obvious . . . awkwardnesses – what's the proper word?"

"Strains? Anyway, I know what you mean."

"And that it was a good thing to talk about them – get them out in the open. Like a wound."

"And it is still a wound, is it?"

He did not answer at once. Then he said, "The trouble with words

169

is that they pin things down. Emotions can't be pinned down. Not the faint ones, anyway – the dying embers and the new little sparks. They're so fleeting – and so changeable."

"Like a candle flame."

"Yes, exactly. Because you can blow out a candle flame and it's gone. But that doesn't abolish the word *flame* itself. The word lives on – like a spirit without a body, or a ghost without a house to haunt. It demands to be applied to *something* out there. D'you see what I mean?"

"You've never told me exactly how you and she broke it off, Michael. Was it she or you who wanted most to end it?"

He sighed. "I was the one who said the actual words – but that doesn't mean a thing."

"It probably did to Diana!" She tried to recruit his agreement with a laugh.

But he remained solemn. "You know yourself, now, that if you had wanted to break off *our* engagement but didn't want to say the dread words, you'd have found a way to provoke me into saying them instead."

"And that's what she did?"

"In my opinion, yes. She might not agree, though. Diana is two people."

"You mean, for your own part, you'd have happily continued the engagement? You'd have married her, too, if she hadn't pushed you into breaking it off?"

He shook his head and, although she was deliberately not looking him in the face, she knew he was lying there, gritting his teeth. "I don't know," he said at length. "How can I possibly know? That's what I mean about words pinning things down. These words I've been using – they're really just comments, guesses, conjectures . . . my own one-sided views. But you're seeking the actual *truth*. For that, you'd have to ask Diana for her version, as well. And any friends she confided in at the time – because perhaps she's tidied up her memories a bit, too."

"Too? You mean that's what you've done with yours?"

She felt him nod. "We've all committed acts we're ashamed of – and said things we'd rather call back and *unsay*." After a pause he added, "The real question is – if it's all in our minds, if all we've got to rely on is our own memories, is there any truth left to discover? That sort of truth is like cloud formations. Once they've gone past, they only exist in the mind, too. Think of all the magnificent clouds you've seen in your life – things that took your breath away and made you say, 'I'll never forget this sight!' Would you stake your life on remembering them accurately now?"

She shook her head. "But I could paint something like them. I could do a painting that would help you understand how it felt to have my breath taken away. And *that's* what I feel is missing when you talk about the time you were engaged to Diana. Not a day-by-day journal but . . . just how you felt."

He put his arms around her and hugged her. "The other difficulty I have, my darling, is that the Michael Raven who loved Diana Powers didn't even know of your existence. The love I have since discovered with you is Mount Everest compared with the mere Mount . . . well, Hill of Howth I felt with her."

She was sure he had been on the point of saying Mount Venus but had remembered the other connotations of the name just in time. Blurred images around the words *Michael, feeling, Diana* and *Mount Venus* stirred her to a sudden rage, so unexpected she could not at once control it. Then, before she could stop herself, she blurted out, "Did you and she ever . . ." She hesitated the merest fraction of a second, long enough to consider saying ". . . kiss?" – but long enough, too, to realize how feeble and hypocritical it would sound – ". . . sleep together?" she concluded.

She held her breath. The shocking words rang on into the silence that now gripped both of them.

"I mean . . ." she stammered. She would give everything she owned to unsay those words now.

"I know what you mean," he said coldly. His arms fell slack, no longer holding her.

"I'm sorry!" She turned and clamped her body tight to his, hugging tight enough for both of them. "Oh, darling! I didn't mean to ask that. I don't know why I said it. I'm sorry, I'm sorry, I'm *sorry!*"

He said nothing, but she felt his heart hammering fourteen to the dozen. Was it anger at her impudence? Fear at how close to the truth her question had probed? Or . . . desire for her?

"Make it up again?" She wriggled her body sinuously against his.

"No!" he cried in a voice tinged with anguish – or, she realized with horror, it could have been disgust. He seized her roughly by her arms and bent his knees under her thighs, turning sideways and heaving her off like a wrestling opponent. Yet for all his determination there was a gentleness at the heart of his action, and he held her firmly but not severely at arm's length at its conclusion.

"Michael?" There was pain and fear – and bewilderment – in that single word.

"Is there anything you want to tell me, Lucy?" he asked calmly.

Tears welled behind her eyelids; she swallowed heavily. "No," she whispered.

"Very well." He turned his back to her. "It's another busy day tomorrow."

The tears began to flow. She cried as stealthily as she could manage but could not help the sudden intakes of breath that punctuated her silent sobs. He must have been aware of her weeping, she thought. His deep and regular breathing was nothing to do with sleep; she knew how it sounded when he had genuinely nodded off. He might as well be saying, "Cry away, my dear – see if I care!"

Eventually, when she had no more tears to shed, she managed to nod off herself – only to be woken in the small hours when Michael rose to pay a call of nature. Normally he would use the chamber pot in the night commode but on that night – no doubt because he did not wish to wake her up and risk a further conversation – he slipped from the room.

She lay in bed, listening to him trying to move without making the floorboards creak – and only then did it dawn on her that he was going the wrong way, not at all in the direction of the water closet. In a flash she was up and, slipping her dressing gown round her shoulders, made a better fist of crossing the floor silently than ever Michael had managed.

Her immediate thought was that he was going to wake Diana – to tell her, perhaps, of their conversation and of her, Lucy's, foul question. The direction he took did nothing to contradict that possibility. Along the passage he crept, past the nursery, past one of the spare bedrooms, down the new stair to the floor below, where the passage led directly to Diana's apartments; true, a new door barred that passage but it was locked on the Ravens' side, so it was no very formidable obstacle. She noticed he was holding something, a small bundle, in one hand. Just before he reached the locked door, he came to his private study, which he then entered.

Lucy longed to creep along the passage and see what could have induced him to slip down here in such a clandestine fashion in the depth of the night, but she realized that if he came out as quickly as he had gone in, she would have nowhere to hide; so she stayed at the foot of the stairs and strained her ears for whatever she might glean.

The only sound she heard, a few seconds after he had entered his study, was of his big, black medical bag being open and shut. Its brass clasp had an unmistakable snap. Then the pale oblong of light from the door, cast upon the passage wall, darkened and she realized he was coming back out again. She just gained the safety of the nursery as he started mounting the stair. By long habit she checked on the children's breathing and then, as he reached the head of the stair, slipped out into the passage again.

"Oh, hallo!" she whispered in surprise as she closed the nursery door behind her. "Sleepwalking?" Whatever the bundle was, he had left it down in his study.

"Sorry," he whispered back, taking her arm. "Did I wake you? I tried to be as quiet as I could."

"Burglars?"

"No." He laughed with little humour. "I woke with a headache. I thought I'd try out that stuff Bayer sent us. Aspirin."

She yawned. "I thought I heard one of the children wandering."

"And they're all right?"

"Sleeping like little logs."

When they climbed back into the warmth of their bed she snuggled against him and whispered, "Sorry."

He grunted.

"D'you know what a watch-baby is?" she asked.

"Mmm?"

"They have them in Vienna. It's a baby who's born about nine months after the night-watch woke the parents up in the middle of the night."

"Mmm . . ." For the second time that night he adopted the deep and regular mode of breathing that had nothing to do with sleep. At length, however, it yielded place to the genuine article.

Then, with dawn already well advanced over Mount Venus, she slipped from their bed and tiptoed out of the room, past the nursery, down the stairs, along the passage, all the way to his study. She had the perfect explanation prepared and ready – she, too, had a headache and had decided to give the new Aspirin powder a try. But, as things turned out, she had no occasion to use it. Nor did she need to light a lamp to tell her what Michael had been doing with his medical bag – and, indirectly, what bundle he had carried down here an hour or so earlier.

From among the stethoscope tubes and bottles of liniment and boxes of pills she drew it slowly forth into the light of the new day: long, soft, and pink, with the neatest imaginable darn over the heel – it was Birdie Kelly's missing stocking.

At the start of each morning the medical director and the matron of Mount Venus (who had so far successfully avoided being Michael and Diana on such occasions) conferred over the coming day's business at the clinic. After his somewhat disturbed night, the medical director's patience was thin on that particular morning. As they ran down the list of patients – Mrs O'Donoghue, Miss English, Mrs Millar, Mrs Stephens, Mr Hely, Miss Skeffington . . . his patience grew thinner still with each successive Miss or Mrs. At length he exclaimed, "It's too much gynæcology, Matron, and not enough cardiology!" – almost as if he were blaming her for the imbalance.

She said frostily that it might have something to do with the fact that they had sixteen female patients under the age of forty and only seven of either sex in the cardio-vulnerable years above fifty. "We are going to need a specialist in gynæ," she concluded.

Michael said he'd have another talk with Dermot Walshe at the Rotunda. "He was in two minds when I last spoke to him, back in April. Perhaps now he can see we're under sail and haven't foundered at the first reef, he'll decide it's safe to join us."

173

Matron said that in that case it would be a good idea if Mister Raven could see Doctor Walshe that very day. There was a hint of personal reproof in her tone, causing Michael to raise an inquiring eyebrow.

"Well, Mister Raven," the matron continued, not in the least abashed, "with the best will in the world you cannot claim to have had much experience in gynæcology. Yet well over half our patients are in that category – which, I don't need to remind you, is notorious for what one might term 'healthy' deaths. In fact, between you and me, I think we may lose Mrs McDermott today. I'm surprised she lasted through the night. I think doctors are sending us patients they would rather like to get off their hands – precisely because their prognosis is so poor. 'Let Mount Venus take the odium of their deaths,' seems to be their motto."

Michael sighed and ran his fingers through his hair. "It was, to be sure, the risk we ran when we decided not to specialize in any particular branch. I thought my well-known interest in cardiology would bias our referrals in that direction."

Matron drummed her fingers on the arm of her chair. "So – will you see Doctor Walshe today?" she persisted.

He nodded glumly and she rose to go.

"Just one more thing . . . Diana," he murmured.

She spun round and stared at him in surprise – which turned to absolute amazement when she saw what he drew forth from his doctor's bag. "I've been hunting high and low for that," she lied. "Where on earth did you find it?"

"D'you want the truth?" he asked.

She shrugged awkwardly and resumed her seat.

"I took it off the line yesterday. Don't ask me why. I don't *know* why. I saw it hanging there and felt" – he hung his head and whispered the word – "compelled. There now." He handed it to her across the desk.

When she made no reply he went on, "D'you think it would have been better for me to lie – say I found it in the grass out there in the kitchen garden?"

"I don't think we ought to say another word about it . . . Michael." She used his name with reluctance.

He snatched the stocking back then and put on a little charade. "Oh, by the way, Matron, I found this stocking in the grass in the kitchen garden yesterday evening. It must belong to one of your girls. See it's returned to her, will you – and I know I can rely on you to put a flea in her ear about her carelessness?"

Diana did her best not to smile as she took it from him for a second time. "If I caught one of them wearing peach-coloured under-clothes!" she said menacingly.

Surprised, he said, "But it's all right for you, eh?"

"Of course. I'm the matron. Matron Rivers was the only one to be

174

let wear coloured underthings at the Adelaide."

"And that's the reason you wear colours now?" he asked in astonishment. "Just copying her?"

"I'm not copying her. She wore pale blue."

"No, what I mean is you never wore coloured undergarments until you became matron here?"

He was horrified to see her eyelids tremble – and tears gather between them. "How can you ask *that?*" she managed to whisper. "You of all people!"

He closed his eyes tight and stopped breathing for a moment. His fingernails pressed hard into his palms. "I'm sorry," he murmured at last. "Of course . . . of course!"

She breathed in deeply and blew her nose. "Why *did* you take it, Michael? I knew it was you. It had to be you."

He shook his head. "I don't know, Diana. It was lunacy." Suddenly he looked up at her and added, "But I did it out of reverence. Not . . . I mean, nothing . . . I wanted to . . . oh, it sounds so stupid now!"

"You wanted to what?"

"Nothing. I did it out of reverence – as I said. I just wanted to have something of yours."

"Something intimate," she added, despite the voice in her head screaming at her to stop the conversation this minute.

He shrugged awkwardly. "I suppose so."

She reached across the table and put the crumpled stocking in front of him. "By all means," she said quietly.

For a long moment their eyes locked and held. What was she doing? he wondered. What obscure pact was she proposing?

"Diana?" he said softly.

"Take it."

He shook his head. "How could I ever explain such a thing – if Lucy found it, I mean?"

She laughed, a little harshly. "There's not an ounce of guile in you, is there!"

Almost as an aside she added, "Not enough to be useful, anyway."

"How then?" he urged.

She tilted her head pityingly. "Oh, Michael! It'd be the easiest thing in the world. You were testing the nurses on first aid and they were all running around like headless chickens, screaming that the cupboard with the tourniquets was locked and you told them not to be such fools because they were all wearing two excellent tourniquets on their persons! Voilà!"

He managed a genuine laugh at last, even though he continued to shake his head. "Lucy'd never believe it. She's convinced this stocking belongs to Birdie Kelly!"

Diana's cool self-possession evaporated and her jaw fell. "You mean she's already discovered it?"

He explained how Lucy had gone out to the pheasant run yesterday and had jumped to the conclusion that the garments could only belong to the Kelly woman. "She doesn't believe you could possibly wear anything so decorative and feminine," he concluded.

"Oh she doesn't, does she!" Diana clamped her jaw tight and her lips vanished in a thin line. "Has she told you she's expecting yet?"

He was going to pass the matter off with a vaguely ambiguous reply but his hesitation answered for him. "For some reason she's set her mind against telling me this time," he said. "I can't think why."

"Can't you?" she asked rather sharply, implying she could hardly believe he was so dense.

He frowned at her. "You mean you can? Has she spoken to you about it?"

"Very nearly. But she held back at the end. Perhaps she was afraid I'd come blabbing to you." Again under her breath she added, "And perhaps she would have been right."

"And why would that be so dreadful?" Michael shook his head as if the whole world were going mad around him. "Why shouldn't I know?"

"Because of what you'd say and do, Michael."

"For example?"

"The world is full of healthy women who have nothing better to do with their time than cultivate an interesting affliction. We have several specimens of the breed under this roof. But Lucy is not one of them."

He stared at her in bewilderment.

"Oh, come, Michael!" she exclaimed. "What's the first thing you're going to do when she finally decides to tell you?"

He shrugged awkwardly. "Express my joy, I suppose . . . the things fathers usually do at such times."

"And they include . . .?"

His face crumpled with impatience – a parody of pain. "I hate this sort of lead-me-by-the-hand interrogation. Lucy does it too. Why don't you just say what's on your mind and be done with it?"

"It's not what's on *my* mind, Michael. But I imagine it's very much on Lucy's – the dread of being treated like an invalid for the next six months . . . or however long it is."

"Has she told you that?"

"I already explained, Michael – Lucy hasn't said a word to me. But she's young, fit, and healthy. And during my time in nursing I've met enough women like her to know that their greatest dread when they're expectant is being wrapped up in cotton wool and not allowed to do anything – which is what you'd insist on with her."

"That's absurd!" he exploded. "It's like accusing me of *treating* patients. What else is one to do with them?"

"You see!" Diana raised her hands in an I-rest-my-case gesture. "I'm surprised you haven't started already – no more laundry scrutiny . . . use the lift, not the stairs . . . stay in bed till ten . . . sleep every afternoon . . . there's really no end once you set your mind to it."

"To what?"

"Power, Michael. The exercise of power." She smiled shrewdly. "Incidentally why haven't you already started? Do you doubt she's expecting?"

He shook his head.

"So why haven't you started handing out the prohibitions?"

"Because she hasn't told me yet. How can I say she's got to rest without giving a reason?"

"Oh, isn't it complicated! The doctor can't lord it over the patient until the patient admits she's ill! And if she refuses to admit it . . ." A delighted laugh completed the thought.

Her point – that he was engaged in some obscure exercise of power that had nothing to do with medical rights and wrongs – escaped him but he felt no desire to pursue it. "You speak as if it's all . . . I mean, it's not easy for the husband, either, you know."

She let the remark go by, though its implications were not lost on her.

"And another baby's the last thing we need," he added bitterly. "Just at this moment."

She made no reply to that, either.

He pushed her stocking toward her. "For God's sake, take it!" he said.

While she rolled it up he continued, talking half to himself. "Six months," he mused. "Novemberish. That means she started it in . . . April."

"She?" Diana echoed accusingly.

"Well, it was certainly no carelessness on *my* part."

She smiled thinly. "I can't spend the entire day passing the same damning comment on your qualifications in gynæcology, Michael."

"Ha ha!" he responded, though his tone was rather kindly. Then with genuine warmth he added, "I'm sorry – truly. I've obviously embarrassed you, talking about such matters. I have no right to involve you. Forgive me. It's just that I'm at my wits' end sometimes, Diana. There's no one else with whom I could possibly discuss such affairs – if Lucy won't say a word, I mean. But I won't embarrass you any further." He began to shuffle the papers on his desk, though not to any great purpose.

It was a Michael Raven she had almost forgotten – not completely, because the moment she saw him revealed once again, now, the memory returned as strong as ever. When he was pushed to the wall, he knew exactly how to turn around and ask a woman for help – to throw himself on her mercy, almost. And he could do it without sacrificing the strength of his character in the smallest degree. He was not a strong man suddenly exposed as being weak at the core, but a

177

man strong enough to reveal a weakness and somehow gain in strength by it. Years ago she had supposed he did it deliberately, choosing his moment and playing her as an angler plays a salmon. But now she realized it was him; he had no more control over it than he had over the colour of his hair. She could like him for it, or dislike him, just as she was free to like or dislike his dark wavy hair; but she could not blame him for it, nor hold him morally accountable.

In short, he did not topple her from her high horse, she fell willingly, even knowingly. "I'm sorry, my dear." She reached across the table and gave his wrist a warm, friendly squeeze. "If I can help . . . if it would help to talk . . . I'll listen. I shouldn't have been so sarcastic just now. I really meant it as a piece of good advice. Don't treat Lucy like an invalid."

He stared uncomfortably round the room, not quite meeting her eye in passing. She realized she had somehow, unwittingly, turned the tables on him. He had tried to quell her sarcasm and general frostiness by tweaking at the tender elements within her. But now, by yielding at once, without even token resistance, she had made it impossible for him to climb back on *his* high horse, too. "But she must be *sensible*," he insisted.

"Why not have a word with Doctor Walshe?" she suggested, crossing her fingers and hoping, for Lucy's sake, that Dermot Walshe's views were as liberal as one or two of her nursing friends had claimed. "Where will he live, by the way? He's married, isn't he?"

Michael nodded. "To Janet Delaney, as was – the Delaneys who have that house by the bridge at Leixlip. They have four children – about the age of ours. Three boys and a girl, I think. Lucy could tell you the seed, breed, and generation of them. I don't know where they'll live. He could even come out from Dublin each day. To get back to what we were saying just now – don't you feel isolated here, as Matron, I mean?"

"You mean lonely?"

He nodded uncomfortably. "Except that the word has other overtones. I mean lonely-because-of-being-Matron – lonely because you're the ultimate nursing authority, just as I'm the ultimate medical authority, inside these walls. We have to decide, and to take responsibility for our decisions. And we can't discuss them with anyone – or not too much – because every time we do so we nibble away a bit of our authority. It's a new sort of loneliness for me."

Before she could respond, however, he added, "D'you feel you've *arrived*, Diana? Because, observing you from outside, that's what it looks like. I didn't really know you as Ebenezer's nurse but Lucy described you as rather shy and retiring. Yet, watching you here over the last few months, I'd guess you were absolutely in your element. You wear your authority as naturally as if it were bespoke for you. Is that how it feels – from your point of view, I mean?"

She smiled, none too warmly. "If it's compliments day today, I want to tell you, Michael – you give a very good performance as medical director, too." As she spoke she rose and crossed to the door.

"Why do you snap at me so often?" he asked. "You fend me off always. Why?" He tried to take his eye off her figure but could not.

"I wonder!" she said as she went out, omitting to close the door behind her.

Dermot Walshe was highly regarded at the Rotunda, but only by the nurses and patients, so that didn't count. As far as those in authority were concerned, he had every conceivable disadvantage. He was young (well, thirty-seven, but young by *their* standards), ambitious, brilliant, good looking, and popular – the sort of fellow anyone in authority would want to take down a peg or two. So Michael's original proposal that he should be in on the ground floor at Mount Venus had seemed decidedly attractive. Even so, he would probably have soldiered on at the Rotunda. It was, after all, one of the greatest hospitals in the world and they could not keep him down for ever. What tipped the balance and made him accept Michael's proposal the second time was a rumour – and it was never more than that – to the effect that his beds were about to be reduced. They would never have carried out the threat, of course, but the very idea that they could let such a scurrilous suggestion circulate, as a way of bringing him to heel, made him so angry that he determined to resign the moment Michael spoke to him.

His wife Janet, however, persuaded him to take a week to think it over – a course that Michael was also prudent enough to urge upon him as well. "Why not spend Saturday and Sunday at Mount Venus?" he suggested. "Bring the children. We can put up camp beds and they can all pig it in the nursery. And you can have one of the rooms that are almost ready to receive patients."

Janet Walshe eyed him suspiciously. "What does *almost* ready mean, Mister Raven?" she asked.

Michael grinned. "It means no doctor has yet seen fit to refer us a patient who might occupy it, I'm afraid."

They accepted the invitation. After Michael had left, Janet said, "I remember him as a student. I like him. I always did – despite what happened at that ball at the RCS. But I can't imagine him in charge of anything. He's far too nice."

Her husband nodded. "It's going to be rather awkward, that – working for a medical director I actually like."

"He married the Honourable Lucinda Fitzbutler, didn't he – her home was just down the Liffey from us."

"Ah yes, of course. I'd forgotten. Did you know her as a child?"

Janet shook her head. "There was about four years between us.

But I knew her by sight – and I'll tell you this: She wasn't that rather stunning young lady he brought to the famous RCS ball! D'you remember?"

"With the blazing red hair? I'll say! Especially after what *you* said about her!"

She gave a conspiratorial grin. "I wonder what became of her?"

"I'll ask him on Saturday."

She punched his arm. "Don't you dare!"

Saturday came and they arrived at Mount Venus, bringing Willy, Meg, Henry, and Timothy with them. "Tiny Tim," being only two, remained piggy-back on his father's shoulders; the others, being nine, seven, and four respectively, invaded the place like marauding Goths.

Lucy greeted them on the front steps, apologizing that Michael was busy with one of the patients. He was, in fact, with Ebenezer O'Dea and their meeting was of a financial rather than medical character.

"I saw your father only last month," she told Janet as they sauntered upstairs to the guest room, which was next door to Ebenezer's set. "Looking wonderfully fit, too. I heard old Gallagher had him under the knife at Easter, was that right?"

Janet, slightly taken aback, agreed that it was.

"Well, he has an enviable constitution, that's all I can say. He must be the same age as my father? Late sixties? But you wouldn't say he's a day over fifty, to look at." They reached the head of the stairs. Tiny Tim, hearing the laughter from the nursery, struggled down from his father's shoulders and toddled off in search of the other children.

Lucy skipped ahead of him and opened the door. The racket doubled in volume. She closed it behind him and they revelled in the comparative silence once more. She, meanwhile, prattled merrily on. "Your room is along this corridor. Oh, and here's Matron. Miss Powers. She trained at the Adelaide at the same time as my husband. This is Doctor and Mrs Walshe, Matron."

Janet Walshe turned and received the surprise of her life.

Diana shook her hand and said, "I know Doctor Walshe, of course."

Janet glanced sharply at her husband. "Do you?"

He echoed the question as he shook her hand.

"By reputation, I mean," Diana added. "It will be a great honour for all of us here at Mount Venus if you decide to move, Doctor Walshe."

When they reached their room Lucy asked if they'd like ten minutes or so to change into something more casual. Janet, who considered their dress to be already casual enough, accepted the suggestion nonetheless. Lucy told them to go back to the door she had opened for Tiny Tim and just walk in and give a shout – and trust they'd be heard above the din.

"Well, what d'you make of *that!*" Janet exclaimed the moment they were alone.

"Just walk in and shout?'" he asked. "The Fitzbutlers always were a fairly casual . . ."

"No!" his wife interrupted. "That matron. Surely you recognized her?"

He frowned.

"We were speaking about her only the other day. She's the flaming redhead Michael Raven brought to the ball that evening – the ones I caught *in flagrante delicto* behind the bust of Hippocrates."

Now it was his jaw that fell. "No!"

"I'd swear it."

He closed his eyes and shook his head. "But this is going to be most excruciatingly embarrassing all round."

She laughed. "Not for me, it isn't!"

"Does he know you know?" Dermot mused. "Probably not. I mean, we've met him enough times since. She doesn't know, either – the matron, I mean. Either that or she's the best since Sarah Bernhardt."

"She hadn't the first notion they were caught," Janet assured him. "Believe me, they were . . ." She waved a hand vaguely skyward. "Over the hills and far away. That's why I say it's no embarrassment to me. But *what* is she doing here? D'you think Lucy Raven knows all about it? She can't, surely."

"Lucy Raven knows absolutely everything. That's almost a Dublin bye-law."

"Not this little nugget, though," Janet said firmly. "No woman could put up with that." Her grin broadened. "But what if she does! What if accepting such an arrangement was her only way of preserving her own . . . No! We mustn't start speculating like this. It's quite disgraceful to go jumping to conclusions when we don't know the first thing about what's happening. All the same – it would explain why they got out of Dublin so fast. They could never hide such a ménage in Dublin the way . . . I mean, this is the perfect place to . . . but no, as I say, it's wicked to speculate." She seized his arm and hugged it tight to her bosom. "All the same, you absolutely *must* accept the offer now. I shan't rest until I know."

A few moments later, when they strolled out to join the Ravens, Ebenezer took the speaking tube from his ear and shook it angrily. "The bloody thing doesn't work at all," he grumbled.

Birdie Kelly kept her ear hard against the bottom of the tumbler, whose other end was pressed equally hard against the wall. "They've gone," she said a moment later, straightening herself up and returning the glass to its shelf in the medicine cabinet.

"What did she say?" he asked stretching his arms toward her. "Sit down and give your brains a rest. I could hear she was doing all the talking but divil a word could I make out."

She skipped across the rooms and settled herself in his lap. "She's after catching himself and Matron in fragrant delight or something. He said Matron looks a bit like Sarah Bernhardt – I heard of her."

"*In flagrante delicto?*"

"That's what I'm after saying."

"Where? And when? Did she say that?"

"She said something about hypocrites going bust. There was a hole in the page there."

"It must have been all those years ago," he said, thinking aloud. "It couldn't be recent, not unless it's *very* recent. And I'll swear it's not recent at all. Did she say anything else?"

"No, it was all about Matron and Mister Raven – and herself, sure. Did she know what was going on under her nose . . . and was she tolera-a-atin' it, like – questions like that."

The oul' fella seemed a bit slow on the uptake today so she undid two buttons of her blouse and fanned the air in and out of her bosom, giving him plenty to see if only he'd bother to look. "Lord but 'tis a warm day that's in it," she murmured.

She might as well not have bothered, though. "Do up those buttons," he said mildly, "and slip across the passage into the laundry room. Take the tumbler with you and see what you can hear."

She pouted and fumbled with the buttons in case he might change his mind. He understood then and, raising his hand, gave her left breast a gentle caress through the silk of her blouse. "My eyes and ears," he murmured affectionately. "You're the shadow of the western world, so you are."

She went with better grace then. When he was alone he murmured, "My zoo!" and chuckled heartily.

I f there was a moment when Michael lost all doubt about the wisdom of inviting Dermot Walshe to join the partnership at Mount Venus, it was on that very first Saturday morning when, while looking over the clinic, they came to Mrs McDermott's room. Despite Diana's pessimism of the previous day, the woman had hung on one more night and, though drifting in and out of consciousness, was still breathing regularly and strongly. He invited Dermot to give an opinion. The speed and confidence with which the man determined the abnormal size and position of her womb, merely by tapping her abdomen, was amazing. But that was only the beginning. He then took a Ferguson speculum – the simplest and cheapest there was – and proceeded to the most thorough examination Michael had ever witnessed. "A text-book lesson in itself," was how he described it later.

Dermot in professional guise was serious and monosyllabic, which was all the more noticeable since he was usually so affable and talkative. "Polyps," he grunted at one point.

"Recent?" Michael asked hopefully.

Dermot shook his head. "'Fraid not old boy. But you'd never detect them by feel alone. Too gelatinous. What treatment has she had?"

"Glycerine pledgets, nightly. And, of course, rest."

Dermot sniffed. "Have you a duckbill speculum?" he asked.

Diana sent the nurse to fetch the item.

"We also have Cusco's bivalve speculum," Michael told him.

"Return it to him at once!" Dermot joked. Then, more seriously, he commented, "You're well equipped, I'll say that." After a pause he gave a dry laugh and added, "You know what the real problem is?"

"We were rather hoping you'd tell us," Michael replied.

"And so I will. I don't just mean our patient's problem here. I mean all of them – all our patients and all their problems. They all boil down to the fact that my wretched profession is split right down the middle over a futile argument as to whether inflammations and congestions are the things to treat or whether it's all due to morbid displacements and abnormal dispositions of the uterus. Is our patient unconscious, by the way?"

Diana lifted one of Mrs McDermott's eyelids and nodded.

He continued. "It's quite clear she has a hypertrophied womb, with some degree of subinvolution. She was delivered about two months ago, at a guess?"

Michael nodded.

"That's the prime cause, obviously. But the cervix is also granular and abraded-looking – which may be pathological in itself or it may be a direct consequence of the displacement – eversion of the membrane and all that. Why can't I tell you for certain? Because my profession cannot make up its mind! And I think that is a thundering disgrace, don't you?"

Michael could not tell whether Dermot was making a veiled attack on him for accepting difficult cases like Mrs McDermott, cases over which even gynæcologists would argue among themselves – or was he simply saying, "You need me here, old man!" Either way, Michael did not see himself putting up much argument. He was out of his depth with this particular patient and the clinic did desperately need someone with Dermot Walshe's skills.

"Which side of the debate do you come down on?" he asked.

"Both!" Dermot chuckled. "And why not? If a thorn in the finger causes inflammation, we remove the thorn *and* treat the inflammation, don't we? The physical and the pathological, both. Why not here? Sometimes we're too clever for our own good."

The nurse arrived with the duckbill speculum and he stooped to complete his examination. As soon as he had placed the instrument in

183

position, Diana took over and held it without being asked. He smiled approvingly at her and said, "Good. You've done this before."

She nodded.

When he had finished he led them outside, leaving the nurse to make Mrs McDermott comfortable again. "I think you were quite right to avoid anything too heroic before now," he said tactfully, "but in my opinion it's time to start. My recommendations are: four leeches on the cervix by day, repeated until the granulation subsides. Irrigation with two gallons of hot water, morning and night. And a glycerine of ichthyol pledget overnight. You should change to an iodized pledget when the abrasions have healed a little. I'd hope to see a considerable improvement within a week. Then one can start tampering with the morbid anatomy. However, a fair degree of cystic degeneration has already occurred, and that, as you know, is irreversible. So I fear she will be unable to bear another child."

He saw a fleeting smile twitch at Diana's lips and raised his eyebrows. She, of course, would never have spoken without invitation, but now she remarked, "I doubt she'll complain at that. She has seven already and the oldest is only twelve."

When they had completed the round of the entire clinic they thanked Diana and then went out into the garden in search of their wives. Michael led him by way of the old stables and outbuildings, where, sometime in the near future, he intended establishing a proper pathology lab.

"What's your overall opinion, old man?" he asked.

Dermot checked that they truly were alone before he said, "Where did you find your matron? She is one of the best, let me tell you."

"We're well aware of that." Michael ran his finger round his collar.

"And so young."

"Mmm." Michael agreed.

Dermot tried another tack. "I have an odd feeling I know her – I mean I've met her somewhere. Not recently. But she's not one you'd forget in a hurry, is she!"

"I suppose not. Perhaps she was at the Rotunda?"

Dermot pounced. "You mean you don't *know*? Surely you interviewed her yourself?" He chuckled, to soften the critical note. "And if our positions were reversed, I'm sure Janet would have insisted on interviewing her, too! Do she and Mrs Raven get on well?"

"Ah . . ." Michael began awkwardly.

Dermot cut in. "Forgive my asking, of course. I mean, in one way it's no damn business of mine. And if I were being invited to consider a post in a large general hospital, it would be impertinent to ask the chief how well his wife got on with the matron. But in a smaller institution like this, such alliances and factions are all-important. I'm sure you understand?"

Michael saw the chance to broaden – that is, divert – the

conversational stream. "Of course," he replied. "In fact, I think there's one thing *you* don't understand, if I may say so. You called me chief, just now. But if you do decide to join us, then, as far as all gynæcological cases are concerned, *you* would be the chief. Cardiology would be another matter altogether."

"And welcome!" Dermot put in fervently. "Cardiology to me seems like trying to mend the gears on a motor you daren't switch off! And good fingertips is hard-got, as a carpenter once said to me! Rather you than me, anyway."

Michael laughed. "And I don't suppose we'll fall out over the assorted patients in between – the hypochondriacs, dipsomaniacs, malingerers, fatties, and professional invalids who, thank heavens, foot most of the bills. Talking of which, we ought to pay a courtesy call on Ebenezer O'Dea this side of luncheon."

There was a thoughtful pause before Dermot said, "Yes, I heard he had something to do with the place. It was the one fly in the ointment as far as Janet and I were concerned. How much say does he have?".

They had reached the engine house by now. Michael flung open the door and said, "How much d'you know about steam engines?"

Dermot took a histrionic step backward. "I know they tend to explode in amateur hands. Why?"

"Oh, I've had an engineer look over the pressure vessel – in fact, all the high-pressure side of it. Polished her up, too." He patted the gleaming flywheel. "She's a two-stage compound engine, double-acting. I thought we might try to steam her up this week-end – if you're game?"

"Don't say 'week-end' to Janet," he warned. "She thinks it's a vulgar Americanism."

"It probably is," Michael conceded. "Give me a better, though. Shall we have a go?"

Dermot tilted his head at a dubious angle. "It's not exactly part of the Live-forever Plan, is it. We'll see.' He turned back toward the door. "You were going to tell me about old Ebenezer O'Dea." As he returned to the courtyard he added, "You've got her *looking* quite splendid, anyway."

Michael showed him how he proposed to adapt several of the outbuildings to form the pathology lab. Dermot asked what they did with their specimens at present. "For bacteriology we use the Eli," Michael explained. "O'Hanrahan's first-rate in that field. Everything else goes to the Adelaide."

"The Adelaide!" Dermot clicked his fingers. "That's where I've seen your comely matron. I'm sure of it."

"You? At the Adelaide?" Michael looked at him askance.

"No fear!" He chuckled at the very thought. "No, it was years ago, at a nurses' ball. They had no objections to dashing and handsome young Roman Catholic doctors at the nurses' balls. *Is* she a Protestant? That would explain it."

Michael nodded vaguely and said, "You were asking about Ebenezer O'Dea."

"That must have been it, then." Dermot frowned pensively. "Come to think of it, *you* were there around that time, weren't you?" He grinned engagingly. "Don't tell me you knew her back then?"

Michael forced himself to laugh and pull rueful faces, as any gay dog would. "Bowled middle stump!" he exclaimed. "I knew her quite well, in fact. She helped me cram several papers. But, funnily enough, we lost touch completely after I qualified. The fact that she's Matron here now owes nothing at all to me and everything to Ebenezer O'Dea. She was his nurse when Mount Venus 'fell into his hands' – I say no more as to how and why."

"And you were his cardiologist?" Dermot guessed.

"I . . . advised," Michael replied vaguely. "But when I put the proposal before him to open a new clinic here, he insisted that Diana Powers should be Matron – otherwise not a penny. Fortunately she is, as you say, superb at her work."

"Does he interfere a lot? Ebenezer O'Dea, I mean."

Michael waved his hands in a gesture of impotence. "Yes," he admitted reluctantly, "but never on the medical side – except when it comes to his own treatment. But never with the clinic. However, he dips his oar in every other water. He likes to play God with people's lives. Oh dear, it's all so complicated. Let's talk about it when we've found the ladies. Lucy will explain it far better than I could – or describe it, anyway. I doubt anyone can explain it."

Dermot dipped his head in acceptance, though he was plainly longing to ask a dozen questions on the topic. "Let's talk about money, then," he said. "The filthy lucre. Does O'Dea hold all the pursestrings? I hear he's the sort of fella as would peel an orange in his pocket. Is everyone here on a straight salary?"

"That's one of the things we need to discuss this week-end, Walshe (if your wife will forgive the word). O'Dea *claims* that his interest is merely to preserve the capital value of the property – keep the fabric maintained, the grounds looked after, and so on. And I have to admit he charges us an absolutely nominal rent."

"Us?"

"Yes, we're a partnership. At the moment it's just three of us – me, Lucy and Diana Powers – as active partners. And then there are odd parents and great-aunts and things as sleeping partners, mainly to guarantee the loan we negotiated with the Royal Hibernian to set the place up. You'd be welcome to join the partnership and sink or swim with us – we're swimming rather well so far, in fact. Or you could work as straightforward consultant on the usual terms. Or you could become wholly salaried. That, as I say, is all to be discussed this week-end."

"While we get your steam engine going?"

Michael laughed. "When better?"

186

For all her pains, Birdie Kelly realized she would have little to report back to Ebenezer. The children had all streamed outside within seconds of meeting; the parents had exchanged conventional pleasantries for a few minutes and then the two men had gone off to do the rounds of the patients; a short while later their wives took their parasols and went out for a stroll through the grounds. Then the only sound she could hear in the tumbler was the rushing of her own blood in her ears, which, like rumbles in the tummy, she always found rather frightening. It was a miserable trawl for so much effort. She then decided that the oul' fella could do without her for an hour or two, and so she followed Lucy and Janet downstairs falling in discreetly behind them as they crossed the terrace.

Janet spoke about her children the whole way – what a martyrdom they were and how one was consumed with worry every second they were out of one's sight. Lucy noted that the children were in that perilous condition at that very moment and yet her companion did not *look* particularly consumed or martyred by anything. And then, Janet continued, what a nightmare it was maintaining them in clothes and bootleather, not to mention keeping it all clean and mended . . . on and on it went, all the way to the top of the steps that led up from the terrace to the glasshouses. There, however, you would have thought that children had suddenly been abolished, for the mother who was supposedly consumed with worry now clasped her hands in delight, folded them across her bosom, and exclaimed "Oh!"

"What?" Lucy asked, fearing that the woman had instantly spotted something she herself had failed to notice all these months.

"The *possibilities!*" Janet wafted a dramatic hand across the landscape before them.

Dead ahead and to their right the ground rose smoothly, forming the northern flank to the modest hill with the immodest name of Mount Venus. To their left it dipped to form a shallow bowl – or *cirque*, as Janet later called it – about three furlongs across, before rising to form the northeastern flank of that same eminence. Although it was, or had once been, garden, it was now a mixture of volunteer saplings and wild shrubs, somewhat tempered by marauding goats and stray sheep.

Lucy looked at her companion and saw a brightness in her eyes that had been entirely lacking when the conversation had been all to do with her children. "Don't you mean *capabilities?*" she suggested.

Janet frowned.

"You know – Capability Brown. It would be far nicer to be known as Capability Walshe, I'm sure, than Possibility Walshe!"

Janet laughed but soon became serious again. "Joking apart," she confided, "I suppose I'm giving away no secrets when I say that Dermot and I have practically agreed between us to accept your husband's offer – barring some quite dreadful discovery. But now I'll tell you – even if we hadn't, the sight of *this*" – again she waved her

187

hand across the slopes of Mount Venus – "would quite determine me. Don't tell me you have plans of your own for it? I couldn't *bear* it!"

Lucy had only the vaguest plans for those outer reaches of the garden, and they all began with the plough and the potato, followed by pigs – the cheapest way she knew of clearing land. But in any case she had been half-watching the antics of Birdie Kelly down on the terrace during Janet's little speech; she turned to her companion with a smile and said, "Let's walk over it together, shall we?" Then, over her shoulder to Birdie, she added, "I don't think Mister O'Dea pays you to play hopscotch, miss. And anyway, you can't play it without a stone."

A smile of petty triumph played about her lips as she watched the girl stroll despondently away.

"Who on earth was that?" Janet asked.

The smile faded and she replied, "Another child, I suppose. A challenge to our charity." Lucy linked arms with her companion and led her off into the landscape she had admired so fervently. "In the bold bad days of my youth," she went on, "when Dazzler O'Dea, the nephew of our landlord here, used to take me to the" – she stared conspiratorially about her and almost whispered the words – "*music halls*, there was a comedian called Kid van Winkle. His forte was that he could mimic children of five, six, seven to perfection – not just their speech but their quite extraordinary behaviour, too – all their odd movements. In fact, it was so perfect that one laughed as much out of horror as at the comedy, though he was extremely funny, too. But the horror was that you were suddenly forced to realize how much children of that age have in common with lunatics. It's much more than we like to admit. If grown-ups behaved like six-year-olds, we'd simply have to lock them away. Well, I want to tell you – Birdie Kelly, the young lady who was pretending to play hopscotch back there, reminds me often of Kid van Winkle."

"And Ebenezer O'Dea is her employer, you say? What on earth for? Not as a nurse, surely?"

"Oh no. He employs her to spy on us. To annoy us. To get us all up in arms. The nurses absolutely loathe her, especially since Ebenezer dismissed one of the best of them, Helen Lynch, and installed the Kelly creature in her place."

"Did you say Helen Lynch?" Janet asked.

"Yes. You possibly know her. She's not here at the present. She's taken two weeks' leave to sell . . ."

"Not Tim Lynch's widow? The Lynch who used to have six medical beds at Vincent's?"

"The same. Why d'you say it in that tone?"

"The poor dear!" Janet said. "And she's reduced to working here!" She saw the shock in Lucy's face and added hastily, "Well, I mean nothing against the nurses, of course. It's an excellent *start* for a girl. But for a *consultant's* wife! You know what I mean."

188

Lucy laughed. "I wouldn't call her 'poor dear' at all. I think she's happier now than she's ever been in her life."

"I'm sure, I'm sure." Janet was eager to make amends for her gaffe. "Actually I was thinking more of her late husband when I said that – such a dreadful case. You heard all about it, of course?"

Lucy was on the rack, stretched between the two most emotive needs of her soul: the desire to be let in on a secret, and the desire not to confess her ignorance of it. The former triumphed. "Only whispers," she replied.

"Well . . ." Janet's tone was conciliatory; secretly she was amazed that Lucy Raven – Dublin's foremost *quidnunc* – had not heard the scandal long ago. "It was kept pretty quiet, I must say – and mostly for poor Helen's sake. The fact is" – she paused and stared dramatically all about them, making quite sure they were not overheard – "old Tim Lynch used to lurk behind the ditches in country lanes – in this very locality, in fact – and knock young girls off their bicycles. He wore a rustic old hat and a false beard – looked a real ruffian. And while the poor girl was lying there all dazed, he'd whip off the disguises and stuff them in his bag and then rush to her aid, saying, 'All right! Fear not! I'm a doctor!' And then he'd caress them improperly under the pretence of feeling for broken bones."

Lucy exhaled through the astonished O of her lips.

"Of course, he did it once too often. One of his victims spotted the false beard in his bag while he was examining her. And the constabulary, too, were beginning to think it odd that his rescues coincided with so many of the bearded ruffian's attacks. Fortunately it never came to court. He retired quietly and took up private practice at Millicent."

"That's the property Helen is selling up now – that's why she's taken some leave."

There was a sudden, speculative gleam in Janet's eye. "I wonder . . . did she ever mention their old house at all? They used to live at the bottom of the hill here, on the outskirts of Rathfarnham. Did they sell that?"

Lucy shrugged. "I know the house, of course. We dined there once but Lynch and Michael never quite hit it off. There *was* something . . . well, *queasy* about him, wasn't there. Anyway, she's never mentioned it. I don't like to inquire too closely because I knew there was a whiff of scandal there. It would suit you perfectly, though – if you decide to join us here. And if she still owns it – and if she hasn't let it already, of course. A lot of ifs."

Janet nodded enthusiastically. "It hasn't much garden though," she added.

Lucy grinned and waved a hand across the landscape, mimicking the other's earlier grand gesture. "All the more time for *this*, then!"

"Yes!" Janet clapped her hands. And for the next ten minutes, as they wandered across the edge of the bowl toward the upper slope of

Mount Venus, she expounded her theory of landscape gardening in general and described, with much artistic hand-waving, what might be done with Mount Venus in particular.

She maintained that the commonly held notion of "a garden" – especially in municipal parks and the grounds of hospitals – was lamentable beyond words. Professional gardeners began their work on winter evenings with compasses, ruler, and graph paper, producing designs that would body forth in an ever-changing kaleidoscope of bedding plants, all summer long. "And," she concluded, "the *army* it takes to sow the seed, to pot them on, harden them off, bed them out, water them, hoe them, dig them up when they're done and then plant out the next wave . . . it's absurd! It's as if we're afraid of nature and have to tie her down in geometrical bondage."

To her a garden should look as if an artist had come in and arranged it, not a mathematician. An artist could make a sort of living sculpture out of the forms of the shrubs and perennials. Professional gardeners, having no imagination, just swept them to the back of the bed as a mere foil to their multicoloured geometries.

"By 'living sculpture' you mean topiary?" Lucy guessed.

Janet almost tore her hair out in frustration. "No! I mean using the *natural* forms of the plants, and their colours. Just imagine this *cirque* now, with paths that meander hither and thither among great beds of shrubs and perennial flowers – tall ones, short ones . . . fat round leaves and long spiky ones . . . and silvery feathers and big green plates . . ." Flecks of foam gathered at the corners of her mouth as the poetry of names overwhelmed her. "Viburnums and Rose of Sharon, pampas grass and mock orange, rhododendrons and guelder rose . . . great arches of laburnums . . . redhot pokers . . . lady's mantle . . ." She gasped for breath and, barely managing to recover it, plunged on: "Surprises round every corner – grassy knolls, sun dials, bird baths, benches in Wicklow granite, pergolas with rambling roses and clematis . . . oh, I can see it so clearly! If only I could somehow photograph this picture in my mind and show it you!"

"Many an architect has wished that!" called a voice behind them.

They spun round and Lucy exclaimed, "Philip! Where did you spring from?"

"Sorry! I made as much noise as I could," he said as he drew near. He was carrying a theodolite and a surveyor's clipboard dangled from his neck.

Lucy introduced him to Janet and then asked what he was doing.

"Going up to the seven-hundred-foot contour," he explained. "We have a spring at just over seven hundred feet at Porterstown and I want to know what parts of the garden could be fed naturally from it."

"And you can't do that from inside your garden, Mister de Renzi?" Janet asked.

Lucy was a little taken aback by her sharpness. She obviously resented Philip's intrusion (as she saw it), but took none of the customary pains to hide her feelings.

"Not all parts of the grounds are mutually visible, Mrs Walshe," he replied with a smile. "As with so many other problems in life, this one becomes soluble by getting well away from it."

Janet now wore a slightly hunted look, which amused Lucy. Janet's difficulty paralleled her own with Birdie Kelly – how do you go on being frosty with someone who refuses to respond in kind? Birdie simply went on laughing and babbling like a child; Philip continued to be charming and attentive.

"I could not help overhearing your remarks on gardening just now, Mrs Walshe," he commented. "It did my spirit a power of good, I must say. You somehow managed to put into words sentiments I have long felt but have utterly lacked the skill to express. I don't suppose you've written it all down somewhere, have you?"

Janet, now torn between her dying resentment at his intrusion and her growing pleasure at his flattery, said, "Why . . . no," in rather a feeble voice.

"What a shame!" Philip sighed. "I cannot seem to make the Flannerys understand. They *say* they want a romantic italianate garden yet they still expect flashy colours and more geometry than Euclid ever dreamed of."

Janet licked her lips nervously and said, "Er, where is this garden, if I may ask? Is that Porterstown House over the fields there?"

"I'll show you," he said, resting his theodolite. They were standing in the shadow of a hawthorn ditch, which had forced them to a halt. Philip consulted his map. "Would you say this is the lowest point of the ditch?" he asked. "It goes uphill both ways from this bulge here?"

The two ladies agreed that it did.

"Then," he announced, "we are *exactly* seven hundred feet above mean sea level." He spread the tripod and set the telescope at five feet above the ground, training it on Porterstown House and its demesne. "Voilà!" He stepped back and invited Janet to see for herself.

While she was thus occupied, he pointed at her and gave Lucy a nod of delighted approval. Lucy looked heavenwards and waited for Janet to be done.

Janet subjected the site to a most thorough scrutiny. "Oh yes!" she murmured ecstatically at last. "It has enormous . . ." She let the word hang as she rose to full height; then, smiling at Lucy, added, ". . . capabilities!"

"All suggestions gratefully received," Philip said.

"I hope I'm not being obtuse," Lucy put in, "but do these romantic-artistic-italianate gardens look after themselves? One just strolls around scattering seed and planting slips – is that it?"

Janet smiled mysteriously. "In certain circumstances," she said, "they can be established and kept up remarkably cheaply."

"For example?" Philip was all ears.

Once again she made a playlet of looking all about her before she replied. "It does occur to me that if one has a clinic for some forty or fifty patients, then between one and two dozen of them are bound to be convalescent at any particular moment. And one of the finest ways to convalesce is to renew one's communion with nature . . ."

"Free gardeners!" Philip interrupted in delight.

She stared at him, pretending to be haughty, and said, "Mister de Renzi! I regard that as an unnecessarily frank way of putting it!"

There was a scream from somewhere down near the kitchen garden, followed by a loud wailing, distressed but not frantic. The two women exchanged weary glances.

"An infant," Lucy said.

"Will there be a nurse in the vicinity, d'you think?" Janet asked.

Lucy sighed. "I'll go. You stay and talk about gardens with Mister de Renzi."

Of course, she did not for a moment expect Janet to agree; she was astonished to hear her say, "Oh, you are a brick!"

Lucy found all the children in the kitchen garden. Timothy Walshe and Portia, aged two and three respectively, were patients, being tended by nurses Meg Walshe and Alice, seven and eight. Charlie and Tarquin, nearly-seven and five, were up on the roof of the pheasant run (or ring-fort, as they now made-believe), defending it from the marauding Mongols, alias Willy and Henry Walshe – who were nine and four.

"Who screamed just now?" Lucy asked Alice.

"Screamed?" Her daughter looked at her in genuine puzzlement.

"Yes. Don't pretend you didn't hear it. I heard it and I was half a mile away up the hill there. Somebody screamed."

"My brother Henry screamed, Mrs Raven," Meg said.

Lucy stared across at the boys, none of whom now seemed to be in any kind of trouble. "Why?" she asked.

"They wouldn't give him back his arrows. Daddy says it's Willy's fault. Daddy says Willy doesn't consider a game a proper game unless he can make Henry scream."

"Ah!" Lucy was relieved. She knew better than to inquire what good arrows were when none of them had bows. "So your father's been here? He's seen all that" – she waved her hands at the boys defending and attacking the pheasant run – "and doesn't mind?"

Meg shook her head. "No, I haven't seen Daddy."

"How d'you know then?"

"Because, if you please, Daddy says the same about every game they play."

Lucy gave up and turned to leave. "They appear to be all right now, anyway."

"Excuse me, Mrs Raven, but aren't you going to say anything to us?"

Lucy frowned and then exclaimed, "Oh yes. You may all play for another ten minutes. Then you must come in and wash your hands."

"No, I mean to the boys – about playing dangerous games."

Lucy looked at her two sons on the roof and called out, "Char-ley!"

They all stopped for a moment and looked at her.

"Be careful how you break your neck falling down from there!" she cried.

To her great surprise both her sons swung themselves over the edge and clambered swiftly down to the ground, bringing great chunks of morning glory with them. It surprised Alice, too. She stared at her mother and said, "They're actually coming down!"

"Just showing off, I expect," Lucy said, and left them to finish their game.

Meg followed her departure open-mouthed. "Isn't she simply . . ." Words failed her.

"What?" Alice asked.

"My mummy would have screamed and gone running over there the moment she saw them."

"Oh. My papa says we should only be stopped doing things that could kill us. He says one broken leg beats a hundred dos and don'ts."

"My leg is mended," Portia announced firmly as she struggled to rise.

Her two devoted nursed pounced on her, eager to prove her wrong.

Actually, Lucy's complacency at the sight of her two boys rampaging around on a roof that was only eight feet high (and only six at its front edge), and that above soft earth and thick grass, had little or nothing to do with Michael's theories. She herself had hardly ever been stopped from doing anything as a child. She could remember incidents that – nowadays – would make her freeze in her tracks, clench her eyes, hunch her shoulders . . . and generally behave as if she were a doting mother to her bygone self. "Tightrope walking" across the top step of the weir by Shackleton's Mill . . . paddling her kayak into the millrace they used to have there before they installed the electric turbines . . . crossing Lord Iveagh's cattle bridge over the Liffey at Strawberry Beds, hanging underneath it, thirty feet above the water – no one had ever stopped her from doing any of these things. As a result, she thought, she was calmer in the face of danger than most other people she knew – although, as Dazzler had once pointed out, perhaps it was the other way about; perhaps she was *born* calmer, which enabled her to do those things without fear.

That was the second time she'd thought about Dazzler in the past half hour; yet before that she hadn't thought about him for a couple of weeks. Come to think of it, she hadn't seen him for a couple of weeks, either. She must ask his uncle where he'd gone.

She went into the glasshouse to cut a bunch of flowers for the luncheon table. She ought to go back and supervise the last-minute preparations, anyway. She still couldn't get over her surprise at Janet Walshe staying on like that with Philip de Renzi, a complete stranger to her. And this passion for gardening. When had *she* done any gardening of that grand, landscaping kind? Certainly not at their present house at Fairview Strand. Her people were gardeners, perhaps. Lucy tried to recall who Janet's parents were and faced a total blank in her mind, even though she'd been able to remember it all a week ago.

Panic seized her. She was losing her skill – her grip on the world. She closed her eyes and the glasshouse seemed to spin around her. And then it all came back. How absurd! The Delaneys of Leixlip! They were practically neighbours of the Fitzbutlers in Hermitage Lodge. They had that house by the Liffey with the long, straggly garden all down the northern bank. Janet could certainly have practised her Capability Walshe tricks there, if her people would let her. Lucy couldn't even remember what they looked like; their families hadn't mixed in the same circles much. Of course, Janet was five years her senior. Five and a half. She must try and work that into the conversation sometime – in a kindly way, of course. Sometime when Philip was around – because he'd never believe it to look at her, unfortunately.

Her rambling search for the finest blossoms took her to the far end of the glasshouse, where she could gain a slant view through the stableyard entrance. She got a glimpse of Michael and Dermot, wandering around the yard; Michael was gesturing at various outbuildings. She waved to attract their attention, though she realized there was little chance they'd notice. Then her attention was attracted by a movement among the heavy festoons of ivy that hung all around the old stone gatepost, which was at least twelve foot high. A moment later a body fell to the ground. When it picked itself up, she recognized Birdie Kelly and burst out laughing. It served her right, whatever she was up to out there.

The men had observed her fall, too, or at least heard her picking herself up. They both came running, though, by the time they reached her, she was on her feet again and brushing her clothing vigorously with the flat of her hand. Dermot folded his arms and stared at her; he was too far away for Lucy to read his expression but she could imagine it was one of incredulity. Michael, however, went round behind her and began picking off wisps of straw and ivy twigs.

194

Lucy, remembering the pink stocking, watched them like a travelling rat. At one stage he did something that made Birdie jump a couple of feet, half-crumpling on her right leg when she landed. She faced him then and shouted something, waggling a finger in his face. Michael brushed it aside and waved dismissively at her as he turned to leave.

She walked past them into the stable yard. Both men turned to watch her and must have noticed she was limping. One of them obviously called out, for she stopped and looked back over her shoulder.

Michael beckoned and she came to him, showing none of the reluctance her earlier temper would have led Lucy to expect; she was, indeed, a child – quick to flare up, quick to forget.

Michael squatted in front of her, with the stone gatestop right beside him. He patted it and she raised her foot and let it rest on the top. She lifted the hem of her skirt with a distinctly coquettish motion.

Dermot turned his back on them. It was probably the instinctive movement of a doctor not involved in whatever medical examination was in progress – in whom it would therefore be prurient to gaze at an exposed ankle. Lucy thought it an astonishing delicacy in a gynæcologist; it had the unfortunate effect of making him appear to be keeping cavey for Michael.

Michael made a careful examination of her ankle, obviously asking her to move it in various ways, and then asking her if it hurt. At length he dusted his hands and prepared to rise – whereupon Birdie, still standing on one leg, raised the other one high, plucked her skirts above her knee, and waved it round like an incompetent cancan dancer, laughing her head off, too. She almost tumbled backward, headlong on the ground once more; in fact, if Michael had not reached up and grabbed the hem of her skirt to pull it down again, she would have done so.

Still laughing, she skipped off into the stable yard, forgetting to limp until she was a good half-way across.

Michael retrieved his panama hat, which had been kicked off in the excitement, and the two men sauntered on toward the terrace, which was immediately below the glasshouse.

The incident, trivial as it was – and all of it explicable in terms of perfect innocence – left Lucy feeling profoundly disturbed. If it had not been for finding the stocking, she would probably have made nothing of it – or she would have teased the two men about it over the luncheon table . . .

The luncheon table!

Her hands were empty. She looked around for the flowers and saw they had fallen to the ground at her side. In some obscure way that only made the incident worse. She had to fight an urge to cry as she stooped to gather them up again. It was so unlike her.

195

They removed all the spare leaves from the big dining-room table, reducing it to its basic oblong. Despite the grandeur of the setting, luncheon was light and informal, with ale rather than wine; everyone admired the flowers. Lucy asked Philip to join them, to balance Diana's presence at the table. However, Ebenezer unbalanced it again by inviting himself at the last minute. Lucy sat at one end of the table, with Philip and Dermot to her left and right; Michael, at the other end, had Diana and Janet for company. Ebenezer inserted himself between Dermot and Diana. A small table was laid with one place at the far end of the room for Birdie Kelly; this had the unfortunate effect of placing her behind Lucy's back – and thus directly in Michael's field of view. Several times during the meal Lucy imagined Michael was smiling at her, only to realize he was smiling over her shoulder at the Kelly creature, instead – though whether it was at her antics or whether the smile was reciprocated she had no way of knowing. The mirror on the wall behind Michael was at just the right angle to show no more than the topmost frills of Birdie's bonnet when she sat up straight. It was most irritating.

Michael began by announcing that they were going to put the engine in steam that afternoon. Janet immediately asked if it would be safe. Lucy recalled young Meg Walshe's hints about her mother's timorousness and smiled. Dermot said risk was part of life, after all, and he wondered how many people had died in sorting out edible fungi from poisonous ones so that she, Janet, could spread her mushroom ketchup (which she was doing at that moment) with such blithe confidence.

Philip said that surely most of the risks people took in life nowadays did not involve physical danger at all. "That's half the problem," he concluded.

There was a silence as people tested this assertion against the circumstances of their own lives – and were left feeling slightly uneasy.

Ebenezer chuckled and said, "I imagine the mention of Vesuvius at a gay luncheon in Pompeii's heyday would have had a similar effect, young man."

Diana asked Philip what he had meant by saying it was "half the problem"?

He pointed out that most of the challenges and dangers primitive men and women faced must have been immediate and physical. The anxiety, the frenzy, the battle, followed by victory or defeat – it all started and finished between one sunrise and the next. "But only children have that privilege today," Philip went on. "People of our age face mental challenges and fight abstract battles that go on for months, even years. We get our blood racing every day – but to what purpose? Victory or defeat are forever round the corner. It's a wonder we aren't all reduced to gibbering wrecks." He turned to Michael. "You're a heart doctor, Raven. You know how the heart beats like a donkey engine when you face a challenge – which is all well and good if you want to put up your fists, or take to your heels, but what if all the fighting is up here?" He tapped his temples. "Where does that leave the poor old ticker as it hammers away in a fellow's chest?"

Lucy saw Michael and Dermot exchange glances in a gesture of medical freemasonry. "Don't appeal to him!" she warned Philip. "You trespass on holy ground. He'll squash you with the heavy boot of medical jawbreakers."

She smiled sweetly at Michael, who smiled sweetly back and said, "Perhaps he prefers that to being gored to death by an Irish bull, my dear."

"I'd prefer a straight answer to my question most of all," Philip said. "We're told it's bad to leave an engine racing away without doing any work. Is that true of the heart as well? And what about when your innards feel all hollow and your palms sweat? That's all part of the same thing – getting ready to fire off the old flinthead arrow. What does it do to us when all the arrows are in the museums?"

Both doctors drew breath to answer but Ebenezer got in first. "From the way you talk, young man," he said, "palms sweating . . . innards going hollow – hearts racing – are you sure you aren't thinking of *Cupid's* arrows, instead?"

The jibe caught Philip perfectly off balance. He could have jokingly yielded the floor to the old man, in high parliamentary style, praising him as the table's obvious expert on the topic. He could have made a parody of his own discomfort – "revealed at last!" – and so forth. But he was too taken aback to do any such thing. Instead he shot Diana a desperate glance, which he immediately withdrew, stared at his plate, cleared his throat, and failed to prevent his ears from becoming red. *I am thirty-two years old!* he told himself – but he could see no possible way of behaving like it.

His embarrassment threatened to turn so contagious that Michael, hoping to rescue the party, said, "Take his pulse, Lucy – quick!"

Philip had the good sense to laugh. Lucy patted his hand and murmured, loud enough for all to hear, "That man is a thundering disgrace." Whether she referred to her husband or to Ebenezer was left ambiguous.

Dermot scooped up the pieces. "Actually, I believe de Renzi has touched on something quite important. We all know – all of us around this table, medical or lay – we all know that half the disorders we treat, even though they may have frank physical signs and symptoms, are actually caused up here." He, too, patted his brow.

"Half?" Ebenezer queried.

Dermot glanced across him at Diana and Michael. "In my view, more than half," he replied. "Something gives way in the mind and it leaves the body vulnerable to demons of every sort. We fiddle around with our lotions and dressings and leeches – and our scalpels. But I often think that if we paid more attention to what's going on in the attic floor, the body would right itself. Good God – the clergy have always known this. Seize the mind and you've got the body *there!*" He flattened his thumb on the tablecloth and squashed an imaginary insect with some glee.

"Holy hour!" cried Ebenezer. "You're a man after my own heart, Doctor Walshe."

Janet smiled comfortingly at Philip, feeling that the old man had taken unfair advantage of him earlier – an unforgivable sin, in her view, when Philip was a guest at his table. Then to Ebenezer she said, "These are the ungodly who prosper in the world. My husband, you must understand, has never quite forgiven Father Clery for curing baby Timothy when he had a very bad colic."

Dermot laughed genially enough, as if to assure the company that his wife was being provocative in the most affectionate manner, but Lucy, close at his side, saw the glint of true anger in his eye. "It was quite miraculous," he confirmed, as if he were one hundred percent on his wife's side. "I never yet saw a medical cure to equal it! A few drops of a rather foul-smelling brew that Mrs Mulligan brought back from the River Jordan – and *Ave Maria,* the colic went! The later attack of tonsillitis had nothing to do with it, I'm sure. What made it even more miraculous was that the same concoction had utterly failed to mend Peter Woods's broken leg – the car owner in Leopardstown – nor had it calmed Mrs Mulligan's palpitations, though she was the bearer of the holy elixir itself. And it probably hastened the calling unto God of half a dozen other parishioners. In fact, no word of a lie, the undertakers of northeast Dublin got up a subscription to send Mrs Mulligan back to the Holy Land for more." He grinned all around him, challenging people not to laugh.

They did laugh, not altogether easily. Even Janet joined in. "These *are* beautiful flowers," she told Lucy for the second time. "Have you only just cut them?"

Lucy nodded. "From the glasshouse above the terrace. And while I was there, believe it or not, I witnessed what was almost a tragedy. Fortunately" – she smiled at Michael and Dermot – "skilled help was at hand to turn it into high comedy. A very thorough investigation was made. No bones were discovered to be broken. And the patient went merrily on her way."

Michael laughed. "Lord, did you see it?"

"More to the point – did they get their fee?" Janet asked, parodying a skinflint and staring across the table at Ebenezer as if expecting his approval.

Lucy half-rose in her chair, apparently to peer over the flowers to see whether the far end of the table required more ale; actually, she wanted to see in the mirror what Birdie Kelly was up to.

Birdie Kelly was scratching a nostril and staring out of the window, envious of two nurses who had the afternoon off.

198

"We were paid in kind," Michael assured her. "A most rural affair. There'll be a gammon at Christmas."

"In a loose stocking," Lucy added, laying just enough stress on the word for Michael (and – though, of course, she had not intended it – Diana) to hear; the others all supposed she was rounding off her husband's little pleasantry.

"And how did you spend *your* morning Mister de Renzi?" Diana asked. "I hope it wasn't too exciting. My head is beginning to whirl."

It was such an uncharacteristic remark for her to make that the three who knew her best – Michael, Lucy, and Ebenezer – could not prevent an ill-mannered stare of amazement, which the Walshes then experienced at second-hand, as it were. Philip alone was unaffected by it, delighted to have any opportunity to address, and thus gaze at, Diana. "We have clothèd the northwestern corner of the Dublin Mountains with gardens that will surely match those of Babylon, Miss Powers. A century hence they will rank as the eighth wonder of the world, I'm sure."

"We?" Michael asked sharply, tempering it with a comic, schoolmasterly glance over the tops of imaginary half-moon spectacles.

Philip spread his hands in benediction, gesturing toward the ladies on either side. "Juno, Minerva, and I!"

Dermot blundered in. "No Venus?"

"She has lent her very name to all our endeavours," Philip replied smoothly.

Lucy smiled at Janet. "So now we are immortal, my dear! Which d'you wish to be – Juno or Minerva? Juno, perhaps, because it starts with a J?"

"Tut tut!" Ebenezer saw his chance at last. "Modern education! Do they teach you nothing of the classics these days?"

The two ladies turned to him with a delight they would certainly not have shown if they had known what was coming.

He addressed Lucy first. "Anyone called Lucinda has to be Juno, for her oldest title was Juno Lucina – goddess of celestial light. She was also the goddess of childbirth – who brought newborn babies into the light of day." At that point Lucy's smile became rather fixed. He continued, "She was the moon goddess, too – which gives her the closest possible affinity with Diana, who was also a moon goddess before she was turned into . . ." – he smiled at Diana and lingered on the word – "a huntress. Juno Pronuba arranged all marriages. Juno Domiduca conveyed brides to their husbands and pushed them over the threshold. Juno Nuxia sprinkled exciting perfumes in the nuptial chamber."

"Goodness, Mrs Raven – what an exciting life you lead!" Janet crowed. "But I do hope you retired from the proceedings at that point and left them to it."

"I'm coming to Minerva in a moment," Ebenezer threatened. "We haven't finished with Juno yet. Junio Cinxia disrobed the bride

199

and . . ." He grinned provocatively at Janet. "Well, there were other incarnations who performed other essential offices but, to spare our blushes, let us say 'and so on and so forth'! Finally it was Juno Lucina, as I said, who brought the newborn babe into the light of day. It was, incidentally, the same Juno who restored fertility to the Sabine women after their little misfortune with the Roman soldiery. Isn't it fascinating – the lessons that history still holds for us today!" He stared round the table with a twinkle in his eye.

"And Minerva?" Lucy snapped.

"Ah!" He turned to Janet, whose heart began to sink at once. "Minerva was the latecomer among the Roman gods of state. The Romans captured her from the Etruscans – or her effigies, anyway – in the middle of the third century BC. She is, I must confess, my very favourite goddess of all, for she soon became the goddess of commerce, the most important of all!"

"Goodness, how vulgar!" Janet splayed one hand across her breast and laughed awkwardly.

"Naturally, too, she was paid particular homage by the corporation of Roman doctors, who, like doctors today, were never backward in *that* branch of worship!"

"Ah!" She began to preen herself and to stare haughtily at the two doctors, who smiled tolerantly back at her.

"Later still," Ebenezer concluded, "probably because her festival was at the spring equinox, which was also the festival of Mars, god of war, Minerva became the Roman god*dess* of war."

"Well!" Dermot exclaimed admiringly before his wife could get in with claims of her own. "She promotes commerce . . . she is worshipped by doctors . . . and she's fond of a good scrap." He paused, gazing merrily at his wife. "One bullseye out of three isn't bad aiming, I'd say."

"Which is the bull?" Lucy asked.

"My wife has a personal interest in that Hibernian species," Michael murmured.

At the same moment Dermot was saying, "Ah ha! That'd be telling."

"How do you know all those things, Mister O'Dea?" Diana asked. She had already reasoned it out that the old fellow could not have known in advance that de Renzi was going to speak of the two goddesses, so he could not have swotted it up especially.

"Weren't they put there with the pandybat once upon a time, Miss Powers," he replied. "I'm sure the Jesuit who beat me for not knowing such things would be only amazed to hear how much I have actually retained."

"We had a hoor of a goat called Juno once," Birdie Kelly sang out from the far end of the room.

Everyone turned and stared at her, where she was sitting.

"It's as true as I'm standing here," she added.

200

No one could think of an apt reply. And if Ebenezer was not going to reprimand her for butting in, Lucy felt it was hardly her place to say anything. They all turned away again.

"Is there any danger of a sup of porter over here?" Birdie added before she might lose their attention entirely.

Lucy's lips vanished and she gave Michael a tight little nod. He rose and carried the ale jug to her. The meal was a cold collation so they had no standing servant in the room.

After that they tended to divide into shifting groups of two and three, with no particular conversational thread and no general point-scoring. And no further interruptions from Birdie Kelly, either.

Toward the end of the meal, Ebenezer rose – that is, sat bolt upright – and bowed rather formally to Lucy, thanking her for a most enjoyable luncheon. He then told Birdie that he required to sleep, and off they went.

"Catch a weasel asleep!" Lucy murmured the moment the door had closed behind them.

"*She* went quietly enough," Janet remarked.

"She has a tongue that'd lick a calf for all that," Lucy replied. Then, to the two doctors: "Are you really intending to get that engine going today?"

They exchanged glances. Michael wiped his lips and threw his napkin down. "We'd better go now, in fact," he told her as they both rose to leave. "We lit the fire just before lunch. She should be singing merrily by now."

Janet tilted her head sympathetically at Lucy and said, "Maternal duties call us to book, I suppose? One can't leave *everything* to the nannies."

"I suppose so," Lucy agreed. She smiled at Philip and Diana. "D'you mind awfully?"

He scratched the back of his neck, muttered that he for his part did not, and managed to look both delighted and desperate at the same time. When they were alone, he licked his lips nervously and asked Diana whether duty called or had she time for a stroll in the grounds?

She replied that she would prefer to take her stroll in the evening, when the sun was less fierce. She suggested they might repair to her apartment and take some coffee, instead.

He stared at her as if he hardly dared believe what his ears had just served him.

Diana smiled wearily. "Oh dear, Mister de Renzi – I am thirty days short of my thirtieth birthday. I am an *old maid!* It is high time I started claiming some of the privileges of that sisterhood, don't you think?"

He swallowed heavily and licked his lips all over again.

Her attitude softened. "Why do you hesitate still?" she asked. "Is

201

your reputation so dreadful that even an old maid of a hospital matron is unsafe with you?"

He blundered into the table in his efforts to reach her quickly. There was anguish in his eyes as he seized her by the elbows, hard at first, then gently. "Don't," he mumbled. "Please don't."

She tried to destroy his solemnity with a laugh but nothing came. For a moment their eyes dwelled in a profound audit, each in the other's. She raised a hand and brushed his cheeks, feather-light, with the tips of her fingers. "Don't *you*," she whispered, echoing him.

"What?" He pressed his hand to his cheek, trapping hers against it.

"You know what," she told him. "Don't be in love with me."

Her hot fingertips against his cheek betrayed the pulse of her heart; it combined with her disordered breathing in a message totally at odds with her warning to him.

A man under compulsion, no longer answerable to warnings and reason, he lifted his other arm and slipped its hand behind her head, pulling her toward him with the feeblest touch. One only half its strength would have brought her to him, though. She raised her mouth to his . . . he felt a sweetness beyond all bearing . . .

And then they heard the maids wheeling the dumbwaiter along the passageway outside. They sprang apart just in time.

"I'd love a cup of coffee, Matron," he said as the door swung inward.

D iana's lips tingled still from the kiss they had not received. Soon, soon, she told herself as she and Philip ambled upstairs to her apartments in the easiest silence she had ever known. But, she discovered, "soon" had no meaning now. Time stretched before her like a scene viewed through the wrong end of binoculars; what might happen a minute from now was made one with tomorrow and next year. The living moment was all she had left; her apartments were a distant shore; the treads of the stairs became a flimsy causeway over unknown and unknowable depths. The living present! The vibrant, exciting *now!*

Suddenly she realized that she had spent her life in a hopeless dependence on the immediate future. Knowing nothing of the glory of the living moment – not just *this* living moment but all living moments – she had sacrificed it for an infinity of moments-to-come, never even noticing that they receded before her like the pot-of-gold rainbow. She looked down at her dress, her matron's uniform which she had bought with such pride, and thought what a sham it was. She had a brief picture of herself moving from room to room in the clinic . . . and of the nurses straightening themselves, smoothing aprons that were starched beyond smoothness, pinching their knuckles with the tension – the authority that had come out of nowhere the day she first donned that navy blue armour. And now it was sham piled upon sham.

Inside her armour she was a frightened child again, lost in a world where authority no longer descended from above but rather welled up from the abyss, too profound to fathom, too mighty to resist.

"And this is my holy of holies," said a calm, steady voice in her throat.

There were confusing changes of darkness and light, of clinic air and the balmy summer drift in her own dear rooms. And then his lips were fused with hers, his lean, muscley mansbody pressed tight against hers . . . and the living moment swelled to claim the world.

After many a summer had come and gone he moved to end his kiss. The calm voice had deserted her by then; all she could muster was a mute's whimper, which struggled out through lips that reached for his, as greedily as if they had been starved all her life – which she would not then have denied.

Occasionally footsteps approached and receded beyond the door against which he held her pinned – or against which she made him pin her. Each time they filled him with anxiety but she could hear them without heed. The oak at her back marked the ultimate palisades of this universe; those strangers moved in a time and space that she had abandoned now.

At last, at long, long last, he broke his kiss – or half-broke it – to say in a rheumy, distorted voice, "My arm has gone to sleep."

She released him then and laughed – because she would not care to name for him those parts of her that were still awake. And then, entirely without warning, she began to cry. That is, tears sprouted behind her eyelids and flowed freely down her cheeks, and her lungs heaved and sobbed with emotion – except that the emotion itself was not there! She felt no sorrow – and few other women were as familiar with sorrow and all its forms as Diana; she felt no elation, either – though she had just established a new criterion for that emotion, too.

His arm was not so dead with sleep as to prevent him from fishing out his handkerchief. A long-forgotten Nurse Powers wondered if it was one he had used. The word "pathogens" hovered somewhere in her consciousness, looking for a sentence to join. It was her first handhold on the old reality of her life and she grasped it with a certain sadness, a sense of deflation.

He had not used the handkerchief before; the folds made a grid of uncreased white linen squares. She buried her face in it and blew the glutinous, salty ocean of her tears into its crisp warm depths – until at last she could smell *him* among the fibres, the once-alien smell of him.

He ran his fingers through the fine hair on her brow. "How long have you wanted to do that?" he asked.

"Cry?" she said.

He shook his head. "To kiss me." His eyes were unremittingly tender, locked in hers, craving to adore her.

"Never," she told him.

Her honesty took him aback. "I have loved you from the moment I saw you," he blurted out.

"I know," she said.

"But you . . . I mean, you haven't . . .?"

She shook her head.

"Then why now?"

"I don't know." She took his arm and led him into her sitting room. "I don't want to know – even if it were possible, which I doubt. Do you? Isn't it enough that it has happened?"

He stopped and turned to face her, taking her head gently between his hands. "You don't regret it?"

"No!" She almost shouted the denial. Her eyes gleamed and she laughed at the very idea. "Regret is a kind of looking back and believe me – there's *nothing* I want to look back on."

Still her answers did not satisfy him. He could not imagine how she could have sat down to lunch, feeling nothing but a friendly sort of indifference toward him, and then, an hour later, kiss him with such passion – to say nothing of bursting into tears. "When did your feelings change?" he asked.

"Philip!" She grazed his cheek tenderly with the back of her hand and murmured his name with reproachful affection. "Were you serious about coffee?"

He nodded.

"You can come and grind the beans, then," she said, leading him to the alcove that now served as her kitchen.

"What was going on around that luncheon table?" he asked when the grinding was over and conversation became possible once again.

She put his handkerchief and her old teacloth in her linenbasket, then took down a new one to wipe the cups, saying, "It's not often I'm after using them."

"Everyone was gently twisting a knife in everyone else – or the two married couples were. It's a fine advertisement for the blessed state, I must say."

"It's Ebenezer O'Dea," she told him. "He's the seed and root of it all. Tip those grounds on top of this water – make a black sugarloaf."

"Is that how you brew coffee?"

"It's the only way, laddie!"

He watched in amazement as she sprinkled a powdering of salt and a little pinch of hot mustard over the conical heap of grounds. "It should be black as night," she said, "hot as hell, and sweet as love. If they don't serve coffee that way in paradise, I shall get up and leave."

His innards melted to behold her, and hear her, and be so close to her. "I've never seen you like this," he murmured.

She took up his hand – for an absurd moment he thought she was about to take his pulse – and patted it. "Nor have I," she said. "Not these many years."

"I was once in love with Lucy, you know – when she was Lucy Fitzbutler. It's only fair to tell you. We grew up almost like brother and sister."

Her eyes dwelled in his. "I think it lasted long after she became Lucy Raven?" The smallest possible lilt in her voice made it the smallest possible question.

He nodded ruefully. "Until I met you, in fact."

She shook her head. "Even then – I don't believe it shrivelled as easily as that, Philip."

The accusation shocked him. He knew there were many uncomfortable truths yet to be told – and even to be faced before they could be told; but he thought this moment too fragile to bear them.

But she was relentless. "I *know*." She nodded reassuringly. "I do know, my dear."

"Because . . . you . . .?" He could not say it.

"Yes, because I was once in love with Michael, too. Hold me?" She lifted her arms to him and settled gratefully inside his ardent embrace. "You must understand this, Philip. It's only fair to tell *you!* No little-maid-from-school am I! I lost my innocence many years ago. I am damaged goods. The colours have faded and some have run. I can no longer tell you what is love and what is hate, nor where self-sacrifice shades into bitterness and bitterness into vengeance." She hugged him hard and pressed her head tight into the curve of his neck. "Should I tell you these things within minutes of our first kiss? Every ounce of common sense says no! *Never* tell him."

She pushed him from her on the word *never* and stared into his eyes with a kind of despair. The water began to boil and he reached past her to turn down the wick, saying, "Go on. I could listen to you until . . . for the rest of my life, I hope."

"Yes!" She gripped his arm urgently and went on staring into his eyes, first one, then the other.

Hers were so large and green and luminous they held him spellbound. "Tell me anything," he stammered. "Say anything you like."

"We *could* be together the rest of our lives," she said. "It would be so easy. You are so . . . so gentle and strong . . . and I have such a temper."

"You?" he asked in amazement. "A temper?"

"Oh, Philip!" She closed her eyes briefly and punched him on his shoulder. "So much to learn! My common sense warns me to be clever with you – and oh, I *do* know how to be clever. I could hide my feelings from God Himself, I think, from now until the end of time. What a *sensible* life we could have together, you and I! With the stupid passions of our youths behind us." She fixed him with an accusing eye. "They were stupid, weren't they!"

205

He shook his head but did not dare say no aloud.

"Bless you for that!" she went on. "Even if they were stupid, they were rescued by their glory." She relaxed and spoke quite calmly then. "Don't worry, my darling, I shall test you less and less as time goes by – though I shall never quite lose the fear that drives me to do it. The damage is not superficial."

"Do you hate Michael now?" he asked suddenly, catching her off guard.

She turned and checked on the coffee before she assembled her answer. "I have hated him ever since . . ." Her voice trailed off and she fell into a reverie.

"Since he broke it off with you?" Philip suggested.

She shook her head, still miles away. "I was about to say 'ever since he used me and threw me aside,' but I've just realized that I used him as much as he used me. There! I haven't been able to admit that, not even to myself, until now. Never mind hiding my feelings from God, eh!"

"Is that because it no longer matters?" he asked hopefully.

She smiled without humour. "Or because I am about to use *you?*" Her eyes pleaded with him not to believe her and she reached her arms toward him; but at the last moment she fended him off, as if she realized she could not forever flee into the haven of his embrace. "I'm all rusty, Philip," she said. "I'm not like that engine those grown-up boys are playing with down there. You'll just have to cross your fingers and hope I don't explode."

"Don't talk like that!" he said angrily.

"You see!" she threw back at him. "I'm not what you expected at all. I'm a disappointment to you already." She turned and stared at the coffee. For just a moment she had no idea what it was. The water had finished seething and all the grounds had been sucked down; she turned the flame off before it could properly boil.

His fingertips rested gently on the nape of her neck, beneath her tightly disciplined bun; he began to caress her.

If he pulls out just one of my hairpins, she told herself, *everything will be all right.* She remembered making thousands of such pacts with fate, all equally futile. Of course, she had been a mere child then! *The hairpin! The hairpin!* she screamed at him inside her skull.

The first she knew of it was when the scalp above her right ear was stretched almost painfully. Then it was above her left ear. This time she heard the tinkle as the hairpin fell to the linoleum behind her – though in her tiny world it rang with a deafening clamour.

When her hair was loose it hung down almost to the small of her back. He began to comb it with his fingers, first with one hand, then the other, spreading the luxuriant redness in an ever-widening train. "Oh God how I love *you,*" he murmured.

Still with her back to him she took his hands and held his arms apart, allowing herself to fall once again into his embrace. When she folded his arms around her she placed them very deliberately on her breasts and let out a great sigh on the one word, "Yes!" She stretched it out over the full exhalation.

But for that he would have plucked his hands away at once. Even then he stood a long moment, rigid and winded with the shock.

She raked her fingernails over the backs of his hands.

"Are you sure?" he asked in a voice neither of them recognized.

A sudden reservation occurred to her. "Wait," she said. "Close your eyes." After a pause she added, "Promise?"

"Yes," he croaked, taking his hands away.

She glanced surreptitiously over her shoulder and was amazed to see he was true to his word. Then, quick as she could, she undid the buttons of her blouse and fished out the gold chain that held Michael's engagement ring – or the replica she had bought. She gathered it in a loose knot and hurled it through the alcove opening into the sitting room, where it would fall silently on soft carpet. She did not care where it went.

Then she leaned back against him once more but this time, when she took his hands, she thrust them into the opening of her blouse. Then she raised her arms above her, behind her head, to pull his face to hers. "Now I'm sure," she said as their lips met.

Incongruously he began to laugh. "I can undo buttons," he complained out of the side of his mouth.

I hope you can undo a lot more than that, my love, my love . . . she said to herself, *if you hope to undamage me!*

T hey filled the dashpots to the brim with oil, squeezed grease into every bearing until it was practically running out by the door, and polished every moving surface until you could see to shave in it. None of it was necessary, since they were doing it for the ninety-tenth time, but turf is a slow fuel and the furnace, as Michael now realized, should really have been kindled after breakfast. The children gave up waiting and drifted off to fight more ancient battles.

"Old Mister O'Dea complains about the cost of this," Michael remarked to Dermot. "He doesn't seem to realize it'll save the work of half a dozen in the house. The gardeners do several hours a day raising the water for the hydraulic lift. And the quantities of paraffin that get carried about the house each day – never mind trimming the wicks each week! The air gets foul . . . we throw open the windows . . . out goes the heat – or it will in winter . . ."

Dermot laid a hand on his arm. "You don't have to convince *me*, old fellow. To have constantly boiling water for sterilizing things is reason enough in my book." He went to the door, glanced quickly all round, and returned, saying, "No little birds in the ivy. You never finished telling me about Ebenezer O'Dea. I must say, he's not at all the man his reputation paints him. All that classical learning! I thought he was nothing but Dublin's most successful and least loved old miser."

Michael set down his oil can and wiped his hands in a bundle of shoddy. "He began life as a teacher, you know. He taught classics at Maynooth. Mrs Lynch told me her father remembers him there. Then he opened a grind in Dublin – very successful, too – in Harcourt Street."

"Up near the station?" Dermot asked. "Good heavens! I did my anatomy grinds there – I'd never have passed but for them."

"Well, he sold his interest there many years ago, before our time. But that was the basis of his fortune. Then there's a hole in his life. Something happened which turned him into the sort of man who deserves his reputation – a maniac for money."

"Was it a woman?"

Michael shrugged. "Who knows? It usually is. Anyway, something *else* has happened to change him once again. Whether we're seeing the man as he was in younger days or a third incarnation of Ebenezer O'Dea . . . I can't say. He doesn't treat money lightly, of course, but it's no longer the be-all and end-all of his life."

"What *is*, then? He seems to enjoy . . . how can I put it? Stirring up friction?"

Michael tapped the pressure gauge, convinced yet again that it had stuck.

"I mean," Dermot went on awkwardly, "Janet and I have our little contretemps – which married couple does not! But we don't usually vent them quite so publicly as at lunch today."

Michael laughed grimly. "By the standards of the Ravens you were the very soul of discretion."

"Ah," Dermot said, even more awkwardly.

Michael, feeling he had been rather too frank, was quick to add, "Ah sure we're like Cuchulainn and Ferdia – we fight by day and bathe each other's wounds all night."

"How did Matron Powers come to be appointed?" Dermot asked.

Michael stared sharply at him for his emphasis implied he did not believe the sketchy explanation Michael had already given him.

At length Dermot lowered his gaze and said, "Actually, Raven old man, I recognized her. It's obviously one of the questions I'm compelled to ask now that I'm nine-tenths inclined to accept your offer." He recruited Michael's understanding with a smile. "Surely you see that?"

Michael inhaled sharply, drawing breath through clenched teeth as if framing himself to an unpleasant task. "It was at Ebenezer O'Dea's insistence – as I explained. She was his private nurse for some months. Oh damnation!" He hammered the pipe to which the pressure gauge was fitted. "You're quite right. You have every claim to be told about it, but if I oblige, then I fear you'll change your mind

208

and turn it down. On the other hand, if I don't, the day may come when I can no longer look in your face."

Dermot raised his eyebrows in some alarm. "As bad as that?"

"I don't know. It depends on what skeletons you have rattling away in your cupboard – you and your wife. Be sure he'll find them – and then he'll scrape off the scar tissue and reach for the salt!"

"O'Dea?"

Michael nodded. "It all goes back to him. Somehow he discovered that Diana and I were old sweethearts. She didn't tell him . . ."

"You're sure of that?"

"Absolutely – as sure as one can be of anything where women are in it."

"Which is very far from absolutely!"

"Well," Michael repeated, "I'm pretty sure of her on that point – mainly because I'm certain I know who did let the cat out of the bag."

"Ah!"

"It must have been Dazzler O'Dea – Ebenezer's nephew who since the old boy's hemiplegia struck him down, has been his eyes, ears, and legs in Dublin."

"Talking of which," Dermot put in. "We are quite certain, are we, that the man *has* lost the use of his legs? We've done all the usual tests?"

Michael explained that Ebenezer had not actually been his patient, so he had no part in the diagnosis. "Why?" he asked.

Dermot shrugged noncommittally. "Just a feeling I had at luncheon. That business young de Renzi was talking about – the suspicion that a lot of apparently physical illness is mental in origin – I'm becoming more interested in it every day. Sorry! This is a complete red herring. You were telling me that young Dazzler O'Dea was his uncle's informer. The question then is how did he know?"

"Because he was once Lucy's sweetheart!"

"My goodness!"

"Yes! It's a hornets' nest – or it could be. And my suspicion is that Ebenezer hopes it *will* be."

Dermot, standing near the window, gazed across the yard at the great pile of Mount Venus House. "You mean to say he's spent all this money . . . set up this whole elaborate" – he gestured at the building – ". . . enterprise . . . just so that . . ."

"Oh no. He already owned the property. Some mortgage he foreclosed . . ."

"The Reilly suicide?"

Michael nodded.

Dermot had a faraway look in his eye. "I wonder if that's when O'Dea became paralysed?" He smiled enthusiastically at Michael. "What an interesting case he'd be, eh? Is it known which room poor Reilly committed the *felo de se* in?"

"Yes. O'Dea uses it now as his private drawing room."

"I say!"

"In a cupboard, actually. Lucy had the door screwed fast and he's never asked for them to be removed."

"I'm not surprised! And what became of the body?"

Michael shrugged. "I should think it went to some anatomy school. He had no family – or none turned up to claim his debts! Perhaps he was buried at the crossroads? That's the usual thing."

"We *must* find out if that's when old O'Dea lost the use of his legs. I'm sure it's not a stroke, aren't you?"

Again Michael was noncommittal. He had grown used to a paralysed Ebenezer O'Dea and, despite his interest in the sort of mental phenomena Dermot was invoking, did not want to inquire too deeply into causes. A thought struck him. "Apropos all this – did you have a word with young Quinlan yet?"

Abraham Quinlan was a recently qualified doctor whose examination results had impressed Michael sufficiently for him to want the young man as RMO, or resident medical officer, at Mount Venus. He had delayed any direct approach, however, until Dermot's own decision was made.

"I did, as a matter of fact," the other replied. "Though I don't see how it's got anything to do with Ebenezer O'Dea and his possibly hysterical hemiplegia."

"Oh, Quinlan's quite interested in all that sort of thing – the mind-body paradox and so on."

"Ah, I see." After a pause he added, "He's a Jew, of course. Quinlan, I mean."

Michael chuckled. "That, too."

"I mean, all these Viennese mind-body doctors – *alienists*, as they call them – they all seem to be Jews. I think Quinlan would make an excellent RMO, anyway."

Neither man pointed out that the appointment of a Jew would neatly preserve the Protestant—Roman Catholic balance.

"I'll sound him out formally, then," Michael said. "To get back to O'Dea and the Reilly suicide – I think he certainly changed character after that. Feeling in Dublin ran very high against him around that time. It must have made him take stock of his life." He paused, having just noticed that the glow from the open furnace door had dimmed. He went round and threw on several more shovels of turf. "We'll have to mix some coal in with it," he said. "This is absurd. Give that relief valve a tap. The boiler's singing like a haggard full of linnets."

Dermot took an open-ended spanner and tapped the pipe beside the valve. It sputtered feebly and two or three drops ran down the pipe, boiling away to nothing in a few inches." "It's looking promising," he said. "What d'you suppose old Ebenezer saw when he took stock of himself?"

"I think he saw a lot of money and nothing to spend it on. He's not interested in lavish entertainment, artistic patronage, a landed estate, a luxury yacht . . . all the usual things."

"What then?"

"Playing God with other people's lives. Perhaps that's been his aim from the very beginning. Teachers play God to their students, in a way. But it wasn't enough. So then he tried doing it with money – but it still wasn't enough – not if your subjects go and commit suicide all round you!"

Dermot felt the hair prickle on the nape of his neck. "So now he's doing it directly! Put the human ingredients in the pot, stir, and leave to cook slowly. Hah! Isn't that *exactly* what God does with all our lives!"

Michael grinned at him. "And didn't the old man discover within five minutes that you and Mrs Walshe disagree profoundly on that very topic! The question is, old man – do you and she really want to leap into Ebenezer's pot with the rest of us? D'you think that is part of your Live Forever plan?"

Lucy and Janet made a perfunctory visit to the nursery, where the younger children were taking a nap and the older ones were reading or drawing in silence. They told the two nannies that their charges could all put on their oldest clothes and go out to the engine house in about twenty minutes' time; they doubted that the steam would be up before then. Then Janet said to Lucy, "Now you simply *must* show me where you picked those wonderful dahlias and chrysanths."

"Did de Renzi discover whether his water-garden is possible or not?" Lucy asked as they made their way downstairs again.

"What an interesting young man he is!" Janet gushed.

"Not to me, he isn't," Lucy told her.

Janet stopped and stared at her in astonishment.

Lucy grinned. "Interesting, yes – but not young." She grinned a catlike grin. "He's almost five years older than *me*."

"Ah," Janet said frostily.

"And will he be able to create this water garden?"

"I think so," she replied vaguely. "He seemed satisfied with his morning's work, anyway. We didn't actually talk about that, though we discussed everything else under the sun."

Lucy got the feeling that the woman was going to make her fish for every little tidbit, especially after that dig at her age. To leap over all the intervening stages, then, she said, "Most particularly about Miss Diana Powers, I imagine?"

Janet, though clearly disappointed, made the best of it with a laugh and said, "How *did* you guess! He's obviously very smitten. I wonder

211

if it was entirely wise to leave them alone together?"

"Two people in their, thirties?" Lucy asked sarcastically, "How would one stop them?"

The other sighed. "My maiden aunt was chaperoned until well into her fifties. But I agree – times have changed. Perhaps we married too young, you and I. Wouldn't it have been nice to enjoy the freedom Miss Powers now has?"

They emerged onto the terrace. Lucy looked at the sky and said it might rain tomorrow, adding that the garden could certainly do with it. Her companion agreed and then said, "We were talking about freedom . . . and Miss Powers."

"Well," Lucy responded hesitantly, "to be honest, I did, in fact, enjoy such freedom myself when I was a girl – not that my parents were terribly free-thinking, mind. Just negligent, I suppose. Not that it made any difference in the end."

"Really?" Janet asked brightly. "That sounds promising! Can the awful story now be told?"

Lucy giggled. "It was nothing awful – sorry to disappoint. But I used my freedom to make a quite dreadful choice. I would happily have married Dazzler O'Dea, old Ebenezer's nephew. Heaven knows what would have happened to us by now. Either he'd have murdered me or I'd have murdered him, probably. Anyway, my parents saved the hangman's fee by insisting I give him up and marry Michael Raven instead."

Janet stared at her in surprise. "D'you mean they said you should marry *someone* else – or did they actually select Michael and say it was him or the convent?"

Lucy screwed up her face to prove how long ago it was and how difficult to remember. "Probably they picked him out for me. I was too numb to care." She laid it on thick because that was the best way of showing how little it mattered to her now. She laughed, too, much as to say what a little fool she had been. "So there are times when even the most neglectful parents know best," she concluded.

"And Dazzler? D'you run across him often nowadays?" Janet's tone was perfectly poised between a polite social question and an invitation to share a confidence.

"Oh, almost weekly." She made it sound old hat. "He lived in Cork for most of the last ten years but he returned to Dublin this spring. I bumped into him in Dame Street which, in a way, led to our meeting his Uncle Ebenezer and . . . all this!" Her spirit exulted; it was like walking along a leaking dyke, plugging each hole with an expert flick of the wrist.

Janet, however, had sunk her teeth in and was not going to let go so easily. "It must have been a bit of a jolt the first time you met, though?" she remarked. "One never knows, does one – meeting ghosts from one's past."

"One never knows what?" Lucy was not going to let her progress by mere innuendos.

"How dead those feelings really are. I know there are some of *my* old beaux – I mean, I can think of them with mild affection now, but that's because they're safely married in America. Or Australia, one of them. But . . ."

"Goodness!" Lucy could not help interrupting. "How *do* you keep track of them all!"

Janet tried to think of a witty reply but could not. "Their *mothers* make sure I know," she said through clenched teeth. "Also how many gold mines they now own and how many million sheep they have to shear each season!"

They both laughed and then, as they entered the glasshouse, Janet returned to her original line: "As to how I would feel if one of them came back out of the blue – if I ran across him in Dame Street . . . I don't know." She pinched one of her blouse buttons and turned the garment into a bellows to cool her breast. "Isn't it warm in here! You're not afraid of rust or wilt?"

Lucy wound the handle that opened the ventilators all down the house. "We'll leave the door open a bit," she said.

For a while they wandered among the flowers, Janet passing admiring comments on their colour and vigour and variety. At the far end Lucy pointed out the stable yard and described the little scene she had witnessed before luncheon.

"One has to keep an eye on them all the time," Janet said ambiguously. Then, as if their earlier conversation had only just concluded, she added, "I sometimes wonder how Dermot might respond if one of *his* old flames turned up out of the blue – all unattached and too old to need a chaperone."

"Why?" Lucy asked. "Has he too many to keep track of, also?"

Janet gave a brittle laugh and, taking Lucy's arm, squeezed it rather hard. "You are a tease!" she said. "And before this becomes part of established folklore, let me assert in the plainest possible terms that I did *not* have too many suitors to count, and I was never formally engaged to anyone before Dermot."

"And he?" Lucy realized the question was a mistake the moment she asked it; her main concern was to keep lobbing the ball back into the other matrimonial court, but this laid her wide open for a smash volley back.

"I believe he was fond of one young lady in Ranelagh – who is now the wife of an eminent barrister. We meet from time to time. Young bachelors have to forage a lot more than would be proper for a young spinster." She smiled and hit the volley: "I expect it was the same with Mister Raven?"

Lucy had seen it coming all the way. "I believe there was a young nurse at the Adelaide when he was a student," she said vaguely. "I have no idea what became of her – nor indeed what her name was. It was nothing very much, anyway."

"Ah, they all say that!" Janet laughed sympathetically. Secretly, however, she was delighted to have established the main fact of the matter: Lucy Raven had no idea that her husband's former lover (in all senses of the word) was the matron of this very establishment.

Let Dermot turn down this offer at his peril!

P hilip rolled on his back, afraid that if he continued to kiss Diana and she continued to respond with such ardour, one thing would borrow another and . . . well, the pressure of time did not permit such a progression. "Time!" he sighed by way of explanation.

"I know," she murmured as she snuggled against him once more.

"We must get dressed."

"I know."

"There could be an emergency. They could send for you at any moment."

"I know." She kissed the soft skin at the base of his neck, below the shaving line.

"One of us must be sensible."

The gentle eddies of her breath around his neck and shoulders as she answered were as thrilling as anything else that had happened to him during the past hour. "I've been ten years sensible, my darling. I gladly pass the torch to you."

"I'll take my clothes into your sitting room, then," he said. "Leave you to dress in peace, eh?"

She raised herself abruptly and stared into his eyes. "You aren't joking," she said in amazement.

He smiled wryly. "I know – it does seem a bit cockeyed."

She rested her head again. "A *bit?* After what we've just done?" The humour drained out of her voice and she went on, "It's as if you think . . ." She bit off the rest of the sentence but he felt her breathing hard.

"I'm sorry," he offered.

She raised herself on one elbow; her eyes were ablaze. "I should think so, too! Look at me, Philip! Look at my body. Look – these are my breasts!" She shook her torso to make them quiver – though her anger was already serving well enough for that. "Do they make you feel ashamed now? Do you feel shame for me? Is my body shameful? Shall we wait until it's dark for me to get dressed?"

Tears prickled in his eyes. He slid down the bed and kissed each breast tenderly, with great reverence.

She collapsed upon him, curling her body round him, crushing his head tight into her bosom until he had to struggle to breathe.

214

"I'm sorry," she said. "Oh Philip, I'm sorry."

"No, *I'm* sorry. It was a stupid thing to say. A courtesy from another world . . . I mean another age . . . oh, I don't know! All I do know is it has no place between us."

"Kiss me." She rolled on her back, pulling him onto her. She was all ready to catch fire again but he was not. She could feel the tension in every muscle. He was worried about time, about what people would say, about emergencies, about being caught.

She quelled her passion, or put it aside for another day, and made noises of mild pleasure, instead.

"I see what you mean about having a temper," he said. "But if after every tempest come such calms, then may the winds blow 'til they awaken hell!"

She reached a hand across and tweaked his nose. "Liar! You're desperate to get dressed again. You don't deceive me."

"I'll show you!" he said, springing to life and throwing himself on top of her.

"Ooh?" she responded.

But he rolled onward and pulled her off the bed altogether. Then, by a heroic contest between muscle and gravity, which he almost lost, he raised her to a standing position, still holding her naked form tight against his.

"Ooh-er!" she cried.

But he left her standing there and picked up her corset. "Does this go on first?" he asked.

She shot him a look of bitter but comic disappointment and reached for the garment, saying "Ye-es!" in a flat, unwilling tone.

But he snatched it out of her reach. "No," he said sharply. "You just stand there and don't do a thing. Leave it all to me. I'll show you whether I'm ashamed of your body or not. I'll deck you like an altar."

She let out a laugh of delight and made to throw her arms around his neck. But again he fended her off. "Do as I say now," he snapped, pursing his lips so as not to smile. "Or I shall show you *my* temper."

She slipped at once into the role of penitent little girl and raised her elbows for him to slip the corset round her. "Have you got a terrible temper, Philip?" she asked. "Is it really fierce?"

"I don't know," he said darkly. "The world has never seen it yet."

"Then it must be truly awesome."

"How does this fit?" he asked in quite a different tone.

She giggled. "You see the two swellings in what you obviously suppose to be the bottom hem? You'll find bits of me up here that fit them quite snugly."

Behind her he said nothing as he turned the corsets the right way up but she could feel he was trying not to laugh. When he had mastered the impulse he clamped the panels around her and began threading the laces. "You don't need corsets at all," he said accusingly. "In fact, Matron Powers, for a decrepit old lady of almost

215

thirty years, you have the body of a sylph." He leaned forward and kissed her lightly on the neck. "I cannot believe this has happened, you know," he murmured.

"How d'you think I feel?" she whispered in reply.

He gave the laces one final tweak. "Uncomfortable?"

She laughed and told him to tie it in a simple bow, not a knot.

"Why d'you wear corsets at all?" he asked.

"Because," she replied.

"Because what?"

"Because it's not proper to leave them off. Suppose I was knocked down by a horse and got taken into hospital. What would they think when they found me not wearing corsets!"

"Aha!" he exclaimed. "So the opinion of others does matter to you! Just now you were behaving as if it had ceased to have any bearing." He picked up her stockings and advanced toward her with a grin.

But she snatched them from him and gave him a quick kiss by way of compensation. "Thank you, darling, you've done enough to make your point. Now go and put your own things on."

"In the sitting room?" he asked lightly.

She raised a fist to him and laughed; but the mood soon faded. "You're right though," she said. "The opinion of others does matter, reputation."

"Reputation, reputation, reputation!"

"Are you going to quote *Othello* all day?"

He chuckled at being caught out, then, with his pantaloons only half on, he hopped toward her, hands raised to strangle her throat, saying, "Put out the light! And then . . . put out the light!"

"Philip!" She pushed him aside so that he almost blundered into her dressing table. "We shall have to find some way of making sure our occasional flashes of seriousness coincide. Otherwise we shall get nowhere."

He pulled his shirt on and said, "Seriously then – may I ask you a question?"

She dipped her head. "I shan't guarantee to answer, mind."

"Why not?" he challenged. "I think you should. I think we both should. Let's try something no two lovers have ever tried since the very beginning of recorded time – total honesty. You can ask me anything and I'll answer as truthfully as I know how."

"All right," Diana responded truculently as she attached her suspenders to her stockings. "After Lucy Raven left you and Janet Walshe alone together up on Mount Venus this morning, did you embrace?"

"How did you know that?" he asked in amazement. The sight of her half-clothed body was so disturbing he had to turn away while he buttoned up his shirt.

She, equally amazed, misinterpreted the gesture as a sign of his guilt. "You mean you did?"

216

"No! I mean how did you know Lucy left us alone?"

She looked at him pityingly. "Don't be such a . . . such an *architect!* When you look at Mount Venus House, don't see windows, see women's eyes! Did you really suppose that with thirty nurses on duty and half a hundred windows you *wouldn't* be spotted up there? *Did* you embrace her?"

"I'll buy you all binoculars," he answered grumpily. "Then you'll know that sort of thing without asking."

"Did you?"

"No," he replied but with a strange lack of conviction.

"You sound very sure of it! Could you do up these buttons, there's a dear?"

He jumped his trousers up his legs and hitched the braces over his shoulders before he came to help her. "How d'you manage normally?" he asked.

"With a button hook and two looking glasses." When his hands touched her she added, "But this is much nicer."

"The reason I hesitated," he said, "was that I'm sure Janet Walshe expected me to . . . embrace her – as you tactfully put it."

She stiffened and then turned to face him. "I meant it literally, Philip. You know – kiss. Nothing more. You mean . . . she . . .?"

He nodded. "I'm a cad for saying it, I know. I wouldn't breathe a word to anyone else. I'm only telling you because of the . . . well, pact I proposed. But she made it clear she expected me to, er, *embrace* her – with all that that euphemism usually implies."

"How d'you know?" she asked in a challenging tone, as if she were preparing to defend a sister. "Or is it just wishful thinking?" She stepped into her dress, which still had its underskirts attached.

"I won't even answer that," he said stiffly. "I know because, well, one gets to know such things after a time."

Without hooking her dress to her blouse, she sat before her looking glass and began to brush out her hair. "Do lots of women throw themselves at you?" she asked speculatively. "No. That's not fair. I'm onto my second question and you haven't even asked your first. Go on – ask away!"

He looked forlornly about him for inspiration and then asked, "Why do you wear pink . . . things. You know – stockings and things?"

Her eyes raked the ceiling. "It's a good thing you're not a barrister, Philip. Your cross-examinations would devastate the court, I'm sure. In the first place they're not pink, they're peach. In the second place – between ourselves, of course – they are not *things*, they're called corsets and suspenders and drawers. And they're coloured peach because I like it. All right? Now it's my turn again. Do lots of women throw themselves at you? I'll bet they do. Are you tired of being totally honest?"

He finished doing up his flies and took the brush from her. "If you really want me to tell you," he said, "I will."

Their eyes met in the glass and she saw he wanted to tell her. Perhaps he even *needed* to tell her. She suppressed her own fears and told him she wanted to hear.

"You know the old code of honour for gentlemen," he began, "back in the days of our late . . . I mean England's late-lamented queen? It held that the virginity of a spinster of good class was as safe with a gentleman as that of his own sister. Maroon them ten years together on Robinson Crusoe's island and she'd be a virgin spinster still at the end of it all."

"Ha ha!"

"That was the code, anyway. It did nothing to protect maidservants, of course, and it enabled large numbers of surplus females, so-called, to imitate the squirrel."

She frowned, not seeing the connection though she knew what he meant.

"They covered their backs with their tails," he said. "That was all part of the code – the unwritten part. But there's an *unspoken* part, too – the part which allows that married ladies are fair game, once they've given their husbands three or four heirs whose seed and breed no one can doubt."

"How very convenient for the gentlemen who live by this code!" Diana sneered.

"And for the married ladies," he responded equably. "In fact, between you and me, my darling, I believe it was the ladies themselves who inserted that little rider."

"On what evidence?" she asked – wondering why the suggestion disturbed her so much.

"Just look at the men they married!" he told her. "They're like incompetent cooks – they can stir the pot but haven't the first idea how to add the spice and seasoning."

His suavity annoyed her – the way he sought to distance himself from it all with his aloof style of wit. "Whereas you," she sneered, "can do both, of course." Then she caught him smiling at her in the glass again, one eyebrow cocked, and despite herself she blushed. "Yes," she admitted as though driven to it. "You can. It makes me seethe!"

"Very well. I shan't do it again," he promised insincerely.

"No!" She caught his hand, with the brush in it, and pressed it to the side of her head. "All those married ladies with their three or four children with whom you perfected those skills! *They* make me seethe! I want to know their names. I want to tear them into little shreds." She held her hands up like leopard's paws. "I want to put these ten commandments on their cheeks!"

"*All* of them?"

Her hands fell to her dressing table. "What d'you mean?"

He laughed at her bewilderment. "Good heavens, lassie – there've only been *three!* What sort of Don Juan d'you take me for?"

She clenched her eyes and pretended to scream. "Three? Oh Philip, that's *worse!* That's the worst of all!"

"But why?"

"Because I can be jealous of three. If you'd said three hundred, it'd be absurd – like being jealous of every pretty girl you ever smiled at. But three! I'll never rest until I know their names." She put her hands to her ears the moment the words were out. "No. Don't tell me – don't tell me!"

He parked the brush in his waistband and began massaging her neck with gentle strokes, using only his fingertips. "Diana!" he murmured soothingly, at a loss for other things to say.

She writhed beneath his touch, luxuriating in it like a cat. This time she looked up at him directly rather than in the glass. "Oh Philip!" she sighed. "Jealousy! I'd forgotten what it feels like. I've been free of it for ten years."

"Have you?" he asked skeptically.

"Oh, you mean Lucy. That was envy, not jealousy – though I'd forgotten the difference until this moment." After a pause she added, "And it wasn't even envy, either. Anger? Chagrin? I don't know. If you imagine I've spent the last ten years cherishing a hopeless love for Michael Raven, you could hardly be more wrong. It's been love *and* hate – and anger, and bitterness, and cold, cold contempt." There was another brief pause before she added, "and outrage, too."

He laid the brush on the dressing table and began to comb her hair with his hands, scratching with gentle fingernails from her temples to above her ears. "I should think simple jealousy must come as quite a relief after all that," he commented.

She gave a silvery laugh and reached her hands up to pull his head down into a kiss. "You are going to be so good for me, Philip," she said. "You're such a rock of *knowingness* – what's the word? Taciturn. I've never felt so safe with any other . . . person, man or woman."

"You mean safe for you to explode in all directions like a bag of penny rockets!"

She let go of him and hugged her own body in a parody of self-indulgence. "Yes!" she exclaimed prissily, as if he had just given her permission to behave in the way he had complained of. Then she shook out her hair and said, "Let's do it in two plaits. Then we can coil one over each ear."

He cocked his head critically and gazed at her, trying to imagine the effect. "But that'll be even more old-maidish than a single bun," he complained.

"Quite," she replied. "Then no one will ever suspect I have a lover." She divided her hair into two hanks and pulled the left one over her shoulder. "You do the other bunch," she said.

For a minute or so he concentrated on getting three even strands and on starting in the right direction, so that when she coiled it up it wouldn't tug at her scalp. When the movements became semi-automatic he felt it safe to say, "Is that all I am now, then – your lover?"

"All?" she echoed in surprise.

"Why not betrothed? Affianced? Your promised one? Why not husband, come to that?"

"I think that would be a little premature," she said primly.

He gave a baffled laugh. "But what we've done this afternoon – here, just now – that wasn't premature?"

She refused to share his mood – or follow that argument. She paused in her plaiting and said, "Well, was it?"

His smile faded – or moderated from argumentative to something more gentle and loving. "No," he admitted. "It was . . . well, the perfect moment. The sort of moment that, if you don't take it, you've lost it forever."

She leaned forward to brush her lips against his and then resumed her plaiting.

"All the same," he went on, "unless the world understands there's some sort of, you know, arrangement between us, it'll be difficult to . . . you know."

"Go to bed together." Her calm gaze challenged him to say that wasn't really important.

It was the sort of insincere disavowal any man might make, especially since countless generations of women had insisted on being told that they were loved for something other than the physical charms on which they themselves lavished so much care and attention and, when they had it, gold, too. He was beginning to realize that in this one respect at least Diana was not as other women are. Her anger when he had proposed to let her get dressed in privacy . . . her astounding carnal appetite, which at times had threatened to overwhelm him . . . her utter lack of shame (which, he now realized, was far removed from shamelessness as commonly understood) . . . he had never known a woman like her.

Her eyes remained level in his, still challenging.

"Well," he told her, "it *is* the single most important thing. But there are also others – like dining out together, going to concerts – not to mention dining *in* together! It's a fan dance, I know, but the world does like to see the fan safely in place."

"D'you give a damn about the world?" she asked, slipping an elastic ribbon around the end of her plait.

"For my part, no. But would it be fair to everyone else – especially to your nurses, who depend so much on their places here? What would become of Mount Venus if word got about that its matron was a notorious evil-liver?"

She closed her eyes and breathed, "The world!" as if it nauseated her.

"I know." He found the other elastic ribbon and slipped it over his plait, delighted to see how well it matched hers.

The smile returned to her lips when she looked in the glass and saw it, too. "Aren't you clever," she said. And then, as if it followed logically, "Let's take a chance!"

"Meaning?"

"Meaning I'm not quite so pessimistic about the world as you are. An eighteen-year-old spinster cannot even dance with a man unless she takes his name down first, like a policeman. But the world lets a fifty-year-old spinster behave as outrageously as she likes. There must be a sort of sliding scale in between, don't you think? Let's see, anyway. We'll be discreet, in public at least. In public we shall not cock a single snook. And I think that as long as we don't rub people's noses in it, we shall be left alone." She gazed into his eyes and smiled, trying to recruit his enthusiasm for her project. "No?" she prompted.

"No," he said firmly.

"Yes," she countered in tones of finality. "Now, help me coil these up and pin them and then we'll go down and watch those grown-up boys play with their steam engine."

He persisted: "You don't understand at all. I *want* to be your fiancé."

She shook her head in an odd mixture of sadness and merriment. "That really would worry the world," she told him. "The world would think that dreadfully hasty. Why, as far as the world knows, we've hardly even met!"

The moment she crossed the threshold Janet said, "Oh dear! Are you quite, quite sure it's safe, darling?"

Lucy shared her doubts though she did not voice them. The engine and boiler had looked magnificent when cold – the condition in which she had known it for the past two months – as safe as anything in a museum. But now it held the menace children first discover in the jack-in-a-box and later in caged carnivores. It still *looked* tame enough but it was hissing at its joints and when bits of water leaked out they did a crackling, tortured dance on surfaces that would obviously blister the skin off you at the merest touch. And worst of all, deep in its bowels, it was making a curious pinging noise. She wanted to snatch up the children and run. Loyalty alone kept her there – loyalty of an order Michael would never understand.

Dermot wiped the pressure gauge one more time. "She'll never be more ready than that," he said. "We can't wait for them any longer."

Michael reached his hand for the throttle lever. Everyone drew breath and held it.

"No, wait!" Janet cried. "I can see them." She leaped to the door and called out. "Come on, cows' tails! You'll miss the great moment."

Philip and Diana broke from a saunter to a trot and joined the others a moment later, smiling apologetically but offering no explanation – not even the vaguest "Didn't notice the clock."

"Now, Pappa, now!" Charley cried, jumping up and down. Willie Walshe joined in and soon all the children were at it.

"Stay behind the hay bales!" Michael warned them. "Or we'll dowse the fire and wait until you've all gone to bed."

The threat had the desired effect, even though none of the children believed he'd actually do it.

"Now!" For the second time he reached his hand for the lever. He delayed moving it, however, for a few tantalizing seconds longer. "No more interruptions?" he asked with a grin. "Everybody absolutely ready?"

"Yes-es!" came a chorus of impatient voices, young and old.

"Shall we send an invitation to Mister O'Dea?"

"Michael!" Lucy called out. "If that machine doesn't explode soon, I will."

Avenged at last for all the delays and doubts, he pulled slowly on the lever.

There was an eerie rushing-hissing-bubbling sound and a menacing rumble; later half of them swore the floor trembled but the others pooh-poohed the idea. However, nothing moved. Michael and Dermot exchanged glances, which swiftly turned to encouraging smiles. The steam continued to hiss and bubble in the pipes. Michael opened the valve a little more. The sound developed a strangulated tone – the sort of noise children make when they pretend someone is choking them. The two engineers exchanged further glances – which did not so readily turn into smiles this time.

"Give the flywheel a tip?" Dermot suggested, laying down his oil can.

"It can't do any harm. Get it going and I'll open the lever all the way."

"Which direction?"

"Try clockwise. Try both. This steam must have *some* effect – I mean, it must be easier in one direction than the other."

The moment Dermot moved the wheel there was a cough like a dog being sick – a dog the size of an elephant – and a great gout of hot water shot out of the relief valve on the low-pressure cylinder. It spurted horizontally, like a bull with a loose bowel, and thudded into one of the haybales guarding the children. The mothers shrieked, the children laughed, and Diana grabbed Philip's arm and clung to it. The tail end of the ejaculation fell to the cobbled floor and lay there steaming.

"Condensate," Michael called out with all the soothing omniscience of his regular profession.

222

"The cylinders were cold," Dermot added in the same familiar vein.

"Oh yes! Cold enough to have boiled our children alive!" Lucy shouted back.

"No harm done." Janet touched her arm soothingly. Diana's instinctive reaction interested her and she wanted Lucy to notice it, too.

"No thanks to them," Lucy answered sullenly – and then saw Diana rather guiltily letting go of Philip's arm. "Are you children all right?" she asked, not taking her eyes off the couple.

The children didn't even hear her. They were watching spellbound as the mighty power of steam began to take effect. Michael still had the throttle at less than half steam but the engine was now turning freely, with a kind of lazy grace that silenced and captivated them all.

Michael laughed. "I don't believe it! It's actually working – look!" He turned excitedly to Lucy.

But Lucy had stepped into the back row, where none of the others could see her without deliberately looking. And her eyes were on Philip and Diana now.

So that was what Michael saw: At the moment of his triumph, the culmination of all his weeks of work on the old engine – this crowning achievement – his wife could not take her eyes off her old flame, Philip de Renzi!

Savagely he opened the throttle wide. There was a momentary illusion whereby the engine seemed to shiver up and down, despite its huge mounting bolts and massive iron bed, itself bolted firmly into the even more massive concrete floor. Seconds later the flywheel was whizzing round, emitting a low, menacing hum.

Dermot stepped forward and eased off the steam. "Not until she's under load, I think," he said. "Which first – the hydraulics or the dynamo?"

"The dynamo! The dynamo!" Charley was near enough to over-hear. He and Willie had been given the special task of turning the fuse handles when the dynamo was working.

Michael swiftly regained his self-control. "Sorry," he said. "Natural exuberance. It had better be the dynamo, otherwise we'll get no peace."

Dermot walked round the far side of the engine and pulled a lever. Above his head the dynamo drive-belt slipped from the idler pulley to the driven wheel and there was a momentary drop in revs as the engine took up the strain.

Michael put his hand to the throttle again.

"Hold on!" Dermot warned as he came back and crossed the engine shed to where the two boys were trembling with impatience. "Oldest first," he said apologetically to Charley as he lifted his own son up onto the bales in front of the fuse board. Charley drew breath

223

to protest but, catching sight of his father's warning finger, thought better of it and fumed in silence instead. Who had polished that fuse board until you could have eaten breakfast off it? Who had spent all those hours scraping the verdigris off the brass? Not mouldy old Willie!

The fuse board was, indeed, a minor work of art in itself. It was built on a slab of black marble, three feet long, eighteen inches high, and almost two inches thick, set in a case of glass and polished mahogany. Along the top were eight engraved labels of ivory: MAIN CELLS, ALTERNATIVE CELLS, KITCHENS, MATRON, DIRECTOR, STERILIZER, WATER PUMPS, LIGHTING. Beneath each label was a U-shaped bridge of brass, some three inches across. Only the tips of the U touched the marble; it was held by a spindle through its middle, connected to a large ebony handle, twice the size of Willie's juvenile hand. At the moment, all the handles (and thus the bridges, too) were horizontal, in which position the ends touched nothing but marble. The electrical terminals were brass circles, almost an inch in diameter, set at twelve- and six-o'clock on an imaginary clockface with the spindle at its centre. Beneath each lower terminal – to complete the fuse board – were two hefty knurled nuts of brass, screwed down tight on measured lengths of stout solder fuse wire.

"Will we charge both sets of cells?" Dermot asked.

"We'd better," Michael warned, giving a significant nod toward Charley. "Or we'll never hear the end of it."

"I mean the dynamo will take it?"

"We're about to find out! Close the first fuse."

Janet made the sign of the cross and shut her eyes. Lucy thought of kidnapping Charley and running for it.

Michael eased the throttle right back, reducing the current to a trickle. Dermot took Willie's hand and said, "Just as we practised it earlier, now."

"I *know!*" The boy shook his father's hand aside impatiently and grasped the ebony handle.

Slowly he turned it clockwise, making it screech in the satisfying way that had sent his sisters screaming from the shed an hour or so earlier; but now it was drowned by all the other noises and only his own ears felt the assault. At the last minute his courage failed him. The ends of the bridge were just fractions of an inch short of closing the terminals when he snatched his hand away and said, "You!"

"Let me! I can do it!" Charley clamoured.

Dermot squeezed his son hard and hissed in his ear, "Don't you dare let the Walshes down now!"

Willie grasped the lever again, clenched his eyes, gritted his teeth, shivered uncontrollably, and turned it the last ten degrees.

And nothing happened!

Or nothing dramatic, anyway. The needle on the ammeter on the

224

dynamo control board swung up to around five, hunted around a bit, and steadied there.

"Good man!" Michael called out. "That's a perfect connection. Not a crackle nor a spark."

"I'll bet I can make a spark," Charlie said scornfully.

"I'll bet you can't," Dermot said as he put his own son down and picked Charlie up. To Michael he added, "Are you going to put the revs up a bit?"

"To make a spark?" Michael asked.

"No but if the current falls too low, the dynamo will think it's fully charged and trip out."

Lucy sidled over next to Philip and murmured, "Can dynamos really think?"

He turned to her in mock alarm. "Oh, Luce! Such a philosophical question! And philosophy was never my strong suit – especially on a Saturday."

She laughed and hugged his arm briefly – a gesture that was not lost on Michael, either. Because of it, he opened the throttle rather more than he had intended. He closed it again but by then it was too late. A delighted Charlie had closed the bridge in a glorious shower of sparks.

"I made it spa-ark . . . I made it spa-ark!" he crowed as he skipped back to join the admiring and envious crowd of children.

"You're not supposed to," Willie told him. "You could have set the hay on fire."

"I know!" he said happily.

"It stinks of fish," Tarquin complained.

Everybody noticed it then. There must have been some trace of fish oil in the lubrication system of the engine, not enough to notice when cold but certainly enough to reek once the hot steam got at it.

"And porridge!" Portia said.

"Porridge?" several of the others shouted at her.

"You must have some funny breakfasts," Meg Walshe told her.

"Mummy? Mummy? It does smell of porridge, doesn't it!" Portia cried.

Lucy sighed. "How quickly everything returns to normal!"

"Doesn't it?" Portia insisted.

"If you think it smells like porridge, darling, then it does smell like porridge. I think it smells like the monkey house at the zoo – so make your own choice."

It was, of course a disastrous carte blanche to issue generally – with the children already in such an excited state.

"Well, I think it smells like toe jam," Willy said, touching off the avalanche.

"I think it smells like cat's puke."

"And I think it smells like Meggie's bottom."

"Out!" Janet roared – and Lucy was only a fraction of a second behind her. "You're just being silly and excited," she added.

"And it will a-all end in te-ars!" Philip murmured in a sing-song in Diana's ears. "Sometimes aren't you rather glad?"

"Sometimes," she conceded. It was touch and go but between them the two mothers managed to prise the children out of the shed.

"What now?" Dermot felt rather deflated at seeing the most appreciative section of their audience disappearing out the door.

Michael, having carefully advanced the lever until the amperage stood at twelve, which the book said was the optimum rate for charging, wiped his hands in some shoddy, like all the engineers he'd ever dreamed of becoming, and said, "You go back to the house and wash if you like, old man. I'll watch her settle down for five minutes or so and then we can leave her to charge up for a couple of hours. Tyndall or one of the other gardeners can keep the boiler stoked."

"And then?"

"Then we can start testing the hydraulic pump and the electrical circuits in the main house." He grinned. "You didn't think you were coming out here for a life of idleness, did you!"

Dermot stood between Diana and Philip for a moment, the only remaining spectators. "Every home should have one," he said.

"A resident lunatic, you mean?" Philip nodded at Michael, who was polishing surfaces that didn't need it, tapping dials to no purpose, and searching in vain for something they'd forgotten to lubricate.

"The kind that makes the world go round," Dermot countered.

"I thought that was love's rôle," Diana put in.

He grinned at her, and then at Philip. "An awful lot of people make that mistake," he said.

L ucy took out her pins and brushed her hair, making little grunts of impatience and frustration in the hope that Michael would take the hint and brush it for her. He had been rather withdrawn all evening. "I think we got more than the steam engine going today," she said. "I feel that with Dermot Walshe joining us the whole place is really beginning to move."

He nodded but she could not tell whether he had really listened. He was passing the door at that moment, moving from his wardrobe to the bed. He paused to switch the new electric light off and on again, laughing at the magic of it.

"You remember what the man said," she warned him. "The bulb won't last if you keep switching it on and off. There are just so many ons and offs in them and then they're dead."

"Why, they're almost human," he said dryly as he headed for the bed. "Last one between the sheets gets up and turns the light off."

"Aren't you going to do my hair?"

She held the brush toward him. For a moment he hesitated and then came unsmiling toward her.

"Oh, such a sacrifice!" she exclaimed.

He took it from her and went to work in silence.

"Ow!" she said after a few strokes.

"Sorry," he replied abstractedly.

She swallowed the rest of her outburst for she did not want to give him cause to drop the brush and leave her – which he was quite capable of doing in this mood. Instead she smiled at him and said, "Ebenezer told me this evening how much he enjoyed our luncheon today. In fact, he wants to make it a regular weekly affair – 'a chance to exchange information that may slip through the interstices of the busy working day and to air petty grievances while they are still pimples and prevent them from festering into septic boils,' was his way of putting it."

"In other words, to find new sores to torment and to pick the scabs off the old ones before time can heal them," Michael glossed the sentiments.

"That's up to us, don't you think?" she suggested. "We needn't let him have his own way. I'm afraid we played right into his hands today. All of us, I mean – not just you and me."

He paused, then looked at her hair and said, "Isn't that enough?"

"I suppose so." She sighed and took the brush from him. Then, giggling, she ran to the bed and said, "Last one between the sheets gets up and turns the light off!"

Grim-faced he went and did so; there was no laughter at the magic this time.

"Oh, who can't take a joke!" she teased, forcing him to smile a little. "Convenient it may be," she went on, "but it's a harsh light, for all that. Don't you think this lamplight is much kinder?"

"You're twenty-eight, Lucy," he responded wearily as he climbed into bed beside her. "You have the finest skin of any woman I know. The only light that could conceivably be unkind to it is the arc lamp in the clinic."

"Why are you taking that tone?" she asked, laying her hand gently on his arm.

"What tone?"

"Oh, Michael – don't jump at everything. It makes reasonable conversation impossible."

After a pause he said, "All right. But it's only *one* of the things that makes reasonable conversation impossible."

"What are the others?"

He drew breath to speak but obviously found it impossible. "I'm tired," he said at last.

She tried another tack, starting with her earlier remark: "We don't

227

have to let Ebenezer O'Dea have it all his own way at these Saturday luncheons."

"*If* we hold them at all."

"I don't think there's any *if* about it, darling. If he wants to arrange them, none of us is in a position to say no. But we could take them at face value – forget that he's hoping to dig up real dirt. Don't you think there's something to be said for airing grievances when they're still small? Before they get out of hand?"

He grunted. It could have been approval of the sentiment or it could have been just a grunt. He was lying in profile to her, chin pressed into his breastbone, staring morosely at his toes. She felt a sudden urge to hit him, and plucked her hand off his arm lest he should feel the tension in it.

"Don't you think the same thing could apply to us, too – you and me?" she pressed.

He glanced briefly toward the ceiling and said, "All right. Fire away!"

"Why me? You're obviously the one who's brooding."

"Ladies first."

His suggestion caught her unprepared, though she ought to have seen it coming; she'd been married to him long enough. Now she had to think fast. Should she counter with some tiny little pinprick of a complaint – a little touch to get the flywheel turning – or drop a bombshell so great it would knock the stuffing out of him and force him to take this moment seriously. A little voice of reason told her to choose the pinprick; but the stentorian roar of her naturally combative soul urged her to knock the stuffing out of him. "All right," she said before she could change her mind. "Tell me – what is your sudden interest in the underwear of a certain . . . *lady* – to give her the benefit of the doubt?"

He stopped breathing. He just lay there and stared at the ceiling. After an excruciating pause he inhaled deeply, to make up the deficit, and then said, in a quiet voice trembling with emotion, "Explain yourself plainly. What are you talking about?"

"A stocking, Michael. But hardly plain. A lurid pink stocking that . . ."

"In my bag?"

After a short silence she said, "Yes." She was beginning to feel the most dreadful misgivings. There were so many other ways she could have broached this topic, and now all of them seemed better than the one she had chosen – or leaped at.

"You mean the stocking I use in order to show the nurses that, in a dire emergency, with the patient bleeding to death, they don't have to go running to the surgical stores for a tourniquet because they all carry two perfectly good ones about their person most of the time? *That* stocking?"

There was a leaden feeling in her stomach now. "But why that colour?" she asked, trying to suggest by her tone that nothing could excuse it.

He was back in his element now. "Because we medical types have always found that a little coarse humour is the best way of conveying serious instruction. And the mere suggestion that any of them would be caught *dead* wearing such outlandish colours beneath the prim navy-blue of their uniforms usually brings the house down. D'you have any other questions, Lucy?"

She sniffed back the incipient tears whose overflow was filling her nostrils and whispered, "No."

"Good. May I begin then?"

"Oh, Michael – don't be so *cold!* I can't bear it when you're like that."

"Like what?"

"Like some medieval inquisitor quietly checking his thumbscrews and branding irons."

He cleared his throat. "That is not part of any religious tradition to which *I* am accustomed," he said. "However, the question is very simple. How did you know the stocking was there at all?"

"Because I was hunting for some of that Aspirin powder you said was so effective with headaches."

"I see," he said thinly. "You marry a doctor and then you tell yourself that the years he spent learning medicine – to say nothing of all the experience he has gained since qualifying – you say all that is worthless as far as you're concerned, eh? You have a headache . . ."

"It was the middle of the night, for the love of heaven! You'd have been delighted if . . ."

He ploughed doggedly on through her objection: "You have a headache – which could be a symptom of some serious condition – but you decide you know best how to treat it."

"You'd have been delighted if I'd woken you at three in the morning to ask *you* to treat it!"

"So you go downstairs and rummage in my bag. And there you find a lady's stocking and you leap to the conclusion that . . ."

"It's not just *any* lady's stocking though, is it, Michael!"

She could feel his confidence draining away again. "What does that mean?" he asked defensively.

"You know quite well what it means. It means I know whose stocking that is."

"I see," he said icily.

"Why *her* of all people?" Lucy blurted out, angry all over again.

"I don't know why you take that tone," he said in the same cold manner. "I may as well tell you that at this particular moment *she* stands vastly higher in my estimation than you!"

Lucy was aghast at the comparison she believed he was making. "How can you *say* such a thing?" she asked.

"Very easily." He slipped out of the bed and reached for his

229

dressing gown. "You heard me do it."

"Where are you going?"

"Downstairs – to sleep in my office."

It took her a moment or two to get over the shock of that announcement. Then she said, "So all the world will know we've fallen out! That will certainly buck up everyone's spirit here."

He hesitated, one arm in, the other out.

She pressed home the point. "But not to worry. Even though all the clinic may eventually know about it, I'm sure all our nurses will move heaven and earth to see that our secret is confined to Mount Venus House. Not a whisper of it will reach the profession in Dublin!"

The dressing gown slipped to the floor. "My God," he said bitterly.

"Yes, Michael!" She was equally bitter now. "That's another former luxury we shall have to give up – the biting quarrel and the sweet reconciliation." She made one last try. "Perhaps we could go directly to the sweet reconciliation?" She smiled at him and lifted the sheet on his side of the bed. "I'm ready if you are?"

She realized she desired him as ardently as she would have done if they really had just gone through one of their old ding-dong battles, which used to progress through snappish exchanges, to raised voices, to outrageous insults, to half-pulled punches, to a physical struggle – which had inevitably culminated in physical love, violent enough at times to move the furniture around beneath them. "Michael?" she prompted in a tone that had only ever meant one thing between them.

But she was too ardent for him, too swift; custom had made that crescendo of hostility necessary for him – not every time they made love, of course, but certainly when they quarrelled. She slipped her fingers inside his pyjamas and began to caress him. At first he responded as she had hoped. But the more aroused he became, the more thwarted he felt – and the more ashamed, too, of the sheer animality of what they were doing. The loving acts that would have purged and cauterized a full-blooded brawl between them had no power to cleanse this lesser squabble; it was like sprinkling cheap perfume over a gangrene and hoping the corruption would go away.

When it was over he felt drained of all goodness. It was as if the very intensity of his physical pleasure, so like a blinding flash of light, had illuminated all that was base and rotten within him. He reminded himself that Lucy was already expectant – "gravid," he called it, but the clinical virtue of the word did not transfer to him – and so, by accepting her invitation, he had not only hazarded the embryonic child but her as well. He had set both lives at something less than his own momentary thrill.

But then it had been *her* invitation. She had proved herself no better than him – worse, indeed, for an invitation is a cause, whereas the acceptance of it is merely an effect. She was the cause . . .

230

The cause! It is the cause! What was that from?

He seized on this chance irrelevance – the half-forgotten quotation – as a way of avoiding his earlier line of thought. Or, rather, his mind divided in two and tried to pursue both at once. Alas, being able to part no wider than any pair of his fingers, his consciousness was soon stretched in perfect immobility over the nothingness in between; and then, like the ass that died of hunger and thirst precisely halfway between a pile of hay and a pail of water, all thought expired and he fell into a profound and dreamless slumber.

At his side a sleepless Lucy listened to his snoring, or breathing on the verge of a snore, and simmered with anger. Something of his self-disgust had communicated to her, not by telepathy, but by touches and gestures too subtle to portray – nuances that her over-sensitive conscience was, perhaps, over-ready to detect. And, as in happier times she had felt his adoration on her skin like a balm, like the warming rays of a fire in winter, so now she felt his revulsion crawl over her flesh in a manner both chill and cloying. For the first time in her married life he made her feel dirty – not that the act of love itself was dirty but that she was now especially unworthy of it.

A great coldness filled her as she lay there, more wide awake than if it were high noon and the sun in her eyes. It was a mercy, though, for it numbed her to her suffering and carried her far beyond misery's reach. She lay as on a floe of drifting ice, half in touch with the infinities of space and the eternities of time – one consciousness floating on many levels, certain that sleep would never come to her again.

But it did, of course, and rather quickly, too. She woke only once that night, at three by the stable clock. She came wide awake – so abruptly, indeed, that at first she thought this wakefulness was continuous with her earlier spell, and she wondered why the clock had failed to strike the hours between. Then she realized that, though her body might have slept, her mind had continued to ponder her problem and had even arrived at some kind of answer – or conclusion, at least.

A voice in her brain announced that affairs between her and Michael were now at such a serious pass that it no longer mattered who was right and who was wrong, nor which of them had started it, nor even what their disagreement was all about; it was grave enough to make all that sort of thing – the matrimonial forensics – irrelevant. The tone of this voice was so grimly certain, she knew it was stating the conclusions of a long-fought debate that she had somehow missed. She could take it, or she could leave it, but the argument itself was over. The voice went on to tell her there was now no quick or easy way back to the marriage she had known. To be exact, it did not precisely *tell* her; in some odd, wordless way it managed to convey the notion: "You *know* there is no quick or easy way." And no sooner had the notion formed than she *knew* she knew it; she recognized its

231

truth as a truth she already possessed.

Part of her mind objected that that could not possibly be, but its logic was feeble when pitted against the strength of those overwhelming truths. There *was* no easy way out of this quagmire. Michael would not even see it was there – not because he was callous or emotionally shallow but because such truths were not available to anyone who had to cast the real self aside for large tracts of the day and shelter behind a professional mask and act to the script of others' expectations. So the burden of it fell entirely to her. *They* could not mend this breach but *she* could.

Just before she fell asleep again another thought came to her, speaking in a very different voice. "Do you want it mended at all?" it asked. Shocking as its implications were, they did not prevent her from drifting back into sleep.

When she awoke in the morning she found Michael already dressed and on the point of leaving the room. "Good morning," she called out as his hand touched the doorknob.

He turned to her and dipped his head, almost formally. "Good morning."

"Smile," she said. "Practise for being in public. We have to keep smiling." She tried to smile at him.

"That's a rictus," he told her.

She knew she had heard the word but could not think what it meant.

"A death's-head smile," he explained. "The smile of *rigor mortis*." And he left without trying to compete.

She knelt beside the bed and said her morning prayers. When she rose to her feet she said grimly, "Give us this day our daily rictus."

When Lucy remarked that something more than the old steam engine had been started that day, she made the understatement of the year. The next fortnight at Mount Venus was busier than any of them would have thought possible. Dermot Walshe took the lease on Helen Lynch's fine old house down in Willbrook, just south of Rathfarnham, and joined the staff as consultant clinical gynæcologist and assistant medical director – and only just in time, for word had gone out ahead of him and seven new female patients with infirmities in that branch were admitted on the same day. And then, as if one reputation recruited the other, Michael's recent specialization in cardiovascular disorders began to bear fruit, too, overturning his earlier disappointment at the slow start. He was so busy, and so cheerful – and so exhausted at the end of each extended day – that he barely noticed Lucy's increasing distress at the growing alienation between them.

From his point of view it was an inevitable consequence of the

232

flood of new work. The work brought money. Money bought a present living and a future security for Lucy and the children. If he was isolated from them for all the working day and half the working night – even though in the same building – it was nonetheless out of dedication to them. Surely they could see that? And if all he wanted to do when at last he come home was read the births, marriages, and deaths in the *Irish Times* and then fall fast asleep . . . well, it couldn't be helped. The situation couldn't last for ever but while they were building up the business everyone had to make sacrifices.

Lucy could not see it in that light at all. On the few occasions when she managed to snatch a word or two with him, and he spoke of sacrifices, she told him there might soon be no altar left on which to make them. He said they were all tired and it was a difficult time and they should think very carefully about making dark statements they might regret when calmer days returned – as they surely would.

He hadn't the energy to brush her hair any more and he usually managed to fall asleep in the time it took her to cross the room from the electric-light switch by the door to their bed. Sometimes she wanted him so much she lay awake at his side, shivering with her longing.

One evening – it was on the Thursday of the third week in June – when she was in the glasshouse, collecting earwigs for the slaughter, she spied Dazzler and Philip strolling up into the kitchen garden. So, feeling the lack of admiring masculine company rather acutely by then, she decided to go up and join them in whatever they were at. She went outside, opened up the slow bonfire and tipped the insects she had already collected into its glowing heart, as she did almost every evening. It always made her think of hellfire sermons as she watched their brief death throes – how they squirmed, spat, crackled, and then glowed. And though hers was the rôle of God – even to the extent that she carefully sorted out the "virtuous" woodlice from the "wicked" earwigs before consigning the sinners to the flames – it left her feeling awful; and she wondered how a God of Love could hold such a threat over His own children?

This petty *dies irae* delayed her so long on that particular evening that, by the time she reached the walled garden the two men were nowhere in sight.

"Is it out walking you are, Mrs Raven?" came a voice from behind her.

Lucy turned round and made herself smile. "Miss Kelly!" She peered at the bundle under the girl's arm. "Been doing a spot of laundry, I see?"

Birdie glanced over her shoulder and then proudly held up a damp pair of drawers and three stockings, as if Lucy were a teacher of household management.

"They're white," Lucy said in surprise.

Birdie laughed as she draped them back over her arm. "Sure and that wasn't aisy."

They started to stroll toward the old pheasant run. "What?" Lucy asked hesitantly. "You mean you bleached them?"

"A touch of the bleach, ma'am. It did no harm. I took a tumble in the grass on Monday, so I did, and 'twas all green streaks here, though you'd never see it now."

Lucy did not hazard a guess at what she meant by "took a tumble." She peered at what she could see of the drawers, all folded over, and said, "But, you mean, they were white before? White cotton?"

"God, I'd never wear anything else. Why? Is white wrong would you say?"

"No no – not at all. I always wear white myself. But . . . I just wondered. With these new fast aniline dyes, colour is becoming popular."

"Gertie O'Hara wore black and you wouldn't want to be sitting next to her at mass too often," she said self-righteously.

"Yes, well, perhaps that's enough about underwear for the moment. Except . . . why d'you have only three stockings?"

Birdie was surprised, as if Lucy had asked her why she had only two thumbs. "Sure I wear them in threes, ma'am. Don't you? I thought everyone did."

Knowing she was going to regret it, Lucy pointed out that she had only two limbs to support them.

"Ah, but I rest one of them, turn and turn about." The stockings were still draped over her arm and she now played a sort of child's pitapat game with them: "Monday, Tuesday, rest. Tuesday, Wednesday, rest. Wednesday, Thursday, rest. Then wash the three together. A day's rest for a stocking is as good as half a wash – did they never tell you that?"

Lucy sighed. "No, Miss Kelly. Obviously my upbringing was severely defective in certain directions." She stepped aside to glance into the old potting shed, which Philip had not yet started to dismantle. The awful thought was just beginning to occur to her that her guess had been wrong as to the true owner of the stocking she had found in Michael's bag. But who else at Mount Venus would wear underthings dyed such a seductive flesh colour? Certainly none of the nurses and *certainly* not their matron!

"Are you after losing something, ma'am?" Birdie asked.

"Two men," Lucy told her. "Mister Dazzler O'Dea and Mister de Renzi – I'm only after seeing them come in here."

"Sure you know where *they'll* be," she commented wearily and then seated herself on the old straw bale outside the shed door. "I'll not hang these out with those gossoons up there!"

"D'you think they are?" Lucy asked.

Birdie clearly did not consider the question deserved an answer.

Still dubious herself, Lucy went quickly to the opening into the pheasant run. In the green gloom she could vaguely make out the dark shapes of some laundry, but nothing living. She called out: "Dazzler? Philip?"

There was a brief pause and then Philip's voice came from somewhere beyond the washing lines: "Up here, Lucy."

She made her way toward them; as she drew near she asked in a schoolmarmish voice, "And what, pray, is the meaning of this?"

Dazzler parodied a slow-witted midlander by way of reply. "We're looooking for a plaaace to lodge two greeayhounds, an it plase ye, ma'am. Have ye e'er an old roll of chicken netting ye could lose without missing?"

"Tonight?" she asked in surprise.

"Ah no." He reverted to his usual voice. "I'm to collect them next week, but I want to get a sort of a kennel ready for them."

"You're not pulling my leg, Dazzler?"

He grinned and slipped an arm around her. "Just give us the chance, Luce!"

She elbowed him away, laughing.

"You're more lovely than ever," he persisted. "Wouldn't you say so, de Renzi? You have as good an eye as me."

Philip smiled at her in embarrassment. "You have to forgive him today, Lucy," he said. "He had some luck on the Gold Cup this afternoon."

"I had a couple of ponies on Throwaway," Dazzler added proudly. "I got them on at five-to-one, too."

"Do *ponies* race in the Gold Cup?" she asked.

They laughed and explained that a racing man's pony was twenty-five pounds.

"I had a very hot tip," Dazzler explained. He wanted her to understand he was no longer reckless and profligate with money.

But the thought of wagering fifty pounds on a horse – no matter how strong the tip – made Lucy feel sick. "So what has that to do with greyhounds?" she asked.

Philip answered for him. "He thinks he can make a bit of steady money at it."

"Well, the nurses certainly won't want you to keep creatures like that here," she said. "The dust they'll kick up. And the smell."

"What's it to do with them?" Dazzler asked truculently.

She pointed toward the laundry lines.

"Lord!" he exclaimed in high innocence. "And I never even noticed!"

"What mark of a fool do you see on me?" she asked sarcastically. "Really, Dazzler!"

Philip laughed and grabbed his companion's arm. "She's right, old man. We'll have to find somewhere else. The place I pointed to first would be driest – foreanenst the kitchen-garden entrance."

"Besides," Lucy added, "there's someone who wants to come and hang her laundry up here and is only waiting for you to go."

"Not Matron Powers?" Philip asked at once.

"No." She was slightly surprised at the eagerness of his question, for she had no idea how far things had progressed between them; he and Diana had, in fact, been most discreet (absurdly so in his opinion) since that Saturday afternoon. "It's Birdie Kelly, why?"

"Ah!" Dazzler tipped back his straw boater and rubbed his hands excitedly. "I want a word with that one. She said I was to come back when I had two monarchs to rub together. She never thought I'd be in the money so soon."

"Just watch her eyes light up with the disappointment!" Philip called after him. He turned to Lucy to recruit her smile but was surprised to see how wan and pinched her expression had suddenly become. Then he was all concern. "Are you all right?" he asked.

She shook her head slowly and, taking his arm, began strolling back toward the opening in the wire. "I'm feeling pretty awful, Philip, if you really want to know," she said.

"Oh, Luce, I am sorry." He squeezed her hand reassuringly.

They were passing the lines at that moment and she said, "You remember the pink laundry that was hanging out here last time you and I passed this way?"

"Yes," he replied guardedly. "It was peach, actually, but still – what about it?"

She turned about suddenly and pulled him back, retracing the few steps they had just taken. "Let's go out through that hole in the wire. I don't want to meet them – Dazzler and La Kelly."

"What about it – the peach-coloured stuff?"

"Oh yes. You don't know whose it was, do you? I assumed it was Birdie Kelly's, but . . ."

He stiffened. "You told me it was Matron's!"

She shook his arm, as if he were being deliberately obtuse. "That was only a joke – and well you know it! Don't pretend. Can you imagine Diana Powers being seen dead in anything like that?"

He cleared his throat. "Sorry – go on. You thought it was Miss Kelly's . . . but?"

"Yes. I've just discovered it couldn't have been."

"Amazing!" His tone was dismissive. "What does it matter, anyway?"

She said nothing. They were approaching the hole in the wire by now.

"Eh?" he prompted.

She leaned her head on his shoulder.

"What's this?" he asked, reached awkwardly across her to push the jagged edge of the netting out of her way.

She squeezed through the gap and turned to face him. When he joined her in the cocoon of woodbine and russian vine, she flung her

236

arms around him and began to cry. "Oh, Philip, I'm so miserable. I don't know who to turn to."

"Well, er," he stammered, "if you think I might help?" He hugged her while her whole body shook with her sobbing, stroking her back. He had to fight hard to quash all kinds of unworthy thoughts and feelings.

After a while she sniffed her nostrils free again, blew her nose in the handkerchief he proffered, and said, "The thing is, you see . . ." and then halted.

"What?" he asked gently after a moment.

"Oh God, if I tell you, it'll be like . . . I mean, it's something I couldn't possibly take back."

"Perhaps you'd better not, then." He tried to bend himself, to ease the touch of her breasts against him. He could never understand that about women. Sometimes they were all too aware of the erotic power of those adorable lumps; at other times they behaved as if such a notion had never so much as crossed their minds.

"But who else is there?" she persisted. "If I do, promise you'll never tell a soul?"

"Of course I shan't, Luce. You don't even need to ask it."

"I know. I'm sorry. Oh, I'm in such a . . . state over all this. The other thing you must promise is not to laugh – because at times even I can see it's the most comical . . . stupid . . . oh, all this fuss about one stupid stocking! Anyway – the thing is, you see, you remember there was only one stocking there?"

"Yes. What of it?"

"Wait till I tell you! I found the missing one that very same evening – or night, rather – hidden away in Michael's doctor's bag!"

She was surprised to feel how rigid he went suddenly; obviously he found it as scandalous as she had done. "Yes," she went on. "Birdie Kelly's stocking in Michael's bag – or so I imagined. As if that wasn't bad enough, I now discover it wasn't hers – so what can I do? How do I find out whose it was? Should I even try? I can't think properly."

Philip swallowed heavily. "Did you ask him what it was doing there?"

"Not at once. It arose a couple of days later when we had an argument – oh, Philip, it was the bitterest argument ever – not hot and fiery like we often have, or used to have. It was . . . *cold!* I can't tell you how cold."

"What did he say?"

"He passed it off as some old stocking he kept for his first-aid demonstrations with nurses."

"Eh?"

"Exactly! I thought it was pretty brazen, too. He said it was something to do with tourniquets, to show them they all carry two perfectly good tourniquets around with them all the time." When she added Michael's explanation for the colour she expected Philip to

237

laugh, if only out of admiration for the quickness of wit that went into such an elaborate tale.

But Philip remained as quiet as the grave – and stiff with tension, too.

"So now I don't know whose it was, you see. All I do know is that it belongs to *someone* under our roof. None of the nurses, I'm sure. Nor the maids – the quality was too good. You don't suppose it could possibly have been Mrs Lynch?"

He shook his head. "She was away at that time, anyway – wasn't she?"

"Oh yes." She sighed again. "You don't have any ideas, I suppose?"

"You're absolutely sure it was a twin to the one hanging on the line when we were here that day?"

"Absolutely. The other odd thing is that when I charged Michael with it, he didn't deny it was Birdie Kelly's – glad to throw me off the scent, obviously."

"You actually *told* him you knew they were Birdie's? You mentioned her by name?"

Lucy couldn't think why it was so important to him but the intensity behind his question made her think again. At last she said, "Perhaps I didn't, you know. I don't believe I did. I just said I knew very well whose it was – something like that. And he assumed I was talking about . . . well, whoever is the real owner. Hah!" The exclamation was bitter. "And all I know about her is that she's worth ten of me!"

"Oh? He told you that, did he?"

She shrugged. "Just the sort of thing either of us is liable to blurt out in the heat of battle, I'm afraid. I don't take it too seriously. Still, I'd like to know who she is, now I know it's not Birdie Kelly."

"Talking of her" – he popped his head briefly back into the pheasant run – "she's a long time coming to hang up her things, isn't she?"

Lucy shrugged. "She probably hid them the moment she saw Dazzler wending his way toward her. Why?"

"Well, if *they* aren't going to make an appearance, *we* ought to, don't you think?"

"Why?"

"Well," he replied awkwardly, "otherwise . . . you know."

She gave a single, grim laugh. "Perhaps *they* are the ones who . . ." But she bit off the rest of the sentence, saying, "No – I mustn't become obsessive."

"Oh, Lucy!" he sighed, stroking her soothingly around the nape of her neck. "What a tangle, eh! But I'm sure it'll turn out all right."

"Are you?" she asked bleakly.

"Quite sure of it," he said in the unsurest tone imaginable.

"Philip?" She closed her eyes and raised her lips in an unambiguous invitation.

He said nothing but she heard him swallow heavily.

"Please?" She slipped a hand inside his blazer and began to caress one of his nipples. "Mmm?"

"Oh . . . please!" he said in an awkward echo of her but in quite the opposite tone.

"You've no idea . . ." she stammered.

"Nor have you!" He pushed her away, harder than he intended.

She drew a deep breath and clenched her fists tight, staring at him balefully – determined not to break down in tears again. "So I disgust you, too!" she said.

"No!" It was a cry of agony – strangulated for fear of being overheard, and all the more compelling for that. "The very opposite, Luce! The very . . . oh Lord, if you only knew how much I . . ." Then he frowned and asked in quite a different tone, "What d'you mean – disgust me too? Why *too?* I mean, who else?"

She shook her head. "It doesn't matter. No one. I didn't mean it."

But each denial only confirmed his increasing suspicion. "It's Michael, isn't it! He's who you meant when you said *too*."

"No." She sounded most unconvincing, even to herself. "Why d'you say that?"

He bit his lip and eyed her speculatively. "I wonder if I ought to tell you?" He pursed his lips tight.

She smiled at him wanly and shrugged, unwilling to say anything that might make him stop.

"It would also explain why I have just declined the sweetest offer I ever . . . that you . . . why I declined. Damn it, I will tell you." He breathed in and squared his shoulders. "I've fallen in love with Diana."

"No!" She parodied surprise. "Who would have believed it! I *wondered* why you've been making sheep's eyes . . ."

"Listen!" He placed a good-humoured hand over her lips. "I never imagined *that* bit would surprise you. It's the bit that comes next. Diana and I have been making more than sheep's eyes lately – d'you follow?"

She felt her cheeks go cold.

"The day the Walshes first came out here? D'you remember? Saturday before last? You and Janet walked off in the garden somewhere and Michael and Dermot were in the engine shed?"

"And you and Diana . . .?" Her mouth gaped – though now she thought about it she could not understand why she felt so surprised.

He nodded. "But the reason I know you meant Michael when you said 'too' is . . ." Suddenly he put his arms around her again and hugged her to him. To the empty air behind her back he murmured, "Oh please, Diana my darling, forgive me this small act of kindness!" Then he pulled away from her – or withdrew his head, at least,

239

though he continued to hug her tight – and said. "And after . . . well, afterwards, I made some slight remark – oh, I remember what I said! I offered to take my clothes into her sitting room and leave her to dress unobserved, and *oh!* She exploded like Mont Pelé! Did her body disgust me? Was I ashamed of her now? Had she defiled me . . . all that sort of thing. Don't ever breathe a word of this to another soul!"

"Would I?" Lucy gave him an accusing look. "However, that doesn't mean it was Michael who . . ." Her voice trailed off when she saw him nodding, a sad gaze in his eyes.

"It does, Luce – I'm afraid. You see, we've talked about it since. I mean, I let it die down for a day or two and then I asked her. And it was Michael. He was the one who made her so sensitive about – in fact, he was the *only* one – until I came along."

Lucy was still looking for a way to minimize anything that had taken place between Michael and Diana, no matter how long ago – not for Michael's sake but because her own spirit required it more than ever at that particular time. "I suppose she . . . you know – made some sort of offer to him . . . sort of thing . . ."

To rescue her he grinned and said, "Like tickling one of his nipples?"

She punched him quite hard on the arm and said vehemently, "If you can't help, just shut up! I mean she made an offer and he turned it down and made some unfortunate remark – and she magnified the whole wretched business, just from that?" She eyed him hopefully.

At once he replied, "Yes, something like that." It was too obviously soothing. The hope fled from her eyes. "Liar," she said.

He nodded. "Forgive me. I don't know where old loyalties end and new ones begin."

"All right. You needn't tell me – I'll tell you. They Did It and then Michael, all noble and full of remorse, tried to take the shame of it all on his own shoulders but somehow managed to say something that left her feeling . . ."

". . . besmirched," he said when she fished for the right word.

"Mother of God, where will this end?" She sank her face in her hands and fought back a fresh wave of tears.

He misunderstood. "It was a very long time ago," he assured her. "Before he met you. Before he qualified, even."

She looked up at him and laughed coldly. "That's not what I mean. I mean I want to know where it happened and when . . ."

"At a ball at the RCS . . . back in 'ninety-two? 'Ninety-three?"

"And did she suggest it or did he? Or did their eyes just meet and their knees tremble? And how much courting had they done before that? And how did she feel while they were Doing It. And him, too – how did he feel? And was she wearing *this* ring at the time?" She almost hit his nose as she thrust it into his vision. "D'you see what I mean by 'where will this end'?"

240

He swallowed and arched his eyebrows. "I think it had better end there."

"Of course it had *better* end there, but d'you imagine for one moment it will? Has he thought about it since? Has he thought *better* of it since? Has he replayed that scene in his mind, over and over again with a different ending? Has he played it over in his mind while his body was Doing It with me! Have I been just a canvas on which he projected *her?*"

He hugged her tight against him, taking her head and turning it forcibly so that her mouth was buried at the base of his neck, allowing her to breathe through her nose but not to go on speaking.

She struggled a moment, with her body writhing and squirming against his . . . and then she felt the effect it had on him, and, though she continued to writhe and squirm, it was no longer with any intention of escaping his embrace.

"No!" he whispered, beseeching her to stop what he could not.

Their knees trembled, their innards went hollow, they almost fainted in the sudden extremity of their desire for each other. And the voices booming "Wrong . . . wrong . . . wrong!" in their minds had the funereal ring of passing bells. The death they mourned was that of conscience.

L ucy and Philip strolled back through the long grass, a careful eighteen inches apart, taking divergent paths around the tall docks and thistles that grew in patches here and there. "If someone doesn't cut these back soon, we shall be in dire trouble next year," she said, adding after a pause: "An ounce of prevention, you know . . ."

Long fingers of westering sunlight caught the downy curls of his beard, just beneath the lobe of his left ear; at that moment there was something so perfect about it, about his head, about Philip himself, that she wanted to capture it, press it in some book of memory. A sharp pang of envy caught her unawares, and it hurt – envy for Diana, whose claim to him was unassailable. Or was she always going to take Diana's men away from her? Was that her real destiny? No, of course not! The very idea was absurd. Indeed, the whole tenor of her life was becoming absurd. Not so long ago she had cherished the thought that Diana must be consumed with envy every night of her lonely life, while she and Michael shared so much. More recently, on the other hand, she had envied Diana her solitude, her independence. Whose life, then, was in a mess?

"Is that a hint about what we've just done?" he asked.

"What?" Her thoughts had strayed so far beyond her latest words to him.

"An ounce of prevention is worth a ton of cure. That's how the

241

saying goes, isn't it? Are you saying what we did was just an ounce of prevention?"

She could barely glimpse the point of his question and had no idea where it might lead. "I don't understand that at all," she replied. "Preventing what? Or *curing* what, come to that?"

He sighed. "Never mind."

She wanted to touch him, to stroke his arm, his face. To soothe him. Instead she stepped away, increasing the distance between them. "You do feel defiled now, don't you – I can tell."

"Of course not, Lucy. Don't be so dramatic."

"You think I've defiled you."

"Nonsense!"

"You're hinting it was an ounce of prevention against my own malady – but at the cost of infecting you."

This time he said nothing.

"So!" she exclaimed, as if she had won the argument.

He sighed again, this time in even greater exasperation. "You clearly *need* to believe this bunkum. Something in you absolutely longs to feel guilty. And equally clearly I can say nothing to dissuade you. So let's drop it."

They came in silence to the unbarred gateway and halted there.

"Point to this and that," she said. "Make it look as if we're planning the garden."

"Do you hold postmortems like this with Michael?" he asked as he wafted an arm in a grand gesture at the grounds to their front. If the question had not been so serious she would have laughed at the incongruity of word and gesture.

"It wasn't my choice of subject," she protested. "You're the one who brought it up. If you remember, I was talking about cutting back the weeds before they seed. You picked on the remark and turned it into a postmortem. Why *mortem*, anyway? D'you feel you died back there?"

"Something did," he replied, referring to the fact that Diana had apparently allowed Michael to have (and treasure?) one of her most intimate garments.

But Lucy was not to know that. "I'll apologize for living and breathing next," she said morosely.

He saw then how she had taken his words amiss and sought desperately for some way to explain himself but without involving Diana and her apparent duplicity. Explain sunlight but leave the sun out of it! "Aquinas called it a little death in the soul," he told her. "Or was it Augustine?"

"Oh well!" she said, as if that made all the difference. "*That* sort of death! It means nothing. Millions of cells in our bodies die every single day. The early fathers didn't know that, of course."

Philip laughed slightly more heartily than her words warranted. "If they had, perhaps we'd now enjoy a less puritanical theology." He could not sustain the humour, however. Conscience compelled him to add: "And we'd both be feeling less guilty, too."

She touched him at last, though to a distant observer it would seem she was simply making him drop his arm. "It won't happen again, Philip."

He stared at her, nostrils flaring, as if she had just insulted him – and then, equally surprising to her, his face creased in laughter.

"What now?" she asked him.

"The Primitive!" He beat his chest like an ape. "The Primitive in me – how close he is to the surface, how ready to take control at a moment's notice! Of *course* it won't happen again. You mean that fervently, and so do I – with all my soul. But when I hear it on *your* lips – like a governess saying primly. 'Now, Master Philip, it won't happen again!' then . . ."

"I didn't say it like that!"

"I know you didn't." He patted her hand comfortingly. "But that's how the Primitive heard it. And his hackles rose . . . and a red mist descended before his eyes . . ."

"Philip!"

"Well – not really. But he waxed jolly wroth, I can tell you. We *are* much more primitive than we like to believe – to be serious a mo. And perhaps a lot of your present troubles boil down to a certain blindness to that fact. What d'you think? Isn't it the case that you expect completely civilized behaviour from Michael and when you don't get it, you feel betrayed and bitter? And you expect equally civilized behaviour from yourself, too, and when you fail that ideal, you feel you've betrayed him and become bitter toward yourself?" He smiled a little sadly as he added, "Or am I just giving myself reasons for sleeping with a quiet conscience tonight?"

When all she did was nod, and smile rather distantly, he thought his efforts to comfort her had failed. But at length she said, "It has nothing to do with conscience. I know you're trying to help but you're too honest. You force me to be honest, too. My real trouble is what you call the Primitive. I mean the Primitive in *me*. I pretend to complain about Michael and the mysterious lady with the pink stockings . . ."

"Peach-coloured."

She bunched a fist and threatened him. "I pretend to complain about her. I say *she's* my problem. But . . ." She swallowed hard and stared at him like someone in a trap.

"Go on."

"But even as I rail against her – and him – I'm forced to confess how trivial it is and how I've really exaggerated it out of all proportion. I'm trying to hide something, you see. And what I'm trying to hide . . ." She turned slowly away from him as she spoke, and lowered her voice, and kept her gaze on the grass at their feet.

243

"What's behind it all is the fact that I'm expecting a baby and that . . ."

"Lucy!" He was aghast.

"No, listen! For the next six months or however long it is . . ."

"You mean you don't know?"

"*Listen!* Just listen, all right? For the next . . . eternity, Michael won't touch me. *That's* what it really boils down to."

"Oh!" He swallowed heavily, trying to take it all in.

"Yes – oh! And I can't last . . . I need . . . Oh damn it – you know!"

"But . . . I mean, are you sure it's all right?"

"Of course it's all right."

"I know less than nothing about it. But he *is* a doctor."

"Ha! But it's *me* we're talking about. My feelings, not his damned books! And I know. Come on, let's walk back to the house."

He set off at once at a cracking walk. "Hey, not so fast!" she cried, taking his arm to slow him to her pace. "The irony of it is, Philip, that when I was first married – the time when everyone seems to think the physical side of love is so all-important – it didn't trouble me at all. It didn't upset me, the way it upset some girls I knew, but . . ."

"You talked about it?"

She laughed. "My dear! Most young wives give tea parties to talk about nothing else! I soon got to learn which of them really loved Doing It and which were only pretending."

"And you?"

"I was in between, as I was saying. I didn't *dis*like It. I hardly ever thought about It – in those days. Nor did I pine like this when I was *enceinte.*"

"And it's different now – obviously."

She nodded. "It gets more and more different with every day that passes. No, that's an absurd thing to say. With every year that passes. I cannot go another six months without being touched – that's all I know."

"And can't you tell Michael that?"

She sighed and shook her head.

"Why not?"

"Because he's a doctor and the one thing doctors cannot abide is to have their noses rubbed in their own ignorance. We know *nothing* about the human body – and even less about the spirit. But if they ever dared admit as much, patients would die like flies all around them. So they say, 'Don't worry your pretty little head about this, my dear – we doctors know all about it. Just trust us and do as we tell you.' And the patients sigh their gratitude and live! Didn't you know that?"

He was still too concerned at her earlier assertion to be distracted by this attempt at humour. "I don't know what you can do, then," he said.

"In other words, don't come knocking at *your* door!"

"Oh, Lucy! I belong to Diana now. I love Diana."

"I'm not asking you to *love* me, Philip. I don't want to take you away from her. Just . . . take care of *me* once in a while. How long did it last? Ten minutes? And don't tell me you didn't enjoy it."

"Aaargh!" He groaned through clenched teeth and shivered as if trying to burst invisible chains.

"You're the only one I'd ever dream of asking. And in fact I'm only asking you *because* you're so stuck on Diana. Are you going to marry her?"

"If she'll have me."

"Well, pretend you're married already. Married men philander all the time."

"You mean Michael does?"

"He would if it were made easy enough. He's too busy with Mount Venus at the moment but if a woman just walked up to him and said come on – he would."

"Like Janet Walshe?"

Lucy missed a step and then found the pace again. "Why d'you pick her?"

"Oh," he replied, rather too airily, "she's around, isn't she? Or she's going to be."

"As a matter of fact, I was thinking of Birdie Kelly. You see the gate over there, into the stable yard? She fell down there the other day and I was in the glasshouse and Michael was nearby and I watched him pretending to examine her for broken bones. If that had all happened up in the pheasant run . . . well, it would have been a very different ending." She sniffed. "Why *did* you pick out Janet?"

He sighed. "I honestly don't know, Lucy. Just a name."

"She set her cap at you, didn't she!"

"Of course not! When?"

"Ha ha! You should have asked when first, my lad! But you *know* when, don't you – the day I left you and her alone together up the mountain. I'll bet she tried to drag you into the furze."

"Ouch!" He tried to make a joke of it.

She stopped in her tracks and began kneading her knuckles.

"Lucy," he said, full of concern. "I've never seen you like this."

"I know." There was a hunted look in her eyes. "Nor have I. You're right to refuse my stupid suggestion. It's not the answer. It wouldn't solve anything."

"You can't go back indoors in this state. Let's just walk once right round the house – or d'you think that wouldn't help, either?"

"What if Diana sees you?"

He laughed. "That's not an *if* question, love. You see all those things that look like windows? D'you know what they really are?"

"What?"

"Eyes! Diana's eyes. Shall we walk?"

"Why not?" She sighed again. "You're right about one thing – I couldn't go indoors like this." After walking several paces in silence she said, "Will you tell me if I'm right about Janet Walshe?"

"Why?" he asked. "What good will it do?"

"All right. Don't tell me about her – tell me about women in general. Have a lot of women set their caps at you? Married women? You didn't seem terribly surprised when I did it. Has it happened to you often?"

He cleared his throat and tugged at his collar. "Perhaps I'll go straight indoors after all," he said, trying to make a joke of it.

"I'm not asking pruriently, Philip. I don't want the incandescent details. Let me make it even more general – do married ladies tend to offer their favours to likely men?"

After a pause – as if he were testing the question for booby traps – he replied: "Not much in the first five or six years of their marriage."

"Meaning more in the next five and very much in the five after that!"

He gave an awkward cough and said, "That sort of idea."

"Next question," she said. "Would a man familiar with the phenomenon soon get to recognize a lady in that sort of mood? I've often looked at my friends and wondered, but I can see no hint of it."

He grinned and said, "That's hardly surprising!"

"I know, dear! That's why I'm asking *you*. Would a man cotton on to it, as they say? Would he twig?"

"Yes!" he said decisively – in a tone that implied that she ought to leave him alone now she'd got what she wanted.

But it wasn't what she wanted. That came next: "Any man? Or any man-of-the-world? A man as old as Ebenezer O'Dea, for example? Would he twig it?"

"Ah!" Now that the conversation no longer seemed to be drifting toward Janet Walshe and her character, he leaped upon it eagerly. "He would certainly be very quick to twig such a thing."

"So that *if* Janet Walshe was that sort of woman – only *if*, mind – Ebenezer would catch on to it like that?" She snapped her fingers.

"Like *that!*" He snapped his fingers far louder than she had done.

"That's what I really wanted to know," she said decisively. "After that lunch – that extraordinary lunch – when he somehow got us all with our claws out at each other – I thought that was why he was so keen to have the Walshes join us – because he could provoke them into arguments, I mean. But he wants to provoke something much bigger than that – I see it now."

"What?" Philip asked, mildly scornful – but only mildly.

"A woman like that . . . she could destroy everything – all of us – my marriage – and yours wouldn't even get started. Were you

246

tempted by her offer? I'll bet you were!"

To her surprise he neither denied nor confirmed it. In fact, for a long time he said nothing – prompting her to ask him if he thought she was going mad.

"No," he said slowly. "I think you probably see it more clearly than anyone. That's why you make the perfect hostess. You have that intuitive understanding." They were passing under Ebenezer's windows at that moment; Philip looked up but they were blank – full of reflected cloud and sunlight. For all he knew, the old boy could be staring down at him through binoculars, counting his eyelashes. He shivered and waited until they had passed along before he added, "I think the same as you about Ebenezer, but I lack the courage of my own judgement. I laugh at myself. But when I hear you say the very same things, I believe them." He shook his head morosely. "I hate doing this. I mean it's so dishonourable, but . . . well, you're right about Janet Walshe. There!"

"And did you . . ." she blurted out before she bit her tongue off. "No. That's beside the point. I've no business to ask."

"We did," he said simply. "And don't for God's sake breathe a word of it to Diana, or I'm dead. I told her we didn't."

Lucy stopped dead and stared at him, open-mouthed. "You actually talked about it with *her?*" she asked in amazement.

He nodded glumly. "And of course I had to deny it."

Her eyes narrowed. "Why are you telling me, then?"

"I don't know. To put what we did this evening into context, I suppose. I'm obviously not a very honourable sort of chap, Luce! I'm more than a bit of a chancer."

She chuckled and dug him in the ribs to provoke a better humour in him. Resuming their stroll she said, "You make too much of it, Philip. You're a handsome young fellow without attachments. Women set their caps at you. You have every right to take advantage of it. As a matter of interest, if she repeats her offer to you, will you accept it a second time?"

He nodded unhappily and said, "Aye!"

The obvious question hung fire between them.

He answered it for her, even though she had not voiced it. "Because there's absolutely no chance I could fall in love with *her.*"

She took him by the elbow and gave him an affectionate squeeze. "Thank you," she murmured. "You've said the one thing that will make me glad *not* to ask you again."

All the good sense he possessed urged him to leave it at that; but something within him was not happy until he added, "You knew that all along, though, Luce. Because you're the same. You could all too easily fall in love with me, too. Am I not right?"

She held her breath until forced to let it out. "Yes!" she said in the same outrush. Then she softened it with a laugh. "Women, eh? We're not at all the sort of creatures we're supposed to be, are we!"

247

He laughed, too. "Oh, my dear! I learned that a *long* time ago!"

The next omnium-gatherum luncheon was held that Saturday, two days after Lucy's fateful encounter with Philip; by then they were all on their guard – best behaviour, best intentions, best hats for the ladies, best cravats for the men . . . they put the whole lot on together. Indeed, they were so sure of themselves now that they were quite looking forward to it, a not-too-easy contest yet one they felt sure of winning.

The only person who resented having to attend was Birdie Kelly. "When I open my mouth don't they all stare like the cat just left me," she complained. "All I do is sit and gaze out the window."

"And listen, I trust." Ebenezer threw off the blanket she had just wrapped around his legs. "I'm warm enough without that. You only do it to annoy me."

"Listen is it?" she asked. "Listen to what?"

"To all the fine talk. You have ears, haven't you?"

"Pigs have mouths but divil a tune they'll whistle."

He grabbed her wrist angrily. "What does that mean?" he asked belligerently. "You come out with these sayings – as if they had the wisdom of the bards behind them – and what do they mean? Nothing!"

"I mean where's the good of all my listening? I catch my death skulking outside windows . . . I crick my neck with my ears glued to the walls . . . didn't I twist my ankle asunder falling out of the ivy, and but for Mister Raven catching the bones and slipping them back in their sockets wouldn't I be in a chair beside you! Is it to kill me you want? And where's the good of it? I'd as well blindfold the divil in the dark for all the use you make of it."

His anger faded and a sympathetic look came into his eye. "Would you houl' your whisht and sit beside me, colleen," he said gently. "And listen till I tell you a thing or two."

Part-aggrieved still, but also part-soothed, she drew his chair a couple of paces to the window seat and sat beside him.

"Listen," he went on. "Did you ever poke a few oul' slips in the clay to see would they grow into bushes?"

She nodded. "I did, of course."

"And how did you treat them? Did you water them when it rained?"

"I did not."

"Did you light candles beside them when the sun shone?"

She looked at him pityingly but he could tell she was just beginning to grasp his point – and to resist it.

"Did you poke them into fertile clay and then bury them under half a ton of fertilizer, that they'd grow to split the skies?"

She compressed her lips and stared out of the window.

"Well," he said admiringly. "At least you're half a good gardener – the easy half. What about the difficult half? Is that where you'll fall down, I wonder? Tell me – did you ever dig them up just to see how the roots were growing?"

She licked her lips and said reluctantly, "I did the once."

"And what happened?"

She tossed her head. "What d'you think!"

He reached across and patted her hand. "Isn't it the hardest thing in the world to do nothing when you're young! And don't you think it's harder yet when you can look at the hourglass and see ten times more sand in the bottom than the top?"

She smiled at him and conceded the point with a sigh.

"And will you sit there and listen with better heart now?" he asked.

"I suppose so."

He beamed at her. "Good girl! If you showed more enthusiasm, I'd trust you the less. The ones to mark are the three ladies and the bachelor-architect. There's something brewing there, I feel. Himself walked past this window the evening before last with the wife of our esteemed director on his arm and you could have read the pocket breviary by the light that shone out of them."

Birdie was suddenly galvanized into feeling. "Jaysus, Mary, and Joseph!" she exclaimed in disgust. "Wouldn't you think women'd have the sense to leave men alone – the troubles they are, and the troubles they bring, and the troubles they leave behind them!"

"Spoken with feeling!" He stared at her in admiration. "You'll never be caught yourself, I'm sure."

"It'll be a fine day for young ducks, the day a man will come round me again – damnation seize their souls!"

"Not even our brave young architect? He's a handsome fellow wouldn't you say?"

She sniffed contemptuously. "One fool is enough for any parish – and we have three!"

"Grand lass," he said. "Now let you stop your complaining. Will we go wrap ourselves around some fine roast pork – if my nose doesn't deceive me?"

At this luncheon the men around the main table threatened to outnumber the women by five to three, for both the O'Deas were there. To make it more even, Lucy invited Helen Lynch – in her capacity as assistant matron rather than as the Walshes' new landlord, "though either would do," as she said. She could think of no good reason for including Birdie Kelly, even though it would equalize the numbers perfectly at five all. When Doctor Quinlan took up his new post as RMO, the sexes would be still further unbalanced; even then, Lucy doubted she'd invite Birdie to join them. Anyway, he wasn't due for another month, so there was time enough. She felt mildly sorry for the girl, sitting all alone like a pariah by the window, but anarchy at arm's length was better than having it at your elbow.

Michael picked on Dazzler as soon as they had said grace, telling him that a greyhound kennels in the grounds was not the greatest possible enhancement to the Mount Venus Clinic. Dazzler explained it was only for a week or so, while he built a proper place for them in the field opposite the front gate, which he'd rented till Christmas to see could he make a go of it.

Janet Walshe chipped in: "Do I understand correctly, Mister O'Dea, that those animals cost a great deal to feed and train?" Her real question, of course, was where the young man had found the money for his new hobby.

Dazzler told her that, properly done, it could pay for itself.

"In time, I'm sure," she agreed. "But it's the starting up, you know. I had an uncle almost came a cropper with a greyhound kennels in County Cavan."

Lucy said, "He should have got a hot tip for the Gold Cup first."

Dazzler looked daggers at her but it was too late. His uncle glared at him and barked, "Is that the way of it?"

"Indeed, it is not," the young man asserted stoutly. "I was after getting a good tip on Throwaway from Poldy Bloom and I passed it on to Mick Brophy in Davy Byrne's, who said he'd put something on it for me – but I never thought he meant it."

"Mick Brophy is it?" Ebenezer asked scornfully. "The last time I saw that spalpeen he was broken, horse and foot. He had a coat off a rag-and-bone man and forty different ways to get into it. How would he have money to lay bets for you?"

"He's after getting good information. That's how. That's the secret. You scratch my back, I'll scratch yours. For instance, I went back to Bloom yesterday and gave him a commission for an advertisement in the *Freeman's Journal*."

"Aren't you the Lord of Lower Egypt when it's another's money you're spending!" his uncle sneered.

"I said 'twas on condition he got a free puff for the Mount Venus Clinic in the *Telegraph* one evening next week. And, well became him, he said he would do that."

"A puff for this place in the *Telegraph?*" Michael asked.

"Sure what else? D'you want the world to think you'll only cure readers of the *Irish Times* – which you're in danger of as things stand."

Michael and Dermot exchanged glances but, since Ebenezer's expression remained inscrutable on this particular point, neither man ventured an opinion. Lucy intervened: "Our present list of patients does have rather an ascendancy cast to it," she informed the table in general.

"Oul' daycency the lot of them," Diana confirmed. "A dying breed."

"God save us from the *living* breed!" Dermot joked. "Divil a doctor's bill *they'll* pay."

Everyone laughed; the risk of a serious challenge to Dazzler's action had passed.

"Have you given up doing favours for Bloom's wife, then?" Ebenezer asked his nephew. "There was a time you couldn't do enough for her."

"Sure wasn't that the trouble," Dazzler replied smoothly. "No man could *do enough* for that one!"

"Mister O'Dea!" Lucy exclaimed. "I beg you will remember there are unmarried females present." She smiled at Diana as if to say what a joke it was.

Diana smiled acidly back and added, "At least one of whom is in danger of dying of boredom at such masculine banter."

"Ah!" Ebenezer wagged a finger at her. "Never dismiss the throwaway remarks of the idle rich, Matron – as I'm sure I told you more than once in Sackville Street. Throwaways do more than win gold cups! If I were a man of the faith, I'd rather defend it with one throwaway word than a whole tome of theology."

"'Twould be cheaper to print, too," Dazzler muttered.

Ebenezer ignored the interruption. "Now what were we talking about?"

"Infidelity, I think," Janet said.

There was an awkward silence as people found things on their plates that suddenly claimed all their concentration; only Ebenezer smiled at her.

"Weren't we?" she asked sharply, trying to encourage the others to beat the old man at his own game by going one or two better. "Perhaps not. The darts were so indistinct one hardly marked where they fell." She turned to him. "Perhaps *you'd* object, though, Mister O'Dea? Perhaps the topic is not to your taste?"

Helen Lynch thought it high time to interrupt. "I think it a most unsuitable topic for a mixed luncheon party," she said coldly.

"I do so heartily agree!" Ebenezer showed his colours at last. "*Delightfully* unsuitable! So will you favour us with your views first, ma'am? I see Mrs Walshe is dying to have her say."

Helen stared at him evenly. "I'm just wondering where you were during the Parnell scandal, Mister O'Dea? Didn't the whole country have its bellyful of the topic then."

"God I remember it like yesterday, Mrs Lynch," he replied. "Christmas eighteen and ninety, so it was. The talk of it filled the whole of Dublin. You could hardly hear the church bells ringing above the clamour."

251

"Well then!" she replied with an air of finality. "Enough's enough."

"I remember, too," he went on, "we had a goose that year which swam down the table in its own grease – and a ham that would have toppled Nelson off his column. But, there's a thing I want to tell you – it won't stop me doing justice to this fine leg of pork, today. D'you follow me, ma'am?"

"All too closely, sir," she replied wearily.

"Talking of Nelson . . ." Philip thought he saw a way of turning Ebenezer aside. "What a contrast between our own times and those of our great-grandfathers! Nelson and Parnell, leaders both, heroes of their nation, adulterers both, too – and each with the complaisance of the legitimate husband. They have so much in common, yet how different were their fates at the hands of their countrymen – the one laden with wealth and honours and buried in his nation's noblest shrine, the other heaped with contumely and buried in ignominy."

"Rise out of that!" Birdie called from her table by the window.

Eating and conversation came to a halt as they all turned to stare at her.

"Sure he's buried in Glasnevin," she said. "Everyone knows that."

Lucy, the titular hostess, raised an eyebrow at Janet and Diana. "Perhaps if she came and sat here at the corner of the table, between me and Mister O'Dea?" she suggested.

Birdie needed no second bidding; she almost scorched the carpet in carrying her plate across; the maid followed with her place setting and glass of water.

"Not a peep out of you now," Lucy murmured as the girl settled in happily beside her.

"Never let the sun go down on an error," Birdie muttered in reply.

"Were you making a point about the lax and easygoing English, contrasted to the stern, intolerant Irish, Mister de Renzi?" Ebenezer asked him.

"Not really. I got carried a little away there. I was really going to say look at all the great lovers of history – Nelson and Emma, Abélard and Héloïse, Dante and Beatrice, Paris and Helen of Troy – maybe they weren't all adulterous but there was a forbidden element in each case. Anthony and Cleopatra – there's one more. Why is it that all the *great* loves of history, the ones mankind remembers, have that doomed or forbidden element?"

"Romeo and Juliet," Lucy said.

"Lancelot and Guinevere!" Dermot added. "There are dozens of them."

"Othello and Desdemona?" Diana grinned at Philip.

"*Othello!*" Michael cried and struck his forehead with the flat of his hand. "Of course!"

Again the conversation halted and this time they all stared at him.

"Sorry!" He laughed. "A private memory. A quotation popped

into my head the other night – 'It is the cause! It is the cause!' Something like that. And I *could* not think where it came from."

"*It is the cause, it is the cause, my soul; Let me not name it to you, you chaste stars!*" Philip quoted, smiling at him. "Othello says it just before he strangles Desdemona. *Put out the light, and then put out the light* . . . Remember?"

"Now I wonder what could have put you in mind of Othello, Mister Raven?" Ebenezer asked teasingly. Then, in case anyone should have missed the point he turned to Lucy and added, "*Have you prayed tonight, Desdemona?*"

She raised a hand to her throat and rolled her eyes in a good imitation of fear. Everyone laughed and the awkward moment was deflected. "Actually," she said, "there's no mystery, surely? Why do children's fairy stories end 'and they all lived happily ever after'? I've never yet met a child who said, '*That's* the bit I want to hear about, Mama.' We're all interested in the *taming* of the shrew but the theatre would be empty for its sequel – *The Tamèd Shrew* – don't you think?"

Ebenezer chuckled. "So the heaven we all hope to enter one day, the abode of perfect peace and harmony, will probably turn out to be hell, instead? That would seem to follow from what you're saying."

Birdie turned to Lucy and murmured, "Do the godless go to heaven, ma'am?"

"What?" Ebenezer asked. "What's the girl saying?"

"She's wondering whether you'll go to heaven at all, Mister O'Dea."

Birdie clenched her fist and raised it but fought shy of striking Lucy.

Ebenezer chuckled. "Ah, but which is heaven and which is hell? To call hell 'heaven' and promise the souls of all the righteous they can live there forever would be quite characteristic of a God who, on such evidence as we have, is rather more malevolent than benign in His dealings with humankind. I'll take limbo if it's on offer."

"What's limbo like?" Birdie asked Lucy in a whisper – loud enough to be heard by Dazzler at least, who replied, "Limbo is a bit like south County Dublin, Miss Kelly. It has interesting scenery and all the best people."

"I always thought limbo was a bit like being inside an Oscar Wilde play for ever and ever," Janet said coldly, managing to include both O'Deas in her gaze. "Endless cleverness and all the exits barred." She shuddered.

"I met Wilde once," Dazzler told her pleasantly. "He said Lady Macbeth lived before her time. A good chemical laundry would have solved all her problems."

Everyone took the opportunity to laugh.

"Your knuckles are all white!" Birdie whispered to Lucy, who looked down and saw it was, indeed, true. She relaxed her grip on her knife and fork, and, looking up, caught Michael's eye on Birdie. His expression was the oddest mixture of affection (to call it by the kindest name) and amusement – the aloof sort of amusement one sees on the faces of visitors to the zoo.

A moment later Michael became aware of Lucy's gaze, though without looking her in the eye. His smile faded and he stared almost angrily at Ebenezer, saying, "Before we allow Lady Macbeth to carry us out of the realms of reality altogether – present reality, at least – may we all pool our thoughts on our present and hoped-for progress at Mount Venus?"

Ebenezer could hardly refuse, of course, but he glanced at his watch as he murmured, "By all means, Mister Raven," making it clear that the discussion was going to be limited.

Lucy watched them talking, watched their lips moving, forming words, delivering them. She watched them fork the last remnants of meat and swirl it round in the gravy, pushing the peas and boiled potato on top of it for transfer to their mouths. She watched them chew and think and talk. And all the while she wondered how she could be so nearly empty of feeling.

Six months ago she could not possibly have tolerated such a void within her. Michael's coolness toward her would have filled her with panic, fear, all the pangs of thwarted love – some powerful response, anyway. His shallow, playful dalliance with Birdie Kelly (and with how many other young females under this roof? she wondered, for she could not follow him round nor grow eyes in the back of her head) would have caused her anger – absurd maybe, but righteous.

Perhaps it was wrong to call it a void inside her; she did not feel empty, exactly. Indeed, she was full of feelings; but none was of that powerful, all-consuming kind. To the contrary, they were mild, light, contradictory. She seethed with light and contradictory feelings – about Michael, herself, their life together, his neglect of her, the wisdom or folly of this new venture at Mount Venus.

She could even wonder if she really minded their drifting apart. It hurt, of course. She could lie in bed in the black of night and unforced tears would flow at the pain of his loss. But then, in another frame of mind, she could see it as the cutting of some umbilicus between them, allowing her not so much to drift away from him as to turn about, look outward, discover a new terrain to explore. Michael's withdrawal might have left an emptiness, but there was no shortage of things waiting to fill it. And painful though it might be to realize he was no longer that twin soul who would do nothing important without her nor allow her to act without him . . . this new independence of spirit was not too disagreeable, either.

So for every negative feeling she might try to indulge, some little imp within her would turn the coin over and show its positive side, too. Small wonder that, though she *crawled* with feelings, none of them could ever develop into full-scale passions, as of old. Perhaps she had died without knowing it, she thought idly. Perhaps Dazzler was right. This could be limbo already.

"All I wish to say," Helen Lynch put in suddenly, and not at all apropos the present conversation, "is that I enjoyed twenty-five years of marriage with a paragon of a husband, a saint who never thought of himself but only of others, who never harmed a hair of anyone's head, and who was the very soul of moral probity."

Birdie considered these sentiments so beautiful she had tears ready to fall. However, she thought the catalogue had stopped one short. "And didn't he leave you rich as Damer of Shronell, ma'am," she added.

Helen turned white with rage. "If that creature is invited to this table again," she said, "I shall not attend."

D iana and Philip stared at the rhinoceros and the rhinoceros stared back at them. The taxidermist had set one of its eyes a little lower than the other but there was only one place from where you'd notice it. Philip was standing in it at that moment, gazing, therefore, at a slightly comical creature – a rhino doing its feeble best to pull a funny face; Diana, a mere eighteen inches to his right, saw instead a beast of unquestionable malice. She leaned forward, threatening it after its own manner, and issued her challenge: "Penny for your thoughts!"

Philip answered for it. "It's thinking to itself, *if that taxidermist comes near me again, I know where I'll bury this horn!*"

She straightened up and stared at him in surprise. "You're in a funny old mood today, Philip."

"Wouldn't it annoy *you?*" he asked. "Or perhaps you can't see it from there." He clasped her shoulders from behind and drew her in front of him. "Look at his eyes."

"Ooh yes!" She giggled. "Isn't that odd."

"The eyes are, certainly."

"No, I meant you only need to move about a foot to one side and he looks completely different. From something clownish to . . ."

"To what?" he asked.

"I don't know. Something almost satanic. They've got vicious tempers, you know. I read all about them in *Illustrated Travels*. They've got a forebrain about the size of a walnut." She put one foot on the plinth and reached forward to tap its hide between the ears. "In there." Then she gave a little cry and leaped backwards, almost overbalancing them both.

"What now?" he asked, splaying his feet to steady them.

She gave the creature a brief, suspicious glance and then flung her arms round his neck, burying her head in his shoulder and laughing with embarrassment. "I thought I saw it move!"

He gripped her tight suddenly; his whole body went rigid. "It *did* move!" he hissed in a panic. "My God, you're right. It's not stuffed at all! Don't move – for God's sake freeze! They react to the slightest movement. Our only hope is to keep quite still."

"Philip! You're joking. Say you're joking – only it's not funny!" She only quarter-believed him – but even a quarter-belief in such a fearsome beast was enough to instil terror. She clung to him all the tighter.

"Actually," he replied in a loving, tender drawl, "I don't think it's funny either. It's heavenly. I could stand like this all day."

"Tskoh!" She pushed him away in delighted exasperation – *and* simultaneously glanced over her shoulder at the pride of the museum's taxidermy department, just to make absolutely sure.

"What else does *Illustrated Travels* tell us about our lop-eyed friend?" he asked.

"They live in a sort of red mist of hatred against all the world. When other animals meet the rhino, they don't just step off the footpath, they cross to the other side of the road."

"And yet it's a vegetarian," he mused. "How significant! I've always had my doubts about vegetarians, you know – vicious people, utterly lacking in compassion or principle. I'm surprised Ebenezer O'Dea isn't one of them."

The rhino still made her uncomfortable. She slipped her arm through Philip's and led him away. "You *are* in a funny mood," she said.

A zebra and a lion improbably shared an even more improbable habitat – a massive case of plate glass and mahogany. Beyond them an elephant from another continent raised its curled trunk as if about to trumpet – a would-be triumphant gesture that some prankster had converted into one of alarm by inking in the silhouette of a mouse on the plinth, between its massive, umbrella-stand feet.

"I love this place," Diana said. "I don't know how many times I've been here. It's like a country of one's dreams, don't you think?"

"Dreams?" He looked at her askance. "You mean to say you dream about . . . Noah's ark and things like that?"

"No! Don't be so literal. You know how in dreams you can be swimming one moment and flying the next? And indoors and outdoors at the same time, somehow? This museum's like that – polar bears and gnus and gorillas and mooses, all cheek by jowl. It's a dream you can touch." She hugged his arm tight, trying to hint that it was not the only touchable dream in her life nowadays.

He placed his hand over hers and squeezed, to show he understood – and yet there was a hint of warding-off in the gesture, too.

"What *is* the matter, Philip?" she asked. "You're so edgy today."

They paused before a walrus with a chipped tusk. "Oh . . ." Philip leaned toward her and did a fidgety little tap dance on one foot. "One or two things I'd forgotten about being in love," he said.

"Such as?"

256

"The impatience, the misery, the despair, the rage . . . you know. The stuff of poetry."

She bent forward and peered at him to see how serious he was. In his smile she saw he was, indeed, quite serious. "Impatience?" She tested the word. "Yes, I can follow you that far. But as for the rest . . . Misery? Rage? The only thing I feel angry about is all the years I wasted. It's a sort of *dead* rage, if you like."

"Rage against Michael?"

"No!" She was quite emphatic. "Against me, if anyone, because . . ." She paused and stared around at all the stuffed animals. "This isn't the right place to hold this conversation. These are all my friends. Let's go out and . . ."

"From the days when you were one of them?" he asked.

She started to laugh and then turned thoughtful. "That's the truth, Philip," she said at length. "I was no better than a stuffed animal. Let's go out and sit in the gardens."

They trundled down the dark mahogany stair, nodded at the curator, collected her parasol, and went out into the bright June sunshine. The Sunday traffic was light and mostly fashionable, driving slowly in order to be recognized. Diana and Philip were able to saunter at ease across the normally busy end of Merrion Square. "It must be one of the few occasions when to travel hopefully *is* to arrive," Diana remarked as an open landau with four gay young ladies, dressed like orchids, and a grave paterfamilias, dressed like a funeral director, ambled by.

They wandered down into the gardens, secretly admiring the brilliant displays of colour and geometry but not caring to admit it. "So artificial . . . so dead!" they murmured as they drifted to a seat at the heart of the most colourful mosaic of all and settled happily to despise it. Diana spread her parasol and created the illusion of a private world in its shade.

"You were saying," he reminded her. "It was a rage against yourself?"

The drowsy scents of summer, the enervating sun, the carefree shouts of children somewhere out of sight – all made it easier to contemplate that dead rage and the dead past over which it had reigned. "Meeting Michael again . . . working close to him – it's forced me to ask myself why I was so bitter when he cast me aside. I could understand it lasting a month. Even six months, perhaps. But not all those years and years." She clenched her fist and patted her breastbone with her knuckles. "The things it does to one, Philip!"

He stroked her forearm lightly with one fingertip. "You say it forced you to ask yourself why. Did you find the answer?"

She nodded glumly. "That was the least welcome part of all. It was, of course, my own inadequacy. The oddest thing, though, is that I really knew it all along. I even told myself – other girls get jilted and they just pick themselves up and dust themselves down and go back into the arena. 'Are you feebler than them?' I asked myself. And even though I knew I wasn't, it somehow seemed better to prove myself by crying a pox on all men and denying myself all emotional entanglements of every kind. I thought I could prove myself strong that way. But that's not strength at all, is it."

"Why did it change so suddenly, two weeks ago?"

She saw he still did not grasp the point she was making; all he wanted to do was wallow in the present glory of their love. "It's all because we're taught it's noble to resist . . . deny . . ." she said. "All that business about the saints going out into the desert to wrestle with their temptations and vanquish themselves. It makes the howling wilderness more noble than all this." She waved a hand at the beauties all about them "But *this* is the true glory of the world. And there never was a saint who wouldn't have been better for staying *in* the world and accepting the very things they were all fighting so hard to deny. That's the truth about myself – the truth I was ashamed to face all those years."

He repeated his earlier question. "And what enabled you to face it suddenly, two weeks ago? I mean so *suddenly?*"

She laughed dryly. "I'm an extremist, you see! I must either be the ice maiden or . . ." She wriggled in the seat until they were touching each other from knees to shoulders. "*You* give it a name."

"Fire maiden?" he offered lightly.

"Maiden?" she questioned with a sly grin and a quick look all round. Then her desire hit her like a great wave. "Oh God, Philip! D'you think we could go in those bushes over there? Would people see us? Would it matter? Would we care?"

He closed his eyes and shivered. "Please, Diana!"

"What? Is that yes or no?"

"It's don't! Don't! You've no idea what a paper palisade my sense of propriety is at this moment."

"Philip?" Her voice shivered as she leaned closer to him and gripped his arm.

"No," he whispered in anguish.

"Kiss me?" she whispered back.

He swallowed heavily. "I'll come if I do. It's on a hair trigger."

Her eyes went wide in shock . . . and then she laughed, as if he had winded her. "I never knew a man so frank," she told him.

"Oh?" he remarked tetchily, pretending to bristle with anger. "Do you disapprove? Are you suggesting there's something unworthy or vile in what is in fact a perfectly natural mn-mnh-mn . . ."

She reached up and pinched his lips together. "Very funny," she said. "I asked for it, I suppose. But there's frankness and frankness, my lad!"

"They sound the same to me."

"There's plain and simple frankness which should arise naturally during the heat of the . . . activity. And there's belligerent, provocative frankness, all out of context. And any naughty little boy who likes to thumb his nose at decent conventions can tell you the difference. Well!" She sat up and tweaked her gloves primly – parodying primness. "That has certainly put the kybosh on passion for an hour or two!"

"Which will give us time to return to Mount Venus, where we have no need of bushes."

"Yes, but in the meantime?" she asked. "What about all this sudden emptiness?"

"There's a question I could ask," he offered. He rearranged his clothing with a rueful smile at her.

"You *haven't!*" she said accusingly.

He shook his head. "Touch and go, though. This question – it's about Michael, you and Michael now."

She became wary at once. "Ask away."

"I believe all is not well between him and Lucy at the moment," he said.

"D'you now why?"

Her tone was so neutral he couldn't decide whether the question was genuine or rhetorical. He played for safety: "Do you?"

"It doesn't matter," she said. "Anyway, what has it to do with me?"

"People in trouble tend to turn to their friends for help."

"Ah." Her tone was wooden. "I see. Now that the maiden has melted, how generous will she be with her warmth? Is that the long and short of it?"

"Sort of."

She eyed him guardedly. "Has Lucy turned to you for help, then? I imagine you'd count as a friend in that sense."

He bridled at her words. "I don't know what you mean – 'in *that* sense'. I'd count as a friend of hers in any sense. We practically grew up together."

"I know. You haven't answered my question. Has she 'turned to you' at all lately?"

"You keep repeating my words with the most awful innuendo, Diana. I don't mean it like that."

"Ah, but I *do*, Philip! I mean it exactly like that. Has she?"

"Oh God!" He leaned forward, elbows on knees, face sunk in hands.

"You asked first," she reminded him.

"I know! I know!" He rolled his head about, exaggerating his chagrin into spurious anguish, which culminated in laughter. "I thought I was firing the starter's pistol – no more than that. Now I discover that not only is it a real pistol, and loaded with live rounds, but I was accidentally pointing it at my own foot! Ouch!"

"This is like calling the banns," she said. "For the third and final time of asking – *has she?*"

"Yes!" he said emphatically. "She has."

"Good man, yourself, Philip! And it didn't hurt much, did it! So here's another one to test you: Did she explain *why* things aren't going too well between her and Michael just now?"

"She said she's expecting a baby."

"Aaah!" Diana let the word out in a long sigh, as if Philip's reply had brought them to some long-awaited destination.

"Listen!" he exclaimed testily. "I'm the one who started asking the questions. We didn't finish that yet."

"Oh, I'll answer you, Philip. I promise you that. Indeed, I think I wouldn't hold my peace now for all the fish in the sea. I'm just trying to discover a little about what lies behind your question. I want to know the context in which my answers will be received. Isn't that reasonable?"

He closed his eyes and nodded morosely. "And yet I am never more wary of a woman than when she invokes reason as her motive." He half-turned and sought out Wilde's old house at the northwest corner of the square. "Oscar!" he almost whispered. "You must have said something to that effect, surely?"

"Never mind all that," she said impatiently. "I want to know how Lucy imparted this vital piece of information."

"How?" he echoed nervously. "She said, 'I'm expecting a baby.' Just like that."

"Or was it just like this?" Diana leaned toward him and, stroking the palm of his hand with the tip of her finger, murmured huskily, " 'Phi-lip – I'm having a ba-by!' And did she add that Michael had therefore ceased conjugal relations with her?"

He stared at her in dismay – but then a slow grin spread across his features. "You're doing it deliberately, aren't you – demonstrating the corrosive effect of suspicion and mistrust. Oh God!" He tipped his boater to the back of his head and scratched, slightly distraught, at the hair that spilled over his brow. "You're too good for me, my darling!"

"Too good a detective?" she asked.

"Too good a person. Both, actually. The answer is yes – the answer to the question you're really asking. Yes, she did make it very clear that Michael and she no longer . . . et cetera. And what did I feel about . . . you know."

"Slipping into the breach?" Diana asked sweetly.

He shrugged. "Every word one can think of is a double entendre! I feel an awful traitor to her, telling you all this."

"The bitch!" Diana exclaimed in the same "sweet" tone, apparently addressing a host of blue delphiniums at her side. "She's going to try and do it to me again! I think I shall pretend to fall in love with Dazzler – that'll send her all the way back to where she started! It's like snakes and ladders, isn't it – except that *she* is every snake on the board."

260

"And who or what are the ladders?" he asked, hoping to lead her away from this dangerous speculation.

"I don't know!" She laughed and abandoned the whole train of thought. "The only ladder around here is the one in my stocking!"

Go on! a voice in his head almost screamed, for she could hardly have given him a better opening. Yet he shied away from the very idea; she was not in the mood for a frank and reasonable discussion, leading to mutual encouragement in facing the trials that lay ahead. "You're quite wrong about Lucy," he told her. "The last thing she wants – and I mean the very last thing on *earth* – is another entanglement. Or something even deeper – another emotional tie. She knows nothing about you and me. All she . . ."

"Philip! What mark of a simpleton d'you see on me! She *must* know – the way you've been mooning around . . ."

"Oh she knows *my* feelings about you well enough . . ."

"Which is why she's determined to snatch you away from me, of course."

"Would you ever just listen! She knows *my* feelings but she has no idea we are . . . you know."

"Lovers."

He nodded. "She envies you, in fact. She envies your freedom, your independence. She's missing the glory of being one of Dublin's most sought-after hostesses. That gave her a *place* in the world."

"A place in the bankruptcy courts!"

"She was someone in her own right – in a place she had carved out all by herself. Now she's just Michael Raven's wife and Mount Venus's housekeeper. But you're different. You're free!"

"Did she say that?"

"Yes."

Diana thought it over a moment and then said, "So you've been discussing me with her!"

He nudged her and said, "It became necessary . . . the moment she made it obvious that there was – how did you express it? – a breach to fill!"

"That's fair," she conceded with a dip of her head. "Actually, you never explained why love goes with misery and despair and rage and so forth."

"Oh . . ." He sighed and looked around, as if for a rescue party. "My little talk with Lucy has unnerved me. I'm not proud of myself, you know. I don't think I'm being at all reasonable – in fact, I know I'm being impossibly *un*reasonable. I want to go storming into Mount Venus a dozen times a day and carry you off. I think of Michael there, at daggers drawn with poor Lucy, and I know how a man's mind can start to get all twisted in those circumstances."

"Really?" She stared at him with provocatively bright eyes. "From personal experience? Do tell me!"

His only answer was a brief flash of a smile. "I just wondered if

261

he'd started to lean on your shoulder yet?"

"Not yet," she assured him. "But if what you say is true, I'm sure he will. I'll be ready for him!"

She was too grim in her promises – too eager to reassure him. "He's said absolutely nothing?" he pressed.

She tilted her head awkwardly on one side. "Well . . ."

"And done nothing?"

Certain overtones in his voice made her decide it would be better to tell the whole truth now than to conceal it in the hope it would never come out. What did she owe Michael Raven, anyway? "One childish prank, perhaps – at least, I hope it was a childish prank."

"What?"

"He stole one of my stockings off the private drying lines up in the pheasant run."

To her surprise Philip let out an enormous sigh of relief. She was onto it at once. "You knew!" she accused. "You already knew that – which is why you kept pressing the question!"

"I didn't know he'd *stolen* it." Philip hung his head in shame – before she could tell him he ought to be ashamed of himself.

"Lord save us!" she murmured, more sarcastic than angry. "You thought I'd given it him!" Her eyes went wide. "Or let him take it off me!" She grasped his arm and shook it. "You did, didn't you! Oh, Philip!"

He closed his eyes tight and clenched his jaws. "That's the point I was stumbling to make, Diana. I *know* it was absurd to think any such thing. I know it's absurd to want to burst down the doors of Mount Venus and kidnap you! I know it's absurd to love you in a way that makes you worth more than all the hundreds of millions of other women on earth all put together – worse than absurd, it's a blasphemy. In a way it's absurd to love you at all – because if I'd never met you, I'd still be a happy . . . carefree . . . shallow . . . you know. It's absurd to claim that my life would be shattered and in ruins if I ever lost you. And yet all these things are the simple truth! I knew there must be an explanation for the fact that Michael had one of your stockings hidden in his bag, and yet . . . and yet!" He made talons of his fingers and mimed the act of clawing out his own entrails.

"How *did* you know, come to think of it?" she asked suddenly.

"Because Lucy told me."

Diana turned pale and put a hand to her throat, as if to help the breath into her lungs. "That blithering eejit Michael! I *told* him what to tell her. He returned the stocking to me with apologies and I gave him the perfect justification for it all."

"Tourniquets?" he asked.

"Yes but . . ."

"He tried that. She didn't believe him."

Diana's lip curled in a sneer. "Doesn't that be telling you a lot

262

about Michael Raven!" Her shoulders collapsed in a dejected heap. "So now Lucy knows the stocking was mine! And if even you were driven to suspicion . . ." She paused when she saw him shaking his head and smiling. "What?"

"She thinks they were Birdie Kelly's! Or, rather, she did until last Thursday. Now she has no idea. But you'd have a hard job . . ."

"What happened last Thursday?"

"I don't know. I think she met Birdie going to hang up her washing and discovered she only ever wears whites. But I was going to say – she asked me whose that pink stocking . . ."

"Peach."

". . . peach stocking could possibly have been. 'None of the nurses,' she said. 'And Diana Powers wouldn't be seen *dead* in anything like that!' Her very words. You're saved by your own icy reputation, love."

"Except in your case. You alone knew the stocking was mine and your mind leaped at once to the worst possible suspicion."

He grinned knowingly. "I said 'your *icy* reputation'. I have every reason to know otherwise."

Diana did her best not to smile. "Next time," she said, "ask questions rather than go leaping to conclusions, eh?"

He frowned. "I'm not quite sure exactly how one would go about it, my darling. I take you in my arms, eh?" He slipped an arm around her. "I gaze into your eyes and I murmur, 'By the way, my angel, there's a rumour going round my mind that you've been spreading the relish for your former lover and that he absent-mindedly walked off with bits of your underwear. Ha ha! I don't suppose there's a word of truth in it, is there! Is there?' And then what d'you do? Laugh and murmur, 'Silly boy!' Somehow I can't see it happening that way."

She reached her lips up and kissed him tenderly. "Silly boy!" she murmured.

"The real lesson," he said, "is that we must learn to repose absolute trust in each other. If you see Lucy take me aside to pour out her heart, or if I see Michael doing the same with you, we must not turn a hair. We must *know* – absolutely know – that whatever comfort we offer them, it is out of friendship alone. Our love is not diminished by it, not one bit. Indeed, it will be strengthened. Agreed?"

She sighed and kissed him once again. "Agreed."

Since the end of June the clinic had been up to its full complement of forty-five patients, so, by the last week in July, the two chiefs were more than relieved to acquire their Indian at last – that is, their RMO, Doctor Abraham Quinlan. He was a stocky, handsome, dark-haired, rugger-playing fellow of twenty-seven. Diana and her assistant, Helen Lynch, had one serious reservation

263

about him, though it was not shared by either of the chiefs. They thought him quite needlessly handsome. It would lead to unhealthy romantic competition among the nurses, which, in turn, would fill the clinic with factions and backbiting. Both Michael and Dermot wondered how anyone would be able to tell the difference between that and the present state of feminine sub-warfare but neither voiced the opinion aloud. On the main point all agreed – Abraham Quinlan was eminently qualified for the post and any patient would be safe in his care at those times when he was the only doctor available.

It was the last week in July before he took up residence. He was given a set of attic rooms at the back of the house, above the Ravens' chambers and accessible only through their corridors or, on the exterior, by one of the newly installed fire escapes; the same escape also served the patients on the first floor and the nurses on the attic floor of the main house. The arrangement was that he would be welcome to use the internal stairs until nine o'clock of an evening – and at any time in an emergency, of course – but in the normal way he'd use the fire escape after nine.

On his first evening he was witness to a curious incident. He had been welcomed by, and introduced to, everyone in the clinic – or so he supposed. Alone at last in his own attic chambers he had gone to the window to admire the westering sun and the crimson glow in which it bathed the rolling hills of County Kildare. While standing there, musing on his good fortune, his attention was caught by a figure gliding quietly through the long shadows below, between the main house and the old stables. He could just make out a female, of indeterminate age by her cloak but young, to judge by her movements. She glanced all about her before she opened the wicket gate into the stable yard and she repeated the gesture before she vanished inside the first of the loose boxes. Half a minute later she re-emerged clutching a fat volume, bound in a rather striking royal blue cloth. Once again she glanced all about her the moment she emerged – an actor playing for children could not have spelled GUILT in larger majescules. She was dark-haired and well built; distance and wishful thinking made her pretty, as well, though she was too far off for a cooler eye to confirm it.

The moment she had assured herself she was unobserved, she took to her heels and ran off into what must be an old walled fruit garden, or kitchen garden, perhaps. From time to time as he unpacked his clothes and arranged his effects he glanced out of the window, hoping to see her again on her return. When his patience was at last rewarded, she was barely visible in the last glimmer of day as she flitted like a ghost across the nearer courtyard. Her sprightly tread made it fairly certain that she had returned the heavy tome to its place (presumably its hiding place) in the loose box. Intrigued, he determined to investigate before breakfast the following morning.

Eight intervening hours of slumber, however, drove it from his mind and, for his first early morning run he went down the front drive and out along the mountainy road, pausing on the way back to chat with Dazzler and admire his two greyhounds. He did not remember the strange incident of the previous evening until the morning was well advanced. He was doing the rounds with Mister Raven, getting to know the patients and those nurses who were on duty, when Dermot Walshe popped his head round the door and asked if anyone had seen his copy of *Sahli's Diagnostic Methods*; gratuitously he added that it had a rather striking blue binding. It was then that Abraham remembered the strange incident of the previous evening.

He drew breath to mention it when native caution made him think better of the idea. The tome the young female had carried from the loose box had certainly been heavy enough for a modern medical text, and the coincidence of the blue bindings added to the probability; but suppose it had been some other book? What sort of trouble might he bring down on the unknown young woman? A caution born of generations made him hold his tongue.

"Yes?" Dermot looked at him hopefully.

"I'm sorry?" Abraham replied.

"You looked as if you were about to tell me something."

"Oh . . . ah, yes. I was only going to say you're welcome to borrow my copy. Shall I fetch it? It's in my room."

"I'll come with you."

They went out onto the fire escape and up one flight. Dermot went past Abraham's door and tested the new nurses' fire-escape exit. "Oh dear," he said. "Bolted on their side. Hard cheese, old boy!"

Abraham rolled his eyes, implying that access to the nurses was the last thing he desired. "I hope these back stairs don't give *them* any ideas," he replied.

"I'm sure you do!"

"Oh, I mean it. Gaggles of nurses together – girls of excellent family who wouldn't say boo to a goose on their own – can egg each other on to the most appalling practical jokes en masse. Especially, for some reason, where young bachelor doctors are in it. And even young*ish* ones, too." Ruefully he touched his temple, where anyone who had known him a few years earlier would discern that his hair had receded almost half an inch.

"Oh, you must walk in fear and dread," Dermot commented in the same ironic tone as he followed the younger man indoors. When he opened the book he saw the inside cover bore a plate saying it was given to Abraham Quinlan as part of the Hunterian Prize for Physiology, 1899. "Ah!" he remarked. "It was modesty – I wondered why you hesitated. Good man, yourself!"

He consulted the section that interested him – on leukocytosis in pregnancy – and handed the book back. Abraham offered him the loan of it but Dermot said it was too good to leave lying around the place – ". . . though you might leave the cover open where some of our patients would be bound to see it," he added. "Since we're forbidden to advertise, we have to learn to blow our own trumpets in the most obscure ways imaginable."

And there the matter rested. Abraham promised to keep an eye out for Doctor Walshe's copy.

All that evening, in between finishing his unpacking and arranging his possessions he kept an eye out for the unknown female and, sure enough, at about the same time as the previous evening, she flitted across the yard and went through the same rituals as before.

The moment she had vanished into the walled garden, he slipped from his room and dashed down the fire escape. On reaching the ground, however, he merely sauntered around in an aimless way, as if exploring his new surroundings with only half an interested eye. When he came to the ungated entrance to the walled garden he hesitated as if he might not go in at all and then walked through it, suggesting that mere thoroughness was all his care.

She was sitting on an ancient and by now well-blackened bale of straw outside a half demolished potting shed, about fifty paces along the western side, and her nose was buried in the book. The sun was now so low in the sky that only her head poked out above the long shadow cast by the wall behind her, making her dark hair glisten with flashes of gold. He stood there awhile, just inside the gate and out of sight of the house, unable to take his eyes off her. Glimpses of other people's lives fascinated him, perhaps because he had always felt a certain sense of exclusion in a society where religious and tribal ties were all-important. He loved travelling by train or on the upper deck of an omnibus because of the chance it afforded to peer into people's houses and gardens and come away with a little trophy of their privacy. There was nothing prurient in his interest; indeed, if he saw anything of an intimate nature, he would avert his eyes at once. What he relished most was the very ordinariness of those vignettes – a woman sitting in an orchard shelling peas in the morning sun . . . a man in heavy veils robbing beehives of their honey . . . things like that. They made him aware of the leisurely hours that had preceded such moments and that would flow serenely on after the train or bus had whisked him far away. He enjoyed the feeling that, just for a moment, he had *belonged*.

And so he stood in the gateway now and watched the unknown female with her head in the sunshine and her nose in a medical tome . . . and he indulged himself in a familiar pang of sentimental envy. But for once there was no vehicle to whisk him away and leave him secure in his petty illusions – that women who shelled peas in orchards and men who gathered honey never quarrelled, nor made much money, nor worried about the lack of it. The fact that he and the object of his scrutiny were both here, wrapped in the same bit of space, did not immediately make her more real for him. She was still a vignette, like a waxworks tableau he could inspect without personal involvement. He started to walk toward her.

A wing-forward on the rugger field, he moved with a naturally lithe grace even without resorting to deliberate stealth. He approached to within ten paces before she became aware of him. She looked up at him calmly and said. "Jaysus, but you'd catch a weasel asleep! Is it out walking you are?"

"It is," he replied. "I mean, I am." He gazed uncertainly at her. He had not expected a girl who was so immersed in reading – and in such a book as that – to speak in so common a manner. Quite a good-looker, too. Not pretty in the conventional sense but with strong, friendly features. "I hope I'm not disturbing you?"

"Not at all," she exclaimed magnanimously. "Them teeth there." She bared her own in a fiendish smile and pointed. "Would they be in-scissors or in-sizers?"

He put her right.

She half-turned the book and faced it toward him. "If you had incisors the likes of them, wouldn't you drown yourself the same day?"

Even from that distance he could see that the book was, beyond doubt, the missing *Sahli*. He walked the few remaining paces and stooped over her, saying, "Oh yes – Hutchinson's teeth."

"The poor colleen!" she exclaimed. "And her only six! It says her elder sister was worse. At least they had the daycency to spare her the public exposure to all the doctors in the world. And her mother had two miscarriages, it says."

He cleared his throat and asked, "Do you have any particular interest in that condition, Miss . . . er?"

A moment later he wished he hadn't, for her reply was: "And all because of secondary syphilis! She must have cot it off her mammy, who cot it off some fella."

"Quite," he said awkwardly. "Er . . . is that Doctor Walshe's copy, by the way?"

"Lorda'mercy!" Her hand flew to her mouth. "Is he after missing it?"

He nodded. She had a guileless quality that was oddly attractive.

"I thought he never would. I slipped a cobweb across it and watched three weeks. That Nurse Geary who says she dusted his consulting room – she never touched it. So I says to meself, 'He'll not miss *this* one, so he won't.' And him with all them hundreds of others to read!" She shook her head at the inbuilt unfairness of everything.

"It may be a stupid thing to ask, Miss . . . er?"

"Kelly." She offered him her hand, not to shake but to kiss. To her surprise (and his) he did so; so that was one more thing she had learned to do. "Birdie Kelly." She watched him through narrowed eyes, wary of his response, but, to her surprise, he did not react to her name at all. "Did no one yet mention me to you?" she asked.

He shook his head apologetically. "I'm afraid not, Miss Kelly. Should they have?"

"'Tis a marvel they didn't. I must be one with the furniture at last." She smiled happily. "You're the *new* wonder, of course."

"You know who I am, then."

"Sure the seals would come up from the deep and the stag descend from the mist-crag – to hear *them* prattle!"

"Them?"

"Them nurses."

"Ah! So you are not a nurse. We shall narrow it down slowly."

"Would you ever sit down, sir!" She moved along the old bale to make room beside her. "You'll give me a crick in the neck."

He settled himself beside her, wondering why he found her company so agreeable – this opinionated, ignorant, muddle-headed girl whose preferred recreation was to read an American translation of a German textbook on diagnostic methods – which she had gone to some trouble to steal from the clinic, where she was *not* a nurse! It was nothing like the fantasies he had spun around the vignettes of life glimpsed from the windows of speeding vehicles; you'd need to be Hans Christian Andersen himself to equal this.

"I'm companion to Mister Ebenezer O'Dea."

"Ah, our illustrious patron. I've not had the honour of meeting him yet."

She snapped shut the book; motes of dust sparkled in the sun's rays above her head, which was now itself in shade. "And he's none too pleased at that, I may say."

"I'm sorry to hear it. What sort of man is he, Miss Kelly?"

"Well, d'you know what I want to tell you – he wasn't behind the door when brains were giving out."

"But I've heard he has his communion money about him still. They say he'd peel an orange in his pocket?"

"Sure a fool and his money are soon parted," she replied. "The wise man knows how to officiate at the ceremony."

Abraham glanced toward the house, not visible from where they were seated. "When it comes to parting with money," he said, "Mister O'Dea's not done too badly. That clinic must have cost a pretty penny."

"Bread upon waters," she told him. "That's what he says. He told me the first week I was here, he said . . ."

"When was that, may I ask?"

"Oh God, a fierce long while ago – when Moses climbed mountains." She laughed at the lie and buried it with a rueful grimace. "No, to be honest with you, I haven't been here a wet Sunday – two months and two days. Anyway, at the beginning he said to me 'twould take a year to see a penny back. And now, thanks be to that flood of drooping women Mister Walshe brought in, we're in profit already." She paraded the knowledge with a kind of guilty pride.

"What?" Abraham asked in surprise – a double surprise, really, for he could hardly believe he was engaged in such a confidential conversation only minutes after meeting this strange young female. "Has the income paid off all his investment already?"

"Be the holy fly, no!" Birdie laughed at his naïvete. "That's not their way, these fellas with all the money. He's after explaining it to me. You and me, now, if we lay out a pound on something, we'd want to see a guinea back before we'd claim to make a profit. But not them – oh no! They lend a pound and if they get no more than the shilling back in a year – 'tis *all* profit! Could you believe it! A shilling on the pound in a year is more profit than e'er they'd make on lending to the Bank of England. I must have been in profit all my life and never knew it! And me as poor as a cow in a quarry!" She laughed. "'Tis a grand world for them as understand it, so it is."

He reached across and took the book from her. "And that's what this is all about, is it?" he asked.

"Well, I want to tell you about that," she said. "Matron was after lending me a book on first aid, so she was, and fair dues to me, I read it all. But I thought it a bit simple like. A bit elementary, d'ye see. I mean, I don't think any grown person needs telling that if someone's lying on the ground and him bleeding to death, 'tis a good idea to staunch the flow. So I thought I'd look into something a bit harder." She nodded at the book, which he now held.

He nodded and asked, "Do you not feel the evening chill, Miss Kelly – now the sun's below the wall there? Would you care to stroll around and show me the gardens."

"I will, of course," she replied happily. "Herself will only cut the head out of me, but I will. She thinks she owns them, earth and sky. And the grand airy notions she has for their beatification! But sure I played here when she was in pinafores in Lucan."

"Herself being Mrs Raven?"

"The Honourable Lucinda Raven," she intoned as they rose to their feet.

"I'll carry the book," he told her. "I don't need to be looking over my shoulder all the time, d'you see." When she passed it over he weighed it in his hand. "And tell me, have you found it difficult enough for your taste?"

"It has words you'd never need outside the dispensary," she told him.

He chuckled. "How else would we have the nerve to charge so much for mere common sense?"

"Isn't that the truth! But I like the little stories, so I do."

"Stories!" The allegation that the great Sahli ever stooped to storytelling surprised him.

"There's a grand one on page nine-five-four about a baby with tetany. 'Twould break your heart in many a day. And another one near that on a little girl with Kernig's sign." She sighed happily.

"With cerebrospinal meningitis?" he asked.

"Well, of course," she said airily. "One of the active contractures, I believe." She broke down and laughed at herself, stumbled, grabbed his arm, straightened up, and then apologized.

He assured her he was not in the least perturbed.

She glanced up at him slyly. "Still, you had no call to lepp in the air like a hen in stubble, as if I'd scalded you. D'you not like to be touched?" There was a hint of demure lechery in her question.

He shrugged awkwardly and lolled his head about before he confessed, "Not really, Miss Kelly."

"No more I don't either," she told him confidentially.

There was a ruminative silence as they walked out of the walled garden to the path that led down to the glasshouse. There she said, "You have a terraced garden along there with the biggest birdbath you ever saw and a raft of diaphanous marble ladies."

"That sounds like something I ought to see," he replied. They set off in that direction and he continued, "You must live a fairly isolated life at Mount Venus, Miss Kelly. Have you many friends here of your own age at all?"

"Divil a one," she answered mildly. "There's things goes on in the world that I can never understand. Why do women ever try to be friends when the moment they've parted company they'll tear the flesh off each other's bones? Riddle me that!"

He chortled. "You have no very high opinion of your sisters, then?"

"I wouldn't walk to the end of my finger for one of them," she declared. "If they swallowed nails they'd cough up screws, most of them."

"Yourself included?"

"Ah, well now," she replied judiciously and with no sign she might be joking, "I'm none too sure of that. Wait till I tell you – many's the time I'd wake up of a morning, full of surprise to find I'm a woman, too, like the rest of them."

"Really?" He peered hard at her to see if she were teasing, and decided she wasn't. "What would you rather be?"

"An angel sure," she said. "But still human, a sort of human angel. They're neither man nor woman, aren't they."

"Well, if you believe in those things," he replied guardedly.

"Ah, you're a Jew-man," she said, having forgotten the fact. "Ye have no angels nor saints nor . . . have ye divils at all? I don't believe in any of them things anyway. I'm with the jury."

"Oh!" He held up a warning finger. "But in Jewry we have angels and divils – and archangels, too, and Satan himself. We have no saints, though – only prophets. But we don't worship *them*."

"Not like Ebenezer O'Dea!" she said. "You never asked that stupid question, you know."

"Eh?" He frowned in bewilderment.

"You said – when you came upon me in the garden beyond – 'It may seem a stupid question . . .' but you never asked it."

"Oh yes – well, you answered it anyway. I just wanted to know why you were so eager to read this particular book. I shall have to return it to Doctor Walshe, you realize?"

"You'll let no word touching me out of you?" she begged. "Sure you may tell him it slipped behind the dispensary bench where that Nurse Geary ought to have found it if she dusted properly and then he'll know she doesn't." She smiled dreamily as she visualized nemesis already descending on the hapless upper-class sloven.

"I will of course," he promised.

"How old would you be?" she asked suddenly. "Without giving away your age, now."

"Without giving away my age," he mused. "Well, now, if you were eighteen, I'd beat you three to two, but if your next birthday comes before mine, I shall only be able to give you nine to your seven."

"You'd be twenty-seven, so," she said at once. "And another thing – if you're a Jew-man, why have you a rosary in your pocket?"

He patted the pocket in question and laughed. "How clever of you to notice! I usually only slip my beads in there when I go into Dublin," he explained.

"But why?"

"Promise you'll not tell a soul?"

She drew a finger across her throat and said, "Cross my heart."

"It's so that if I get knocked down by a tram they won't carry my unconscious body to the Adelaide."

She laughed and said he'd better not let Mister Raven hear him saying that.

"I know. That's why I made you promise to keep it to yourself. There's no Jewish hospital, you see, not in the whole of Ireland, and I'd rather wake up in the care of the nuns than be surrounded by those fearsome Protestant nurses."

They arrived at the terrace garden but the twilight was now so well advanced that individual shrubs and features like statues and pergolas were no longer discernible – only the muffled and mighty resonances of shapes, jostling one another as if impatient for darkness to come and liberate them entirely.

"That would be a lonely occupation in this country, I'm thinking," Birdie said at last. "Being a Jew-man. You haven't even a hospital of your own!"

"Loneliness . . ." He began. There were thoughts about loneliness in his mind but they would not coalesce into words; they were like the elements of this garden, powerful, vibrant, but only half-glimpsed.

When he said no more she continued: "Don't you sometimes feel there's a land somewhere you belong to? I do. Lord but I tried my hand at a raft of trades, and divil a one e'er put me in God's pocket.

The time I've wasted – I'd have done better at the zoo, helping the blind monkeys to eat bananas.''

"Do you not enjoy your place here?" he asked.

"Indeed, 'tis good work, wet and dry. But one day they'll say to me the same as they said in all them other places: ''Tis time to gather all you can wrap, Birdie, and run, for you don't belong here.' Sure I *know* I don't belong here. I don't be needing the likes of them to tell me that. What I want them to tell me is where I *do* belong. But they're shook for an answer."

Abraham, now barely visible at her side, sniffed and cleared his throat but said nothing.

"D'you folly me now?" she asked.

"Indeed, I do," he assured her. "And I'll tell you another thing – I never hoped to hear it so beautifully put."

The following evening Lucy knocked timidly at the door to Diana's private apartment. Diana, who had been half-expecting Philip to call, barely managed to conceal her disappointment. Her cry of "Do come in!" was, however, welcoming enough.

"I hope I'm not intruding?" Lucy said.

Diana glanced sharply at her. A cold "For instance?" was on the tip of her tongue but it died when she saw how nervous and strained her visitor was. Instead she said, "Of course not, Lucy." Then, to show she was keeping nothing back, she added, "Philip de Renzi may drop by." She spoke casually in case Lucy should go jumping to conclusions.

"I shan't be staying long," Lucy promised.

"I don't mean it that way. I mean we could play three-handed whist or something – or perhaps get Doctor Quinlan to join us for some proper bridge. If he plays at all, that is."

"Or" – Lucy smiled wanly – "if he's not out spooning with Birdie Kelly again!"

"I beg your pardon?" Diana stared at her in consternation "You jest I hope?" She waved a hand at a chair and seated herself facing it.

"I would have thought the whole clinic was agog with the tale." Lucy pulled a face. "Perhaps I'm the only one who saw them. Why do you hope it's not true?" She smiled teasingly. "Have you plans of your own in that direction?"

"Not at all! But I must be the only nurse who hasn't. The other forty can talk of little else but our divine RMO. The news that he is spooning with *that* one would be the last straw."

"Well," Lucy's tone was apologetic, "*spooning* is perhaps stretching it. I'll tell you what happened – or what I saw of it. I was doing the day's accounts yesterday evening, about half an hour before sunset,

272

when I heard a great clattering on the new fire escape. The noise on that cast-iron is unbelievable, especially if you're just on the other side of the wall to which it's bolted. None of your nurses need think they'll be able to creep in after hours that way, I can tell you! Anyway, I ran to the window, and there he was – our divine RMO, as you call him, strolling off into the gardens. I was just about to pull on a cardigan and join him – because I've been longing to show off what Janet and I have achieved already – when I saw him vanish into the kitchen garden."

"Oh dear!" Diana mimed a weary collapse. "Not him too! What *is* this fascination with . . ."

"That's what I thought to start with," Lucy interrupted. "But a few minutes later he emerged with who-d'you-think in tow? Birdie Kelly!"

"Arm in arm?"

"No, no – in fact, he had rather a large book under his arm, as big as some of Michael's medical tomes. And they . . ."

"Blue?" Diana asked. "The book – was it bound in blue?"

Lucy frowned, trying to recall the scene. "I believe it was. Why?"

Diana explained how Dermot had lost his *Sahli* and how Abraham Quinlan had claimed to discover it that very morning. "Odd, what?" she concluded.

"Even odder," Lucy added, "was the fact that he hadn't been carrying it when he went into the kitchen garden. However, the pair of them wandered off toward the terraces, talking like two old chums."

"And?"

Lucy shrugged. "I don't know. Darkness fell. He didn't go back by the fire-escape, anyway. I'm sure of that."

"Not good news," Diana said glumly. "He's an odd fellow altogether – affable, charming, smiles a lot, delightfully shy . . . and yet I get the feeling there's nothing there. Nothing at the heart of him. Don't you agree?"

Lucy made an awkward, not-exactly gesture. "I think there's a public Abraham Quinlan who's all those things you say, and a private one who's hidden away behind a high wall. Perhaps that's saying the same thing?"

"Anyway," Diana said, "you probably didn't come here to tell me about our new RMO and his fire-escapades. Would you like a cup of tea – or shall we hold back ten minutes in case Philip comes?" She answered her own question by rising and saying, "I'll put the kettle on, anyway."

Lucy followed her to the kitchen alcove and lit the wick while Diana filled the kettle. "Really I came to say I don't think I can go on being . . ." She sighed. "I mean, I may just have to take a holiday soon. If I don't . . ." The words petered out.

"Oh?" Diana asked in as neutral a tone as possible.

"I know. We can't afford it financially yet, and even if we could, the clinic couldn't do without me for . . ."

"If you fell ill, Lucy, we'd have to."

"For an illness, yes. But not just for a . . . a whim."

Diana set the kettle over the burner and touched Lucy's arm gently. "I'm sure it's not just for a whim, my dear. What's the real difficulty? Is it, ah, you and Michael?"

Lucy nodded. Her lip trembled.

"Are you sure I'm the one to discuss it with? I should think Mrs Lynch has far more experience of . . ."

"No, no! Absolutely not! She's incapable of saying anything other than that she and Timothy had the finest marriage in the western world and their only difficulty ever was how to hide his wings and halo from mere mortal sight. No thank you!"

Diana laughed and led the way back to the sitting room. "If you're sure, then . . ." she said.

Privately she wondered if she was in her right mind. She hadn't believed everything Philip had told her about Lucy Raven; her opinion of men was understandably jaundiced. She believed Philip when he said Lucy had made it fairly clear she was available, but she felt less certain he had spurned the offer in so noble a fashion. She also had her doubts about him and Janet Walshe. In both cases, though, it was the women she blamed – and would gladly have murdered. Yet here she was, preparing to listen to Lucy with a sympathy that was quite genuine, and to take her side in any complaint she might make against Michael. She was thus possessed by two emotions, completely at odds with each other, and yet she could feel no conflict between them. Was that not a kind of madness?

It was all because Michael was in it, of course. If Janet Walshe came to her for sympathy over the way Dermot was treating her, she'd get short shrift and no cups of tea!

"I wouldn't breathe a word of this to anyone else," Lucy began. She watched her hands fidget and wondered if she could wait even ten minutes for a cup of tea.

"No, of course not," Diana replied soothingly.

"I mean, you know him – or knew him – so well, too. Has he changed much? D'you notice any great change?"

"In some respects not at all." Diana was grim.

After a longish pause Lucy sighed. "Oh dear! I thought it was going to be so easy."

"It is. Just say what comes into your head."

"But that's the problem. I've held this conversation with you a hundred times over the past few weeks. In here." She tapped her brow. "When I say the words to myself they sound like me asking for help. But when I open my mouth to say them to you, I just know they're going to sound like a dreadful confession of failure."

274

Diana let no silence grow between them. "If it takes two to love, and two to quarrel, it also takes two to fail, you know. Anyway, I'm sure it's nothing that can't be turned around and made into a success. May I hazard a guess? It might save us both a lot of beating about the bush."

Lucy stared at her, eyes full of hope all of a sudden.

"Michael has made you feel grubby . . . sordid – unclean, unworthy . . . that sort of thing. Am I warm?"

The hope turned to amazement. "Why, yes! But I wasn't going to . . . I mean, well – you've leaped over everything in between! That's the final conclusion, the last straw, if you like." She frowned. "Did the same thing happen to you?"

Diana nodded; she bit her lip, wondering whether to say more.

Lucy smiled bleakly. "Which of us goes first?"

Diana shrugged. "I was first in anno domini. But I've recovered from it those many years. You rank first in terms of hurt and pain – but, for that very reason, perhaps, find it hardest. As long as we both agree to . . ." She hesitated.

"Stab Michael in the back? Make his ears burn?" Lucy suggested.

Diana chuckled. "I was going to say pool our experiences – as long as we both agree, it hardly matters which of us begins." She closed her eyes and pinched the bridge of her nose.

"Headache?" Lucy asked.

Diana shook her head. "I just hope it *is* dead – that's all. One thing I *have* learned is how superb we are at self-deception."

"Before you start," Lucy said quickly, "can I ask a truly awful question? Do you hate me?" It was easy to ask when Diana's eyes were not upon her. She added, "Throw me out now if you like, only I feel it would be important to know. Does *part* of you hate me?"

The other looked up. Their eyes locked in silence. At length Diana said, "How easy it would be for us never to quarrel and never to be friends! We could go on forever, just being formally correct and cool. I even thought of trying it, you know."

"I know. Me too."

"The reason I never did is that it would mean freezing myself in a certain attitude for ever and ever. You know how people with strokes get a fallen eyelid – or some part of them left permanently dead? It would be like doing that to oneself, only deliberately. We have to quarrel, *or* be friends – or both. We can't just freeze bits of ourselves away, can we. Or I can't."

"Nor me," Lucy agreed. "I'll answer my own question for you – in case you were thinking of asking it back. Part of me *does* hate you – a very primitive, unlovely part, but it's there. I can't reason with it. I wish I could. I'm not proud of it, but it's the part of me that can never forget you owned Michael once. No, not owned – more than owned. You haunted him. Possessed him. Obsessed him. Filled his nights and days. And you say that for your part you've recovered from it,

275

but I *know*, Diana" – she tapped her breastbone – "I know it's something one never really recovers from. It's always *there*."

Her vehemence took Diana by surprise. "But how can you possibly know any such thing?" she challenged.

"Because I feel the same about Dazzler," Lucy said simply.

"Dazzler!" Diana sat bolt upright – she almost rose to her feet – in her amazement.

"Didn't you know?" Lucy asked.

"Well yes . . . I mean . . . yes, I did. But you hardly give him the time of day when he's around here."

"Oh yes – I've *recovered* from Dazzler, the same as you've recovered from Michael. I'm not talking about actual living feelings. I'm talking about the memory of them. And memory's a tenacious stuff." Her eyes narrowed. "You're very fond of the stuffed-animals museum, aren't you."

Diana nodded warily.

"And have you never had a pet cat or dog?"

"Several, why?"

Lucy looked about the apartment. "But you never had one of *them* stuffed."

"Oh, I couldn't *bear* it!" Diana exclaimed.

Lucy smiled. "Then you know exactly what I mean!"

Diana thought it over and then gave a baffled sort of laugh. "Yes!" she said, "I suppose I do. And by the same token, you understand what I mean."

Lucy nodded. "So we can trundle them out quite safely for each other to look at – these tenacious memories. We're not in danger of mistaking them for the live animal."

Diana laughed again, frankly this time. "Funnily enough I was in the stuffed-animals museum the Sunday before last – with Philip de Renzi. And he came within an ace of convincing me the rhinoceros was still alive. Oh!" She fanned her face for the shame of it and giggled.

"I can imagine," Lucy assured her. "He's always been like that. We used to play together as children. Turn a nursery table upside down and he could magically transform it into a four-masted tea clipper – and two seconds later, a lion's cage!" Then, with the barest perceptible pause, she added, "You don't need to tell me about Michael and you, Diana. You jumped over all my reservations, now I'll jump over all yours."

The kettle rose to the boil. Diana rose. "I'll just go and turn that down to simmer," she said. "Or let's have a cup now, eh? I'll make a fresh pot when Philip comes. I mean *if*."

Lucy realized it would be much easier to say what she had to say if they were both occupied, with employment for their hands. "I'll set out the cups," she said, following Diana to the alcove. Then, in the same casual voice, she went on: "Did I tell you I'm expecting a baby?

276

There's been such confusion I'm no longer sure who I . . . apart from Birdie Kelly, that is."

Diana swung round, clutching the warmed pot in her hands. "You told *her*?"

Lucy shook her head. "I didn't need to. She guessed. She came straight out with it – about a week after Ebenezer took her on. She is extraordinary."

"Well!" Diana tipped the water from the pot and measured two spoons of tealeaves into it. "And one for the pot," she added. "She's never said a word about it."

"No, I know. She's not a gossip, is she. She'd talk the cross off an ass's back but it's never mere gossip. That's just one of the extraordinary things about her."

"I guessed, too," Diana said quietly. "You haven't told me before now but I guessed, anyway."

Lucy smoothed the lace runner beneath the cups on the tray, quite unnecessarily, and carried it into the sitting room. "And, of course, Michael also guessed," she said with a heavy sigh.

"You mean you didn't tell him?" Diana pretended to be amazed.

Lucy shook her head. "Has he . . ." She swallowed nervously. "I mean, has he dropped any hints to you?"

Diana decided to take the goat by the ears. The horns could follow later. "Not yet," she lied, with an odd sort of gaiety – almost flippancy – in her voice.

It surprised Lucy, of course. "Not *yet*?" she echoed. "You mean you expect it?"

"Any day now," Diana fired back. "Now that he knows I'm safely in love with Philip de Renzi . . ." She saw Lucy's eyes widen and added, "Come, come, my dear! You surely knew it, too? Anyway, he'll reason that it will be safe to unburden some of his woes to me. Or to *some* sympathetic female – except who else is there?"

Birdie Kelly, Lucy thought, but kept it to herself. Since she had been proved wrong over the incident with the pink stockings her assurance was dented.

Diana continued: "A man will never confide such things to other men, will he. The only marital confidences they'll share are things they can laugh about. If sighs or tears are in it, the cat has their tongue."

Lucy let out a single grim laugh. "What a holy show it'll be!" she said. "The man who once turned his back on you – and the woman who made him do it – each crying on your shoulder by turns!"

Diana smiled, but more in sorrow than in triumph. As she stretched the cozy over the teapot she said, "And that's only the half of it. Ten years ago I'd have sung alleluias at the very thought it might one day happen so. But now it only saddens me. You put a sword into my hand, Lucy – and I cannot even lift it!"

"I'll give you the buckler as well, then," Lucy said. "That man

277

who once turned his back on you now performs the same office nightly . . . against me. There!"

The smile faded from Diana's face. She said nothing as Lucy babbled on: "I don't know what to do about it. Am I being unreasonable? Every advance I make . . . I mean, I try. God alone knows how hard I try. But no matter what I do, he just lies there, dead to the world. No – dead to me. Am I unreasonable? D'you know what it's like – can you imagine – lying next to the man you love, wanting him, wanting him, *wanting* him . . . and nothing but his cold shoulder for your share? I don't think it's unreasonable. But who am I to judge when it's driving me out of my mind." She stared at Diana as if from the bottom of a deep well. "I sometimes think I'll go with any man. The men who call here to visit their wives and mothers – I see them look at me . . . our eyes meet. And, you know, if it wasn't for civilization and that, almost any man and any woman could tumble in the grass together. I can see it in their eyes. *Go on!* I think to myself. *Suggest it – little enough argument I'll give you.* And even that doesn't seem unreasonable to me. D'you think I'm being unreasonable?"

Diana shook her head but continued to hold her peace.

"You don't know how much I envy you," Lucy went on. "What you've never known you never miss. I always kept a paper knife in my bedside cabinet, you know. One of *the* pleasures of life – opening the first post in bed. Not any more, though. I had a battle royal with myself one night – when I'd gladly have pushed it to the hilt between his shoulderblades! I'm not exaggerating, Diana. I lay there sweating with the effort . . . clenching my fists . . ." She shivered at the memory.

"It's so easy for men," Diana ventured. "A quick visit to Eustace Street . . ."

"You know about that house in Eustace Street?" Lucy asked in surprise.

"Housezz." Diana emphasized the plural and, smiling for the first time since Lucy had begun her confession, added, "Nurses and nuns – the two at the 'angelic' end of the feminine spectrum – are far more likely to meet the women at the . . . what can one call it? – the *venal* end than are all the classes in between. Have you never realized that?"

"Of course." Lucy was thoughtful. "It never struck me."

"The real shock is to discover they don't have horns and tails and don't reek of brimstone – indeed, how very like nuns and nurses they are in almost every way. Still, we're straying from the point. As I was saying, it *is* much easier for men, though I don't envy them for it. You might as well envy boars and stallions in the farmyard. But you're wrong in another of the things you said – that I've never known these feelings you speak of."

Something in the way she spoke – the care with which she selected each and every word – made the hair bristle on Lucy's neck. "No!" she whispered.

"Yes," Diana insisted quietly.

"You?"

"Yes."

Lucy closed her eyes and held her breath. "Tell me!" The words were barely audible. "I cannot ask. I dare not ask."

"I have also had a baby. I know very well what . . . temptations, what torments you are undergoing."

Lucy opened her eyes at last, which were now shimmering with tears. "More?" she pleaded. "You know there is more I dare not ask."

Diana nodded. She, by contrast, was calm as the grave. "A boy," she said. "He's just turned ten. You remember when I went back home to my parents a few Sundays ago? That was his tenth birthday."

"Oh, Diana!" Lucy closed her eyes again, forcing the tears to brim over and course down her cheeks. "Diana – I'm so . . ."

"What?" the other asked when Lucy's voice trailed off. "Sorry? There is absolutely no need for that, I assure you. He is the joy of my life."

"Does he know? What's his name?"

Diana laid her head on one side, implying that was one question she need not have asked. "Mick," she said. "What else! He 'knows' I am his aunt. He knows that my sister Agnes, who died in America on the very day he was born – and that's a genuine coincidence – was his mother. I was there, in fact. I went to America, you see, to avoid the scandal. I was in labour and Agnes ran to fetch the doctor – and just collapsed and died on the way. We never really knew why."

Her matter-of-fact words – for, of course, these incidents lay ten years in her past – cut like knives into Lucy's heart. She broke down completely and wept her eyes out.

Diana let the worst of it pass and then went over and, kneeling at the side of her chair, put her arms around her and cradled her head against her shoulder, saying, "There, there. It's of little consequence now."

When she judged that Lucy was looking for some reason to stop altogether, she went on, "Half an hour ago I'd have gone to a martyr's grave rather than reveal a word of this. How can you look to me for comfort when I'm as unpredictable to myself as that?"

Lucy even managed a little laugh. "Because you're born to it, my dear," she said, sniffing heavily – and so glutinously that she was forced to make a little exclamation of self-disgust.

It was Diana's cue to rise and go to one of her dressing-table drawers. She returned a moment later saying, "I always keep a couple of masculine handkerchiefs handy for moments like this." Then, realizing that her confession made it seem as if she often gave way to tears, she added, "I hope it doesn't smell too musty – it's lain there, unused, rather a long time."

"I'd love to see him," Lucy said wanly – as people say they'd love to see the Taj Mahal by moonlight or the Pyramids at dawn.

"Indeed you will," Diana responded. "He's to start at Saint Columba's this coming term. He'll probably spend the weekends here with his Aunty Di!"

It was Diana's practice to make three rounds of all the beds each day – morning, afternoon, and evening. She knew every patient and every detail of his or her condition and treatment – and Lord help the staff nurse or sister who knew less than she or who let any aspect of her care slide back. Michael said you could hear the very rafters sigh with relief when each round was over.

That Thursday, the 28th of July – the morning after her confession to Lucy – was her thirtieth birthday, but her behaviour made not the slightest concession to the event; she was as severe and demanding as on any other day and no one dared even whisper a festive greeting to her on her morning round. As it came to an end Michael asked her gravely if she would mind accompanying him to the senior common room, which was the preserve of the doctors as well as of the Matron, her assistant, and the two most senior sisters. Her heart sank, for she knew the room would be deserted at that hour and she suspected that Lucy, despite all her promises, had blurted out her secret to Michael. Why else was he so solemn?

The room in question was next to Ebenezer's private apartments at the western end of the main house; as they walked in sepulchral silence up the corridor she turned over half a dozen excuses to prevent this painful interview. She was even willing to closet herself with Ebenezer O'Dea for the rest of the morning, rather than face Michael and his inevitable accusations. She was about to blurt out some rigmarole when he took her by surprise; he grabbed her wrist and dragged her swiftly over the last few yards, stretching out his other hand and throwing open the door the moment its handle came within reach.

And then there was a chorus of cheers and cries of "Happy birthday!" from within and she found a whole crowd of well-wishers facing her – everyone who was entitled to use that room, of course, as well as Lucy, Dazzler, Philip, Ebenezer O'Dea, and his ever-attendant Birdie. Their ragged greetings coalesced in an ironic chorus of "She's a Grand Old Irish Lady," during which the two other doctors and Lucy stood aside to reveal a cake with thirty lighted candles, almost burned down to the icing.

"Quickly!" Lucy plucked her into the room by her starched cuff. "Before they die on you."

Diana drew the deepest possible breath and managed to extinguish the lot in one go. There were cries of "Speech! Speech!"

Then her smile faded. "Very well," she said ominously as she squared her shoulders, clenched her hands in front of her, and assumed the grimmest of visages. "I realize that Miss Huxley was only twenty-six when she was appointed matron at Sir Patrick Dun's, but she was then as she is now – exceptional in all things. For my part I have never considered it possible for the more run-of-the mill sort of woman, like me, to become a hospital matron under the age of thirty – which explains why I have so far been rather *shy* and *reluctant* in asserting the authority vested in me here at Mount Venus."

Hoots of disbelieving and derisive laughter greeted this blarney but Diana continued implacably, still not smiling. "Take heed, however, and let the word go forth from this gathering. Now I have achieved the age of maturity, all that will change. *This* Diana will henceforth become the huntress of legend. Where I have been mild, I shall be fierce. What was bland until today shall be stern and pitiless tomorrow and all tomorrows."

There was plenty more in that vein until they began to stir in a kind of restive silence. Her relentless delivery had convinced them she was in earnest and, though they could not challenge the sentiments, they considered this the worst possible occasion to ventilate them. Then at last she gave way to her laughter and concluded, "But chiefly I hope that none of you here – good friends all – will be able to detect the slightest difference in me!" Then, as they sighed with relief and joined rather sheepishly in her merriment, she thanked them for their surprise party and explained her stern remarks by saying that one good deception deserved another.

Just before she cut the cake her eyes lingered briefly in Lucy's, then in Philip's; both of them supposed they knew what wish she was making. They all drank her health in thimble-sized tots of madeira, after which Doctor Quinlan, Mrs Lynch, and the two sisters returned to their duties. Michael and Dermot noticed that the slightly guilty glances they gave on leaving were directed not at them but at Matron Powers. Her ascendancy could hardly be more strongly and more delicately underlined.

Ebenezer took a second tot and toasted her again. "In future, Matron," he said, "whenever I hear of the iron fist in the velvet glove, I shall think of you."

"Hear hear!" Philip put in.

She turned to him and laughed. "I spoke entirely for your benefit, Mister de Renzi, to pay you back for the rhinoceros."

"Grand slam," he replied.

Michael and Lucy drifted across and joined them; she had also recharged her glass but he had not. To see them together in public like this Diana would never have guessed there was a hair out of place between them – which was why Lucy's outburst of the previous evening had so surprised her.

"I hope you can look in on the children this Saturday afternoon, Diana," Lucy said. "Tarquin has written a play and they're all dying to perform it in your honour."

"Oh? Is it about nursing?"

"Alas no. It's about runaway slaves and bloodhounds and chains and whipping, as far as I understand it. But no doubt the victim of the whipping will need to be nursed at some stage."

"*Victims*," Michael corrected her. "Tarquin would never stop at one where a dozen will do. Talking of festivities, Matron, I don't know if you've glanced through the latest roster of patients and realized the implications for the second week in August?"

Diana frowned. "No? I have noticed that things seem to come in waves. We've had thirty-one acute or surgical cases this July, which is now almost over, thank heavens. And as the first of them won't be discharged until the middle of next month, we'll practically be a convalescent home for the next two weeks. Is that what you mean?"

Michael chuckled and looked at the rest of the group. "Can't hide a thing here," he said. "But it gave me an idea. Since we are compelled to be a convalescent home, however temporarily, why don't we organize a couple of outings – half of us to go on the first, half on the second? The first on a Friday, say, the other on the Saturday after it. Take all the convalescents who are capable of benefitting from it, plus an appropriate number of nurses. Hire a charabanc and go down for the day to Glendalough or the Meeting of the Waters at Avoca . . . something of that sort." He turned to Ebenezer. "D'you feel up to it, sir? Would you enjoy that?"

He grinned heartily. "Nothing would suit me better, Mister Raven," he replied. But then, with a tinge of sadness, he added, "Though, of course, it's not up to me. In this, as in all important matters, we are in the hands of our implacable and newly matured Matron. What says she? A factory outing to Saint Kevin's Kitchen? Is it 'just what the Matron ordered' – to adapt the ancient saying, which is now quite passé?"

Diana did not rise to the barb; she said it would be as well to organize the two outings now but to leave the final decision until one could see how the weather turned out on the actual day.

"If you're free now," Michael said, "we could draw up some preliminary lists?"

On their way to his private consulting room Diana said, "That was rather crudely done, Michael."

Over his shoulder he replied, "I don't suppose anyone else was of that opinion. Don't you think it odd that Birdie Kelly didn't let a single peep out of her at that meeting? I've never known her so reserved. Is it too much to hope she's sickening for something?"

"That's a dreadful thing for a doctor to say," she snapped.

282

"Oh, come on! Don't imagine that turning thirty gives you the right to be pompous." He grinned as he held open the door for her.

"I don't wish to be spoken to like this," she said coldly as she walked in past him. "If you persist, I shall leave. In fact, I'm only staying because I know you're behaving like this deliberately. You *want* to provoke me to anger. I can't imagine why, but that's my only reason for staying – to find out." She seated herself without waiting to be invited.

When Michael took his own chair he was serious again. "I don't know why, either," he said. "I'm sorry. You are, in fact, half right. I wanted to make you angry, not for any particular purpose but just to serve you out – because you've annoyed me."

"I?" she asked in surprise.

"Yes. It's not your fault. In my more rational moments I realize I'm being highly unreasonable . . . but I find it increasingly difficult to be rational these days."

"Is this all because Lucy came to talk with me last night?"

He lowered his eyes and fiddled with the paraphernalia on his desk. "That was the last straw."

"It was also the first straw, then," she shot back. "Lucy hasn't called on me once, not since . . ."

"No – the rest was nothing to do with you. I told you it's not rational. The thing is, she's also been unburdening herself to Janet, to Philip de Renzi, even to Birdie Kelly. And to Dazzler O'Dea for all I know."

"I don't know why you say 'also,' Michael. You're simply assuming she unburdened herself – as you express it – to me last night. For all you know we were talking of forming a bridge circle for the coming winter. In fact, that's one of the things we *did* touch upon. Perhaps she also *unburdened* herself of a few cake recipes? Or a complaint about my nurses making a racket on the new fire escape?"

"Did she?" he asked in surprise.

"I'm not saying. The point I'm trying to make is that you simply don't know."

He nodded morosely at the logic of her words, which was, of course, irrefutable. He stared at his hands for a long time and then said, "I don't know who else to turn to."

She felt a little flame of pity kindle in her heart – and instantly quenched it. "You have a funny idea of how best to turn to a woman for help!" she said.

He inhaled deeply through his nostrils and then out. "Can we start again?" he asked.

"It depends on what you want to start," she told him.

"I'm not looking for a shoulder to cry on," he said. "And nor do I seek to revive . . . well, anything that might have been between us."

To his amazement she rose to her feet and thumped his desk. "God Almighty, Michael!" Spittle flew from her lips and her eyes gleamed with intimations of battle. "Did you say 'might have been'?"

He closed his eyes and slumped, as if she were being infuriatingly pedantic. "All right, then: 'anything that *was* between us'! Better?"

She thumped the table again.

"*Everything* that was between us!" His voice softened and he murmured. "Wonderful though it was."

Nothing other than that gentle afterthought could have penetrated the armour of her anger. Her tone, too, was slightly less abrasive as she responded. "Oh, you remember it, do you?"

"Just lately," he replied, "I've remembered very little else." He raised his hands as if to ward off words he knew she was going to say. "I'm not trying to revive anything – everything – in saying that. But that doesn't mean I'm not allowed to remember. It doesn't warp my ability to judge things. I can still say such-and-such was better . . . this was good and that was bad."

"You're rambling, Michael," she snapped. "I'm not interested in your memories these days. Nor – though I'm sure it comes as a great surprise – do I wish to hear what you judged good or bad."

He raised his eyes and stared balefully at her. "You don't need to tell me what Lucy spoke of last night. I hear it in every word you utter. You've already judged and condemned me."

"I did that many years ago, Michael. You'd have to kill Lucy in some unspeakably vile fashion to change my opinion of you very much."

He swallowed hard and then just gaped at her in disbelief. At last he said, "You mean your opinion could *only* change for the worse? Truly?"

"Truly. Why? Surely you can't be surprised? If so, then your memories and mine can hardly coincide on any particular. Tell me one thing you did – just one thing – that would allow me to judge you kindly?"

Her bitterness left him completely bewildered. "How can you go on working here with me?" he asked.

"That's easy," she replied dismissively. "Because I think you're one of the finest doctors I know. I'd champion you against any other – *as a doctor*. I regard it as a professional privilege to work with you. Ours is a professional connection."

He was already shaking his head before she finished. "No," he said at once. " No, that cannot be so. That is not *all* you derive from being here. If your opinion of me, as a man, I mean – if that's as low as you say, then you must be cock-a-whoop to see what's happening to Lucy and me. It must be the crowning of all your bitterness." He compressed his lips and squared his shoulders as he came to a decision. "Well, I'm sorry I inveigled you here on such a flimsy pretext, Matron. You're quite right – we can discuss our charabanc outing at some more convenient time. Now – is there anything else before I go and see my patients?"

284

Diana rose and went across to the window. Down on the terrace below Ebenezer O'Dea was playing a sort of sedan-chair polo, with the Kelly girl manipulating his chair, shrieking encouragement and hooting with laughter; their sole opponent, keeping goal, was one of the convalescents, a Mrs Probert, whose prolapse might return if she wasn't careful. "Oh, Michael," she whispered, and was amazed that her breath should cloud the pane, however briefly, on so fine a day.

"What now?" he asked tetchily.

"Why me? Can't you see the dangers?" She turned and accused him with her gaze.

"Not if you hate me so much," he replied.

"Never mind my feelings – what about yours? How honest are you being with yourself? If you and I were castaways, the only castaways, on some remote island, what would . . . I mean how would . . . well, you know what I'm unwilling to put into words."

"Are you hinting it'd be a cure for your hatred?" he asked. "By heavens, it'd be almost worth it!"

"I said be honest, my dear – not funny."

His smile died. "I don't know," he confessed. "Perhaps the reason I turned to you for help is precisely that. I fear I might fall in love with you all over again, so I am compelled to challenge that fear, meet it head-on – because if I turn and run, I yield the contest to it without a struggle. And that would be to build a lifelong prison for myself."

She returned to the chair and seated herself. "Tell me, then." She raised her watch and consulted it. "No. We ought to go and do your round, otherwise I'll be keeping Doctor Walshe waiting." She put her fingertips to her forehead and massaged hard. "Duty!" she said bleakly. Then at last she smiled at him. "Perhaps a little cooling off won't come amiss with either of us, eh? Shall we meet again this evening?"

"Here?" he suggested.

She hesitated a long moment before she said, "In my apartment. As you say – meet the challenge head-on!"

Oh look!" Janet called out. "I thought as much. This isn't just a wild rose that's volunteered. These are all suckers and there's a dainty little bourbon struggling for survival in the middle of it there." She cupped her hands to her lips and called out, as if to the rose, "Can you hold out, little thing? Help is on its way." When Lucy had picked a careful path among the plants they had already rescued she pointed it out.

"Oh yes," Lucy said. "It looks a bit like *Belle de Malmaison* – the Empress Josephine's favourite rose."

Janet darted a suspicious glance at her. "You're making it up."

Lucy grinned. "One day I'll learn how to say things like that with absolute authority. Actually, we both ought to be rather good at it – we've heard our husbands play that game often enough."

"What? Sounding completely confident when really they haven't the first idea?"

Lucy nodded. "Shall I hold the suckers out straight while you snip away?"

It was a superfluous question for she was already holding the first and Janet was already bending to snip. "This is the sort of thing one could never leave to Slattery," Janet said, "good man though he is. He'd rather root the whole lot out, have a nice big bonfire, and start again. Women are much better suited. We should get a few women up here and start training them as gardeners. I've never understood why females are considered perfectly acceptable for field gangs but you never see them gardening."

"It's not a bad thought, Janet." Lucy used her secateurs to shorten the long suckers that her companion was severing at the rootstock. "They'd be cheaper, too."

Janet stood straight and surveyed her handiwork with pride. "There! Doesn't that feel better?" she asked the rose, half of whose suckers were now removed. "We're going to have trouble with those lads at the back, where they're all mixed up with the wistaria. I think we'll just cut off the bits that show and leave the rest to rot and fall away, don't you?" She turned to Lucy, as a sergeant might turn to an officer. "Permission to be slovenly, sir?"

Lucy parodied a drawling type of Guards officer they both knew very well. "Cawwy on, sah-majah!" and tipped her a languid one-finger salute.

They both laughed. "I know exactly who you're imitating," Janet said. "In fact, between you and me, I dashed neah mawwied the oaf, once." She shivered theatrically at the narrowness of her escape and bent again to snip out the visible bit of the suckers on the farther side of the rose. "Actually, I wasn't entirely joking about getting some females out here and training them. You're connected with the Ranelagh Female Rescue Society, aren't you? D'you think they might cough up a few females for us to experiment with?"

Lucy had begun gathering the thorny snippets and was carrying them to the site of their next bonfire, about twelve paces away. "I was," she called back over her shoulder.

"D'you think they'd be suitable probationer-gardeners? The younger ones, anyway. It calls for a certain stamina."

Lucy dumped her armful and trod it well down before she answered. "Your question implies that there is a *them* – as distinct from an *us*, I mean. But what struck me most forcibly was how varied *they* are. Before I became engaged in that work, I held the same opinion as most women, I suppose – that they were uniformly lazy, greedy, pleasure-seeking, disease-ridden, drunken, thieving, untrustworthy women who had entirely abandoned all moral principle."

"My!"

Lucy grinned apologetically. "Sorry! That was part of a speech I used to give."

"Heartfelt, obviously."

Lucy took off her thick gauntlets so as to shake out some withered rose hips that had fallen inside. She stared wistfully at the skyline as she answered. "Of all the things I had to give up, I think I miss the Ranelagh FRS the most." She turned her gaze on Janet. "D'you think we could manage a sort of women's gardening school here? It would mean so much."

Janet, who had finished her pruning, began to gather up the debris on her side of the rose. "Tell me more about them. You listed all the things they *aren't* – but you're not going to tell me they put the nuns to shame?"

"No!" Lucy chortled. "Though for charity of heart some of them could have taught *some* nuns I've known a thing or two. But no – obviously one could find hoors who were all those things I said, just as you can find respectable women who are lazy, greedy, pleasure-seeking . . . et cetera. So the whole point of that speech I used to make was to show respectable women that when it came to ordinary human qualities – like friendship, mutual support and comfort, innate sense of what's right and what's wrong, thrift, truthfulness, care of loved ones, snish snish – you couldn't slip a visiting card edgewise-on between 'them' and 'us'. That was all, really. Therefore – to get back to your original question about how suitable 'they' are – the answer is precisely the same as for any other group of women taken at hazard, phew!" She rose and mopped her brow. "This talking is hard work!"

"The next question is – would the Ranelagh FRS pay for their training? Or at least for their board and lodging? Actually, that's a point – where *would* we house them? We can't have them associated with the Mount Venus Clinic, and apart from anything else, the nurses and female domestics would probably walk out en masse."

They began pulling the weeds around the salvaged rose, weeds no longer protected by the profusion of thorny suckers.

"The FRS would certainly be willing to pay if we could issue some sort of recognized diploma at the end of the women's time here. We must look into it. There must be one. There's a diploma for just about everything these days."

"Except for wives and mothers," Janet quipped. "And how many of *us* would pass, eh?" After a pause she said, "It's funny I should think about old Hawwy Twumpington-Stuart again. He hasn't crossed my mind in years. I wonder what life would have been like if I *had* said yes to him? I was very tempted. They had a wonderful house in Esher. Eight acres of garden with a river running through it and a divine Japanese bridge. When you sowed seeds you had to flee before the plants could rise and throw you to the ground. *Very* tempted! D'you ever think about your old beaux? Oh, careful! That's bugle – *Ajuga reptans* – we want to encourage that."

Lucy bit her lip in vexation. She knew very well that it was bugle – *and* that it was called *Ajuga reptans* on Sundays – but Janet's chatter had distracted her. "I was dividing it," she lied as she replanted the bit she had pulled.

"Do you?" Janet asked. "Ever think about them, I mean? I also nearly married Lord Oxmantown . . ."

"They've got *two* rivers running through *their* garden," Lucy teased before her companion could launch into another panegyric. "I can't imagine why you ended up marrying a man with no garden at all."

"Nor can I." Janet giggled. "Still, it hasn't turned out too badly. Did you have impossible ambitions – no, I mean irrelevant ambitions – before you settled for Michael?"

Lucy decided to meet her head-on. "The only man I seriously considered was Dazzler O'Dea – if 'seriously' is quite the right word, which it isn't. But he was great gas, which seemed all-important in my giddy youth."

"Dazzler?" Janet asked in great surprise. But since she had drawn breath several times to make the exclamation, the final effect was a bit damp.

"Come! Surely you knew that?" Lucy chided.

"I heard a vague rumour but of course I didn't believe it. Dazzler, eh – what an escape! It would have been a disaster." She bit her lip like a naughty girl. "Sorry – perhaps you don't think so?"

Lucy made a vague gesture with her hands, to imply it was all water under the bridge by now. "It would certainly have been different," she agreed.

"D'you ever catch yourself looking at him and wondering? It must be odd to live almost cheek-by-jowl with someone who once meant so much. I can't imagine it."

By now Lucy had a shrewd idea of where this seemingly idle conversation was leading. From time to time she'd caught Janet with her eye on Michael and Diana, filled with a speculative gleam. In the beginning she'd dismissed it as the normal interest any woman would show in a situation where a friend's husband was forced to work in close proximity to an attractive and unmarried female – and both of them well furnished with opportunities to make something of it. More recently, however, she had begun to suspect that Janet's interest had some more solid foundation. And now she was almost sure of it; these questions were not mere chatter to fill out the hour until the luncheon gong sounded. She decided to tease the game out a little. "Actually," she said, "if you promise not to breathe a word to a soul about it, I'll tell you."

"Promise-promise-promise!" Janet's eyes were aglow.

"Well, the truth is I'm rather glad to live cheek-by-jowl, as you put it, with dear old Dazzler. Because make no mistake about it, I was heart-sick in love with that man once upon a time. I couldn't breathe for sighing, nor eat for the havoc inside me when I'd just say his name. He was the world to me. And yet now I can look at him and wonder what all the fuss was about. Not that I despise him now – I mean I haven't jumped from the bakestone onto the griddle. I still see all his good qualities but I cannot *fathom* how I ever thought he was any different from other men."

"But why does that make you glad?" Janet was forced to ask. "I don't understand that."

"Oh, I thought you knew that, too. Surely there's a little rumour about that as well? About Michael and . . ." She paused before denying Janet the name: ". . . his old flame?"

"No!" Janet was now consumed with frustration. Not only had Lucy volunteered the information – thus cutting short all the fun of dragging it out of her bit by bit – but she had omitted the all-important name. "Here?" she asked in astonishment. "Actually at Mount Venus?"

Lucy shook her head. "It's a bit more complicated in Michael's case. Sadly, his 'old flame' is . . . er, extinguished, one might put it. She went to America – and got married there – and then died a year or so later, in labour, alas."

"Oh dear!" Janet allowed a few seconds for her sympathy to register and then frowned. "But, in that case, I don't see . . .?"

"I said it was more complicated. Her living image is here at Mount Venus, as you correctly surmised – her twin sister – our birthday girl – our revered and beloved Matron!"

Janet's conventional cries of "Good heavens!" and "Well I never!" could not mask her intense disappointment that the dormant-volcano of scandal of Mount Venus (as she must have thought of it) had, in fact, been extinct those many years.

"So," Lucy chattered on happily, "if I find that my feelings for Dazzler, once so all-consuming, are now mere dust, it helps me feel entirely sanguine about Michael's closeness – professional closeness, I mean – to one who merely resembles a love that was equally all-consuming to him. But *isn't* life just absolutely extraordinary!" She bubbled over in merriment.

"Ye-es!" Janet drew the word out thoughtfully. There was a pensive and disbelieving glint in her eye and Lucy saw she was not going to be cheated of her juicy morsel quite so swiftly as all that.

Not that Lucy worried. Janet could hardly probe into every detail of this new gloss on ancient events. She might, with some ingenuity, work a conversation with Diana round to the subject of her siblings. Then she'd learn that Diana *had* had a sister (all right, not a twin, but that could be explained as a simple misunderstanding), and the sister had gone to America and had, indeed, died on the very day Mick was born . . . But the probing would probably not even get that far; it would almost certainly die as soon as the sister's existence was confirmed. Besides, if Diana intended putting the boy through St Columba's from this September, she'd better start spreading the story herself, quite unprompted by questions from Janet Walshe or anyone else.

No, Lucy decided, all things considered, she had little doubt that her new version of Diana's story would hold water as far as Janet was concerned. There was nothing to worry about.

"Well!" She removed her gloves as the gong rang for luncheon and ran her eye over the rich dark loam of the border, now almost entirely free of weeds. "What a splendid morning's work!"

It was Dermot Walshe's night on call at the clinic, which came round every twelve days. He went down the hill to Willbrook, bathed, dined lightly on cold mutton and blancmange, and returned to Mount Venus. About twenty minutes after he had gone, Janet realized he had left without his nightshirt – or, rather, that she had forgotten to replace the rather threadbare one she had removed from his room there. She set out after him on her bicycle, thinking the exercise might do her good; her back was rather stiff after spending all day in the garden with Lucy Raven.

It had been an outstandingly successful day as far as the gardening went, but rather disappointing on all other fronts. The news that she and Dermot had been mistaken about Michael Raven's amour that night at the RCS Ball was particularly galling. All the excitement of observing the awkwardness between the chief and his matron simply evaporated when one knew that the female in question – or, rather, *in flagrante* – had been her sister. Even a twin sister wasn't at all the same. Nonetheless, all was not lost. One never knew what sort of twists and turns Michael's residual sympathies, denied a natural outlet by that untimely death, might take. The pair of them would still be worth observing.

Then again Lucy might be, quite frankly, lying – taking a chance that no further inquiries would be made. Yet somehow Janet didn't believe she'd be as rash as all that; the risks were too great. But suppose it had been only half a lie? Suppose Diana Powers had a twin sister who had gone to America and had died in childbirth? It would surely be a most convenient thing to put about that *she* had been Michael Raven's sweetheart. Diana herself would surely, and gladly, connive at the lie; there was positively no advantage to her now in letting the world know she and he had ever been so close.

The more Janet thought about it, the more she seethed with frustration. A conjecture that had been simple to verify, given time and patience, had now been supplanted by a story that would require the resources of Scotland Yard or Sherlock Holmes to confirm. It began to look as if the truth would now never be known – by any outsider, at least.

She turned these thoughts over and over as she walked down the passage that led to Dermot's room at Mount Venus. It was, in fact, the governess's old room in the days when the place had been a private house; the staircase that led through it, up to what were now Matron's apartments, had simply been boarded off at the top. In fact, Dermot used the treads as a series of staggered bookshelves, with only the outermost twelve inches being left free to go up and down. The moment Janet entered the room, all thoughts of ancient scandal fled from her mind, for there, doubled up on the topmost steps of that disused staircase, sat Birdie Kelly. Guilt was written all over her face.

"What . . .?" Janet began at the top of her voice – and then remembered to close the door behind her. When she turned round again, the Kelly woman had her fingers to her lips and was pointing urgently to the ceiling above her. "What is the meaning of this?" Janet asked in a vehement whisper.

Birdie rose to a sort of crouch and began to descend the steps backward; from the way her joints creaked, she had been there some time. "Lord, my feet can feel stars in them boots," she complained. "And I have lemonade for blood."

"What d'you think you're doing here?" Janet asked her the moment she reached the floor and could turn round.

"Listening out, ma'am," Birdie said, quite unabashed, as she pointed again at the ceiling.

"To whom? I mean, how dare you? That's eavesdropping. You should be dismissed for it. Whose chambers are those?"

"Matron's, ma'am. She's up there with Mister de Renzi and he's knocking the stuffin' out of her. Go listen for yourself an it please you."

"I'll do no such thing! The very idea! What . . . d'you mean they're . . . fighting? Or what?"

Birdie sniggered.

"And you're just sitting there listening? Bold as brass! But that's dreadful. I simply can't believe it. It's . . . it's . . . I mean, it's simply not . . . are you *sure* that's what they're doing?"

Birdie stood aside in obvious invitation.

"Well . . ." Janet said dubiously. "As a matter of plain duty, I suppose . . ." She compressed her lips and began a hesitant ascent.

"You'd best hurry, ma'am, if you don't want to miss them. They've been at it those forty minutes already."

"Forty!" Scandalized, Janet raced to the top and pressed her ear to one of the new floor joists, where the boarded-off section lay. After a few seconds she exclaimed, "This is outrageous!" and pressed her ear even harder to the timber. "Absolutely scandalous!" she said, trying a different position but hastily returning to the first. "They must be lying on the floor!"

Watching her, Birdie could tell the progress of affairs above by the height of her eyebrows and the O-ness, so to speak, of her mouth. When her eyes almost fell out of their sockets even Birdie could hear it for herself.

"Unbelievable! Simply unbelievable!" Janet muttered as she crawled gingerly back down. "Our own Matron! And that *nice* Mister de Renzi! I still cannot credit it. Are you sure it's him, Kelly?"

"*Miss* Kelly, if it's all one to you, ma'am, please."

"Don't you dare take that tone with me, girl! You're trespassing in this room. I could have you dismissed for that alone."

"I don't think so, ma'am. Not wishing to pick bones with you, but 'twas himself sent me here."

Janet frowned. "My husband?"

Birdie shook her head. "Himself."

"Mister O'Dea!"

Still Birdie shook her head. "I'll name no names, ma'am, but I could lick that finger and carry it to him wet. So now! 'Tis best not to tangle with that one, ma'am. Best to know nothing and tell less, as the man said."

Janet sniffed haughtily but did not pursue her threats. "But you *are* sure it's Mister de Renzi?" she asked.

"It always is, ma'am."

Again Janet simply gaped at her. "*Always?* D'you mean this isn't the first time? How long has it been going on?"

"The fourth of June was the first time."

Janet swallowed hard; her voice fell to a shocked whisper. "But that's two months! It *can't* have been going on for two whole months. The minx! They must be exposed. She must be dismissed. And Mister de Renzi – *such* a gentleman!"

Birdie smiled, slightly pityingly, Janet thought. "She'll not be dismissed, ma'am. Himself would take out all his money before he'd allow that. 'Tis best – like I said – to hold your whisht and count all the pretty clouds in the sky."

Janet frowned suddenly. "Did you say the fourth of June – the Saturday Doctor Walshe and I first came out here to Mount Venus?" Her tone suggested she had caught Birdie out in a lie.

Birdie, who had been waiting for her to make the connection, merely smiled and said, "Isn't he the hero, ma'am? He could give any churn three good turns, as me mammy used to say."

Janet swallowed again, even more audibly than before; but this time the dominant emotion was fear rather than amazement. A chill frosting had settled round her guts. "I see," she said quietly. "It's not just those two you spy on then!" She nodded toward the ceiling.

"Himself does be wanting to know the way of things, ma'am. 'Twould be worse for all if he had the use of his own legs to carry his own eyes and his own ears about his own place. 'Twould be worse for all if he knew *everything* I've seen and heard – which he doesn't." She sniffed and added, "Yet."

Janet squared her shoulders. "I see," she said calmly. "Well, Miss Kelly, I think I understand you."

"Glad I am to hear it, ma'am. And I'll be obliged if you'll say nothing to Doctor Walshe about this book I fecked off him." She reached behind her and brought out from the folds of her skirt a small leather-bound volume, which she passed to the other. "I read all them bottom two steps and now I'm started on the third," she added.

Janet turned the spine to the dying light from the window and read the battered gold lettering: *The Nature of the Universe – Lucretius.* Bewildered again, she handed it back. "If you say so," she murmured feebly.

"Doctor Quinlan does be helping me folly the arguments," Birdie added as she left.

Janet went to the former staircase and began picking the volumes up, one by one, and turning them to the light: *The Republic – Plato . . . The Poetics – Aristotle . . . The Imitation of Christ – Thomas à Kempis . . . The Compleat Angler – Izaak Walton . . .* all the books that Dermot had cleared out of his shelves at home – the books he'd bought off barrows down on the quays because he "thought he ought to read them one day" but never had.

And this strange, uncouth, ignorant little hoyden was chewing her way through them like a bookworm!

And Doctor Quinlan was helping her "folly the arguments"!

"The world's gone mad!" she murmured.

Philip ran his hands down the smooth blue cylinder of linen that encased the darlingest body (and now, also, proclaimed the darlingest person) in all the world; even the bits that weren't starched looked and felt as if they were. Ten minutes earlier what riots of passion had fired that now imprisoned flesh! Where had it all gone? Where did she keep the memory of it in between? And when she reprimanded some junior staff nurse for unseemly behaviour – being observed taking tea with a young man in a Dublin café, for instance – did no remnant of that fever stir in its dungeon, and give a discreet little cough, perhaps, and whisper a seditious "remember me?"?

"If the whole world was mad," he said to her, "no one would know it, would they. Or perhaps one or two might – but *they'd* be the ones the rest of us would call mad!"

"And if you're not out of here soon," she replied, "you'll have the pleasure of driving Michael Raven mad."

"I daydream about you all the time," he went on, as if she had not spoken. "That must be a kind of madness, don't you think? I cannot understand how a woman as beautiful as you, as fine as you, as good as you, is *there* at all – for me to love, I mean. And why me? I'm not worth one single drop of your blood."

She grinned meanly. "I can only agree with every word you say, darling. And with every word you say the mystery of what on earth I see in you grows even deeper. Now pull your tie straight and run along." She inspected her coiffure minutely in the looking glass, a little disappointed to find nothing out of place, no tress that needed a comforting little pat. She distributed needless light touches here and there at random.

He bent at the knees and looked over her shoulder to straighten his tie. "Why wear your uniform, anyway?" he asked.

"To remind him of who I am nowadays. I think he's beginning to live dangerously in the past." She gazed tenderly at him in the glass. "Don't say you're worried!"

"Will you wear your engagement ring?"

She shook her head. "Not until after we've made the announcement all official."

"When?"

She rose and kissed him on the nose. "All in good time."

He stood his ground stubbornly and took her in his arms, or, at least, held her by the elbows. "I'm not worried that anything's going to *happen* between you and Michael," he said.

"I should jolly well hope not!"

"I'm just afraid he'll upset you."

"Well, that's very sweet of you, Philip. Now *do* cut along!"

"It's the only power he still possesses over you. I'm just afraid he'll use it, that's all."

She jerked her arms out of his grip and walked away from him. "Are you trying to start a quarrel with me, Philip? You want me to be roaring up and down the banks by the time he gets here – is that it?"

He raised his hands in a warding-off gesture that reminded her of Michael's, earlier that day. "I'll say no more," he promised.

"For this relief much thanks!"

"I can't come back later because Abraham Quinlan said he might cry in."

"*With* Miss Kelly in tow, no doubt."

"What of it? There's nothing romantic going on there, you know."

"If you say so." Diana's tone implied that she cared little either way.

"But," Philip added, "he seems to be the one person who can hold a conversation with Birdie Kelly without . . . " He sought for the *mot juste*.

"Vertigo?" Diana suggested. "Schemes of murder?"

Philip laughed. "Without losing the thread all the time – was the idea I was straining after."

"You see!" Now it was she who grasped him by the arms, propelling him backwards toward the door. "You even lose the thread when talking *about* her. Now go!"

"Will you come over to Porterstown and join us if there's time after?" he pleaded.

She reached for the door handle behind him, nimbly avoiding any contact between their bodies. "If I feel the need for fresh air," she promised.

Desperately he surveyed the room over her shoulder. "Hide me in one of the cupboards," he suggested. "Or let me stay out of sight in the bedroom – just in case he . . . you know, tries anything on."

"Philip!" She pushed him out into the passage.

"You have no idea how I feel," he complained bitterly as he plodded away.

She closed the door and leaned her head against its smooth panelling. "And d'you think you have the smallest inkling how *I* feel?" she whispered.

She was glad of the ten minutes that elapsed before Michael knocked at that same door, a knock that was neither hesitant nor peremptory. She was quite composed again by the time she answered. "Punctual as ever," she said, stepping aside to allow him in.

He was rather surprised to find her in uniform but immediately understood the gesture; he even gave an approving nod as he came in. She, in turn, understood that passing nod; it frightened her a little to find so much rapport between them, so little need for simple words.

"A wee dram?" she suggested, not knowing why she used a Scottish phrase.

He thought he understood, however. "Old McKechnie!" he exclaimed. "I've not seen him since the Adelaide. Have you?"

"A wee droppeen, then?" she replied. "I have a half-bottle of Powers somewhere."

"And so you should!" he joked. "I'd be glad of 'a wee dram'. Isn't it odd how a little phrase like that can take one back?"

She found the bottle and poured out two generous measures. "I hope we're not going to dwell too much on the rare oul' times, Michael. Haven't we cares enough in the present! *Sláinte!*"

"Good health!"

They sipped and then sat down, Michael taking the same chair Lucy had occupied a mere twenty-four hours earlier; Diana saw no humour in the irony as she took her own seat, facing him.

"Are you on call, tonight?" he asked, though he knew very well she was not.

"It feels like it," she replied.

He turned his gaze to the window, where day had almost fled. "It's hard to talk if you're going to be so prickly."

"Then stop asking tendentious questions. You know I'm off tonight and you know why I'm in uniform, nonetheless." After a brief silence she added in a softer tone, "Let me start, then. This trouble between you and Lucy . . ."

"*Trouble* is a very Irish word. 'I'm sorry for your trouble.'"

It was the standard condolence at a funeral. "Now who's being prickly?" she scoffed. "What would you prefer? Brouhaha? *Contretemps?* Is it better in French?"

He inhaled deeply and let almost all of it go again. "I'm sorry. This *trouble* between me and Lucy . . .? What were you about to ask?"

"Am I in any way its cause? Do you argue about me?"

He shook his head; she could see he was wondering why she asked.

"I merely wish to know whether I'm an unwitting third party at each . . . fracas, or not."

"You're not. If anything, she feels a little guilty toward you."

"Hah!" Diana thumped the arm of her chair. "So it *is* about me!"

"I'm only guessing, mind," he warned.

"You don't understand at all, do you," she accused. "Guilty about what? About having stolen you away from me? There's nothing else to feel guilty about." She shook her head sadly as she gazed into his still-uncomprehending eyes. "Even if I wanted to help – which is by no means certain, Michael – that makes it very difficult."

He closed his eyes, frowning as if in pain. "I just want to *talk*," he said. "You're only adding complications when you look for things like that. I have to talk to someone, and who else is there but you?" He opened his eyes and pleaded with her.

"Alas," she replied, and sipped her whiskey, and waited.

He took a deeper draught and smacked his lips, relishing the afterburn. "Lord but it goes down like a torchlight procession!" he murmured. "The thing is, you see . . . I don't really know how it happened. Such little things started it. And such little things keep pushing it along. But always in the same direction. Always making it worse."

"They may be little things to you," she complained. "But thanks to your stupidity and lack of self-control, I've had to put all my nice underwear away in the bottom drawer and buy horrible white!"

He waved his hand impatiently, unable to cope with her problems on top of his own.

"I'm sorry," she went on. "I suppose that is a bit like Lady Muck in the lifeboat, complaining about the service. You were saying – every little thing that happens only makes it worse?"

"I do love her," he mumbled; it was obviously something of a strain to say it in these circumstances. "I really do. And yet I'm full of hate, too – no, not hate. But anger. Definitely anger. And resentment. And bitterness."

"Because she . . . what? Or because she *doesn't* . . . what, perhaps? Can't you be less vague?"

"Because she won't admit she's expecting a baby," he responded awkwardly. Then, hastily, he added, "But that's only one thing among many."

"Have you asked her?"

He shook his head and could not meet her eye.

"Because you can't? Is yours the sort of marriage where you simply don't discuss anything below the navel?"

"Hardly!"

"Well I'm not to know that Michael. I can't read your minds."

A strange shiver ran right down him; it put her in mind of a wet dog shaking off the rain. "All right!" he exclaimed with some vehemence. "We enjoy a very frank marriage in that respect. And, ah, a very *full* one, too – until lately." He stared uncertainly at her. "I'm not embarrassing you?"

Not these days, was the answer that occurred to her but she choked it off and said, "Of course not. When did it stop being 'very full', as you put it?"

"Since we moved out here to Mount Venus, I suppose," he admitted reluctantly.

"And you're still sure it has nothing to do with me? Even the mere fact that I'm *here?*"

Again he shook his head. "I honestly don't think so. It's something between us alone. Between her and me."

Diana let a little silence intervene before she asked, "Why do you suppose Lucy has said nothing about being pregnant?"

He canted his head awkwardly and bit his lip.

"Was it the same when she was expecting Alice, Charlie, and the rest?"

"No! She couldn't wait to let me know, then. She even told me the times when it turned out to be a false alarm. If we'd had every baby she told me she was expecting, we'd have our own rugger team by now!"

"Doesn't it make you wonder all the more – why she's behaving differently this time?"

"No. In fact, it makes me wonder why she was bursting to tell me all those other times."

Diana laughed, with no trace of humour in it.

"What's so amusing?" he asked.

"This disgusting haste with which you brush the question aside, my dear – and then, for good measure, stand it on its head! I'll put it to you straight, then: Why has Lucy said nothing *this* time? See if you can answer straight, too!"

He stared at his hands which were soaping each other in his lap. "Because . . ." he began slowly – and then lapsed into silence.

She did nothing to help him.

"Because she . . . um, because she's afraid I'd stop her doing anything."

"Anything?"

"You know. Housekeeping . . . gardening . . . she's at it all hours now."

"With no ill effects?"

He sniffed. "Nine months is a long time. She's not even half way yet. I think she's being entirely unreasonable. She complains I'm never home. Yet she knows very well this is our last chance to clear off our debts and make a success of our lives. If Mount Venus fails, we lose everything. The best I could hope for then would be Poor Law physician in Ballypreposterous or somewhere. She understands that full well. She knows I must work every hour God sends to make this place a success, yet she complains she hardly knows me. D'you call that reasonable? I'm damned if I do."

"Does she mean *know* in the biblical sense, perhaps?"

"Oh, don't *you* start! I come home exhausted – working my lights and liver out for her and the children, mind! – and she expects me to . . . eurgh!"

Diana put down her drink, rose, hurled herself at him, and slapped his face hard.

He dropped his glass, spilling whiskey all over the carpet, and stared up at her, mouth agape, hardly breathing. He was, however, more shocked than hurt. "What did you do that for?" he asked in a small, strangulated voice.

"I should have done it ten years ago," she spat back at him.

She forced herself to stand again, to pace up and down the room, well away from him, for fear she might have another go. "The look on your face!" she said. "I'd forgotten it – that revulsion. It took years and years to forget it – years and years until all I could remember was the *fact* of it. And all I could feel was the *hurt* of it."

"Have you gone mad?" he asked, rubbing his cheek and beginning to feel the hot smart of it.

"I haven't even begun!" she shouted. "There was the shame, too – the shame you put on my flesh like a brand. How many years did that . . . I thought it would grow out. I thought it *had* grown out. And then tonight I see your face and it all . . . Oh my God!" She bit the knuckle of her thumb to stop herself from crying. The last thing she wanted now was to break down in tears.

"I haven't the first notion of what you're trying to say," he told her, half pleading, half accusing.

She forced herself to stand still, facing away from him. She made a tent of her fingers and pressed its edge tight against her lips . . . gathering in her passion. Then, in the calmest voice she could manage, she said, "I will try to be reasonable. I will try to make you understand." She took up the whiskey bottle and refilled his glass. "You'll probably need it," she said in a bleak attempt at humour.

Then she went back to her chair, took up her own glass, and seated herself on the arm, the way she could look down on him. "You're a ladies' man in your own way, Michael – in the best sense of the phrase. I mean, you're charming, considerate, thoughtful . . . you don't patronize . . . and I believe you're genuinely more fond of women's company than men's."

"But?" he asked. "I can feel a big *but* coming!"

"Yes – you're right. And what d'you think I'm going to say? If you can guess, you'll half prove me wrong."

He shrugged awkwardly. "That I don't really understand you, I suppose?"

She smiled indulgently. "Quarter marks, anyway," she said. "I'll tell you *what* you don't understand – starting with the simple facts. Women are angels, of course – that's the best-known fact of all. We have these lovely pure voices like honey and blameless white skin like alabaster and faces that launch thousands of ships and no disfiguring hair on them at all and necks like swans and booosoms like milk (which is only fair, I suppose) and . . . well, then it all gets a bit vague until you get to the well-turned ankles and the dainty feet." She snatched a breath and plunged back in again. "And our breath smells like – cachou and the perfume off our skin is all innocent and floral and we have extra chambers in our hearts labelled hubby and babies and we're sugar and spice and all things nice and sweetness and light attends us all the days of our lives and if it wasn't for us being the way we are, mankind would still be living in caves. That is the General Catechism for all Good Girls."

She gazed down at him in silence then, waiting for him to look up into her eyes.

When at last he did so, he saw nothing of the anger and bitterness he expected – only a great weariness, a despair that he would ever understand her. And for a fleeting moment he did – not her words, not her rancour, but something even more important. He understood that he had wronged her . . . deeply, profoundly, more than he could ever imagine. He had inflicted upon her some wound that would never heal.

The moment passed but it left him with a determination to try to understand. To *actively* try – rather than just sit there and hope that understanding would somehow wash over him and wash this stain away. And the ancient rapport between them – which she had noticed the moment he walked in that evening – was strong enough to let her see the change in him, too.

The relaxation it brought in its wake enabled her to drop her hectoring voice and speak in a near-monotone, which, by contrast, was almost alluring. "We all know it's arrant nonsense," she said. "We women know all too well what devils we are, what shameful passions stir our sinews, what murderous intrigues our souls can embrace, what mountains we can make of a molehill's grievance, and . . ." She watched him carefully as she spoke the next few words: ". . . how *unclean* our bodies really are."

His face twitched in distaste.

She pounced like a travelling rat. "Yes, Michael! *That's* the bit which sticks in your gullet, isn't it! You can accept all the other contradictions but not that! D'you think it's any easier for us, then? Eh? Answer! D'you imagine we don't need all the help we can get?"

He closed his eyes and nodded, miserably. He was beginning to understand at last that . . . But, hard as he tried, no words came. Yet somewhere beneath the reach of words he could feel his understanding taking shape, for all that.

"You nearly killed me, Michael," she said softly, with no hint of a challenge. She was stating a fact of long ago. "You let me see that I disgusted you. You had your porcine pleasure and left me no better than a sow. You showed me a self I could not destroy – because she lived in *your* eyes. You took her away in *your* eyes and left me with nothing."

"In the rare oul' times!" he murmured. He could say no more. His voice broke and two or three meagre tears ran down his cheeks. He wept briefly and in silence.

"But then I'm probably being hysterical," she said dryly, thinking that softness and open sympathy were not what he most needed at that moment.

He sniffed heavily and then blew his nose clear in a large handkerchief. "Now I'm supposed to rise and go unto my wife and say, 'Wife, I have sinned against thee and before' . . ."

"That's blasphemous, Michael."

He dipped his head in acknowledgement. "Well, I'm supposed to be a reformed character, eh?"

"Have you understood a single word I said?"

"Of course. Truly. Not only understood, but felt its truth. There is a defect in *me*. I have to face that. But it will make little difference to the present state of affairs between Lucy and me."

"Then I don't believe you have understood."

"No, Diana, it's you who hasn't understood. The simple fact is – I no longer love her."

She stared at him, speechless. It was the one possibility she had not considered. How could she have overlooked it? "That's just tiredness speaking," she said at last. "It will pass."

"Thank you!" His smile was withering. "That might be true if I'd gone from one extreme to the other – the pendulum effect and all that. But I haven't. I still like her – perhaps even more than when I loved her. I can live with her happily to the end of our days – I'm sure of that. I see so many good qualities in her and admire every one of them. There is no one whose friendship I value more. You spoke of being castaways on a remote island this morning. If I were cast away with Lucy, I should not struggle very hard to return to civilization. I suppose elderly people in their sixties talk and feel like this?" He sniffed again. "I'm senile at thirty-seven!"

"I can't help you there, I'm afraid," she said, plucking out her

300

watch and tut-tutting at the hour. "And now I have to go. I promised Philip and Doctor Quinlan to join them at Porterstown for whist. Anyway, I'll bet before the year is out, all will be well again with you and Lucy."

"Is prophecy in your gift, then?" he asked.

"We medical people call it prognosis," she replied. Then, tapping his glass, she added, "Drink that down and go, like a good man."

He laughed. "That's a part I can play in my sleep!"

"Wake up and try it!" she said.

When he rose to his feet he felt the carpet gingerly with his toe and said, "The floor seems to give way a bit there."

"It's the old boarded-off staircase," she explained. "Don't you remember – it came up here, and there was a wall across there, and this was a passageway to the young spinsters' bedrooms."

He screwed his face up, trying to recall it as it had once been. "How quickly things change!" he said.

"That's what I've just been trying to tell you."

After he had gone she poured herself a second tot of whiskey, something she rarely did. Then she sat there a long while, replaying their conversation in her mind and wondering if it had done the slightest bit of good to anyone.

A mere twelve inches beneath her feet Janet Walshe was suffering agonies of pins and needles – and praying with heart and soul that Diana had spoken the truth about changing and going out. Her clothes reeked of the whiskey that had seeped between the floorboards and dripped upon her.

Ten minutes later, still smelling like a taproom, she mounted her bicycle and set off down the hill to Willbrook. In the interval all her pleasure had dwindled away to nothing. She had caught their stern and noble matron *in flagrante*. She had learned that Lucy's tale that morning was a pack of lies. By all past experience she ought to be cock-a-hoop to be the possessor of such secrets. But there was the rub – nothing in her past experience had prepared her for intrigues on this scale. These were not minor embarrassments in the lives of those concerned – little mortifications they might prefer to keep dark; they were the very stuff of their existence. She could not drop the vaguest hint about them without causing such distress as to brand herself a monster of spite.

It was worse than being a priest with the secrets of the confessional. She could never breathe a word of her discoveries to another living soul. Not even the feeblest hint. Not a wink. Not a nudge. Not a whisper. At least a father-confessor could hand down a homily and dish out the penances; he could respond after *some* fashion. But to say nothing? She wondered if she had enough strength of character to do that.

Then she remembered the appalling Kelly creature and her hints about what had happened with Philip de Renzi on that Saturday morning last month – and then Janet felt the strength of character simply flooding into her.

W hen Michael had gone, Diana changed out of uniform and set off along the three-quarter-mile path that led by way of the stables and across the fields to Porterstown House. The moment she entered the stable yard she became aware of a fleeting movement in the shadows to her left. She paused and held up her lantern, shielding her own eyes from its glare with her other hand. "Miss Kelly?" she asked.

"No." Lucy stepped into the feeble ring of light. "Only me. I'm sorry if I startled you." She was dressed for rain and carrying an umbrella, which made Diana wonder if she ought not to turn back and get hers.

"What are you doing out here, anyway?"

Lucy came to her side. "I hoped you might be going over to the Flannerys' . . ."

"To Philip's, actually."

"Yes, well, the Flannerys' *house*. May I walk with you? I promise I won't stay once we get there."

"By all means." Diana hoped she made it sound more welcoming than she felt. "And do stay if you wish. Doctor Quinlan will be there, too."

They fell in side by side and resumed their walk. "And therefore Birdie Kelly, too, I suppose?" Lucy asked, with the first trace of levity in her voice.

"Yes, to make my birthday complete," Diana responded.

After a pause Lucy went on, "I should think you're just about sick to death of the Ravens today."

Diana sighed. "I should be, but I'm not. I don't understand *why* I'm not. You know Michael called on me, then. Did he tell you he was going to?"

"No. I saw him." After a momentary pause she added, "And that's not all I saw."

Diana's patience, thin enough before she met Lucy, was ready to snap. "I'm sure I don't know what you may mean by that!" she retorted.

"Nothing to do with you. Cool down! Well . . . it's to do with you in a way. Your sitting room is directly over Dermot Walshe's room, isn't it?"

"Ye-es?" Diana's tone was guarded.

"Well, I spotted Birdie Kelly coming out of there – about ten to fifteen minutes before Michael called on you. I was gardening until the light got too bad. And on my way in I saw her."

302

Diana's pace faltered. "You're not suggesting . . . she and Doctor Walshe . . .?"

"Not at all." The idea was so comical that Lucy laughed. "He's hardly *ever* in his room, on or off duty. He's much too fond of the crack with the nurses. He just uses that place as a dumping ground. But I think Birdie Kelly takes full advantage of his absence to go in there and spy on you. Or eavesdrop. Did you know that where the old stairwell was blocked off there's just one set of floorboards between your sitting room and Dermot's room? They never finished it off below with a proper ceiling on his side. So she *could* – I only say could, mind – sit there and eavesdrop to her heart's content."

Diana's stomach felt like lead but there was no trace of it in her voice when she replied. "She'd fall asleep of boredom, so." Then she gave an ironic laugh. "But then she missed the best bit tonight – if she left before Michael called."

Lucy cleared her throat. "Yes. I was wondering about that. *Was* it the best bit?"

A light rain began to fall in warm, well-spaced drops. It was so scattered that Lucy, on her own, would not have bothered with her umbrella; but, as there were two of them, she raised it and moved close to Diana's side.

"I didn't break a single confidence of yours," Diana said.

"But I'm sure you made it clear how I feel – I mean, assuming you talked – about *us* at all. I don't know *what* he came to see you about. He hardly says a word to me nowadays."

Diana halted and stood there with her eyes closed and fists clenched. "Oh, Lucy . . . Lucy! If only you knew how reluctant I am to get embroiled! I know exactly what'll happen if I tell you what I think is on Michael's mind – or try and give his point of view. You'll think I'm taking his side and you'll jump down my throat. You won't mean to but with the best will in the world you won't be able to stop yourself."

"Yes-yes-yes!" Lucy stamped her foot. "I'm sorry! It's utterly unreasonable of me, I know. But that's only to be expected, isn't it! I am, after all, losing my reason."

"You married him and he married you. It's between you now. You can't expect . . ." She sighed with exasperation. "I mean, me of all people! Me of *all* people! Is there really no one else?"

The umbrella dropped from Lucy's nerveless grasp and rested awkwardly on both their bonnets as she flung her arms around Diana and burst into tears. "I'm sorry," she kept whispering. "I'm sorry . . . I'm sorry . . ."

Diana swallowed the sudden lump in her throat and, after a moment of fierce resistance, put her free arm around the poor woman and stroked her soothingly, murmuring, "There, there!" and feeling angrily inadequate.

The emotional storm passed as the meteorological one broke.

There was a flash of sheet lightning across the whole southern sky, to their left, and, as if at a signal, the rain began to fall in ramrods. They raced for the shelter of the nearest hedgerow, where they were fortunate enough to find a blackthorn infested with traveller's joy – which now lived up to its name by providing a roof more watertight than many a canopy of thatch. "It'll be over soon," Diana said above the rumble of high, distant thunder. The lightning was now quite frequent, though none of it seemed to be coming to ground.

"Everything passes in time," Lucy said.

"If you want to know the full of it, Michael didn't say enough for me to be of much use to you. I can understand now why these alienists take hours and hours just talking to their patients."

"What *did* you talk about then?" Lucy asked. "Without giving away what you said." She laughed. "That sounds very Irish but you know what I mean."

"It sounds very Birdie Kelly," Diana commented dryly. "I told him how he made me feel once upon a time – how unworthy he made me feel . . . how unfeminine . . . worthless . . ." With every word her voice grew more bitter, less controlled. "How he almost ruined my life," she said firmly, to nip off the flow.

"And?"

The corners of Diana's lips twitched down. "I don't think it did any good. He didn't understand what I was driving at. Men don't, you know. They have no intuition about the business of being a woman. If their thoughts ever stray remotely near the subject, they just wish we could be more like them – and then they give up. I think we've just got to accept it. We could scald our hearts and weep enough tears to fill the Shannon but it wouldn't change them."

Lucy felt suddenly chill, though the storm had brought a cloying warmth to the air. "How bleak!" she murmured. "D'you even feel that about Philip? Even him?"

"Especially so, because he's the only man I really care about in all the world. So I'm not going to make the mistake of giving him power over me – that power I once gave Michael – though I didn't realize it until he . . ." She relapsed into silence and then sighed. "Well, enough of that." Suddenly she raised a fist and shook it at the sky. "Damn Ebenezer O'Dea! This is all his doing."

For an absurd moment Lucy thought she was blaming the old fellow for arranging the storm. Even when she realized that, of course, Diana was talking about the human storms and rumblings around Mount Venus, she thought it much too wild an assertion. "Come!" she chided.

"It is," Diana insisted. "You don't know him. You weren't his nurse for months and months. He saw all our weaknesses . . . he knew just how to seduce us . . ."

"Michael and I made it rather easy for him," Lucy commented. "But you?"

"Oh, he knew, all right! The chance to be matron of a *new* hospital! What? He knew."

The rain stopped as suddenly as it had started. The sky was still clouded over and there was plenty of lightning beyond the Wicklow Mountains. The warm, moist air seemed to magnify the sounds from dripping branches, gurgling shores, and the grateful crackling of the parched earth as it guzzled up the puddles.

"I'll go back by the road, I think," Lucy said, mainly to explain why she didn't turn back at once – for what more could she or Diana say on the topic that had brought her thus far?

"There could be another reason why the Kelly creature creeps in and out of Doctor Walshe's room," Diana mused. "To steal his books."

"Steal them?" Lucy was shocked.

"Well . . . borrow them without asking. Perhaps 'steal' is a bit strong. She puts them back. You know it *was* she who borrowed his *Sahli's Diagnostic Methods?* Doctor Qinlan covered it all up for her."

"Did he tell you that?"

"No but Nurse Talbot saw him coming out of his room with it yesterday morning – before he claimed to *find* it behind the bench." She gave an angry sigh. "I don't know why we bother to try and lead separate lives here at all! Why don't we just tear down the walls and enjoy a completely communal existence! Living in Ireland is bad enough, but living at Mount Venus is impossible!"

Lucy wondered what secret anger was gnawing at Diana now – what might Birdie Kelly have overheard in that apartment *before* Michael called on her? "Isn't it odd that Abraham Quinlan should go out of his way to help little Kelly?" she said.

"They're kindred spirits," Diana replied at once.

"Eh? I wouldn't have thought they had a shred in common – an educated man, qualified, shy, sober . . . a man who keeps himself to himself . . . and Kelly, who is none of those things – nor comes within an ass's roar . . ."

Diana interrupted "But they're both outcasts, don't you see?"

Lucy was about to hoot with derisive laughter when it struck her that Diana might have the truth of it after all. "Because he's a Jew?" she asked.

"That must play a part, obviously. But maybe it's in his character, anyway – as it is with her – and being born a Jew has only deepened it. They're both outsiders, so to speak, stuck out there with all the luggage in the wind and the rain, listening to our conversation – we who travel inside the coach by right – but never able to join in. And if you think that's fanciful, Lucy, just remember how you used to seat Birdie Kelly at a separate table for our Saturday lunches!"

"And a fat lot of good it did!" Lucy commented morosely.

"I know. Perhaps that's what Doctor Quinlan sees in her. He's the sort of outsider who accepts his lot, but she's going to fight it until she's in her box. And she might win, too. She beat you quick enough!"

"True," Lucy sighed. After a moment's thought she continued, "And is that why she's borrowing these books all the time – looking for the key to the universe?"

Diana gave a contemptuous snort. "Some of her efforts are reasonable, others are just absurd."

They climbed a stile onto the road directly opposite the lodge to Porterstown House; the house was well lighted but the lodge was dark.

When Diana took the first step across the road Lucy put out a hand to stay her. "Just one thing," she said.

Her companion turned to face her but said nothing. Distant, fitful lightning froze her expression in unrevealing and contradictory snapshots.

"You didn't say anything to Michael about . . . you know – Mick and so forth?"

The only answer was a contemptuous snort.

"Does that mean you never will?"

"Lucy-y-y!" She drew the name out in a blend of annoyance and discomfiture.

"I'm not suggesting you should. If I could be perfectly selfish about it, I'd much rather he *never* knew – but don't take that as a plea to keep silent, either. It's your feelings, not mine, that should prevail, and if you want to tell him, you have a perfect right. Oh God, this is like treading on eggshells."

"What are you really asking?" Diana interrupted, in a more kindly tone than the words themselves implied.

"I can commit myself to the fiction that he's your sister's boy. Here!" Lucy patted her breastbone with her gloved fingertips, hard enough to make quite a resonance.

"Healthy sound," Diana could not help commenting.

"But I don't want to make that commitment if you intend telling Michael the truth. Not in my heart, I mean. I'll make it here as far as the rest of the world is concerned." She tapped her skull with the same gesture.

When Diana made no reply she added, "I take it that *wasn't* a healthy sound!"

The other chuckled. "Unfortunately there's no such easy test for the brain." She inhaled deeply and her tone became serious again. "The answer is I simply don't know. I certainly shan't tell him idly – just for the sake of it. Nor do I think he has any *right* to know, independent of my feelings in the matter. But circumstances might arise in which it would seem the only proper thing to do . . ."

"For instance?" Lucy asked quickly.

Diana let out her breath as if winded. "I don't know. If he pestered me? If he started to wax all lugubrious about the rare oul' times? I don't know."

"Why?" Lucy's tone was even sharper. "Did he show signs of it tonight?"

Diana turned angrily on her heel and started across the road. Lucy caught up with her and, once again, stopped her. "I'm sorry, my dear. I know how it seems to you. You give me an inch and I take two. You give me two and I take four. But try and put yourself in my shoes. Think how low he's brought my spirit. Think what I went through, knowing he was with you – and the secret you bear. The *power* it would give you over him!"

"I'm sorry." Diana hung her head. Then she looked up again, a bright smile on her lips. "I'll make you the easiest promise I'm ever likely to utter even if I live to be a hundred – and the one I'm most confident of keeping: I shall never tell Michael about Mick in the hope of bringing him nearer me. If I do tell him, it will only be to put a high wall between us for ever. There!" She reached out and touched Lucy's arm. "Are you sure you won't come up? You won't be interrupting any billing and cooing, I assure you."

"Well . . ." Lucy still hesitated. "I'll only stay if the two 'outsiders' are there. I wouldn't mind seeing them together. It never struck me until now, but what you say about them may be absolutely true."

And so together they strode up the short drive to the main house.

B irdie helped Lucy and Diana out of their capes, shaking the rainwater off them with such vigour that a spaniel, which had been lurking around, summoning the courage to bark, fled to some other part of the house. When she had finished, one wall of the entrance hall looked as if it had been left out in heavy rain. She studied it for a crestfallen moment or two and then brightened, saying, "Sure the man who made wallpaper made plenty of it."

The curtsey with which she favoured the two ladies was ironic. "Thanks be to God ye came," she said breathlessly. "And I sitting in there with the two gintlemen, like one egg on a dresser!"

Philip, the minimal host, greeted them as they entered his parlour; to Diana he gave an offhand kiss, to Lucy a surprised cry of welcome and a buss on each cheek. Birdie watched these civilized antics with secret amazement, for she knew what connection there had been between him and both those ladies that summer – indeed, with one of them that very evening. Yet there they were, dancing on cobwebs. Somehow she expected it of men but it made her uneasy that women could be hot as brood mares at one moment and cool as pebbles in a brook the next. She, being so much more constant in her own emotions, thought it very like cheating at cards – worse, in fact, for life was the most important game of all.

307

Abraham joined his own greetings and added the interesting information that a large building in the Egyptian style was to go up by Waterloo Bridge in London, a fact he had just gleaned in Philip's latest *Journal* from the RIBA. Birdie asked if Gypsies were originally from Egypt – which was a more intelligent comment on Abraham's announcement than either of the two ladies could muster on the spur of the moment.

"A drop of something to drive out that rain?" Philip suggested as he lifted the stopper out of the whiskey decanter.

Diana declined, adding with a smile in Lucy's direction that she had already fortified herself once that evening.

"Sure a bird never flew on one wing," he replied dismissively, making ready to pour her a tot despite her refusal.

She then admitted she'd flown at Mount Venus on two wings.

"With Mrs Walshe, if I'm not mistaken, Matron?" Abraham said pleasantly.

"Why no, Doctor Quinlan." She turned to him with a quizzical expression. "What gave you that idea?"

"Ah, well, I'm mistaken, so," he replied awkwardly.

No one said anything to help him; they were all too curious to know how the idea arose at all. He hooked a finger in his collar and moved it a few degrees. "She came into the dispensary when I was on my way out," he said. "Looking for Doctor Walshe. I don't wish to malign the lady, but . . . well . . ."

"She had the angel's share of the malt about her?" Birdie suggested helpfully.

He laughed. "You might say so. Did you meet her, too?"

"I did. She was after bringing up a nightshirt for himself that he forgot. She left it in his room. I saw her meself."

"And what might *your* interest have been?" Philip asked; there was a note of jocular accusation in his voice for he knew Birdie borrowed Dermot's books without asking.

"The nature of the universe," she replied airily – at least, that is what they heard, for none of them recognized it as the title of a book. "Sure you'd find it all on that oul' staircase there."

Diana, remembering how Michael had spilled a good measure of whiskey in her sitting room, turned pale at this; she took it to be an artfully veiled taunt that her secrets were known. Or was it a covert warning that Janet Walshe had been eavesdropping, too? And, in that case, was Doctor Quinlan in it with Birdie Kelly – had the two outsiders brewed it up between them? For it was he who said Mrs Walshe had reeked of whiskey.

No. The suspicion was absurd. How could they have known that Philip would offer a drink and that she would turn it down in quite the way she had done? And without that they would have had no peg on which to hang their end of the conversation. Absurd.

Unless Philip was in it, too?

Her innards hollowed. He was so resentful when he left her, just before Michael came calling. He'd have been seething with it ever since, and he was not, thank heavens, one of those sly men like Ebenezer O'Dea, who can smile and banter away even when his heart was plotting his interlocutor's destruction and ruin. Philip would have passed some remark to the two outsiders and they could have . . .

No!

She was not going to start down that trail of delusions again, where the whole world was giggling at her behind her back, pointing the finger of scorn (which turned to the glad-hand of welcome the moment her eyes fell upon it) . . . and all that.

She forced herself to laugh. "You've talked me into it with that glib tongue of yours, Philip," she said as he measured out generous tots for the others. "If a bird can't fly on *three* wings on her birthday, when can she?" Her unaccustomed recklessness, she realized, was born of anger at the climate of intrigue and prank that ruled all around Mount Venus.

"That's the spirit," he exclaimed as he poured her the most generous tot of all. "Will I light a little fire to pop the Guinness corks?"

"Why not?" Lucy encouraged him gaily. "Is that your new gramophone?"

"Well, it's not an ear trumpet," he told her as he stooped to set a match to the kindling. The fire had been laid several weeks earlier and was dry as tinder; soon there was a merry blaze, with the turf glowing bright as sea coal.

Lucy was meanwhile looking through his pile of records with growing excitement. "*Floradora!*" she exclaimed, "And *The Country Girl!* And *Merrie England!* And *The Earl and the Girl!* Philip – you have everything!"

"Everything a girl could want," he said, handing her the glass she had left by the fire. "Don't leave this lying around, or *someone* will scoff it!" He grinned accusingly at Diana as he spoke.

"What shall we play first?"

"The latest?" He picked up a carton Lucy had not yet explored. "*The Geisha* – waltz, two-step, turkey-trot . . .?"

"Turkey-trot," Diana voiced her vote; she read the label as she speared the record on the spindle: "The Pipes of Pan by Bessie Jones."

"Can you do any sort of a ga-lopp to that fella?" Birdie asked as she gave the machine a few experimental winds. She peered down the huge horn and shouted, "Bessie Jones? 'Tis no use hidin' – I know you're in there! Would you ever come out and eat your dinner before it goes cold!"

This preposterous fancy made the others laugh so much they all ended up sprawled in chairs and on the sofa, fighting to breathe – all except Birdie, who hadn't thought it as funny as all that and half-suspected they were laughing at her. But it released so many of their tensions that it marked a turning point in the course of the evening. Inhibitions that might have taken several more tots to dissolve were melted at once, with the benefit of sobriety rather than "heartiness" to go with it. The parlour was, in any case, too small to permit proper dancing, much less the spirited gallop Birdie had hoped for; all the two couples could do was adopt a dancing posture and move from foot to foot, slowly gyrating in time with the music. They didn't even bother to roll back the carpet.

To begin with, Birdie stayed by the gramophone while Lucy danced with Abraham and Diana partnered Philip. But then Lucy grabbed her by the wrist and pulled her onto the "dance floor," saying, "Ladies' choice!" She thrust Birdie into Abraham's arms and did a little solo dance herself, making the longest possible way of it to the other two. Then she cut in on Diana, saying "Keep going round," and nodding toward Birdie. Diana made such a slow circuit of it, however, that the gramophone was going hissssss! before she reached them. She went to change the music, instead.

She looked at the back of the record but it was blank. She selected the next from the carton without looking at it; Birdie meanwhile wound up the spring again.

"What is it?" the others asked.

But Diana shook her head. "Mystery number!" When the music started she called, "Turn down the lights."

"It's Wonderful Rose of Love," Philip murmured when the intro was only a few bars old. He began singing it with more lugubrious passion than sense of key but Lucy hadn't the heart to ask him not to.

A moment later Diana cut in and left her to dance solo. Almost immediately Diana said, "What is that caterwauling?" and Philip stopped.

Lucy closed her eyes and let her feet carry her where they would as she swayed and shuffled round. *Voluntary blind man's buff*, she thought. *The first man who touches me must kiss me. And all this on one glass of whiskey!*

But she knew it had nothing to do with the whiskey. This sense of liberation was genuine. What had she said to Diana on their way over? Or what had Diana said to her? She tried to recall their walk but the only bit she could remember was running for shelter – and flashes of lightning.

She bumped into someone and opened her eyes to discover Abraham Quinlan disengaging himself from Birdie Kelly and preparing to dance with her. "You're all right," she told him, pushing them together again.

Birdie was looking at her rather curiously.

"I'm all right, too," she told the girl and laughed as she continued on her solo round.

She closed her eyes again and tried to remember something, anything, of what she and Diana had said on the way here, but again all she could remember was a few odd remarks she'd made on the drive— about the history of Porterstown House. She concentrated on the memory for a moment.

The good thing about it was that it recalled the old days, before they left Clyde Road.

She remembered now – she'd put her arms round Diana's neck and wept. She'd been sorry about something but she didn't want to recall it now. She'd never have done such a thing in the old days, back in Clyde Road.

Diana had reeked of whiskey then – no, not reeked. There had been a good hint of the malt around her. Oh yes, of course, she had explained that – she'd "fortified" herself with it. Would that have needed *two* glasses? Perhaps the other had been taken with Janet Walshe. Who knows how many visitors she'd entertained that evening? Knock twice and ask for Diana's room! Dazzler's old joke. If Dazzler were here, she'd have a partner . . .

Actually, Dazzler might be the answer to all her little problems concerning the delicate matter of partners. No danger of a romance, there! He couldn't and she wouldn't – romance, that is. As for the other thing . . . ever ready! Present arms and fall in! Another of Dazzler's jokes.

She bumped into someone and opened her eyes to find it was Quinlan once more. "You do get round quickly," she chided. "Same again!"

And off she floated once more, solo, not round the tiny patch of floor but across it, toward the fire. Warned of it by the heat she halted and lifted the front hem of her skirt a daring eight inches to warm her ankles and half her stockinged calves.

"Warming up the old man's supper," Birdie whispered to Abraham, directing his attention to Lucy with a nod.

When he caught her meaning he stared at her askance and then burst out laughing.

"What pearl has the dear girl cast before us this time?" Philip asked as they swayed within sotto-voce distance.

Abraham leaned across to whisper it, with Birdie plucking urgently at his sleeve and Diana straining to hear, while maintaining a look of weary asperity . . .

But before a word could be said there was a loud pop as a cork shot out of one Guinness bottle – followed by an even louder yell from Lucy as it went up her skirts and hit her on the inside of her left knee. She then rubbed the spot ostentatiously to show that this piece of unintentional marksmanship had not found a more embarrassing target.

"Serves you right!" Philip taunted as he raced to catch the overflow of foam in a tankard. "That was a truly shocking display of ankle.

Though it's rough justice on the knee, I must confess."

"What's that tune called?" Diana asked, for it had come to an end.

Abraham read the old label as he put on the next record. "I Can't Refrain From Laughing," he told her.

Every one laughed, repeating the words, and laughing all the more.

Michael and Dermot considered that about half their convalescent patients – twenty-one in all – would benefit from a day in the country. After a full and frank democratic debate between the pair of them they divided the lucky excursionists into two roughly equal groups, one for the Friday outing, the rest for Saturday – weather permitting, of course. They had heard unfavourable reports of the new motor charabanc and so had decided to take the old-fashioned jaunting car – four cars, in fact – from Tom Gallagher's livery down in Tallaght.

The plan was that each party, fortified by a good breakfast, would go down the wild and picturesque military road to Laragh, pausing en route to view the spectacular falls on the Glenmacnass River; then on to a brief stop at Glendalough. It would have to be brief, since there was little to see there apart from the lough, a round tower, and a cluster of ancient churches; and there was nowhere for a party of about two dozen to spread itself. They would then take a short drive to the ruined abbey at Killasheela, where they would have a picnic luncheon and a pleasant stroll before returning to Mount Venus by the less challenging road through Roundwood and Enniskerry.

Dermot and Helen Lynch were to lead the Friday group, Michael and Diana would take the one on Saturday. Ebenezer O'Dea claimed the privilege of going on both days; Lucy, the organizer, lubricator, and factotum of Mount Venus, would also accompany both parties, though for her it was a duty rather than a privilege. The children and their nannies could go directly to Kilasheela with the servants.

They chose the third Friday in August, which fell some three weeks after Diana's thirtieth. But from the moment they began their planning, the heavens opened and the rain poured down almost without ceasing. No month in Ireland is reliably dry, but August is hardly even dry*ish*, and that particular reincarnation of it was the wettest anyone at Mount Venus could remember, even the octogenarians. When the Thursday came around – the day on which they were to confirm or postpone their provisional booking of the four jaunting cars, the consensus was that they should postpone for a week. "It can't rain for ever," they told one another; however, as they had all lived in Ireland for most of their lives, they spoke with a sort of ha-ha in their voices.

Lucy decided to convey the message in person, rather than send a boy with it. She had been working on old Tommy Gallagher for some time now and thought he might be just about ready to let slip a thing or two concerning the childhood days of Birdie Kelly. Braving the rain, she set off in her gig with Brutus, her favourite gelding, between the shafts; she always felt twice as safe with him as with any other horse in the stable – especially when the roads were greasy in the rain. When she came to the corner of the Porterstown demesne, however, where the Tallaght road leaves the ridge and plunges steeply to Oldcourt and Ballycullen, she saw a sight – a celestial marvel – such as people are lucky to witness once in a lifetime. From Knockanave in the south, which was to her left, to the dear-dirty-Dublin haze that obscured the Phoenix Park and Castlenock in the north, it was as if the Clerk of the Weather had ruled a sharp line across the sky. To the east of that line, where Lucy now stood her horse and watched, the drizzle danced like vapour from an inhaler; but to the west, the sky stretched in one unclouded vault of blue. She could see the knife-edge of the shadow clear across the landscape, dark and brooding to either side while before her all was sunlit and beckoning; it was like a romantic painting viewed inside out.

Soon the drizzle ceased though she was still bathed in shadow; she waited there, watching as that sharp edge advanced toward her, its shifting peaks and troughs defining the restless forms of hills and valleys, displaying their contours in a way that seemed almost shocking – for, like men and women of a certain age, such gentle, rolling landscapes rely on ambiguity for their charm.

While she waited she took her binoculars and surveyed the far horizon. Already it was shimmering in the heat, and a haze of rising vapour had reduced it to a purple-sandstone-pinky-ochre grey that would defeat the efforts of even the greatest colourist to match. Nonetheless, quivering in that pale-upon-pale conjunction of land and sky, she could just make out the serrated ruin of Carberry Castle, two dozen miles away due west, and, more northerly and farther off still, the unmistakable twin peaks of Croghan Hill in the King's County. If Fate had wished her to change her mind about cancelling the outing, it could not have written a promise of fair weather in a clearer hand. She collapsed the overhead canopy and drew off her oilskin cape.

At last she was able to watch the shadow come sprinting up the hill toward her, and with a speed that Pegasus himself would envy, for the hill was so steep that she usually came home by the Willbrook road rather than set her poor horse at that fierce incline. The way down had its perils, too, and she had to keep a strong pull on the brake almost all the way; but today, with the bright sun splitting the trees all around her and everything new-washed and glistening, she felt a pleasure that not even her aching brake-arm could alloy.

What a difference a little sunshine could make! For three weeks now these hills had looked like the back half of nowhere – cold, gray, and miserable; and Mount Venus, with its northerly aspect robbed of

313

the charm of sunshine, had come to remind her of nothing so much as Dartmoor Prison, which she had seen in pictures. The portents for the approaching winter had been grim. But now, with the sun turning the roads to steam and even the birds singing a different tune, life itself began to look better all round.

As she hauled on the brake, pondering these commonplace mysteries, she realized that her return to a happier, or at least calmer, frame of mind was not as sudden as the coming of these blue skies now above her, nor did it owe as much to that meteorological improvement as it might seem. Rather, the dreary weather had masked the general easing of her mood – and so successfully that she did not notice it until that mask was pulled away. So it was with some surprise that she realized she was now so much easier in her estrangement from Michael than she had been on that night when the weather first broke, the night of that alas-unforgettable party chez Philip at Porterstown House. Sadly, however, she realized it had little to do with any improvement in her relations with Michael (for there had been none) but rather was a measure of her own ability to take life as she found it, forgetting old dreams of how it might be.

And what a humdrum sort of estrangement it was, too! She could almost wish Michael had been a monster of cruelty, flagrant in the betrayal of his vows, a gaoller to her in both body and spirit. Instead, what insignificant causes had wedged their lives apart! Suspicions that even Shakespeare could not have milked for more than half a dozen of Othello's lines . . . an idiotic misunderstanding over a lady's stocking . . . glimpses of each other in gestures and looks that would have passed unnoticed at any earlier period of their marriage . . . and stubbornness they would have laughed out of court before they moved to Mount Venus – what a catalogue of petty shame!

Was it altogether too fanciful to blame the house itself? Not one of its previous incumbents had ever prospered there – which was surely food for thought? Diana would blame Ebenezer O'Dea, of course, but without giving him credit for the good things that had come her way, too – Philip, her enhanced status, and her greatly improved income and prospects. To Lucy that seemed not alone ungrateful but also rather simplistic. Perhaps it was too easy altogether to go looking for outside forces to blame – the ghosts of Mount Venus or the games of uncaring neighbours. "The fault, dear Brutus," she told the horse, "lies not in our stars but in ourselves."

She laughed aloud, not because the quotation was apt to her horse's name but because she remembered saying it to Michael once and he had told her she was in danger of becoming a Protestant. Her laughter turned melancholy at the memory of those happier days.

At the foot of the hill she passed the ancient and now ruined gateway to the remains of Mount Pelier House, or "Mount Peelya", on the local tongue – a vast Gothic fantasy of the seventeen sixties, built by Henry Loftus, Earl of Ely, as a hunting lodge. Though it was only a hundred and forty years old, it was already a ruin. To construct it Loftus had deliberately plundered an earlier Mount Pelier, built as a summer residence at the top of the hill by Speaker William Connolly in the seventeen twenties – a residence that has passed into legend as the meeting place of Dublin's Hellfire Club. And to build that resort of debauchery Connolly had, in his turn, deliberately ruined a prehistoric fortification, all of whose stones had been incorporated into his clubhouse. What an essay those stones could write on the impertinence of human ambition, on the folly of all grandeur!

Did the ghosts of Stone Age sentries, doomed to guard their ancient fortress for a twinkling of eternity's eye, ever come face to face with the phantasms of Connolly's rakes and bawds, still seeking life's most fleeting illusion of all? And were both in their turn surprised to stumble across the peacable shades of the Earl and his wife, Frances, their heads eternally together as they planned the woodlands and rides, the lawns and fountains, the terraces and arbours that were never to grace these slopes? And what when warrior-plunderers, peaceful builders, and hellfire's lechers met in that bewildered conclave? As the winds keened through the eyeless walls, and cellars filled with the unhindered rain, did they stare about them at this folly out of a folly out of a folly and ask the only honest question mankind may ever ask: *Why?*

Lucy closed her eyes and shivered. It was not good to know too much. Especially of history; there was altogether too much history here. One should be more of a tourist in this life. How delightful it would be to pass this place and exclaim, "Oh, see the pretty ruin!" and so trot on to the next bright wonder. By contrast, her private landscapes of Ireland teemed with memories of alliances that failed, feuds that ended in maimings and death . . . right down to the petty level of "things one dare not mention when so-and-so is near." These smiling fields and graceful woods were like a painted voile in the theatre; change the lighting and they would dissolve to reveal a graveyard in a treacherous mire beset by thorns.

Brutus must have wondered why she clucked him to a faster trot on a lane whose bumps and bends made a walk more advisable. Even as she did so, Lucy knew that the gauntlet she was running could not be escaped by any mere change of pace. But she came to Oldbawn all the quicker, and felt all the easier for it, too. The place bustled with people going about their daily lives, worrying more about tomorrow's bread than yesterday's broken heads . . . people busily forgetting.

Now that it was safe to trot she called Brutus back to a walk and breathed deep lungfuls of that easier air.

"A fine day the sun found itself again!"

"Wasn't it fierce fond of the rain those weeks!"

"Ten days of this and we'll save the hay."

"Another ten and we'll bring the turf home, too."

The chants and responses of forgetfulness were intoned all about her and she joined in with a will.

The smith at the forge called after her, "Don't be leaving that left fore much longer, ma'am!" and she waved her whip in gratitude for the advice – always happy to acknowledge a chancer.

In Tallaght a tram vented its steam suddenly and nearly made Brutus bolt, but she aimed him at a big Guinness dray and good sense soon halted him. Then she made him go back and stand near the tram until the safety valve shut down again.

Tom Gallagher watched the whole thing from the feed door to his stable loft. "Well it became you, Mrs Raven, ma'am," he said admiringly when he joined her on his own front yard. "There's fierce few ladies these days with the sense to do a thing like that." He gave an approving nod. "And how is your good self keeping, ma'am?"

"Pretty well, thank you, Mister Gallagher – all that's left of me. And yourself?"

"Sure I'm back on the baker's list, Mrs Raven."

"I'm sorry – I hadn't heard you were poorly."

"Arra 'twas little enough. I found my death in the rain. 'Twas my own fault." He made this last remark loud enough for his wife in the office to overhear.

He was delighted when Lucy confirmed the booking and confessed he'd had his doubts when he'd looked at the sky that dawn. She told him she'd still had her doubts until twenty minutes ago, when the sun made such a clean sweep of the sky.

"I'll change pencil to ink, so," he said, tipping his hat and turning to go into his office.

She realized her best chance of a bit of crack was receding and so called after him. "Will you not take a deposit, Mister Gallagher?"

The moment he turned to her she saw that he would. "Whatever you think yourself now, ma'am. I'd never seek it from such quality as yourself, you follow."

They had previously agreed a fee of £4. 10s. 0d, a day, or 12s. 6d, per car, making an extravagant £9 in all. "I thought two pounds down?" she suggested.

He licked his chops greedily and repeated, "Whatever you think yourself, ma'am. 'Tis entirely up to you entirely."

She descended and left the reins to one of the lads. Solemn money did not change hands on the forecourt. "We may put a liquid seal on the transaction, I suppose?" she suggested. "You have the approved solvent?"

It took him aback, though he recovered swiftly enough. "Indeed I have, ma'am. Divil mend me for not being the first to say so."

Mrs Gallagher looked up from her ledgers, amazed to see her husband taking out the crock of whiskey and three glasses. The serene anticipation on their customer's face dispelled most of her

316

doubts; the presence of that third glass did the rest. "'Tis welcome you are, Mrs Raven," she said.

"If I'm as welcome as this sun, I'm welcome indeed," Lucy responded. She laid two sovereigns on the desk, saying, "I don't suppose that will do much harm, either."

The business was concluded before they'd swallowed half a sip; then Gallagher asked if the clinic took in more people in fair weather or foul. What he meant, of course, was, "How is trade?"

Lucy told him that the general experience was that they got fewer cases in the cold weather but they tended to be the more serious ones; the warm days brought people who wanted to rest and be pampered. In other words, she treated his question seriously, as an inquiry between one person in business and another.

The nuance was not lost on him and so, as proprietors the world over are wont to do, they began talking of the difficulties of getting, training, and keeping good servants. Lucy, though delighted to have got so close to her quarry and with such ease, was careful not to go charging in all at once. Indeed, she waited for him to say – as she knew he would sooner or later – "And what of the Fair Maid of Tallaght herself, ma'am – our own, dear Birdie Kelly?"

Lucy explained that Birdie was neither nurse nor servant at Mount Venus but was maid-of-all-work to its owner and founder, Mister Ebenezer O'Dea. "But have you not seen her yourself, Mister Gallagher? Does she not come down here to visit her parents in Tallaght?"

Both of them stared at her in bewilderment.

"Her mother, anyway," Lucy persisted. "Doesn't her mother live here?"

"Lordamercy, Mrs Raven," he said, "those Kellys moved away when . . ."

"When she was barely tall enough to pick shamrock," his wife interrupted quickly.

Lucy looked duly amazed though, in truth, the discovery that Birdie had been out varnishing her life story yet again had lost all power to astonish her. "I must have misheard," she said. "I felt sure she told me her mother still lives hereabouts."

They both shook their heads. "Sure they moved to Lucan, it would be seven or eight years ago, mother and daughter both," he replied. "Her man, of course, was dead."

"Or well gone, anyway," his wife added.

Lucy thought furiously. Lucan? Seven or eight years since? Two people called Kelly? It rang no bell. To be sure, she'd been several years out of Lucan by then. Even so . . .

"Had they family there?" she asked. "Or did they leave family here?"

Neither of them could say whether the Kellys had family in Lucan; they were both quite certain that none were left here in Tallaght.

317

And there the matter had to rest, for Lucy could not pursue it further without revealing that her interest in the Birdie Kelly enigma was more than casual. She did, however, gain the strong impression that Gallagher himself wished to say more than his wife on the topic, and her presence was the only thing inhibiting him.

She then did all the other businesslike things expected of her – asking about the drivers' references and experience, going to look at the cars and the horses that would pull them, and so on – before returning to her own gig. And still Gallagher had said nothing, despite several opportunities.

She asked him what he thought of Brutus and did he need new shoes? She got him to lead the beast out onto the road and walk him a bit. And finally, at the very last minute, he picked up one of the horse's forelegs and, while pretending to pare something out of its hoof, said, without raising his voice or looking up, "That question you're after asking beyond, ma'am. Listen till I tell you. When Birdie Kelly was a wee colleen – thirteen or fourteen, she'd have been – she frightened the jackdaws all summer for Mister Shaw at Boherna-breena, and he gave her an oul' bicycle for her pains that his own daughter had grown out of. Lord but she was proud as a turkeycock on that bicycle. But the very next week wasn't it all destroyed on her!"

"Run over?" Lucy asked, bending down as if to inspect the hoof more closely.

"Worse, ma'am. A great wild divil with a beard on him like a furze bush knocked her off it and, pardoning the term, ma'am, *interfered* with her, so he did – and only for old Doctor Lynch, God rest his soul, coming along to chase the blackguard away she was kill't on the spot."

"Poor soul!"

"That Doctor Lynch was a saint, Mrs Raven. Didn't he pay for the Kellys' removal to Lucan himself."

"Oh did he?"

"He did. And called to visit them, I'm told, to see she'd suffered no permanent harm. A saint, ma'am. I doubt we'll see his like again."

"He certainly was a most extraordinary doctor," Lucy felt justified in saying.

On her way home she considered this story and found nothing that tempted her to believe it, even though it fell in with her own conjectures about Birdie Kelly's erratic past. Gallagher had delayed too long in telling it – which meant that he had been sizing her up – which, in turn, meant he had some purpose of his own in coming out with it at last.

And the telling had been perfect – a deft sprinkling of tiny details that would mean nothing to someone who was ignorant of the Lynch case but that would blackguard the poor man utterly with anyone who did. She did not doubt that Gallagher (or his wife, or his father,

318

or aunt, or fifth cousin) had it in for Lynch, God rest him. Any stick to beat a dog.

To be sure, the handiest stick might have been the plain unvarnished truth. Its use had been known to occur from time to time in Ireland, despite the best efforts of the populace.

In short, she was no nearer learning what had really happened.

It looked like a spell of settled weather; at all events the next day, Friday, dawned bright and clear and with only the faintest breeze to stir the air. For the past three weeks everyone had wished for a little warmth; now they gazed up toward the mountains and said hopefully, "That will be the coolest place today, thank God."

The menservants, maids, and picnic hampers were sent on ahead, together with the nannies and the children; they left at seven in three ass-carts. The four jaunting cars arrived a short while later, all drivers sober. Each car was, in fact, capable of taking nine people – two rows of four, back-to-back, and the driver. So three cars would have been enough. However, to make better time and to let the patients and nurses travel in greater comfort, the clinic had splashed out the extra twenty-five shillings and hired four. Each car carried one nurse, and there were two reserve nurses who rode with Mrs Lynch in a gig behind. And behind them, bringing up the rear in an open carriage and pair driven by Dermot, came Ebenezer O'Dea and Birdie together with Janet and Lucy. Leading the entire procession was Lord Ussher's phaeton containing his son, Lord Glanbeg, and two Honourables, all three of whom – though patients at Mount Venus – had condescended not to travel with *hoi polloi*. It was quite a military procession that set off shortly after eight to take the old military road through the Wicklow Mountains.

The first mile or so was a steep climb, almost due south, up to the ridge of Mount Pelier, past Porterstown House and the demesne of Killakee. Of course, Mount Venus was already 650 feet above sea level, so the climb to over 1,100 feet was not the daunting prospect it would have been to lowland Dubliners. Even so, when they gained the ridge they were glad of the rest and the chance to admire the last splendid view of the city before they vanished into the glens and mountains. Lucy's binoculars were in great demand in Ebenezer's carriage for she was the only one who had thought to bring such an instrument.

It was just possible to make out the gap-tooth ruin of Lord Ely's Mount Pelier House from where they halted. Lucy pointed it out to Ebenezer and asked if he had ever visited it. He shook his head and said the mere sight of it had been enough to make him shiver. The place had once been finer than Mount Venus yet a single careless tenant had managed to reduce it to a decaying pile; a squatter had then completed its ruin. "It had no history, anyway," he said. "It was a parvenu palais from the start."

A week earlier Lucy would have put him right; now she held her peace and thought how lucky he was.

They set off again, southeastwards now, along the sunny side of the glen carved by the River Dodder, a tributary of the Liffey, which nonetheless grudged its tribute until a mere mile before Dublin's great river enters the sea. This was still half-tame country, where rolling moorland was often interrupted by an orderly patchwork of cultivated fields and game covert.

"That was the Hellfire Club back in the olden time," Birdie announced suddenly.

Only Lucy realized what she was referring to. "Mount Pelier?" she asked. "How do you know that?"

"Sure everyone knows it."

"And what does everyone say about the goings-on at that place?"

"They say it's haunted, Mrs Raven."

"By what, or by whom?"

"By ruin'd maids, so they say." She spoke as if it were a variety of cottage-garden flower – love in a mist, lords and ladies, and ruin'd maids.

"What ruined them, I wonder?" Dermot asked lightly.

Surreptitiously Janet pinched his forearm.

"The whole place is a ruin," Birdie told him, making it clear they'd get no sport out of trying to embarrass her.

Halfway along the glen they came to that stretch which makes every passer-by feel he or she is losing touch with reality. Some trick of perspective – the slope of the ridges that form the glen, the course of the Dodder below, and the looming bulk of Kippure away to the south – all combine to convince the traveller that the road ahead leads gently downhill. In fact, it rises rather steeply, as one can tell from the straining of the horses. And, since the illusion worked in both directions, it had lately become a favourite trick of automobilists at this spot to face the car at what looked like a hill climb, slip it out of gear, release the brake, and then marvel as it apparently free-wheeled uphill. No such jape was possible with a horse-drawn vehicle but the opposite illusion – of pulling hard to go downhill – was compelling, nonetheless.

"The easy life, eh!" Ebenezer wafted a hand at the apparent downhill slope ahead of them. "A sermon in rock and scree. How often are we tempted to rest on our oars and let the world do our work for us! And how swiftly we slide back and downwards when we succumb to that temptation!"

Lucy caught Birdie's eye and knew she was wondering when Ebenezer O'Dea had last done a day's honest toil – in all those years since he sold his grind school and took up moneylending instead.

The man himself grinned all round at them, looking very like Mr

Punch. "Harking back to the Hellfire Club, I always suspected that debauchery was a close cousin to hard labour. It looks like an easy downhill, the primrose path of dalliance. But once you're committed to it, you have to struggle like these horses to maintain the pace. No wonder they all die young."

"Who do?" Janet asked. "The horses?"

"No! The rakes and hellraisers, of course. It's a well-known fact."

Lucy could see Birdie was about to jump in with both feet, though precisely what she might jump into Lucy had no idea. One could never be sure of anything with that one. But she considered that the morning was too young and the carriage too crowded to risk it. So she jumped in herself instead. She began counting out the names on her fingers: "What about Lord Kilpool, then? Or Francis O'Donoghue of Twickenham Lodge? Arbuthnot English in Blanchardstown? My own Uncle Felix Marsh of Music Hall . . . 'The Divil' Darcy Dalgliesh of Shillelagh . . . rakes and hellraisers to a man – all alive-oh and not one of them under eighty."

"Collapse of stout theory!" Dermot said, turning around to grin at Ebenezer.

Janet stared at Lucy in amazement. "How do you do it?" she asked.

"Do what?"

"Remember all these people? And know all these things about them?"

"Sure you know them yourself!"

"I do – once you say the names. But divil a one could I trot out off my own bat, except Kilpool, perhaps."

"She means where d'you dig up all the dirt?" Ebenezer put in, unhappy at the way she had so swiftly punctured his comforting theory.

"I don't dig anything up at all," Lucy protested. "Sure if you write three or four letters to friends each day and receive a like number, it's not long before you know what's really going on in the world."

"But to remember it!" Janet went on, not to be cheated out of her amazement.

Lucy sighed, "Well, that's as much of a curse as a blessing, let me tell you."

They came at last to Glencree Reformatory, with its splendid vistas down the thickly wooded valley and, at its eastern end, the Great Sugarloaf Mountain, blocking their view of the sea. Here their way led south again, rising another three hundred feet over the next two or three miles as it skirted the massive eastern flank of Kippure, the highest of the mountains in the northern half of the Wicklow massif. Now the landscape was all moorland – blanket bog for the most part. Yesterday, when the rain first eased off, it must have been the most desolate scene in the whole Garden of Ireland, but today it was almost crowded, as people took advantage of the fair weather to stack or restack the turf they harvested earlier in the summer and must have feared they'd have to carry home by the gallon rather than the lump. Turfcutters and excursionists exchanged greetings almost all the way – or, rather, exchanged elegant variations of the same greeting. By the time they reached the summit of the road – and, at 1,000 feet or more above the altitude at Mount Venus, the summit of their outing that day – they had established in thirty different ways that this Friday was, thanks be to God, a grand day for the race and that the turf would be home, please God, before September.

In any other land but this, it would have put the weather for the next eight hours beyond all possible doubt. But this was Ireland, and Irish eyes scan every little cloud on each and all horizons for its rainbearing potential, even on the grandest day for the race. From the high flank of Kippure, they had plenty of clouds to practise on, though they were all fleecy, wispy things with divil a threat of malevolence in one of them.

A little way beyond the summit they came to the bridge over the headwater reach of the Liffey.

"If it's landscapes-into-sermons you want, Mister O'Dea," Dermot said, "here's one for you. The Liffey at its source is but eight miles from the sea. Yet how far does it wander before it reaches anything that even sniffs of salt? Why, ten times that distance!"

Lucy knew it was closer to fifty miles but kept it to herself. Never in her life had she let facts spoil a good story. Probably every single one of Dermot's hearers was thinking the same, she realized. "Isn't it in the nature of the country," she said. "Its estuary lies somewhere to the northeast of here. So what direction does it start out in? Southwest, of course. If it didn't, we'd be sure the English dug it."

They all laughed, but her words made them realize something that had not consciously occurred to them before – that they were all Irish in that carriage. They were of that stratum in society that spent six days out of every seven in Anglo-Irish or even straight English company – a sort of limbo in which a certain well-mannered reticence became so much second nature that they easily forgot what they were being reticent about. More often than not, then, they carried the reticence over into those periods when it served no purpose – like that very morning, indeed.

Before anyone could comment openly on the fact, however, Birdie cast her latest pearl. "The shortest distance between two points," she said, "is not long enough to be worth looking at." While people pondered this, she added, "Besides, if light didn't travel in straight lines, you'd never know where anything was. I could be looking at you *there* and you might really be over *there*. Now isn't that amazing?"

They agreed that it was – and prayed no one would be so unwise as to ask for an explanation.

Birdie, however, had dropped into a self-sustaining mode. "On the other hand," she went on, "if space itself was curved, you'd never know a thing about it. You could shoot bullets and they'd go in curves only you wouldn't know it because *everything* is curved."

"If all the world was mad," Lucy put in, "they'd lock the sane up in the lunatic asylums. The thing is – how do we know that isn't, in fact, the case already?"

Ebenezer looked from one to the other in a kind of mild despair. "I want to tell ye something," he remarked. "I'd not send either one of ye to find out."

Lucy and Birdie smiled at each other. "I know what I mean," Lucy said. "Don't you, Miss Kelly?"

Birdie laughed. "I did when I started, Mrs Raven."

The emotional division in the carriage was no longer between the Irish inside it and the sprinkling of Anglo-Irish and English in the cars ahead, but between Lucy and Birdie on the one hand and the smugly sane on the other. And, since any group or society divided into *us* and *them* is inherently more stable than one where all are united in common cause, this vaguely collusive spirit lasted for several miles – down the road to the Sally Gap and onto the military road proper.

In fact, it lasted all the way to their first halt, near the foot of the spectacular Falls of Glenmacnass, a mere five miles short of Glendalough. Indeed, the sound of the rushing water strengthened it, for, as Lucy helped Birdie out of the carriage, the girl muttered, "Jaysus, would you hark at that water! I'm kill't if I don't find a bush or a rock."

Lucy, who felt the same, could have agreed openly if the thought had been more delicately phrased; all she said was, "I'll come with you and keep cavey."

They left Ebenezer comfortable, with his relief bottle at hand, and set off across the stone-mottled pasture toward the falls. Their carriage had rather lagged over the last few miles, for the military road traversed some of the wildest and most romantic scenery in the kingdom and they had drawn up often to view it through Lucy's binoculars. The cars had therefore arrived at this halt some fifteen minutes earlier, which explained why their occupants were now climbing aboard and preparing to set off once again. The laggards just had time to exchange greetings and agree it was a splendid start to a most promising day before they had the falls to themselves.

"Ay splaendid staaht!" Birdie mimicked the English lady who had said those words and laughed at her own embellishment of them. "Me Mammy said I should learn to talk like them, could you believe! 'Twas the way to better myself, she said. When we see the back of them at last, Mrs Raven, won't they be easy forgot, the way they talk!"

"You think we will see the back of them, then?" Lucy asked.

"It must be the tannin in the tea that gives them the hide thick enough to stay here."

323

"Anyway, you don't think to better yourself by talking like them? You *could* talk like them, you know, if you didn't seek to make a joke of it. Try it seriously."

"A splendid start!" Birdie repeated in a faultless English accent. Then she burst out laughing to hear herself. "Be the holy fly – would you hark at that!"

"I told you you could. You have a gift for mimicry. You should get Dazzler to give you a part in one of his amateur productions. You might end up with a career on the stage."

Birdie stopped between one rock and the next; something kindled behind her eyes. "Do you think so? Honest?"

Lucy nodded firmly. "At least you don't look like making the mistake of marrying and settling down."

"Hah! Who'd have me?" Birdie replied bleakly.

"Go on!" Lucy chided. "None you'd welcome, I'm sure. Keep your fancy free!"

Birdie did not quite know how to respond to that. It was as much intimacy as the hour of day and their present association could bear. Lucy looked back toward the carriage and then drew Birdie's attention to Dermot Walshe, who was already climbing back into the carriage. "There's one who's not fond of the falling water," she commented.

They continued to pick their way across the few remaining yards to a large boulder by the side of the rushing stream – for, although the falls were spectacular in their height and in the arrangement of the scarps over which they plunged, the volume of water was that of a stream rather than a river, even when, as now, it was swollen by recent rains.

"Doctor Walshe has a month's mind to talk Mister O'Dea out of his paralysis, ma'am."

"Eh?" Lucy was suddenly all ears.

"He told me it's all in his mind, if you please! Paralysis in the mind – and him with legs on him no bigger than a redshank!"

"Save it, save it!" Lucy exclaimed. "I can't hear above all this rushing water. D'you want to go behind that rock? Actually, there's no one about – I'll join you."

They slipped behind the rock and hitched up great swathes of their skirts before they squatted – "Like kitchen-maids at a horse fair!" Lucy exclaimed.

A moment later, however, they were both distracted by a piteous bleating from somewhere over the water. "It sounds like a lamb in trouble," Lucy said.

"Sure there's no such creature in the middle of August," Birdie pointed out.

"Oh all right! A youngish sheep, then. It certainly isn't a crocodile out of the Limpopo!"

They stood up and shook down their skirts and then saw at once

324

that it was, indeed, a hogget – something between an elderly lamb and a young ewe. It was not, as they had supposed, on the far bank but trapped on a large, flat rock that divided the stream.

"How in the name of God did you get there?" Lucy shouted at it.

The creature bleated pathetically in reply.

"Shoo! Shoo – g'wan – shoo!" Birdie flapped her arms at it and made lunges that stopped dangerously at the edge of the rushing torrent. "Would you look at the eejit! It could lepp that gap as soon as lie down. G'wan!"

The ewe favoured her with the same bleat as it had given Lucy.

They chucked a few pebbles at it and a scraw of rank grass that Birdie managed to uproot, but all it did was panic and half-slip into the water – fortunately at a point where it was fairly slack, so it managed to extricate itself again.

"I could almost jump across to it from here," Lucy said, hitching up her skirts to get the feel of the thing. "If I took my boots off, too."

"Begod, Mrs Raven, it's not worth a human life so it isn't. Sure she'll lepp ashore again when she's hungry enough. She's only bleating to torment us. She's not been there ten minutes."

"How d'you know that?"

"She's left none of her calling cards on the rock."

"Ah, yes, so I see." Lucy's eagerness to be doing something humane subsided. "You seem to know the book when it comes to sheep, Miss Kelly. Are you sure she'll be all right there?"

Birdie assured her all would be well. "And if it's not, sure aren't we back this same way tomorrow? We could do something about her then if she's still there. Twenty-four hours is nothing but a lesson to a thing like that."

Lucy would not have yielded as quickly if she had not been so eager to hear about Dermot's hopes of ending Ebenezer's paralysis. As the roaring of the waters receded behind them she reminded her of the topic and asked, "Is it some kind of faith healing, or what? We'll walk slow enough to give him scope, whatever it is."

And so, as they ambled back over the sheep-nibbled sward, Birdie gave her own particular – not to say peculiar – gloss on Dermot's reading of the latest theories of the mind. Most of it she had merely inferred from the questions he'd asked her. "He says there's whole rafts of people who go blind or deaf or lose the power of speech from being guilty. Or they get paralysed. And I said I never heard of one except meself – and Mister Ebenezer, if it's true. And he said they mostly seem to live in Vienna. I don't know why that should be. Maybe they have a special home for them there or something. So I said if Mister Ebenezer was going to feel guilty about the mortal sins *he's* done, it would have started a fierce long while ago, not last year. But he said it only goes back to when that fella Reilly hanged himself there at Mount Venus. Mister Ebenezer woke up paralysed from the waist down the very next day, it seems. But I says to him, says I – any sort of quills'll make pens!"

Lucy cleared her throat hesitantly; she did not wish to stop this informative flow but there were so many things she desired to ask, too. "I'm sorry, I didn't understand that last bit – about quills and pens?"

"I mean, Mrs Raven, any fool can stare at a cloud and see a face. You may make pattrens – shite! I mean patterns – sorry I said shite . . ."

"Yes. No matter – I've said it myself in my time. Go on!"

"You may make patterns out of anything – clouds, old walls, a heap of turf – if you're so-minded. If Mister had gone paralysed the day after winning a three-horse accumulator (I know he doesn't bet, but *if*), you could say it was guilt over gambling. If *you* went blind tonight, he'd say it was guilt for abandoning that sheep. D'ye folley me now?"

"So – apart from the coincidence between Mister O'Dea's affliction and Reilly's suicide – there's no other evidence that the paralysis is mental rather than physical? Did he question you about that?"

All at once Lucy felt the girl become evasive. Birdie's pace slowed still further, she moved a little way apart, moved her head about awkwardly . . . "Well, he did, ma'am, I want to tell you that," she said.

"And were you able to tell him anything? Any hopeful signs?"

Birdie hesitated again, cleared her throat, and replied, "Sure he seemed to think so. I wish I'd said nothing. Lord but he'll murther me if he knows I said it."

"Mister O'Dea will murder you?"

"Himself, ma'am. The thing is . . . d'you see . . . oh Jaysus!" She spun on her heel and faced away from the carriage – as if she were afraid that Ebenezer could lip-read a whisper at a furlong and a half. "The thing is I felt sorry for him so I did. There's women who do be feeling sorry for the priests that they can't touch a woman with a loving stroke. Well I want to tell you I never felt sorry for any gentleman of the cloth, for didn't they choose it of their own free will? But I own I felt sorry for Mister Ebenezer, who never *chose* to be paralysed – no matter what jesuitical twists Doctor Walshe may give it. So . . ." She breathed in sharply. "One day, and me after giving him a bath . . . and going at it hearty with the soap . . ." She turned to Lucy with great, desperate eyes. "Well isn't it yourself would be curious, too, Mrs Raven, to be knowing how much of a man is paralysed when they say it's *everything* below the waist?"

Lucy saw that it was all or nothing, no hems, no haws, no half-measures. She laughed and put her arm round Birdie's shoulder and hugged her hard, crying. "My dear girl! I'm only *dying* of that very curiosity at this moment and I *beg* you put me out of my misery! Was he? Is he?"

326

Birdie stared at her, eyes wide, mouth agape. "Honest?" she asked.

"D'you know any woman who *wouldn't* be on the edge of her seat to know?"

The younger woman let out her breath in a great rush. Then she threw back her head and laughed. "You may knock me down with a feather!" she exclaimed.

"I'll knock you down with something a great deal more substantial if you don't answer me," Lucy threatened.

"Well, Mrs Raven, the long and the short of it is – he isn't. He'll stand as good as any howitzer – and fire like one, too – if you take my meaning, now."

"It would be hard not to, Miss Kelly! I shan't press you for details – for fear they'd embarrass *you*, not me, I do assure you. But I take it this was no flash in the pan?"

"Lord no – 'twas in the bath, as I said."

"No, I mean . . . oh dear! It wasn't a fluke? It's happened a couple of times? Two or three times, perhaps?"

"Oh, every day. But d'you know what I'm going to tell you now – he's never laid a finger on *me*. He's never touched me. You should know that – honourable man that he is. Not even slipped a finger inside my bodice now, nor even asked for a peep, which his nephew's after asking every time. We manage it most elegantly. I slip a hand between his sheets and work away, and him lying back with his eyes closed. And he says, after, 'Thank you, Birdie, you make an old man very content with his lot.' And I'm sure I'll answer for it on the Day of Reckoning. But I'll confess it then to a God of Mercy, not some celibate culchie who couldn't stand a woman the right way up."

If Dermot Walshe had been hoping for a miracle cure he must have been disappointed, for Ebenezer's legs remained as paralysed as before. The expression on Dermot's face, however, was rather cheery, so the two women surmised that he must have made *some* progress by his own estimation. Birdie watched Ebenezer closely for any sign that the doctor might have dropped a hint that he knew what sort of comfort she had been providing, but she detected none. Not that that meant much where the old fellow was concerned; he could have hidden the torments of hell from the devil himself until it suited him to scream. Mrs Raven's suggestion about going on the stage began to find echoes in her own mind now – which was odd. If she'd conceived the notion all on her own, she'd have laughed herself to scorn. Such fancies! But because a grand lady like Mrs Raven said it, the fancy could be indulged while the laughter got shown the door.

Yet how grand was she, really – that Honourable Lucinda Raven? Wasn't that a curious thing she said, about not getting married and keeping your fancy free? And her like a hen in stubble with Mister Raven, too. She felt glad she'd confessed about her doings with Ebenezer O'Dea. She felt no shame about it now. In fact, she never had. In the beginning she'd done it for divilment, then to see would she feel any shame, then to see would the shame come over her in the course of time . . . and now she did it because he was grateful and it softened his heart and the day went the easier for it. Perhaps the reason she'd told Mrs Raven was really just to discover was this shamelessness hers alone or would any woman understand? The answer, anyway, was encouraging. Birdie had grown so used to people telling her she was a few cards short of the full deck, and that she'd end up a wandering familiar, muttering to herself and begging for crusts . . . it was good to have that support from an Honourable lady. Unless, of course, the said Honourable lady was herself a few cards short of a full deck! How would one recognize another? If all the world was mad . . . Didn't she say that herself not an hour since!

Birdie's perplexities were still unresolved as they drew into the village at Glendalough, where they were greeted by four empty cars, a gig, a phaeton and a huddle of four drivers shying pebbles at the twigs that were drifting in the stream. It was gone eleven o'clock now and the sun, near its zenith, was pouring down upon the lake and its girdle of mountains, on the old stones of the cathedral and its acolyte chapels and churches, and on the people, picking a random path among the higgledy-piggledy of graves ancient and modern. This way and that they peered, gazing at the time-worn stones with a kind of bemused tolerance, learning nothing except that priests and their bishops must have been recruited exclusively among the Little People in those far-off times.

"Could you imagine Father Corcoran and Father Riley trying to fit in that little chapel?" Birdie asked at the doorway of the diminutive structure popularly called St Kevin's Kitchen. "They'd roll up their sleeves and beat the bejaysus out of each other in five minutes."

"Have you heard the story of Saint Kevin?" Lucy asked her as they wandered on down the path toward the Deer Stone, where the deer were supposed to have left milk for the saint during a period of famine.

Birdie admitted she hadn't. "I saw a print of it once in the *Catholic Girl*. He lived chastely in a cave you could only reach by boat."

"Yes, but d'you know why?" Lucy asked while she pointed out the escarpment of rock where the cave was still to be found. "Have you heard Moore's melody about it? Saint Kevin was haunted by the beauty of a colleen called Kathleen, and he was afraid he'd fall in love with her."

"Exchange sainthood for manhood," Birdie suggested.

Lucy chuckled. "So he fled to this desolate spot and hid in the cave and prayed night and day for strength to resist her beauty. But the women of those times weren't the milksops you find today. Kathleen pursued him to his hideaway and when the saint woke up one morning, there she was – bending gently over him with the light of love in her eye and her heart overflowing with devotion. So what did he do – guess?"

"Baptized her and made her abbess of her own house?"

"No."

"Preached chastity to her and sent her away reformed?"

"No."

"Took leg bail from her as fast as he could?"

"No. He slew her! He picked her up and dashed her to pieces on the rocks below."

"Jaysus, Mary, and Joseph! And him a saint!"

"And him a saint!" Lucy echoed. "I'd like to hear the sermon they preached at his canonization."

"'Twas her fault," Birdie asserted, "for tempting him so sorely. When a man gets a bee like that in his bonnet, a woman's a fool who seeks to talk him out of it, or tempt him out of it, either."

"What should she have done?" Lucy asked, a little miffed that Birdie had chosen to draw so practical a moral.

"She should have looked elsewhere," Birdie replied – then, with a cheeky grin: "Kept her fancy free!"

Lucy had to laugh, though somewhat ruefully.

At that moment they saw Lord Glanbeg coming toward them with his two noble friends. After mutual greetings Glanbeg showed her a small fragment of stone he was carrying. Half of its faces were freshly broken but the rest were well weathered; one of them bore an Irish Á and part of some other letter. "It's a bit of an old O'Toole gravestone," he explained. "One thousand and three years old! All the great O'Toole kings were buried up there, it seems."

Lucy was aghast. "And you've broken up one of the gravestones, Lord Glanbeg?" she asked.

He laughed. "Lord, no, Mrs Raven, I do assure you. It's a group of the local guides. They usually sell the fragments at the gate, but they ran out last week. So they're breaking up another stone now." He assumed a mocking Irish accent: "A spicimen, yer onner, of the grave of a rale oul' Oirish king!" He laughed again. "Rather charming, I thought – and only half-a-crown. Very reasonable."

Lucy thanked him for the information. But when she and Birdie were alone again they did not take the path up to the old church and the O'Toole burial ground. "Who's the villain?" Lucy asked despairingly. "Them for seducing us with their half-crowns, or us for pandering to it? Solomon himself could not answer, I think."

It amazed Birdie that an Honourable lady like Mrs Raven would lump herself in with the desecrators of the grave rather than the purchasers of the spoils – two of whom, after all, were Honourables like herself. It was a quare old world when you saw it close-up! "'Tis the same question as with Saint Kevin," she said. "Was it Katherine's fault for having such charms or his for taking such hearty notice of them?"

"Solomon had nine hundred wives, you know," Lucy replied. "So I don't suppose *that* question even crossed his mind. Such is progress!"

They had gone a few dozen paces down the path that led around the smaller lake – far enough to realize how long a walk it was. They glanced at each other and turned back by common and unspoken consent. Lucy went on: "Back there by the waterfall you said something that puzzled me. I meant to ask about it but we got on to, ahem, other things."

"And what might that have been, Mrs Raven?" For some unknown reason Birdie felt her spirit begin to sink already.

"You were talking about what Doctor Walshe told you – how people go blind or are struck dumb and so on, not because of physical injury or disease but because of something in their minds. And you said you'd never heard of it happening to anyone *except yourself*. Did you mean that? Were you ever struck blind or . . ."

"Dumb!" Birdie laughed. "Could you imagine! *Me* – with a tongue that'd lick a calf – struck dumb! Me Mammy says that for them three months – *those* three months – she knew the music of heaven."

The hair began to bristle on Lucy's neck. "And what caused it?" she asked. "Did anyone ever find the reason?"

Birdie let out a sigh, as if to suggest it was all rather tedious and trivial – and a very long time ago. "They said I fell off my bicycle. But sure I don't remember having a bicycle in those days."

"And do you remember being struck dumb? How old were you?"

"Fourteen, so she says."

"Not being able to talk for three whole months – surely you recall that if you were fourteen at the time?"

"Not at all," Birdie answered scornfully. "But for the numbers who'll swear the truth of it, I'd swear she was codding me. Yet I have no memory of it at all."

Lucy took her heart in both hands and said, "I must say it doesn't *sound* very likely. Where would you have got the money from to buy a bicycle. Is this when you were still living in Tallaght?"

There was a long silence before Birdie said, "So you know we moved away?"

"Tallaght is a small village, my dear – and we do live rather close by," Lucy replied gently.

"I was a fool, so," Birdie said. "And I suppose you know we moved to Lucan, ma'am?"

330

"Yes. Why didn't you want me to know that?"

Birdie shrugged awkwardly. "I don't know, I'm sure. I thought the less ye all knew of me, the less reason ye'd have for breaking me."

"Well, I've made no inquiries there," Lucy assured her. "And nor shall I do so – you may have my word on that. I'd trust my own high opinion of you before any poison your friends and neighbours might pour in my ear. I hope you believe me?"

"I do, Mrs Raven. I believe you and thank you."

"So – to get back to you and the bicycle – what work would there have been for a girl of fourteen in Tallaght? Scaring the jackdaws for farmers, I suppose, but precious little else."

Birdie's pace slowed to a halt. She frowned and a faraway look stole into her eyes.

"What now?" Lucy prompted.

Birdie closed her eyes. "A dream, I think, ma'am," she replied. "I never frightened the jackdaws for anyone, farmer or gentleman. But I had a dream of it once."

"And what happened – in the dream, I mean?"

Birdie shook her head. "It has all gone now."

Lucy made a further try. "Anyway," she said in a soothing tone, "there's only one farmer near Tallaght big enough to afford a girl to frighten the jackdaws – Mister Shaw of Bohernabreena."

Birdie agreed. With no show of any particular emotion she said, "His daughter Helen had a bicycle I remember. They say she lent me the ride of it once – and that's the only time I ever rode a machine in those days."

"And what happened?"

They were re-entering the cathedral precincts now, where the excursionists were drawing together from their diverse promenades around the ancient site. Lucy realized her chances of pursuing this gentle line of inquiry were dwindling – and no bad thing, perhaps. More haste less speed.

Birdie laughed. "I fell off and hurt myself, of course. I didn't laugh at the time, I may say. To be honest, I passed out."

Lucy sneaked in one final question. "Was it bad enough to make them fetch the doctor?"

Birdie's smile faded and she shook her head. "I have no memory of the incident at all, ma'am. They say it robbed me of the power of speech, that fall. But I can't even remember that."

"Maybe it's just as well, then. It can't have been a pleasant memory, anyway."

"But there's no *guilt*, you see, Mrs Raven. That's the thing I'd put to Doctor Walshe if I'd dare. No guilt." The point seemed to agitate her remarkably.

"Of course there wasn't!" Lucy replied in the most soothing tones as she patted her on the arm.

331

S ince the arrangements for the first outing had gone perfectly, the second should have been perfection with cream on. In fact, it began to unravel even before they set off. Birdie came down to the courtyard, where the assorted forms of transport were being marshalled, to say that Ebenezer would not be coming that day – but that she was to accompany the outing nonetheless and make herself useful in any way Mrs Raven thought fit. Then Philip, who had hemmed and hawed all week before deciding not to accompany them, turned up and said he'd changed his mind yet again and would, after all, like to go along. Then two of the patients, who were already in one of the cars with the rugs wrapped snugly around them, succumbed to the excitement and had to be sent back to their beds – which left the Misses Wilks alone in that car. Nobody wanted to join them, since the only thing that had sustained them for the past sixty years was an endlessly renewable quarrel. Diana, who was driving the gig with the two spare nurses, sent one of them to sit with the Wilks sisters and distract them. And so at last, a mere fifteen minutes late, they all set off.

Michael drove the carriage and pair, with Lucy, Birdie, and Philip behind him. Lucy sank back in her seat and said that if that was all the upset they faced today, she'd be well pleased. "I knew it couldn't be absolutely plain sailing," she added, "because yesterday went so well."

"That's because I wasn't here," Michael said over his shoulder.

He meant the remark humorously, but the tone of his voice was lost in the grind of the iron tyres on the gravel. So, because they could not see his face, either, they did not know how to respond. In the ensuing silence he said, rather bitterly, "It was a joke, dammit! Oh I give up!" He shook the rein savagely and, a moment later, had to pull the horses in.

Philip and Birdie glanced at Lucy and then averted their eyes. Michael's angry "I give up!" obviously referred to a sequence of fruitless attempts to improve his and Lucy's union – of which they had just witnessed the latest. If the gray tiredness in Lucy's eyes and the lines of strain upon her brow were tokens of the night just past, the skill these two had shown in keeping their differences to themselves and presenting a united front to the world was now inadequate to the labour.

"Well, it's going to be another lovely day," Lucy said brightly.

Alas, coming on the heels of Michael's bitter outburst, it sounded like the sort of stiletto sarcasm to which women are driven in the company of angry men.

"I thought the same, myself," Michael replied.

On another day, in another context, his use of the past tense would have seemed mere colloquialism; now it was a little flick of the gauntlet on Lucy's cheek. A couple more exchanges of that

332

nature and they would no longer care who overheard them; they would take the first step down that road the Wilks sisters had trod all their adult lives – being now unable to argue *unless* they had an audience.

The two old dears were at it now – I-said and you-said by the yard. Diana realized her mistake in sending one of the nurses to control their spleen; she had merely supplied them with a captive audience. Her horse seemed more upset by the racket than any of the humans, who were used to the pair of them by now. She was having some difficulty in ruling him.

"I wonder if that poor little hogget is still stuck in the waterfall?" Lucy said to Birdie. "We should have taken the gig and come back that way."

"And if she was there all night?" Birdie asked. "Sure 'twill only teach her a lesson. She'll never stray again." She did not understand why Mrs Raven stared at her so balefully; the trouble was, no matter what anyone said now, it fell into a pool of vitriol; it seethed with unintended nuances. Silence itself was even worse; or at least, it was no answer.

They endured what seemed like an eternity of it up the long climb to the point where they could rest and enjoy a final view of Dublin and the Liffey plain. There Diana sent the one remaining spare nurse forward to help her colleague with the querulous sisters. Then Michael, seeing that Diana would now be alone in the gig, passed his reins to Philip, saying, "You take over here, old chap." He waited until he was half-way there before he called back: "Matron won't be able to handle that brute on her own."

Philip looked about him angrily, unable to decide whether to ask Lucy or Birdie to hold the reins while he went forward and took Michael's place in the gig – but then he saw the expression on Lucy's face and held his peace.

Then, as they all set off again, he began reassuring himself. After all, what could Michael *do*, in the middle of such a convoy in this wild, open moorland? Talk, that was all. And what about? They could talk shop – and no harm in that. They could talk about old times – in which case she'd surely make him wish they hadn't! And it would be the same if he tried to talk about the state of his marriage . . . surely?

He bit his lip. The trouble was that the instincts which had impelled Diana toward nursing couldn't be switched on and off like an electric light – except, paradoxically, where her own emotions were engaged. She could be hard as cobbles with him, Philip, because she loved him. But a sick stranger could try her patience beyond what the saintliest saint would endure and she'd continue to be as soft and sympathetic as ever. If Michael were wily enough to pretend he needed her *impersonal* love, he'd snag her fast. Philip sat and watched them like a hawk.

"Did Mister O'Dea give any reason for not wishing to come today?" Lucy asked Birdie.

"Divil a one that I'd believe," she replied.

"That's a shocking thing to say about your master." Lucy grinned hugely, her first genuine smile for some time.

Birdie relaxed. "Him and that Doctor Walshe are up to something," she said darkly. "He has a mind to talk the quare fella into walking again. You know that cupboard with the door screwed fast?"

Lucy sat up, all else suddenly forgotten. "Yes?"

"He was at it with a screwdriver when I left, so he was."

"Mister O'Dea?"

"No, Doctor Walshe. He said there'd be skellingtons in it that should be laid in a quiet grave."

Philip turned round and stared at her. The shock in his eyes bordered on horror.

"What's the matter?" a surprised Lucy asked him. "D'you know something about it?"

"No," he replied at once. Then, "Well . . . I'm not sure. You know we finished taking down the potting shed last week?"

"Yes?"

"I didn't say anything about it because . . . well, there was no point, frankly. But we found poor William Reilly's grave."

"We?" Lucy was aghast.

"Ryland and me – he's the bricklayer. We thought it was an old lime pit. Can you imagine – they buried him in quicklime, just like a hanged felon!"

"Lordamercy!" Birdie exclaimed.

"No one else did," Philip told her bitterly.

"But how d'you know?" Lucy asked. "I mean, doesn't quicklime eat a body away in a couple of days? I always heard that."

He shook his head. "Everyone'll tell you that, but it's wrong. In fact, the precise opposite is the case. It dries the body out and leaves it mummified – perfectly preserved." He shuddered. "If perfectly is quite the word!"

"And why d'you think this might have something to do with . . . whatever Dermot Walshe is planning for today?"

Philip sighed. "Only because he showed such an interest in the find and asked me to say nothing about it."

"That's all?"

"He didn't *say* any more but his whole attitude was that he might have a use for it. I thought he was going to do . . . I don't know – medical tests on the body or something."

Lucy flared up suddenly. "Oh, and that would have been perfectly in order, would it? It wasn't enough that poor old Reilly was hounded to his death and laid to rest – to *rest* by God! – in a pit of quicklime in the kitchen garden. He now has to be subjected to the final degradation of . . ."

"Lucy!" Philip cajoled. "Do you really think any purpose would have been served if I'd announced my find to all and sundry? Don't you think there are enough . . . cross-currents, or whatever you want to call them – eddying and swilling around Mount Venus? What good would it have done?"

Lucy closed her eyes and shook her head in bewilderment. "I think we should turn around and go back," she said. "I have the most awful premonition. I think something dreadful is going to happen at Mount Venus today."

The carriage trundled on in silence for a while. Then Philip said, "Well I don't know *what* to do now."

After a further long pause Lucy asked Birdie what she thought they ought to do.

"D'you know what I'm going to tell you," Birdie replied. "'Tis the same opinion as I voiced yesterday concerning Katherine and Saint Kevin. When a man gets a bee like that in his bonnet, the women might as well go out and enjoy a picnic as seek to change his mind."

Philip laughed loud enough to make Diana and Michael, half a furlong ahead, turn round. "Dear God, Miss Kelly!" he exclaimed, "I believe there's more sense inside your head than in the whole of County Dublin."

Lucy reached across and patted Birdie's arm gratefully. "You're probably right," she said. "The whole thing baffles me. It has from the very beginning. I never understood why Mister O'Dea should sink so much money into Mount Venus. The fact that it seems to be paying back is mere fluke. The investment went far beyond commercial calculation. And all those things Diana told us he said about building a zoo for humans! That didn't ring true, either – though I'm sure he forced himself to believe it quite sincerely."

"What are you saying?" Philip asked.

"I'm saying it had something to do with Reilly's suicide. I'm not talking about spirits and ghosts. I mean those dark, shadowy fringes of the human mind that love to dwell on such phantasms. Dermot Walshe is dabbling in things he doesn't understand. He could unleash forces that will destroy Ebenezer O'Dea – the forces he *hopes* will make him walk again. They could destroy him instead. And it's no good saying 'I meant well' then. The way to hell is paved with those intentions."

They digested this in yet another silence. Then Birdie said brightly, "Sure what good is all the gold in the world to a man when his wife's a widow!"

Lucy was about to point out that Ebenezer wasn't married when it struck her that – as with almost everything Birdie said – although it didn't quite match the real world, the discrepancy was not the part that mattered.

Diana yielded the reins to Michael with a heavy heart – and an angry one, too. For, though she'd concede that she and the horse were not the best matched pair in the world, she would rather have handed control of it to anyone other than him. "You're not welcome," she said gruffly. "But I suppose you realize that."

"Shall I call for Philip, then?" he risked asking.

She almost said yes.

He turned half round and drew breath to shout.

"Oh, go on then!" She struck him furiously on the arm, angry at her own lack of horsemanship, angry that Michael was going to beg for her help, angry that she was going to give it – against all her better judgement. "It'll look ridiculous if you swap now. You can change over at the waterfall."

The moment they set off again she consulted her watch and added, "So you have something like forty to fifty minutes to whine and nag and bleat away at me."

For half a mile she enjoyed the silence while he stared glumly between the horse's ears at the road. Then he said, "Perhaps I'll just get off and walk home. I could send Quinlan on after you. Back there in the carriage I couldn't even make a joke without Lucy jumping down my throat. And now, whatever I say to you, you'll turn it into a complaint, no matter what."

She sighed. "I'm sorry, Michael."

"Yes, but for what?" he asked.

"I'm sorry things aren't going well between you and Lucy – but we've already talked that subject to death. There's nothing more I can usefully say. I'm sorry you turned out to be the sort of man you are – or were ten years ago. Eleven years? Oh, who cares any more! Donkey's years ago. We could have had a splendid marriage – lovely children – snish-snish! But we didn't. So that's that. God, how many times have I told you this already? Ten million in my mind, I'm sure."

"You say 'that's that' very glibly, but . . ."

"D'you know what I think we *ought* to talk about?"

"What?"

"This idiotic faith-healing business, or whatever it is that Doctor Walshe is intending to practise on Mister O'Dea. I'm sure that's why he's stayed behind today."

"Of course." Michael nodded glumly. "But what can I do?"

"Put your foot down. Forbid it."

"But Ebenezer owns the whole place, Diana. He owns you. He owns me. And now he's pretending to take poor Dermot seriously – which is just a different way of owning him."

"He doesn't own *me*," she said vehemently.

"Control, then. He controls you. It's the same difference, putting my foot down wouldn't stop anything. I'd just be left looking foolish."

Diana thought of several answers to that but kept them all to herself. "That's that, then," she said again.

This time he did not pick her up on it. After some thought he said, "All I really wanted to tell you – this is apropos our last conversation, on the evening of your birthday . . ."

"I thought I made it clear, Michael. There's nothing more to be said about all that."

"There is on my side."

"I don't wish to hear it."

"We killed the subject," he said, "but we didn't bury it."

"What was left to bury?" she asked sarcastically. Then, after a pause, "Oh very well! Go on then – for there'll be no peace until you've got it off your chest."

"I want to tell you everything," he said. "Just this once. And then I'll never tell you again. I want you to know it . . ."

"Why?" she asked.

He discarded a number of answers before he said, "So that I can hope to sleep again, perhaps?"

"It's for your good, then, not mine."

He smiled wanly. "I'm afraid so, my dear."

She stared at the road, her face now quite blank. "At least you're being honest, I suppose. All right – go on, then."

"Here's another bit of honesty: I love you . . ."

"Michael!"

"No listen – please! I said I'll only say it once and then I'll never plague you again. I'm married to Lucy and I'll die married to Lucy. And I'll never be unfaithful to her, even though she . . . well, never mind."

"Never mind! How were you going to finish that thought? Even though she may think you are unfaithful? Or even though she may break the vows on her side? Never mind? D'you think the difference is too trivial to bother about? And in any case, d'you imagine you're breaking no vows of your own in telling me these things?"

"I just want to tell you. I *must* get it off my chest."

"Become a Roman Catholic then – get it off your chest every week! And break your vows as often as you like. As long as you still feel miserable about it and take care to tell the priest, you'll still go to heaven."

"All right!" He sighed. "I won't say anything, then."

"I think that's a very wise decision."

"I just wish I could do something to cure your bitterness."

"Good!"

"I feel responsible."

She stared at him and laughed harshly. "You *what?* You *feel* responsible! Michael, you *are* responsible!"

"Clever!" he sneered. "That's what I meant."

"And you think talk is going to do any good? This isn't some ghastly slice of realism down at the *Abbey*, Michael – where people talk for two and a half hours and all the world's problems get solved. This is real life – where people talk-talk-talk for years and years and *nothing* ever changes. Listen to the Wilks sisters – they're just caricatures of all of us."

Michael said nothing.

She resumed in a quieter, more conciliatory tone. "Perhaps when we were young we could talk *and* change. But then we did that, didn't we!" She smiled sadly at him. "You did change. Now you seem to regret it but it's too late." Almost under her breath she added, "Ten years too late."

"Eleven," he said.

"Ten," she insisted.

He stared at her sharply. An oddly speculative smile played at the corners of her lips. "What?" he asked.

"I wonder," she mused. She drew breath to speak but just at that moment Philip laughed loudly in the carriage behind them. They turned and gazed all around without seeing any obvious cause for merriment. "Someone's happy, anyway," Michael said.

"Perhaps it'll help if I tell you what I think you were going to say," Diana suggested. "Then you can disown it if it sounds too stupid."

He closed his eyes and shook his head. "You do know how to rub salt in a wound."

"It cleans it of corruption in half the time." She chuckled. "Now let me tell you some other things you know. You love me. You love me still. Perhaps you always have. You cannot now understand why we ever parted. When you try and think back to it your mind just goes zizz! However, there it is – we did part, and you did marry someone else, and get children on her, and she's not a bad old sort, taking the rough with the smooth. So, looking at it all round, you think you'll stick with her until you die. But, just in case I should be so foolish as to imagine that sets me free, you want me to know this all-important fact – namely that I am the *real* love of your life. And you're going to be terribly good about it and never say another word after today. But you want me to *know* it. And if ever I'm in *real* trouble, of course, of course, of *course* you'll help. Like a shot. Like the trooper you are. And you'll be able to jump to it because, wonder of wonders, you've been sleeping quite well since you got all this off your chest! Am I close?"

He let out a deep breath as if she had winded him. "Thank God I never told you," he said.

It stung her into the reply she might otherwise never have given him. "If it's getting-the-truth-off-one's-chest time, Michael, let me tell you why I said it's ten years too late, not eleven. Ten years ago I went to America to stay with my sister . . ."

"Agnes?"

"I didn't think you'd remember. Yes, Agnes. She died in child-

338

birth. Her husband, Tom, went to pieces. The baby survived and I brought him back with me. My parents have reared him." Her great dark eyes rested in his. "You've guessed," she concluded.

He swallowed hard; his voice had to fight its way out. "Only because you said ten years too late. He's ten years old, I presume?"

She nodded. "His name is Mick. The story I've just told you is the one we shall all live by."

He frowned. "Live by?"

"He's starting at Saint Columba's next term. He'll be spending quite a few Sundays with his *Aunty* Di."

Michael stared grimly at the road ahead. "Never tell Lucy this," he said, adding "please" as an afterthought.

Diana laughed harshly.

He turned to her in amazement.

"That's one great difference between you," she said. "Lucy made it clear she'd rather you did not know, but she gave me carte blanche to decide whether or not to tell you. You, by contrast, simply issue an order. Think about that, Michael. Take it to heart."

It did not seem to perturb him to hear that Lucy already knew of the boy's existence and, presumably, origin. "Ten years!" he said quietly.

"I flew them," she declared.

"You've kept it to yourself for ten years. All these months . . . you never said a word."

"Does it hurt?" she asked with an odd kind of relish.

"And why have you told me now – after Lucy made it clear she'd rather I didn't know? Are you trying to punish her, too?"

"On the contrary, Michael. I'm keeping a promise I made her at the time."

"What?"

"Ask her. You've got to start speaking to her again sometime. I can't think of a better question to open with. Try it."

T he carriage and pair dawdled so much that, as on the previous day, they arrived at the waterfall when everyone else was just about leaving. Michael was standing out in the road, in the obvious attitude of a man fretting and waiting. And, though he must have seen them at the first of the hairpin bends by which the road descended into the valley, he continued to stand thus until they arrived at the bottom of the hill – "not simply making his point," Lucy said angrily, "but making a parade of it, too."

He took the reins from Philip and tied them to a fencepost. "The others are all going on," he said. "You can take over Diana's nag, if you want." To Lucy he murmured, as a kind of peace-offering, "I was beginning to get worried."

But she was in no mood to let him off so lightly. She was still furious with him for his lack of self-control when they set off – and even more so for the brusque way he'd gone to ride with Diana on the flimsiest pretext. "You wouldn't care whether I were alive or dead," she sneered, wanting desperately to wound him – and feeling desperately pleased to see how well she succeeded, too.

In fact, he was so hurt – and angry – that he simply turned on his heel and walked away, back toward the gig. Lucy's last sight of him – for she would not deign to turn her head again – was of the gig setting off toward Glendalough, with only Philip and Diana up; Michael having covered only half the distance to it, just stood and watched it depart.

She skipped across the turf to catch up with Birdie, who was going to see whether her theory about the hogget had proved right. Lucy was suddenly so light of heart that, as she drew level, she slipped her arm through Birdie's and hugged her elbow warmly.

The girl looked at her in amazement.

"Pay no attention, dear," Lucy said. "It'll pass. But I feel very . . . *good* at the moment. You don't mind, I hope?"

"Go first in a wood, last in a bog," Birdie said.

Lucy roared with laughter, though she could not have said why. "And how should one go on Saint Bridget's turf like this?" she asked.

"Side by side." Now it was Birdie who laughed. "All will be well, ma'am."

"I think it will, you know," Lucy agreed. "I can't explain it but I feel an incredible lightness. Not light-headed, you understand, but a lightness of spirit. Did you see that cloud go across the sky the other day? All darkness and drizzle on one side and clear blue sky the other? It's like that. I wouldn't be surprised after all to find Mister O'Dea up and walking again by the time we get back this evening."

"Wouldn't that be grand," Birdie said with little enthusiasm.

"Don't you worry," Lucy assured her. "You've a place for life at Mount Venus if you want it."

But before the girl could say anything in reply they crested a small ridge and came in sight of the rock where the hogget had been stranded the day before.

And she was still stranded there – bleating away, though much more feebly now. And the rock was mired with hundreds, if not thousands, of little droppings. They were mostly concentrated around the rim, where she had been standing – presumably thinking of leaping but not daring to try.

"Oh, the poor thing!" Lucy cried, looking all around in her anguish.

Where was the farmer? Why did his shepherd not keep better control of his flock?

"Shall I fetch Mister Raven, ma'am?" Birdie asked.

Lucy was about to say yes when that unforgiving element in her spirit rebelled. "No," she snapped. "We're perfectly capable of managing this ourselves. Look how much the water's gone down since yesterday. I can easily leap across there now. I shan't even need a run up." She started to gather her skirts.

Birdie wrung her hands. "Oh dear, Mrs Raven . . . I think 'twould be best to send for himself beyond."

"Watch!" Lucy cried. And before she could have second thoughts she sprang toward the rock and landed well into the middle of it, beyond the ring of droppings. "There!" She even surprised herself.

The hogget, panicked by Lucy's sudden appearance at her side, made the leap she could have made at any time within the past twenty-four hours and landed in a backwater pool among some boulders, out of the reach of the current. From there she scrambled onto the farther bank, where she gambolled away, bleating continuously and shaking her head.

"There!" Lucy said again. "And now watch me jump back."

If she had delayed just long enough for Birdie to break off a nearby sally and use it to brush away the droppings, she'd have flown it. But she was so flushed with success she didn't think it necessary. She slipped at the very edge of the rock and, with a half-somersault backward, fell flat on her back in the rushing torrent.

She heard Birdie's scream, just before the water closed over her. It was black and cold and full of roaring. Her only thought was that she was now as good as dead. Then Birdie's hand reached into the foam and plucked her to the surface. She breathed again, hugely, as if she had been under for a minute or more. Her hands found a hold on one of the boulders. The current swung her round into a backwater. Her feet felt the solidity beneath her. And the next moment she was standing up, rubbing her eyes, blowing rivulets of water off her lips, and exclaiming – of all things – "Bother!" again and again.

Birdie collapsed into laughter and had to sit on a rock. "Is that all you have to say, ma'am?" she asked.

"I could say a great deal more, my girl!" Lucy shook down her hair and wrung gallons from it and her bonnet. "I feel such an eejit! Lord, but that water is *cold!*" She began to shiver.

It was thus that Michael found them. "If you've nothing better to do than laugh, Miss Kelly," he said, "you may pick up your skirts and run. Bring the travelling rugs from the carriage."

Birdie's heels flashed in the sunlight as she sped to obey.

"She saved me from being swept away," Lucy said. "She was only laughing because she saw I'm all right."

He took her by the hand and led her into the lee of a large boulder, out of sight of anyone on the road. "Take those wet things off," he said. "You can wrap my coat around you." He took it off as he spoke and left it by her, intending to retire to the other side of the boulder while she undressed.

"Michael?"

341

He turned to her.

"Stay by me?"

He gave a wan, uncertain smile and came back.

She faced away from him and began unbuttoning her bodice. "The dress unhooks at the back," she said.

Her icy fingers made better work of it than his. "D'you remember the last time you undid a dress of mine?" she asked coyly.

"When you boasted you could drink me under the table any day?"

She gave an exasperated cry. "All right! The time *before* that. God! Talk about marriage being the enemy of romance!"

He did remember the evening but she realized he wasn't going to admit to it. "For a moment I truly thought I was going to drown," she went on.

"And did your life flash before your eyes, the way it's supposed to?"

"No. I thought . . ." She hesitated.

"What?"

"Promise you won't laugh?"

"It's an easy promise to make these days."

"I thought of you. I thought, *I'm going to lose you – I'll never see you again!* . . ." Her voice broke but she pretended all she needed to do was clear her throat. "It was desolate," she managed to add.

The wet swathes of clothing peeled themselves off her; the sun was like a fiery salve on her shoulders and thighs. He slipped his overcoat round her and pulled her into his embrace. After a while she dabbed his cheek with her knuckles and murmured, "Here! Don't you think I've had more than my share of water for one day."

Lucy sat in a borrowed dressing gown before a roaring fire in the best bedroom of the Royal Hôtel at Glendalough; meanwhile Birdie and Philip raced home in the gig to fetch another dress from Mount Venus. It was useless for Lucy to protest she had been under the water less than half a minute . . . that it was a warm August day . . . that the fire would be the death of her. Michael was a doctor and doctors know best. He kept feeling her forehead and taking her pulse until even he was convinced that her pleas to sit by the open window and enjoy the balmy summer air were not mere bravado. "I think you'll have sweated any febrile tendency out of you by now," was how he put it.

The window was not a bay but the walls were so thick that the seat took the form of a bay within it. They sat, three-quarters facing each other, knees almost touching, and found they were suddenly as shy as a newly courting couple.

"Did you really think you were going to drown?" he asked hesitantly.

342

She nodded. "I suppose the reason my past life didn't flash before my eyes was because . . ." She paused.

"Because it's been doing nothing else for weeks?" he suggested.

She smiled at him. "How did you know that?"

"Snap!" he replied. He fretted with a knot in the woodwork. "Diana told me, you know – about . . . the boy."

"Mick."

"Yes." Still he could not look at her.

"And?" she prompted him.

He inhaled deeply. "She told me you'd have preferred me not to know. But she also . . ."

"That was a stupid thing for me to say," she put in. "The first Sunday he's let out of Saint Columba's and comes to stay at Mount Venus . . . you'd have guessed. *Aunty* Di, indeed!"

He nodded. He still could not look her in the eye but his gaze drew closer. "She also said she'd made you a promise – about certain conditions under which she *would* tell me. But she wouldn't say what they were. She told me to ask you."

"She promised she'd only tell you if she thought it would . . ." Lucy balked at repeating Diana's exact words. Instead she said: ". . . if it would help us, you and me." She swallowed. "Has it?"

He met her gaze at last and smiled. "I'm sure." His tongue flickered nervously over his lips. "Did you . . . I mean, you and she . . . have you told her everything?"

"Everything?" Lucy echoed warily. "That's rather vague. I unburdened myself to her, if that's what you're asking."

He reached out and brushed her wrist with the tips of his fingers; she snatched at his hand and clamped it tight between hers. After a moment's silence she said, "I'd forgotten."

"What?"

"The feel of your hand in mine. Even a simple thing like that, I'd forgotten. I suppose you unburdened yourself to Diana, too?"

She watched him weighing up his reply. Part of her hated him; part of her – most of her – wanted him more desperately than ever. In those few seconds when she had been convinced her life was at an end, the agony had all been for the loss of this man. Not her own life, not her children, not her friends, but Michael, and only Michael. It surprised her now that she could find any part of her that hated him and rebelled against his power to move her like that. For the first time in her life she had an intimation that love and hate were not the simple opposites of everyday usage but parts of something even bigger, something for which, as yet, she could supply no name. "A sort of him-and-her-ness," was her childish best.

She realized, too, that she could no longer contemplate herself without a simultaneous reference to him. Remove him and she, too, was diminished.

"Whose stocking *was* that?" she asked, cutting across all his careful calculation.

"Eh?"

"That pink stocking you took from the pheasant run. It was Diana's, wasn't it!"

The colour that flushed the tips of his ears was all the answer she needed. She began to laugh.

He looked so shocked that, in a panic, she leaned forward and kissed him warmly; the touch of his lips was another of those intimacies she had forgotten. Then it was no longer a question of love or hate. Such refinements of feeling flew way over her head. Every fibre of her was now consumed with simple need – raw, urgent, ungovernable.

Her lips devoured him. Her fingers ransacked his buttons, the folds of his clothing, peeling him, bursting him out for her. For her.

"Lucy!" he croaked as they fell to the carpet, too wild to go the extra yard to the bed.

They were calm again – silent and serene – by the time they heard Birdie come racing up the street in the governess cart.

"Just when my own clothes are almost dry anyway," Lucy said.

"You'll change dresses – and no argument," Michael told her.

She grinned archly. "Is that my doctor or my husband speaking?"

He drew breath to reply but then stumbled over his own thoughts.

She laughed. "Will those two men ever agree!"

He bit his lip ruefully. "The husband won over the doctor just now, anyway."

"And quite right, too. There's more sense in his big toenail than in the whole of the doctor's head."

Michael's expression became dubious. "I don't know," he sighed. "It was taking a risk . . ."

"Michael!"

Her sharpness surprised him – and so did her earnestness as she leaned toward him, bringing her face within inches of his. "The risk lies in what we've been doing these last few months. Or *not* doing, rather." When it looked as if he still might argue, she added, "Trust me, my darling. I *know* what's safe and what's not safe."

He relaxed and his expression turned to one of humorous challenge; she knew he was going to ask, "Safe for what?"

Before he could speak the words she said, "Safe for the little fella."

He drew a deep breath and let it out without speaking.

"All right," she said, "I was wrong not to tell you at once. I . . ."

He raised a hand and put a finger to her lips. "Shh," he whispered. "There's nothing to be gained by going back over all that – who was wrong here, who was wrong there . . . Nothing to be gained by it. The best thing of all is to be able to talk about it at last – to tell you how glad I am. Glad? What a flabby word! Ecstatic . . . overjoyed . . ." His voice broke and he leaned his forehead against hers.

344

"How I've longed to say that! Why didn't I? What a . . . what an utter . . ." He choked.

A large, hot tear rolled down her cheek. "Oh Michael!"

After a moment of silent communion she sat upright again, sniffed deeply, and said, "Birdie will be here at any mo, now. We'll look a fright."

He rubbed his cheeks into his sleeves and for once she said nothing – or, rather, she wanted to say something grand and poetic to crystallize this moment before Birdie, the world, and life in general reclaimed them.

But no words came to her.

In the end, all she could think of to say was, "At last our hearts are open."

He smiled wryly. "All desires known – and no secrets hid!"

As a Roman Catholic she did not recognize his borrowing from the Book of Common Prayer; instead she was filled with the simple joy that he had found the words that had failed her: "Yes!" She sighed. "All desires known and no secrets hid!"

And at that moment Birdie came galumphing up the stairs with a change of dress for her. "Himself has stood and walked!" she cried even before she knocked at the door. "Could you believe it!"

"Come on in," Lucy called out. "Tell us all about it. I can believe anything today. It's been set aside for miracles."

"No but isn't it the truth I'm telling ye!" Birdie advanced breathlessly across the room, laying the dress out on the bed as she passed. "I hope this was the green one you meant," she added.

"Did Mister O'Dea really walk, Miss Kelly?" Michael asked. "Did you actually see him with your own eyes?"

"I did, sir. And I want to tell ye, if ever ye saw a new-dropped calf rise to its legs for the very first time, then ye'll know the way of it. He shook like a sally in the storm. But he rose from his chair and he *walked!*"

"Where did all this happen? Up in his room?"

The girl's eyes went wide with delighted horror at the choicest revelation of all. "Into the very cupboard where old Reilly, God be good to him, took his oyster and artichoke. Three bold steps in and four tired ones out. And down he flopped. But he did it, so he did!"

"No crutches? No stick?" Lucy asked.

"Divil a one, ma'am. He spurned them aside." She turned back to the bed, to Lucy's dress, which she picked up again, saying, "Would you be wanting an ignorant, willing colleen, ma'am, to train up as lady's maid? I'm between positions myself, now."

Lucy took the dress from her with a laugh. "You may help me into this if you will," she said. "But as to your reward, my thanks will be all your pay."

Michael left the room, kissing her warmly, easily, on the neck as he passed. "I'll settle up, darling," he said.

Lucy shivered but did her best to hide the response; the world had reclaimed them with a vengeance. After he had left, she went on: "If you suppose Ebenezer O'Dea has no further place for you, my girl, then you don't know the first thing about him. Nor, I may add, about yourself, either."

"Me?" Birdie asked dubiously. "What can I do?"

Lucy stared her straight in the eye and said something she had been longing to say to the girl ever since she had known her: "Whatever you think yourself, now, colleen."